MW00448653

Other titles in the Library of Modern Jewish Literature

Of Lodz and Love

Of Lodz and Love

Chava Rosenfarb

Translated from the Yiddish by the Author

Syracuse University Press

Copyright © 2000 by Chava Rosenfarb

All Rights Reserved

First Edition 2000

00 01 02 03 04 05   6 5 4 3 2 1

The paper used in this publication meets the minimum requirements of
American National Standard for Information Sciences—Permanence
of Paper for Printed Library Materials, ANSI Z39.48-1984. ∞ ™

Library of Congress Cataloging-in-Publication Data

Rosenfarb, Chawa, 1923-

[Botshani. 2. teyl. English]

Of Lodz and love / by Chava Rosenfarb.

p.   cm.—(The library of modern Jewish literature)

ISBN 0-8156-0577-3 (cloth : alk. paper)

I. Title. II. Series.

PJ5129.R597B5813   1999b

839' . 134—DC21   98-54858

Manufactured in the United States of America

For my children, Goldie and Abraham

Chava Rosenfarb was born in Lodz, Poland. She is a survivor of the Lodz Ghetto as well as the Auschwitz and Bergen-Belsen concentration camps. She is the recipient of numerous literary prizes. In 1979 she was awarded the Manger Prize—the highest award for Yiddish literature—for her trilogy *The Tree of Life, (Der boim fun lebn)*. She now resides in Canada.

Of Lodz and Love

◎ 1 ◎

LATE IN THE EVENING of the same day that she had fled from her father's home in the shtetl of Bociany, Binele arrived in Lodz. The flour merchant's wagon, in which she had been taken along in order to watch over the merchant's sick wife and baby, was now making its way through endlessly long streets. It seemed to Binele that she was riding through a river filled with darkness, whose banks consisted of the incredibly tall walls of brick or stone houses—some of them three or even four stories high.

She sat in the rear of the wagon next to the merchant's sick wife, who moaned quietly, and held the woman's sleeping baby in her lap. In spite of her exhaustion from the long trip, she was afraid to shut her eyes lest she miss out on the dream-like sights that greeted her. Here and there the dark streets were lit by the yellow lights of gas lanterns or by lights shining from the windows. Every time that a drosky with lit side lanterns or a wagon with burning torches fastened to the rear passed her, she turned her head and followed the lights with her eyes until another vehicle came into view. Who were the people who occupied these vehicles? Where were they heading to? And who were the people whose figures she saw moving behind the lighted windows in the tall, dark walls? Why were they still up and around now, at an hour when all of Bociany would have been fast asleep? And to whom did those shadowy figures who moved in clusters along the sidewalks belong? In Bociany only demons and ghosts walked between the huts so late at night.

The mysterious, dark world unfolding before her eyes filled Binele's heart with apprehension and awe. Her mouth watered as she stared on, wishing that this ride would never end. But the wagon was already approaching the middle of the main street, the Piotrkowska, and the flour merchant who drove it turned toward her and asked whether she had any relatives who would take her in for the night.

"Of course," she answered distractedly.

"So where should I let you off?"

"A little bit further on."

"You mean in Baluty?"

"Sure."

They drove into the heart of the slums of Baluty. Here too the streets running through rows of tumbledown houses were still alive with people. Near the Church of the Holy Virgin Mary the merchant slowed down and turned to her again. "Can you find your way from here?"

"Of course," she said, put the baby on its sick mother's lap and jumped off the wagon through the rear.

"Thank you very much!" the merchant called after her.

She was too preoccupied to answer. Slowly she moved ahead, walking around in circles as she tried to get her bearing. Dark masses of people came in a surge toward her and passed her by. She stopped by the entrance to the church. Bright shafts of light beamed at her from inside. She allowed them to guide her into the church along with the men and women who surrounded her on all sides.

Evening mass was being celebrated. Binele sat down on a long, hard bench. It seemed so comfortable and hospitable after all the hours that she had sat hunched up in the covered wagon, that her eyelids immediately began to droop. She tried to fight off her sleepiness. She had to keep herself awake in order to decide what she ought to do. But the priest's voice droned on so monotonously that despite herself she rested her arms on the back of the bench in front of her, nestled her head in them, and drifted off into slumber. When she awoke, the crowd had begun to leave. Sleep still lingering in her limbs, she heaved herself up heavily and dragged herself toward the exit. The prettily carved wooden confessional caught her eye. She pushed her way through to it, stepped inside, and hid behind the curtain. When the lights in the church had dimmed and only a few oil lamps remained lighted near the altar, she stepped out of the confessional and moved along the walls until she came to the sacristy.

For a while she stood there, in the dark, undecidedly. By the faint light shining in through the stained glass window, she could make out the shape of a priest's soutane suspended from a peg. She took it off, folded it, and reentered the church hall with it. She decided to postpone making any plans for the next day. All she wanted to do now was to sleep. She was about to stretch herself out on a bench when she noticed a rolled-up carpet under the altar table. She went over, unrolled it, and lay down on it, putting the folded soutane under her head. Then she deftly rolled herself up in the carpet until it was back in its former place under the altar. After having set her inner clock to wake her before the bells tolled for the first morning mass, she drifted off into a deep sleep.

She woke up on time, rolled herself out of the carpet, and put it back in its place. She hung up the soutane on the peg in the sacristy and hid in the confessional again. The bells started to toll.

Workers on their way to work and peasants from the surrounding villages, who had come into the city to deliver their woven fabrics or their dairy products, filled the church. Binele sneaked out from behind the curtain of the confessional and sat down among the worshipers. She wanted to get some more sleep. It was still gray outside and she could not keep her eyes open. Her head hung limply and her body began to sag sideways and forward. As she was about to spread her arms over the back of the bench in front of her, for support, she noticed the canon, a tiny old man, walking between the rows of benches, collecting donations.

She quickly reached into her bodice and removed the rag in which she kept the four kopecks that the boy Yacov had given her in Bociany. She saw that people were tossing coins into the canon's plate and taking change, so she did the same. She put in two kopecks and took five in change. Then she stood up, crossed herself, and left the church as the drawn-out howl of sirens filled her ears.

She wandered the streets, staring at everything in wide-eyed bewilderment. The rhythm of life pulsating around her was so odd, so incomprehensible that it seemed funny. People rushed to and fro as if they were being chased after, looking awfully angry or as if they were all suffering from toothaches. But mostly she gaped at the clanking streetcars passing her at a dizzying speed. Her first thought was that these wildly rushing horseless wagons served for transporting the gold that she had heard was "swept up" in the streets of Lodz to be stashed away in distant, secret places. They moved so fast, she thought, so as to prevent even the quickest thief from catching up with them. But then she saw the gray, unhappy faces peering out from the streetcar windows and was forced to discard this explanation as unlikely.

After she had walked about for many hours, she bought a couple of bagels for the five kopecks which she had taken from the canon's plate. Again she heard the disturbing, baying sound of sirens. They seemed to be penetrating her through every pore in her skin. She asked the little bagel vendor about the sirens. The boy laughed smugly, "You've just arrived in Lodz, haven't you? Why, the factories do it. How else would people know the time?" She walked on, deciding to be thrifty and allow herself to eat only one bagel and save the rest.

Gradually she became accustomed to the masses of people pushing and prodding her, and with less rigidity she allowed them to carry her along. Now and again they brought her to a large brick structure with hundreds of small clattering windows. She saw the front gates each swallow a part of the throng, shutting behind it like the gates of a prison, and she realized that these were the factories that the bagel vendor had mentioned and that Yacov had told her about. She turned hastily away and moved on. Not for a single moment did it occur to her to return to Bociany. The rhythm of Lodz mesmerized her. It corresponded to her own restlessness. But to become trapped inside one of those roaring monsters, those prisons called factories, she had not the slightest intention.

She survived the day on the sustenance of the two bagels. At nightfall she went back to the Church of the Holy Virgin Mary. These quarters pleased her, and she made them her permanent abode. The church stood open day and night, and no one bothered her inside. Soon she felt quite at home there. In the sacristy she had discovered the decanter containing the communion wine and a dish full of wafers. When the hollowness in her stomach nagged at her too persistently before she went to sleep—rolled up in the carpet beneath the altar table—she refreshed herself with a few communion wafers and a sip of wine from the decanter.

Mass was celebrated three times a day. On Sundays and holidays it was celebrated every hour. Whenever Binele had run out of kopecks, she also attended mass in the middle of the day. She made a nice contribution when the old canon came over with the plate and took back an even nicer number of kopecks as change.

On the third morning, when her stomach had begun to crave a bit of warm food, Binele braced herself and approached the nun who was polishing the sacred vessels on the altar. First she crossed herself, then, with her hands folded as if in prayer, she knelt down before the nun and burst into sobs. "I'm a poor orphan," she mumbled in the peasant Polish that she had learned from her friend Yadwiga in Bociany. "I've come from the village to scrub floors for a bit of warm food."

The nun took hold of her hand, helped her stand up, and led her into the presbytery. "This poor orphan here is starved for a bit of warm food," she whispered to the fat housekeeper who wore a black apron and a white, heavily starched kerchief on her head. "She'll scrub the floors of the presbytery and the sacristy for us."

The housekeeper grumbled something into her goiter, filled a bowl with kasha from the breakfast cauldron, and placed it on the table to the left of the shortsighted canon. The old man was sitting hunched over the table, counting the coins which he had collected during mass. Binele's stomach rumbled. Without thinking, she sank into a chair, and immediately attacked the food. It was only when she had scraped the bowl clean of kasha with the spoon that she became aware of the canon's rasping whisper as he counted the coins.

"Poor child," she heard the nun say compassionately with a sigh. "She was so hungry that she even forgot to thank the Lord."

Binele crossed herself a couple of times. With great fervor she pressed her palms together to form a steeple and bowed her head. She thanked the Lord with the words that she had learned so well at her friend Yadwiga's home in Bociany. All the while her eyes stealthily measured the distance dividing her bowl from the canon's collection plate. She went back to loudly scratching the bottom of the empty bowl with the spoon. The kasha had had a heavenly taste. The housekeeper decided that to offer the poor orphan another scoopful of kasha would make for a good Christian deed. As she did so, she asked Binele, "Can you do a decent job at scrubbing floors?"

At the sight of her refilled bowl, Binele cried out enthusiastically, "I can make them as white as chalk!"

Startled by her outburst, the old canon popped up his head. Jingling coins dropped from his small palm, which seemed to be shaped out of creased parchment. He forgot where he was in his counting, shoved the coins back into the plate, and started counting all over again.

Binele ate more slowly now, concentrating her attention rather on the shortsighted old man than on the food. A bright thought lit up in her mind as she kept time with his rasping voice counting the coins. "You made a mistake, Father!" she finally exclaimed.

Before the housekeeper had time to recover from her astonishment, Binele was already on her feet, standing beside the canon, her back turned to the gaping woman. She emptied the collection plate onto the table, and began to count loudly and quickly. She bent so low over the table that the loose left sleeve of her caftan, which she had "taken" at the inn in Bociany before leaving, touched the pile of coins like an open drawer. As she counted, she turned her head carefully and looked around. The nun had gone back to the church hall, but the housekeeper was keeping an eye on the table. Binele then and there placed herself so that the woman could see nothing but her back. Then she spread out the coins and made separate piles of the ten-kopeck pieces, of the fives, the twos, and the ones. She stacked them up into columns and as she did so, she shoved a few coins from each pile into her left caftan sleeve.

"May the Lord reward you, my child," the canon said, wiping his strained eyes. "How much did you count altogether?"

Binele slowly folded the sleeve around her left wrist and holding it tightly with her right hand, she bowed deeply before the old man. "Four rubles," she announced. She called out to the housekeeper, "May the Lord bless you!" and holding on to her sleeve, rushed into the church hall, and hid between the pews. Once there, she shook the coins out of her sleeve and hid them in the rag she carried in her bosom, the same rag that held the two kopecks parting money which Yacov had given her, kopecks she had decided never to part with. She approached the nun who was still busy at the altar and asked her which floors needed scrubbing. She was given a pail, a floor brush, and a pile of rags.

That day she bought herself half a loaf of bread and a whole herring.

From then on, every time she wanted a bit of warm food or a piece of bread and herring, she scrubbed the floors of the presbytery and helped the canon count the coins in his plate. If remorse began to nibble at her conscience, chiding her for repaying a favor with theft, she scolded herself for having such thoughts. Could what she was doing be called stealing? Did she not deserve the same charity as other hungry people? Was she not an orphan without a single relative in the entire town? And was she not a Jewess on top of it all and consequently leading a harder life than any Gentile? And weren't the Gentiles cruel people who deserved to be taken revenge on in every possible way?

The rest of the time she spent looking for work in her trade as a maid servant. She quickly realized that in the slums of Baluty where her lodgings were, she would find nothing. So she set out for the center of town, which was called Wilki. She strolled along the crowded elegant main street, the Piotrkowska, and went into the large backyards that were surrounded by three- and four-storied buildings on all four sides. Each yard was like a small shtetl. She climbed stairs, one story after another, and knocked on doors. It soon dawned on her that both the cellars and the top floors of these huge buildings were inhabited by paupers. The wealthy lived on either the first or the second floor. Their doors carried small brass signs with fancily engraved names in Polish letters. So she concentrated only on those doors.

She had no luck with the women who answered these doors. Either she came face to face with a maid who slammed the door on her nose, or the lady of the house opened the door, grimaced when she saw Binele, and, without giving her time to enumerate her qualifications, shut the door with a thud. If Binele was a little luckier, she was called back and offered a piece of bread.

So she walked from house to house, from the main street to the side streets, from one part of town to the other, until she had covered the city in its length and breadth. A strange feeling took hold of her that although she was in Lodz, she somehow was not really there. It was as though the town were fenced off from her by an invisible barrier that prevented her from throwing herself into the town's exciting bustling life and partaking of it like one of its own.

When she grew tired of walking and her courage faltered, she recalled one of Yacov's sayings, "Even if you see your grave open, you must never give up hope." All she needed, she told herself, was to catch her breath and rest her legs. So she entered one of those large backyards walled in by tall buildings and sat down on the water pump located in the center of the yard. People were milling all around her. Hordes of children chased each other, or kicked ragballs, or skipped rope, or fought amongst themselves. Neighbors chatted in groups at the doorways or quarreled through the open windows. Peddlers of various kinds entered the yard, loudly advertising their goods in drawn-out Yiddish. A peddler with a box of glass panes on his back called with a lilt, "Ladies of the upper and lower floors, I put panes into your windows and doors!" Another peddler called, "Honorable and charming ladies, I will mend your broken pots while you play with your lovely babies!" Or a rag collector arrived with his cart and cried in a whining voice, "Whether you're a beauty, or whether you're a hag, I'll still give you a plate for a bundle of rags!"

She watched a street singer give his concert while holding himself by an ear with one hand and clopping with his walking stick with the other. Then a family of acrobats showed off their acrobatic tricks as they performed on a sack full of holes that they had spread over the cobblestones in the very middle of the yard. She listened to an entire orchestra of cripples performing on their crooked and lame instruments, or she listened to an organ grinder with a guinea pig sitting on top of his playing box. The organ grinder sold cures for headaches, toothaches, and heartaches and told fortunes as well. He called loudly, "Ladies and gentlemen, who wants their fortunes told? All of your past, all of your present, and all of your future for only two kopecks!"

Binele badly wanted to have her fortune told, so as to know what awaited her in this breathtaking, strange city. But she could not afford to spend two kopecks on it, and she was also afraid that the fortune-teller might tell her that her father would soon be coming to look for her and that he would find her one day.

In the midst of all the to-do in one yard or another, she noticed dainty, elegantly clad ladies pass by her now and then, their ravishing splendor lighting up the humdrum surroundings like wandering stars would a gray sky. Dressed in coats with fur collars or with silver fox furs thrown around their necks, their delicate hands hidden in large fur muffs, they cautiously trotted by on their high heels, attracting the attention of one and all. To Binele they seemed more splendidly decked out than even the lessee's daughters on a Sabbath in Bociany. It made no sense to envy such magnificent creatures; they seemed to belong to an entirely different race. Binele could only admire them, her mouth filling with saliva. When she saw the same ladies peering out from behind tulle curtains from the windows of the upper floors, it made her think that serving one of these glamorous creatures would make her happy beyond words. Jealously she looked on as these 'ladies' maids, dressed in white aprons, descended from the regal heights of the first or second floor, loaded down with pillows and featherbeds, or with rugs large and small that they hung on the special stands in the yard and then beat the dust out of them to the last mote with their straw swatters. Why were these maids so fortunate? And why was she having such bad luck? Why were the chains never removed from the doors when she knocked?

Finally, the thought struck her that it was her dress that was causing her all the trouble. Her appearance stood between her and this fascinating city. The noble ladies could by no means judge by her looks how neat and meticulous a worker she really was. Appearance was important in Lodz. Even in Bociany there was a saying, "The outer dress covers the inside mess." So as soon as this became clear to her, Binele remembered the barber shop with the large mirror in the window that she had seen on a neighboring street. She quickly made her way to it and, peering in through the pane, gave herself a long critical look in the mirror inside.

Now she saw herself in the full extent of her ugliness. Her sloppy dress with the loose seams had a thousand threads dangling from it, and the threadbare cotton caftan that she had picked up at the inn in Bociany had tips of cotton sticking out like white tongues from every hole. Her reddish yellow braids were undone and full of knots—as they had not been touched by a comb for days—and these tresses framed a face full of brown freckles and smudges of dirt that extended from her ears to her very nose.

"Marzepa, stupid cow!" she yelled at herself in the mirror, and banged her head against the glass as though she were intent on breaking it. She stuck her tongue out at her reflection in the mirror and made distasteful grimaces at herself.

Having composed herself somewhat, she turned around and started to observe the women in the street who passed her by. Not all of them were dressed like the elegant ladies who lived on the first floors. Far from it. But even the plaid shawls that most of them wore looked neat in comparison with her own clothes. She resolved that she must immediately "become a *mentsh*," even if she had to steal for that purpose.

She continued to walk from one large backyard to another, but refrained from looking at the "rich windows" any longer. She concentrated her attention on the laundry and on the clothes that hung airing on the clotheslines in the back of the yards. There was no doubt in her mind that these garments and the laundry were well guarded. Who would leave such treasures unwatched? So she resolved to wait for two opportunities to present themselves simultaneously, namely, to find both a fine piece of clothing hanging on a cord and some kind of racket creating confusion in the same backyard at the same time. But such happy coincidences were not easy to come by.

It took a couple of days before Mother Fortune finally smiled on Binele. She noticed a cord hung full of wonderful clothes and there was a funeral of an important member of the Jewish community taking place in the same backyard.

The backyard was black with gabardines, traditional caps, and hats; the air was permeated with the sound of sobs and the lamentations of the mourners. Binele had to cover her ears in order to gather her thoughts. She decided to snatch a decent-looking dress and perhaps a coat as well from the cord in the rear. But then she changed her mind and postponed this for another time. Now she needed something that would solve her appearance problems in one shot. She needed, for instance, that red and green plaid shawl that fluttered so attractively behind the backs of a group of Hasidim.

To her dismay, a tall teenage boy stood clasping the cord that held the plaid shawl. He seemed to be guarding the treasure, since he made no attempt to push himself forward. All he did was balance himself on tiptoe and stretch out his thin hairy neck so that he seemed taller than the Hasidim around him. He was obviously intent on securing for himself a good view of the entrance through which the honored deceased would soon be carried.

Binele pushed herself through the mass of people so as to emerge right beside the clothesline. She squeezed herself in behind the backs of the Hasidim and reached a spot between them and the lank teenager. The latter, having felt the sudden touch of her arm, gave her a frightened look and jumped away as if she had burnt him. She took this opportunity to place herself between him and the plaid shawl. She too raised herself on tiptoe and stretched out her neck, as her face displayed an expression of deeply felt grief; she even moaned. And meanwhile, with her hands behind her back, she pulled at the plaid shawl, until she had it off the cord. As quickly as she could, she rolled it up behind her back, then moved it to the side, away from the boy. Once again she pressed her way through the cluster of Hasidim and plowed ahead in the direction of the gate.

At that moment the coffin of the deceased was being borne out through the entrance. Binele was sure that she heard the voice of the teenage boy amid the spasmodic wailing which erupted in the yard. The crowd swept forward, everyone pushing ahead to get a glimpse of the honorable deceased man's widow and judge with their own eyes how close she was to fainting. In this manner the crush of people carried Binele along and helped her get out of the yard. And with her came the red and green plaid shawl.

Once in the street, she immediately wrapped herself in the shawl and felt herself instantly transformed into a woman of Lodz. She paraded down the Piotrkowska. Whenever she felt herself being pushed, she pushed back, or proudly prodded the mannerless passers-by with her elbow, like any other citizen of Lodz would do.

The plaid shawl did wonders for Binele. She began thinking along altogether different lines. She grew disgusted with knocking on doors, with the very thought of being a maid servant and constantly being ordered about, serving others and never for a minute having a moment to herself, not even at night. She wanted to be on her own, to live for herself, at least after work. Granted, she would have to pay dearly for her leisure, but when, after all, had she ever received something for nothing, except when she stole? And since she did not want to steal, yet wanted to remain a citizen of Lodz, she realized that she had no other choice but to do what most of the women of Lodz, those who wore plaid shawls, were doing.

The next day, as soon as the factory sirens came on, she sneaked out of the church. In the gray of the morning the streets looked as though they had mobile sidewalks. Processions of dark shadowy figures streamed in all directions. The men wore sloppy jackets with long, shaggy shawls wrapped around their necks; on their heads sat creased, grimy caps with cracked visors; bottles of coffee stuck pointedly out of their pockets. The women wore their plaid shawls over their heads. Braided straw baskets dangled from their arms. They walked herded together in groups, holding each other by the arm, the pallor of their faces shone out from the frames of their shawls.

Binele followed the streams of people first in one direction, then in another, until she reached Plocka Street, a narrow street with textile factories on both sides.

The throngs grew increasingly dense. They forked out in separate groups, each heading for one or another of the open gates. Binele looked around and finally decided to follow a group of women who spoke Yiddish among themselves. The sound of the language made her feel a bit more at ease. She even had the impulse to ask one of these women how she ought to go about finding work at such a factory, but gave up the idea. The women would laugh at her, or perhaps tell her lies, or even chase her away. People did not like others to have the same good fortune as they had.

The Jewish women passed through the gate of a factory and Binele followed right behind them. In the yard the mass of workers split into smaller groups, the men separately and the women separately. At the entrance, the women were squeezed together as they pushed and shoved each other. A woman whose back was pressing tightly against Binele's bosom, turned her head halfway and sighed, "My little bastard has the runs again."

Binele failed to understand what she heard. Then she caught herself. "Curds are the best medicine," she answered.

The woman shook her head impatiently. "Where will I get curds? I don't even have enough for a bottle of milk until payday. My old man, may he never live to grow old, is already on vacation." Binele had no idea what "on vacation" meant, but she dared not ask for an explanation. Instead, she pulled from her bodice the rag that held the kopecks from the charitable donations at the church and without hesitation gave the woman the five kopecks that were supposed to go for her daily consumption of bagels.

Only now did the woman turn around and gave Binele a closer look. She grabbed herself by a cheek. "Oy, good Heavens!" she cried. "I thought I was talking to Minda. That's how crazy I've gone! Where do you work? Upstairs?"

"Yes, upstairs," Binele nodded. "And where do *you* work?"

"I work under Handsome Moshe," the woman replied with obvious pride. "If we live, with God's help, until Monday," she added as they pushed themselves toward the stairs, "I'll pay you back the five kopecks, may you live in good health. And what did you say your name was?"

"It's Binele. And there's no hurry with the five kopecks. Perhaps you'd like me to have a look at your little one? I used to work for a barbersurgeon," Binele said with great pride. "What's your name?"

"Ziporah's my name. Wait for me outside the gate after work."

The woman vanished in a hall on the first floor, the others climbed higher. Binele followed them. She came up into a large dusty hall with cracked plaster walls. Long rows of narrow tables, covered with unwound bolts of fabric, were set up parallel to the blurred dirty windows. Some of the women sat down at one row of tables and took out all kinds of *pincettes* and needles similar to the ones that Binele had used at the plush factory where she had worked as a *shtoperke* before she had escaped from Bociany. Another group of women occupied another row of tables and took out similar tools, plus magnifying glasses. They began to look for faults in the weaving. Binele relaxed a little. She was familiar with the work done here. Perhaps her trade would stand her in good stead.

Once the women had taken off their shawls, she could see how much better dressed they were than she. None of them wore a torn uneven skirt, or a blouse full of holes, or a caftan with the cotton showing through it. She stood in her plaid shawl for another few minutes. A shawl made one woman resemble another and she was afraid that if she removed it, she would be recognized as a stranger. But neither was it wise to stand around like that. She did not know what to do next, except that she had to find a free place at a table and quickly sit down.

As she made a wavering gesture to remove the shawl, a woman approached her, snatched the shawl by a corner and smacked her lips admiringly. "Look at this beautiful thing! Pure wool too!" She rubbed the corner of the plaid between her fingers, and in a moment all eyes were fixed on Binele. The women stared not at the shawl, but at her.

Binele, at a loss, jerked the shawl out of the woman's hands. Then she checked herself and threw the shawl over the woman's shoulders. "It suits you," she giggled nervously.

The woman stroked the plaid over her bosom and asked, "Handsome Moshe sent you up to work here, didn't he? And how much did you pay for the shawl? A fortune, I suppose."

"Not a kopeck!" Binele shrugged.

The woman smiled suggestively at Binele and blinked, "A bridegroom, eh?"

"Of course," Binele smiled back.

The woman, realizing that this was not the right time for a chat, swiftly removed the shawl, rolled it up, and thrust it on a table where other shawls lay piled up in a heap. "All we need is that The Bandit should find us here chatting first thing in the morning." She pulled Binele by the sleeve and pointed out a free seat at a table not far from her own. "You can call it yours," she said to Binele, indicating the seat. "Bronia is already expecting a visit from the Angel of Death."

Binele took the seat, cast stealthy glances at her neighbors to both sides, and decided to copy what they were doing. She picked up a pinkish piece of chalk-soap which lay on the table, passed her palms over the surface of the material spread out before her, and began to look for bulges in the weaving. Her neighbor to the right caught Binele's sidelong glance. "Why did Handsome Moshe send you up to this hell?" she asked. Obviously all the women in the hall already knew how Binele had come among them. "And why do you work like a clay golem? The Bandit will be here any moment. And where is your *kooker,* your magnifying glass?"

"I lost it," Binele answered in a whisper.

"Fine story! You don't need much more!" The woman stood up and vanished somewhere. The next moment she was back, pressing a magnifying glass into Binele's hand. "Here," she said. "It's a *kooker* from *kooker-*land, it'll make you go blind. Good for the garbage. But at least hold it in your hand. He's crazy about *kookers.* I don't give a kopeck for your life if he catches you without one." She turned her attention to her work, and Binele continued to copy her. When she had worked with plush, plucking out the snarls and smoothing the bulges in the fabric had been done in a slightly different manner. Again she heard her neighbor's question, "But how could you have sinned so greatly against Handsome Moshe? After all, he doesn't make an issue of trifles. It's paradise to work for him. He's already promised me that as soon as a table is free in his hall, he'll take me down. Maybe he'll take me in your place. You can build a fortress on a word of Moshe's."

Binele pretended to be so engrossed in her work that she did not hear what her neighbor was saying. But then she ran into trouble with a knot in the fabric that could not be plucked out without making a hole. She turned to her neighbor. "Say, how does he, The Bandit, like these snarls to be fixed?"

The woman moved over to Binele's table and quickly smoothed out the knot. "You didn't work for long under Handsome Moshe, did you?" She looked at Binele disparagingly. "Quick, watch me and I'll show you how to do it." She took Binele's left hand and made it glide over the fabric, teaching her to feel for the swellings in the weaving with her fingertips. Then she showed her how to pluck out the threads so that the lumps would vanish and how to cover the traces. "It's about as complicated as plucking chickens," the woman sighed. "The trouble is that the worries carry you off some place else and you don't see what's in front of your nose. The main thing in this profession is concentration."

The woman barely managed to return to her table when the head supervisor, Yone the Svolotch, or Yone the Bandit as the women dubbed him, entered the hall. He was balancing a bolt of material called a "beam" on his shoulder. It grew so quiet in the hall that the buzzing of the weaving machines on the other floors seemed to be coming directly from above one's head. Yone himself looked as if he had descended straight from a fiery storm cloud, with the roll of material like a sacred scroll over his shoulder. His head was full of flaming red curls and he wore a smart-looking skullcap on the tip of his head. He had a red mustache, a red beard, and curly sidelocks. In his high boots, with his black turtle-necked *roubashka* tucked into his belted pants, he looked more like a Cossack than a religious young man from Baluty. His red eyebrows were wrinkled and sparks shot from his dark green eyes.

He zoomed through between the rows of tables with the "beam" on his shoulder. "Whose bloody piece of work is this?" he thundered, while the women let their heads sink deeply over their work. With his free hand he slapped the sitting women on their behinds. "Yours? Yours?" he bellowed. The women squirmed and popped up from their seats, shaking their heads in the negative. Yone did not miss Binele and he planted a smack on her behind as well. But then he raised his brows and gave her a good look from out of his forbidding questioning eyes.

"It's mine!" she pointed to the roll of material on his shoulder before he managed to open his mouth.

"Yours?" he squinted and roofed his eyes with his hand as if in order to see her better. He riveted his gaze on Binele's neighbors. Pale and frightened, they kept their heads lowered. "And who are you?" he asked Binele, a raw grating edge in his tone of voice. She could read in his face that he had no need to ask.

"Handsome Moshe sent me up to work here," Bravely, Binele looked straight into his eyes.

"Who sent you?" He took a step toward her, sizing her up with his green eyes. He already knew all there was to know. Before him sat a young woman with healthy red cheeks, a fresh-looking skin, and a lively sparkle in her slanted eyes. She did not belong here and was a greenhorn in the trade. Her behavior proved it: the way she stared him straight in the eyes, her nerve, claiming to have done the faulty work that she had never seen before. It was clear as day that this suspect girl was putting on an act. He decided to play along until he found out what she was after. So Yone started to fume, letting on that he believed her. "Handsome Moshe is sending me up all the garbage, the stinker! Come over here!" He pulled Binele by a braid into the middle of the hall. "You're all witnesses!" he called out to the other women and faced Binele. "If you don't fix this 'beam' good and proper by tomorrow morning, so that there is not even one lump left in it, you'll fly from here to where the black pepper grows!" He pinched Binele once more on the rear while all the women watched, and thrust the 'beam' of material into her arms. He then rushed along the rows of tables, pinching and smacking the women on their rears. When on his way back, he again passed Binele, he blinked at her meaningfully as if to let her know that he had seen through her trick.

The minute Yone the Svolotch left the hall, a surge of nervous whispers went through the rows of tables. Binele had barely managed to recover from her encounter with Yone, when a middle-aged, round-faced woman walked over to her, grabbed her hand, and shook it firmly. "Thank you, comrade," she said loudly, beaming at her with a pair of warm maternal eyes.

Binele stared at her. "You're mistaken!" she yanked away her hand.

The woman shook her head emphatically. "I'm not mistaken. You saved my life, comrade!"

"My name is not Comrade," Binele insisted. "My name is Binele and I never saved your life. I've never seen you before."

"Many comradely thanks," the smiling woman repeated with hearty enthusiasm and walked off to the other end of the hall.

"Very nice of you," Binele's neighbor on the right said in a whisper. "We of the proletariat must stick together and support one another."

Binele wondered what kind of "yat"—which in Yiddish meant simply a guy—this "proletar-yat" was, and why her neighbor had said "we," although she was a woman, and why they had to stick together. But she refrained from questioning the woman, lest she betray her ignorance. She heard a whisper pass from one table to the other, "Her name is Binele . . ."

She grew aware of the friendly, curious eyes beaming at her from all the tables. These were the first friendly looks she had been given in this town. She rejoiced in the good feeling. Her neighbor on the right informed her that the women in the hall would each give a bit of her own time to help correct the faulty work on the "beam," and that she would be especially helped by the comrade who had originally made all the mistakes. Binele considered this a good augury. Perhaps she could continue working here. The women were doing her a favor, one of those favors that had rarely been done her in her life. She had no idea how she would ever repay them. There was no such thing as getting something for nothing in this life, unless one stole. Everything had to be paid for. And then there was Yone's pinching her on the behind. The thought bothered her. Not that the pinching had hurt, but it made her feel disgusted with herself, as if she were filthy all over.

Before long Yone was back in the hall with another "beam" of badly fixed material resting on his shoulder. He set out to rush from one table to the other as he bellowed, "Yours? Yours?" Binele did not turn her head, but remained watchful so as to avoid his pinching. The moment he took aim at her rear, she deftly shifted to the other side of her seat.

At the far end of the hall someone was quietly confessing to having produced the faulty piece of work. Yone's jarring voice reached Binele's ears, "You'll fly from here like a balloon to where the black pepper grows!" Then he addressed himself to the entire hall full of women, "Remember, all of you! There is no lack of *shtoperkes* dying to get a job. A working *shtoperke* is still a 'ristocrat among the textile workers. Bear that in mind!" Binele heard him approaching. This time however she did not shift in her seat quickly enough and he pinched her. She turned abruptly, but he was gone.

Somehow her first day at the factory had passed. As soon as the sirens had begun to wail, Binele joined the flood of workers streaming out of the factory gate into the street. Ziporah, the mother of the sick child, was waiting for her outside. They went on foot, passing through the familiar streets of the center of town and then of Baluty until they reached the Faifer Street. On the way Binele told Ziporah about herself and how she had gotten herself into the factory and had worked there the whole day.

"If you're familiar with that kind of work," Ziporah said encouragingly, "you might have the good fortune to stay on. Where do you live?"

"Not far from here. At the Holy Mary's," Binele answered.

"The way you say it shows right away that you're a provincial." Ziporah remarked. "You don't call that square 'At the Holy Mary's.' You call it Church Place. That's the right name." Binele did not care to tell her that she lived not in a house on Church Place, but in the Holy Mary Church proper. As they walked along Faifer Street, Ziporah said to Binele, "Don't give yourself the idea that my living on this street means that I am a you-know-what. I'm *vitish* from head to toe, and in case you don't know what *vitish* means, let me tell you that it means to be straight. I never was a such-and-such and never will be. I earn my piece of bread with my own two hands and not with my you-know-what. My father is a Hasid, a follower of the Gerer Rabbi. He walks the backyards selling plates in exchange for rags. An honest occupation. I'll tell you the truth, I do work for Hand-some Moshe, but I'm not a *shtoperke*. I'm one of the floor cleaners, and I earn a ruble and fifty kopecks a week."

Binele could hardly understand what the woman was trying to tell her. "And where did you say your old man was?" she asked.

"My old man?" Ziporah's face twisted into an expression of bitterness and revulsion. "May he never live to grow old. He's on vacation. Would he stayed there forever. Wintertime he goes thieving, so that they should catch him and send him to jail. There he spends the cold season like God in Odessa. Paradise! No wife, no children, no worries about making a living. They take care of him and serve him food to eat, may the worms eat him, while I am left to manage here alone with his bastards, may they live and be healthy. Luckily I have a suitor, a puller, who lends me a few kopecks per week when my pay runs out."

"What's a puller?" Binele asked.

"You're a real provincial! Don't you know what a puller is?" Ziporah gave her a kind of haughty yet compassionate look. "It's a trade like any other. You saw the pullers when we passed the shops. The puller hangs on to a passer-by, to a peasant for instance, and talks to him for so long, until he talks him into entering a shop, or he just pulls him inside, willingly or not. And you can rely on my suitor. He's got a tongue like a polished diamond, may he deal in real diamonds one day. He can talk you into believing that what's black is white, and what's garbage is gold. And before you have time to look around, you're leaving the shop happy as a lark, with a piece of filth in your hand. He makes a good living at it, may he live a long life, and he's *vitish* from head to toe."

Binele observed Ziporah from the corner of her eye. Only now, as Zi-porah talked of her suitor, and her face lit up, did it become clear that Ziporah was not a middle-aged woman, but rather a very young one. Ziporah's face, like the faces of most of the women at the factory, was the color of yellow mud. Her forehead and the skin under her eyes were densely wrinkled, but she had a fresh and beautiful mouth. Her black eyes, nestled in puffy bluish folds of skin, were themselves clear and were fringed with long eyelashes that curled upwards. She had a finely shaped small nose and a dimple in her chin.

They arrived at a decrepit mildewed house which resembled most of the houses in the slums of Baluty. A row of women stood in front of the house like a guard of honor. The women wore tightly fitting dresses in screaming colors with deep décolletés and had cheap shaggy "foxes" thrown around their necks. Large black purses stuck out from under their armpits. They smoked cigarettes as they leaned against the wall with one shoulder. Their legs in high heels were crossed, while one of their hips protruded toward the street and the passers-by. They shivered with cold. The thick layers of powder and rouge on their faces distinctly revealed their goose pimples. It was cold in the street.

"How is my kid doing?" Ziporah asked one of the women.

"He doesn't stop doing," the woman shrugged. "May my enemies do just as well."

Ziporah rushed into the dark entrance. Binele followed her. They came up the creaky wooden stairs into a long dimly lit corridor with many doors from which strange sounds issued. Ziporah reassured Binele. "It's the most decent of all the houses on the Faifer Street, believe me. The girls pay my rent, because I do their laundry on Saturdays and Sundays, when the rush is on for them. They keep an eye on my kids, too, and give them something to eat while I'm at work."

Ziporah and Binele entered a dank slovenly room. The first things that greeted the eye were the window panes which were so dirty that they were devoid of any transparency. The room contained a table, a partly sunken stove, and a few straw mattresses strewn on the floor. Two children with bare behinds crawled on all fours toward Ziporah, a third one, wearing a diaper, lay asleep on one of the mattresses. Ziporah walked over to the sleeping child, picked it up and put it in Binele's arms. Binele felt the humidity of the dirty diaper as its strong smell attacked her nostrils.

"Well, what do you say?" Ziporah searched Binele's face with a worried restless look. The child whimpered faintly.

Binele grimaced and said quickly, "You must hurry to a barber-surgeon with him. You can see for yourself. He's barely alive." She grabbed a rag from the mattress, wrapped the child's behind in it and took the child under her plaid. The other two children tugged at Ziporah's skirt, and screaming wildly, hung on to her. She smacked them loudly on their bare bottoms and tore them away from her.

Binele was greatly moved as she held the warm trembling body of Ziporah's child pressed against her bosom. The smell it gave off was ugly, but it did not really bother her. She thought of her own mother, who had died while giving birth to her. She thought of her mother with the kind of tenderness and warmth she usually felt whenever she held a child in her arms. For a moment she imagined herself being her own mother, holding her, Binele, in her arms.

As soon as they came out into the street with the child, the women outside surrounded them. "Listen to me," one of them said. "The best thing to do is to hurry to the gypsy camp with him. They sell the best remedies."

Binele shook her head emphatically. "She must get the child to the barber-surgeon's!" She turned to Ziporah. "Where does he live?"

Ziporah shrugged her shoulders. "May I be as ignorant of evil as I am of where a barber-surgeon lives."

"Go to see Gaiger," another woman advised, and the others seconded her.

On the way to see Gaiger, Ziporah explained in a desperate sounding tone of voice, "Gaiger is a horse doctor, may he soon kick the bucket. The girls go to him when they need a favor. Maybe you could go in with the kid instead of me, what do you say?" Her anxious eyes looked pleadingly into Binele's. "You're a stranger. You can get away. . ."

Binele failed to understand. "I can get some money later. Tell him that you'll pay him in an hour or so."

"There is no 'later' with Gaiger," Ziporah wagged her head desolately. In front of Gaiger's house she stopped as if she were trying to make up her mind. Finally she pulled Binele with her. "Well, come on. I have no other choice, do I? And I must pay him myself, right away."

Gaiger, the horse doctor, lived in a house built partly of wood and partly of bricks, which stood on the very corner of Faifer Street. Upon entering his dwelling from the backyard, one first found oneself in a stable strewn all over with straw. Two burly men attended the few horses which stood by the walls. As soon as the two young women with the child entered, one of the men called out, "Gaiger! Two brides are here to see you!"

From a side door deep inside the stable, Gaiger stepped out to make his appearance. As if he did not see the women, he first went over to the sick horses and walked around them, one after the other. Holding on to their manes and putting his mouth close to theirs, he pretended to kiss them. "How are you, lover?" he asked each horse, smacking his lips. Then from a corner, he took the measure of the two "brides." Finally he approached them, observing them closely and allowing them to observe him.

He was not a tall man, but he was sturdy and heavyset, with a massive neck and a pair of protruding ears which seemed doubly large since they stuck out from a bare, closely shaven head. Binele sized him up. He seemed taller than he actually was, wearing a pair of heavy knee-high boots on raised heels. The boots tightly hugged the leggings of his blood-stained riding pants. Binele stared at his firm round face which looked as if it had been hewn from stone and at his tiny eyes of a steely gray, eyes whose gaze was devoid of any expression. He cast a dread upon her. The demons of Bociany seemed more human than this human being who stood before her.

Before Ziporah had time to explain anything to Gaiger, he had brushed the child's diaper aside with a short stubby finger on which he wore a large signet ring. "Dysentery," he said in a dry voice. From the rear pocket of his riding pants he drew out a creased wad of scrap paper, removed a blunt pencil from behind his ear, and scribbled something on one of the scraps, which he then handed to Ziporah. "A spoonful three times a day," he said and took hold of Ziporah's arm. "The little bastard is yours, isn't he?"

Ziporah nodded as Gaiger led her off in the direction of the door in the rear. "I beg of you, Panie Gaiger, . . . " Binele managed to catch the sound of Ziporah's pleading voice before the door slammed shut behind them.

Binele carried the baby out into the street. She paced up and down the sidewalk in front of Gaiger's house, biting her lips, her mind racked by both rage and helplessness. A terrible ache invaded her heart and seemed to creep over her entire body, penetrating her whole being and destroying something tender, sweet, and innocent within her. Gaiger was a wild bull, worse than the Evil One himself, of whom she was not afraid. Gaiger's fleshiness, his human form, was awesome and threatening. Ziporah had suddenly grown so near and dear to her heart that it seemed to Binele that she herself was Ziporah, alone inside with Gaiger. She wanted to help Ziporah, wanted it badly—but how? She trembled. Beside herself with frustration and nervousness, she rocked the child in her arms with quick jerky movements and stalked back and forth in front of the house. "Come out of there, Ziporah, come out of there already . . . " she whispered. An eternity seemed to have passed since Ziporah had vanished behind Gaiger's door.

Finally Ziporah emerged at a run from the gate, her face all aflame, her dark eyes fiery hot, red blotches on her neck, and a crooked smile on her puffy lips. She adjusted the plaid shawl over her disheveled hair. "It's nothing, nothing at all," she muttered. "Finished and done with, thank Heaven. As long as the child gets well . . . " As if she were drunk, she raised the piece of paper with the prescription on it and kissed it loudly.

Binele went up to Ziporah's room with the child, while Ziporah left to see her "suitor" to borrow the necessary money for the medicine from him. When she returned home, Binele proposed, "I'll sleep over with you and help you take care of the child."

So Binele moved in to live with Ziporah in her room on Faifer Street.

⊚⊚ *2* ⊚⊚

ON PAYDAY AFTER WORK the women at the factory formed a circle around Yone the Svolotch. He called each of them by name and paid them cash, the ordinary *shtoperkes* two, the first class, most qualified ones three rubles each. Binele gasped. So much money! When he had called out all the names, she pushed herself through to him. "I haven't been paid!" she exclaimed boldly.

His shifty eyes began to creep over her, from her head down to her toes. Somehow he looked undecided, as if he were weighing something in his head. It was clear that he could not make up his mind what to do. Then his green eyes lit up, becoming pointed, penetrating, piercing her with a gaze as sharp as a blade. The expression of his face changed. He smirked, took a step backward, puckered his eyebrows, and finally raised the list of names to his nose. "What's going on here?" he pretended surprise. "Your name is not on the list."

"Then put it down on it," she said with not a trace of fear in her tone of voice, although her heart stirred uncomfortably in her bosom. Nervously, she twiddled the edge of her braid around a finger. "You've seen me working here all week, haven't you?"

He scratched his head under the skullcap with the tip of his pencil, and asked, "And what's your name?"

"My name is Binele."

"Bi-ne-le," he copied her tone of voice, baring the two rows of his large, healthy teeth. "What a name! One can choke on it. Did you know that, my beauty?" The women who stood around, satisfied with themselves, thrust their pay into their bodices. Some smirked, mimicking Yone. Others tittered, squeaked, and blinked at him with eyes full of flattery. He came closer to Binele. The women nodded their heads at him encouragingly. "And what's your family name?" he asked.

Her family name. Binele felt as though someone had poured a pail of icy water over her head. What was her other name, the one called a family name? Her mind worked feverishly, trying to recall it. She had never used it. In Bociany, if she was not called by her heinous nickname Marzepa, she was called Binele, Yossele Abedale's girl, while Abedale was her father's nickname. Nor did her father ever use his real family name, which had been used only for registration in the county official's books. But how could she explain to Yone the manner in which people were addressing each other in Bociany? She had heard him call out the family names of the other women. She would not make a fool of herself. Nor would she call herself in the diminutive, Binele, any longer, but call herself Bina. Her face was all aflame.

The women dispersed and gradually disappeared through the exit. Only the middle-aged woman whose life Binele had "saved" on her first day of work, remained standing a few steps away from Yone and Binele. The woman spoke up, "What do you want of her, Panie Yone? She was working for Handsome Moshe before. That's why you don't have her on your list."

"Really, for Handsome Moshe?" Yone rejoined with fake seriousness. "Then let her go to Handsome Moshe." He lashed out against the woman, "And what business is that of yours, dear lady? You'd better put your legs on your shoulders and vanish!" He pointed to the exit with a long, sharp-nailed finger.

As soon as the woman left the hall and Yone was alone with Binele, his demeanor changed. He looked neither angry nor boisterous, but rather serious and even more than before he seemed unsure of himself. "I'll pay you next week. I'll find a way. And . . . I asked Handsome Moshe about you." Suddenly he grabbed her by the waist and with his face very close to hers, added heatedly, "Beware of taking me for a fool. I know all your tricks by heart. The Bundists have sent you in to trap me with those thievish eyes and that wriggling behind of yours, damn you! So that you could either poison me or bury a knife in my heart."

She had not the faintest idea what he was sputtering about. Fascinated, mesmerized by his feverish grip on her, she peered at his face. Its expression made it seem as though she were not in his hands, but he in hers. Fear, genuine fear lurked in the depth of his eyes. These Bundists, who were they? She vaguely remembered something. There had been a group of young men and women at the factory in Bociany where she had worked, who called themselves Bundists, and Yacov too had mentioned them to her. Of course! They were the fools who wanted to overthrow the tsar.

"Don't make such a face," Yone smirked uncomfortably, still holding her tightly by the waist. "I'm not a stool pigeon. I'm a good Jew. It's they who are the enemies of the People of Israel. They've seduced you with their sweet talk, they've misled you. Soon enough you'll find that out for yourself." With a sudden, rough tenderness he clumsily brushed his hand against her cheek and pressed her more tightly to his chest. "If you let me kiss those juicy freckles of yours, I'll let you spy on me as much as your heart desires." She felt the touch of him with her entire body. "You're Lilith the Seductress . . . "

"I'm a Marzepa!" she cried out and tore herself out of his arms. A thought passed through her mind and she added, "Don't meddle with me and don't try to flatter me, because it won't help you! And if you don't stop bothering me or pinching me, and if you don't give me my pay next week, and if I lose even one hair from my head, I'll tell the Bundists and they'll finish you off even before they finish off Tsar Nicholas!" She dashed out of the hall.

The friendly middle-aged woman was sitting on the landing, waiting for Binele. She stood up, took hold of Binele's arm, and they went down the stairs together. "Aren't you going in to see Handsome Moshe about your pay?" the woman asked as they passed the hall on the first floor.

"I'll take it from him . . . later," Binele answered, distraught. She could not shake off the impact of the moments that she had spent alone with Yone.

"Do you know him personally? I mean socially?" the woman asked cautiously.

"Whom?" Binele asked her back.

"Handsome Moshe."

"Of course . . . He is . . . he was my . . . suitor."

"You did not see eye to eye politically, I suppose."

"Of course."

"Now I understand." The woman pressed Binele's arm to express her satisfaction. "That's the reason why he sent you up to work for Yone the Svolotch. There you have it, the entire Poale-Zion morality on the palm of your hand. They want to dance at two weddings at the same time, that is, make the revolution here and build a National Home there, and that's why they can be trusted neither here nor there. Don't you agree?"

"Of course," Binele agreed. She asked herself whether the woman was speaking plain Yiddish, or was mixing it with another language.

In the street the woman once again squeezed Binele's arm. "I'm very glad that you're one of us. I heard how well you told off Yone Svolotch."

"Because he deserves it!" Binele nodded proudly. "Sure I'm one of yours. I may come from Bociany, but I'm a woman of Lodz like everybody else, rely on me."

The woman let out a heavy sigh. "In the year nineteen hundred and five, my dear child, I was even more enthusiastic than you are now. I was there, you know."

"In Bociany?"

"No, in Lodz, at the very heart of the revolution, as a member of the Bund. What life, what spirit! I stood on the barricades on Volborska Street. And the strikes, the demonstrations I participated in, and the blows from the Cossack knouts that I endured! We thought that any moment the revolution would come to a victorious end and we would be liberated. But now . . . Well, you can see for yourself. Dead times. And you'd better not overdo it in your quarrel with Yone Svolotch, because we may run into trouble. He's right in saying that a *shtoperke* is unlike any other textile worker. We are the aristocracy of the proletariat. And in our factory, conditions are still better than in any other. It's the only factory in Lodz that hires Jewish male workers. You yourself surely know that the struggle for accepting Jewish workers at the factories is lost just as badly as the rest of the revolution. When it comes to the Jewish proletariat, the Jewish capital-ist is just as anti-Semitic as the goyish. Only we, the Jewish *shtoperkes* have the good fortune to be accepted everywhere, for the time being. You un-derstand? That's why you must watch out for Yone Svolotch as for fire." The woman saw Binele nodding, moving her head up and down at every statement that she made, so it did not occur to her that Binele understood not a single word of what she was saying and had already given up the ef-fort of trying to understand.

@⊚

Binele worked for another week without pay. In order not to become a burden to Ziporah, who made it through the week thanks to her "suitor," she went to the church every day, contributed her kopecks for charity, and took change from the canon's plate.

One day the following week, Yone the Svolotch appeared in the factory hall with a "beam" of material on his shoulder. As was his habit, he sped ahead between the rows of tables, bellowing, "Whose is this bloody piece of work? Yours? Yours?"

Binele became restless. By the design of the fabric on the "beam" she recognized it as one on which she had recently worked. When Yone ap-proached her, she saw his green eyes light up, not with anger, but with the little flames that she had discovered lurking inside them when she had been face to face with him. She spoke up uneasily, "It's mine."

"I know it's yours," he bent down to whisper in her ear. Then he burst out with booming guffaws and exclaimed as he faced the other women, "I, your chief supervisor, am telling all of you that this is the best piece of work ever produced in this hall! Let this be an example for you all!" And to Binele he added in a loud voice, "That's why I'm putting you to work in the first class category next week, among the best of the good." He dashed out of the hall with the bolt of material on his shoulder.

Binele's head swam. Her face burnt. Had she heard right? What had happened to Yone Svolotch? Was he really so afraid of her? He had not pinched her in the rear even once during her entire second week at the factory, but rather had pretended not to notice her.

"Her eyes are still good," she heard her neighbor to the right whisper to the woman next to her.

"He has a good eye on her," the other woman murmured back envi-ously. "Who knows which of the first class *shtoperkes* will be fired next week, so as to accommodate her." There were no friendly eyes beaming at Binele from the tables anymore. Just the opposite. The women eyed her with open resentment.

When payday came at the end of the week, Yone pushed himself through the crowd of women who surrounded him and asked Binele, "What did you say your name was?"

"My name is Bina," she answered.

"I know that already," he grew impatient. "What's your family name?"

As if her father were standing behind her back, whispering into her ear, she called out, "My family name is Yoskovitch!"

Four rubles lay in her palm. She could not believe her eyes. She was rich. She was singled out by Mother Fate to be showered with kindness. Somehow the four rubles seemed to have no connection with the two weeks of work that she had done. They were rather like a winning lottery ticket, like a stroke of good luck.

On their way home, Binele and Ziporah stopped to buy the curds that were to remedy Ziporah's child's chronic diarrhea. Binele refreshed herself with a few sips of the curds and gave the mug to Ziporah to carry, so that she would not be tempted to have another sip. When they passed the bazaar, Binele bought herself a second-hand skirt without holes. She still could hardly believe that the money was hers, that the skirt was hers, and that it was earned, not stolen. It was a powerful feeling. The world seemed to have expanded before her, along with her fantasies and hopes. One day she would perhaps have saved up enough money to buy herself an embroidered white blouse with frills around the collar, and perhaps a hat to go with it, such as she had seen the young women wear when they promenaded through the streets of Lodz on the Sabbath.

The following day was Friday. Binele held onto Ziporah's arm as they walked home from work. The preparations for the Sabbath in the slums of Baluty reminded her very much of Bociany. The streets were more crowded than usual. The clopping of the looms heard from the windows of the small weaving plants and home workshops, a clopping that was an eternal accompaniment to the noise in the street, seemed to have accelerated its rhythm. Everyone in the street rushed by at a double tempo. The hosiery makers, the knitters, the glove makers, the spinners, the tailors, the shoemakers, all loaded down with sacks, boxes, and parcels, were hurrying in both directions to deliver their finished work. Women and girls rushed to the baker's with pots of *cholnt*. The heder boys, free for the day, were everywhere. The shops were crammed with people.

At length Binele let Ziporah go home by herself, while she wandered on through the streets. The houses of Baluty, small, untidy, decrepit, so much resembled the houses of Bociany that they made her forget where she was. Her thoughts carried her off toward her home shtetl and she saw herself wandering along the Wide and the Narrow Poplar Roads. She saw the special beadle of Baluty running through the streets, knocking on the shutters as he called, "Time to light the Sabbath candles!" and it seemed to her that she heard the beadle of Bociany. The flicker of lit Sabbath candles began to reflect in the windowpanes. Washed, combed, and neatly dressed children appeared in the yards. Their hair newly washed and arranged, dressed in their Sabbath dresses, girls appeared on the thresholds of the houses. Even the gentile janitors, the only non-Jewish inhabitants of Baluty, looked subdued and solemn as if they too were about to welcome Queen Sabbath.

Processions of men streamed out from the synagogue, group after group of men in shining black capotes, fur-trimmed hats, white shirts, and white stockings. Binele peeked in through the windows of the houses and saw families gather around tables covered with white tablecloths. Candle light. The aroma of Sabbath food. She heard the singing, "Welcome ye angels of the Heavenly Chariot . . . " She saw a paternal figure standing at the head of a table. He picked up the goblet in front of him, and raised it as his lips moved. He was saying the kiddush. She saw her own father in her mind's eye, saw him at home, in their hut, surrounded by all of his seven children. Faigele, her sister, was still alive, and was playing with their Sabbath guest, Abele the Town Fool. The children's laughter was reflected in her father's gray eyes, shining through them like sparks through ashes.

She saw Yacov in her mind's eye, standing in the middle of the Wide Poplar Road; saw him becoming increasingly smaller as she sat in the rear of the flour merchant's wagon, moving away from him and away from Bociany. She remembered how the haunting gaze of his warm brown eyes had penetrated her and had remained within her, despite the distance growing between them, despite his figure growing smaller and smaller, transforming into a speck, a dot, then vanishing at the point where the receding rows of poplars met. She still felt that gaze, fresh and sharp, imbedded within her. It gnawed at her somewhere deep inside the hollowness that his disappearance from sight had left in her heart.

That Sabbath, Binele and Ziporah decided to celebrate. The first thing that they did in the morning was to roll up their sleeves and devote themselves to the housecleaning. This meant that Ziporah cleaned while Binele looked on, watching and learning how housecleaning was being done in the metropolis of Lodz. Ziporah boasted proudly that she was renowned in the neighborhood for being a *vitishly* clean woman.

The first thing Ziporah did as an expertly and punctiliously clean woman of Lodz was to dust out the straw mattresses. She stirred up the straw inside them so vigorously and thoroughly that soon she was engulfed in a cloud of dust. The cloud of dust infused a smell into the room that bore no relation to that of any perfume, but was rather so odious that Binele wished that her nose were blocked with cement, to enable her to bear it, or at least to hold her back from sneezing. Then Ziporah pounded the mattresses with the broom, and another dust cloud formed in the midst of the previous one. It penetrated the throat, scratching and grating inside as though the broom itself had made its way into it.

Finished with the mattresses, Ziporah embarked on cleaning the floor. "I sweep the floor every single Sabbath," she boasted as she first sprinkled the floor with water as sparingly as if each droplet of water had the price of gold. She explained to Binele, "If you sprinkle too much water, the floor gets muddy and looks dirty." When she started to sweep the floor, the layer of dust on it, disturbed in its rest, shot up into the air as though in protest, stirring up and mixing with the lazy immobile dust clouds which had previously formed from the mattresses. When she was finished with that, Ziporah sprinkled yellow sand all over the floor to protect it from dirt. The sand dust rose to join the dust of the mattresses and the floor in mid air, thus creating one thick homogenous fog.

In the thickness of that fog, Ziporah's naked children crawled about, rejoicing in their mother's presence at home. Ziporah never opened a window in fear that the draft might, Heaven forbid, attack her children. And then the windows were not supposed to be touched because they hung on single hinges. Binele stared at the hole in the pane which was stuffed with a rag, in the hope that a breath of fresh air would, at least from there, penetrate into the room.

That kind of cleanliness which made one's throat grate and burnt the eyes made not much sense to Binele. "What do you need this kind of housecleaning for?" she argued with Ziporah. "At least, if you didn't clean the room, we would not be coughing. When I worked as a servant at the barber-surgeon's in Bociany, we had to keep all the windows open during housecleaning."

Ziporah waved her hand dismissively and said with a supercilious grin, "What do you provincials know about such things? In Lodz housecleaning is done in the most modern way."

Binele did not think much of such modernity. She longed for the sweet fragrances and the pure transparent air of Bociany.

They took delight in their festive lunch, meat soup with barley, with bones instead of meat. They ate chunks of bread with it and finished the meal with cups of chicory coffee. The children, their bellies full, played on the floor. Binele and Ziporah, their heads freshly washed with naphtha, as a protection against lice, sat in their Sabbath skirts, engrossed in a serious discussion about Binele's future and the sad state of Ziporah's marriage. Binele argued heatedly with Ziporah, urging her to break with her husband.

"Send that good-for-nothing to where the black pepper grows. Let him go to hell!" Tears welled up in her eyes when she saw Ziporah's eyes brimming over.

Ziporah wept and scoffed at her as she smiled a bitter, tearful smile, "Are you out of your mind? Where would I get another man like him, may he rot in his grave? After all, he's more precious to me than words can tell. He spends the whole winter in jail and I have a winter of perfect peace and quiet."

"Your suitor is probably a more worthwhile find," Binele argued.

"My suitor? You don't know what you're talking about, for heaven's sake! You think he'd marry a beggar like me, with three small children into the bargain, and hang a heavy load of worries around his neck? Are you out of your mind? A suitor is suited to be a suitor, not a husband. When he becomes a husband, he's finished as a suitor, can't you see?"

Binele shook her head resolutely. "I will never marry. I need a husband as much as I need a hump on my back."

Again Ziporah disagreed with her. "Do you prefer to lead the life of an old maid?"

Binele laughed. "How can I be an old maid, if I'm not old?"

"Go ahead and laugh. Another year and then another and you'll laugh no more. A woman without a man is like a doormat for everyone to rub their feet on."

"And if she has a husband, then she's her husband's doormat. That's the only difference. And for your information, I'll be a doormat under no one's feet, no matter husband or not." She was thoughtful for a long while. With less self-assurance she confessed to Ziporah, "I don't know how to deal with Yone the Svolotch, you understand? I'm always afraid that he'll come over to me at work and pinch my behind, and that I'll smack him in the snout and all will be lost. Not that he's done it ever since I quarreled with him the first week, mind you."

Ziporah assumed a didactic tone of voice, "The only choice you have, if you want to stay on the job, is to wipe your mouth and keep quiet about it. Be happy that you please him, that he wants to make a first-class *shtoperke* out of you and raise your pay by a whole ruble. Fancy that, a fortune! That's why I'm telling you, a woman should never pull at the rope too strongly, because it might break."

"I will pull at it strongly, if he starts up with me," Binele contradicted her.

Ziporah took hold of her hand. "For how long do you intend to remain a provincial, tell me. Listen to me, get used to him and that's that."

"I cannot get used to him."

"Why not? What harm does he do you, silly head? He gives you a little squeeze, a pinch on the rear, a smack with his lips on your face? What's the great to-do about that? It's better than collecting blows, isn't it? And even if he really does start up with you, there is always Gaiger to go to if you're in trouble. You're not alone in this world. And don't worry, Yone will soon get tired of you. He likes fresh fruit. Then, you see, you won't be as haughty and honorable as you are now. You're plain spoiled, that's what you are."

In the evening, after Ziporah's children had collapsed on the straw mattresses and fallen asleep, Ziporah and Binele went for a stroll on the Faiferovka, as the Faifer Street was called. It was dark outside. The street was illuminated by only two gas lamps and by the lights from the windows and pub doors. In the nocturnal light "grooms," "brides," and "madams" with their entourages thronged the sidewalks as did the other inhabitants of this infamous street of amusement and earthly delight.

Ziporah nudged Binele, pointing out passersby to her, and telling her spicy stories about them. "Do you know why this street is called Faiferovka?" she asked. "Because a man only has to 'fife' through his teeth, to whistle that is, and a girl will appear before him. If you ask me, this is the liveliest street in Lodz. I wouldn't move from here even to Wilki, if you paid me. Who needs to go downtown, if all of downtown comes here every night, the richest and the poorest. It's so boring there that you can fall asleep walking. Here at least you see real life. Do you know what I mean?"

Binele nodded. Ziporah was right. It was fascinating to stroll with Ziporah and watch the colorful parade of beggars, drunkards, toughs, and dandies who strolled about with their dolled-up women. Ziporah, who was on neighborly terms with all of them, kept stopping in order to introduce her new girlfriend to them. Binele thought of the demons that caroused in Bociany at night. There they were rarely seen by anybody, while here in Lodz they were tangible. Lodz was their city of delights, their fair. On the one hand, Binele felt herself strangely attracted by this reveling atmosphere, eager to throw herself into this bewitching life full of secrets and excitement.

She wanted, like Ziporah, to become part of this city within a city. But on the other hand, she wished to escape it and find a corner for herself at the furthermost end of Lodz. Because here in this secret city she felt herself to be a provincial in a completely different manner.

She was made increasingly ill-at-ease by the way some male passersby pierced her with their glances. She felt still worse when others called her or whistled at her, or when, in passing, some man quickly whispered something in her ear, something which she did not understand and which made her feel stupid. What did they want of her? How come they noticed her at all? She was a Marzepa, ugly and unattractive, while all the girls who swarmed past her were a thousand times prettier and more elegant than she was.

Ziporah reassured her, "If you're walking with me, you have nothing to fear. They know that I am *vitish* from head to toe and they respect *vitish* people. Aside from that, my suitor sends them so many clients that they tremble before him like fish on the Day of Atonement."

"Where is he, your suitor?" Binele dared to ask for the first time. She had been living with Ziporah for two weeks and had noticed that Ziporah ran to her suitor only when she needed money to get through the week.

Ziporah shook her head coquettishly and pressed in the waves of her hair with her fingers. "How should I know where he is, may he live in good health?" She quickly changed the subject and pointed out a house in front of which stood a group of dandies with their women. "If you're game, we can go into the pub, have a glass of beer and we won't lose a singe hair from our heads. Have you ever tasted a glass of beer, my provincial?" She checked to see the expression of Binele's face. "Good Heavens! I bet you don't know what a pub is!"

"You mean an inn?" Binele asked.

"Some comparison! An inn is frequented only by peasants, yokels or petty Hasidim who count their kopecks, whereas in the pub you'll find the cream of Baluty. Have you ever heard of Berl the King? Of course not. Nowadays they call him Lame King, may all his enemies be lame. He's the best safecracker in Lodz; he specialized only in robbing safes. Last year he had an accident. He jumped from a second-floor window during a theft and broke a leg. You should see the man! True, he's not overly handsome and has black teeth from chewing too much tobacco, but his personality, Good Heavens! He's as strong as Samson and as clever as Haman the Wicked. But he himself isn't wicked, believe me. Crazy Moshe Gootnick, whom the weavers call "Tsokrates" and who presides over the tables at the weaver's pub, has made a real *tsocialist* out of Berl the Lame King. Besides that, Berl can read the Bible smoothly, and he can read a newspaper, too. When Berl is at the pub, I have nothing to fear because *tsocialists* are like the goyish priests. They take an oath to live like saints and they make sure that the rich should pay for it. And Berl the King, I wish he were a real king, straightens out the quarrels between the thieves, the 'grooms' and the 'brides' and even between the 'madams' and their clients, because everyone knows that he stands for justice. Then they empty the beer barrels and devour tons of goose-fat crackers until they burst. Well, do you want us to have a look inside?"

Binele glanced briefly at the dandies and their women who were crowded around the entrance to the pub. The smell of cheap eau de cologne tickled her nostrils. "All right, let's have a look inside," she agreed, allowing Ziporah to push through the crowd ahead, pulling her along by the arm. The open door of the pub was hung with a swaying curtain of colored strips of oilcloth, the interior made visible through the slits. By the light of the burning naphtha lamps inside, Binele could see a thick fog of smoke in which rows of heads seemed to be suspended over the tables, one above the other, right up to the ceiling. Mugs of beer lit up the darkness with their ruby-brown shine. Pair upon pair of shining eyes. Hands like flocks of birds flying about in the air. Noise, screams, and laughter mingled with the drunken singing around the tables. To the smell of eau de cologne was added the smell of *monopolka,* beer, cigars, and cigarettes; the odors penetrated Binele's nose and made her head begin to swim.

A pair of hands spread the door curtain apart. A shaven head poked out from between the strips of oilcloth and one of the hands grabbed hold of Ziporah's wrist. A voice asked, snickering, "Why are you looking in, little bride? You'd better come in and look out!" Ziporah had already put one foot over the threshold when the hand began to pull her inside. But Binele, at the sight of the shaven head—which she had immediately recognized—gave Ziporah a powerful pull backwards, and Ziporah fell back into her arms. Her features twisted into an expression of revulsion, Binele dragged Ziporah away from the cluster of people who, clinging together, stood around in front of the door. Binele cried frenziedly, "I don't want to go inside!"

"You're a stupid cow!" Ziporah laughed falsely. "You recognized Gaiger, didn't you? But the Lame King and Moshe Tsokrates and other *tsocialists* are also inside. So Gaiger would have paid for our beers and we wouldn't have lost even one hair from our heads. And you would have seen Shaye the Magnate with your own eyes, too."

"I don't want to see anybody!" Binele kept pulling her away from the pub.

Ziporah gave Binele a derisive glance. "Because you haven't got the faintest idea who Shaye the Magnate is. Did you know that this pub belongs to him? They call him Magnate because he got rich making first-class *monopolka* in secret, in a shed in the backyard. Apart from that, he has a gambling den behind the pub. Inside, they don't bet mere kopecks on the cards. They bet entire houses. The cream of Baluty, the bigshots of the underworld, as they call it, and the biggest 'poultry' merchants who send their chickens, girls that is, to Argentina, play a twenty-one inside. And to Shaye the Magnate, may the Angel of Death play a twenty-one with him, belong all the houses on the Faiferovka, may a grave in the cemetery belong to him. He evicts people every Monday and Thursday. Fortunately, there are such people alive in this world as Berl the King and Moshe Tsokrates. There are *tsocialists* around who risk their heads for the poor. Shaye the Magnate trembles before them like a fish on the Day of Atonement, may a shark devour him once and for all."

Ziporah was in the middle of pouring out her entire lexicon of curses on Shaye the Magnate's head, when they heard screams and the breaking of glass and the cracking of wood coming from behind them, from Shaye the Magnate's tavern. The entire street, like a river suddenly reversing its course, made an about turn and lurched forward, racing in the direction of the shouts. "A fight! A fight!" people yelled from all sides as they rushed toward the tavern. Ziporah and Binele took hold of each other's hand and ran along, panting with excitement and tension. They pushed themselves through the crowd to come as close as they could to the sight of the spectacle.

"Scram! Make room!" a burly fellow in front of the tavern yelled at the top of his voice. A pair of hands tied up the loose strands of curtain over the entrance, shoving them to both sides like two long braids. A bleeding man was carried out, then another. The men who had brought out the wounded laid them down near the wall and then resumed fighting among themselves. Another group of heated-up toughs emerged from the tavern, stepped over the bodies of the moaning wounded, and with their fists flying in the air, plunged into the knot of fighters. Soon they were all entangled in one wriggling, twisting mass of hands, legs, and faces with mouths howling or moaning. The crowd of onlookers reluctantly receded to avoid an accidental blow and looked on with burning eyes, gasping, saliva dribbling from their mouths.

Binele lost Ziporah in the crowd. As she stood there, all alone among the onlookers, she suddenly grew aware of a hand making its way down her body. She tore herself away from her place, drilled a passage for herself with her head and elbows and got herself out of the human mass. She ran toward Ziporah's house. Ziporah appeared before her, smiling nervously, "Why did you run away, you provincial dumbbell?"

"Where were you?" Binele grabbed her by the arm, feeling safe again.

"Where should I have been? I was standing right beside you." She pulled Binele along. "Every Saturday night they scuffle and fight a bit. It's like a theater without tickets. Don't worry, no one calls the gendarmes here. They'll straighten it out among themselves and still manage to empty all the beer barrels and devour all the goose rinds tonight. Come," she dragged Binele forward. "Let's go and see what's doing at Burke's pub." Binele allowed herself to be dragged along. She was not really frightened.

She was curious. But she could not bear it when a stranger's hand ventured to creep over her body.

"There are so many pubs here," Binele remarked as if she were paying Ziporah a compliment.

"What did you think?" Ziporah raised her head proudly. "We're not living in some hole called Bociany-Shmociany. Here every trade has its own pub, the butchers, the wagon drivers, the weavers, the tailors. Over there, for instance, is the weavers' pub," she indicated the pub with her chin. "That's where the long-haired *tsocialists* in their *roubashkas* used to gather. Nowadays you can only see a few of them. The tsar has sent the rest of them to Siberia. But our Moshe Tsokrates still goes there with his cronies, and goes to the other pubs, too. He gives speeches to the thieves and the 'brides' and 'grooms,' and he reads to them out of all kinds of books. He makes up his own rhymes, too, which is called "povetry." That's why they call him Tsokrates. He's afraid of no one. There are no stool pigeons here, unless there is a raid. Telling on someone is the greatest sin in Baluty. That's why there is a price on Yone the Svolotch's head."

"Why?" Binele grew red in the face, she herself did not know why.

"Because he is a stool pigeon, a telltale."

"On whom did he tell?"

"On the *tsocialists* . . . on whom else?"

"I don't understand a word you're saying." Binele became strangely irritated.

"You don't understand because you're still a provincial greenhorn," Ziporah said, then she pointed at the windows which they were passing. "Can you hear the weavers' looms clopping inside? Have a look," she pushed Binele closer to a window. Binele peered inside and saw a sparsely lit room full of cupboards, tables, beds, and looms. From above each loom a lighted candle illuminated a disheveled man, his sleeves rolled up, sitting stooped as he threw the shuttle back and forth. "You understand," Ziporah explained, "It's Saturday night, and those inside sit down at their looms right after the Sabbath is over, and they'll stay there until dawn. So the *tsocialists* want that a man should at least have Saturday night to himself." She heaved a heavy sigh. "If you ask me, they'll keep on wanting it forever."

Binele looked through the other windows which they passed. "They're working everywhere," she remarked.

"So they are. A Jew must earn his piece of bread with his sweat and blood. The men can't get a job in the factories, so the owners of the work-shops suck the marrow from their bones." Ziporah looked at Binele with pride. "Well, and you thought that the Faiferovka is only inhabited by 'grooms' and 'brides' and thieves, didn't you? Look here, for example," she pointed to a house that they were passing. "That's were the rag collectors live. Every day they swarm into the city like locusts. They make their living from the garbage, like my father for instance, but they make it honestly. The same goes for the organ-grinders and the street singers who live here, not to mention the acrobats and beggars. They all earn their piece of bread honestly. You think it's easy to walk around begging all day, with one eye covered, pretending to be blind? Or pretending to be lame, with one leg tied up, hobbling about on crutches all day? Believe me, you could go blind and lame just from the effort. And if you think that the people of Baluty, because they work so hard, are like corpses and haven't got a spark of life in them, you can see the truth for yourself. Nowhere is there as much singing going on as in Baluty, nowhere do they tell as many stories or crack as many jokes. And I swear to you, no one in Baluty is drawn to Wilki. True, twice a day you can see them going there. In the mornings to work and in the evenings when they go to their *tsocialist* cells. If I didn't have any chil-dren, I would go there myself. Moshe Tsokrates wants to take me along."

"You mean to jail, to see your husband?" Binele asked.

"No, silly provincial! A *tsocialist* cell is where they meet secretly. There can even be a cell in the Konstantine Woods, or in a park." Ziporah no-ticed that Binele was thinking hard and she shook her arm. "What's the matter now?"

"Nothing. I was just thinking about the beggars' profession." Binele frowned. "To me it's not a real profession, even if you are blind or lame."

"What do you mean? Aren't they human beings, too?"

"They are, but not my kind. I'd rather steal than beg."

"It's a question of habit," Ziporah resumed her didactic tone of voice. "A person has to make a living one way or the other, so what difference does it make how one does it, as long as one doesn't kill?" They were ap-proaching Burke's pub. Ziporah offered further information, "I wouldn't say that they don't fight at Burke's. Here the bodies which they bring out are sometimes so dead that no doctor could help. But they settle it amongst themselves quietly. Because even a better sort of clientele comes here than to Shaye the Magnate's. For instance, this is where Pesach Katzap comes. He's the owner of his own restaurant on Piotrkowska

Street and he also deals in 'poultry.' He's already shipped hundreds of girls off to the whore market in Argentina. But he associates with the biggest brains of Wilki. He's even on personal terms with the actors."

"What are actors?" Binele asked.

"Actors are the same as artists. That means they're the best sort of clowns or Purim players. They don't work in the streets or in the back-yards. They work in halls which are called theaters and the people come to them, not they to the people, and you need a ticket to see them, which costs money of course. And here, at Burke's, most of the clientele are not thieves but *potachniks,* you understand?"

"No, what are *potachniks?*"

"They are a band of decent fellows. They don't steal from houses. They just stand on street corners or in the gates. If a wagon with mer-chandise passes by, they quickly grab whatever they can from it. Then they sell it to their men here in Baluty and make a good living out of it."

"In Bociany such people would be called thieves just the same," Binele remarked.

Ziporah had no time to answer. Suddenly her face lit up. The 'brides' from her house where strolling by with their 'grooms.' They were sur-rounded by a group of other 'brides' and 'grooms.'

"You want to join us, dollies?" asked a dainty short 'groom' who had a barber's mustache and wore a black top hat; a thickly pomaded curl dan-gled smartly over his forehead. He twirled his walking stick in the air as he grabbed Ziporah by the waist. "We're going to the gypsy camp to dance."

Ziporah and Binele joined them.

The gypsy camp was located in the fields on the outskirts of town, within walking distance of the Faiferovka. The house, number twenty-six Zgierska Street, that led up to the gypsy camp was called The Point, and as a rule no Jew ventured beyond it. But the inhabitants of Faifer Street were not usual Jews. They were themselves a kind of gypsies. So the promenad-ing tailors and their apprentices, or the young cobblers, or the weavers and their girlfriends, walked along the Zgierska up to The Point and turned back, while the 'brides' and 'grooms' continued leisurely in the direction of the fields.

After a few minutes' walk beyond The Point, the fancily clad 'grooms' were transformed into different people. Up to then they had behaved in quite a *vitish* manner. Now, however, they made themselves comfortable, removed their stiff collars, unbuttoned their tight vests and jackets, took out bottles of *monopolka* from their pockets, and started to sip from them as they walked. One of them looped his arm around Binele's waist, linking her to the rest of the gang, all of whom walked knotted together, arm in arm. Then he boldly let his hand slide lower down her back as he intimately rubbed his smooth cheek against hers. Without thinking, she flung the stranger's hand away, edged herself away from the boisterous noisy group, and darting forward, walked on by herself. Her eyes followed the route of a drowned rat carried afloat by the swiftly racing water in the gutter.

Ziporah approached her while scolding her companions, "What do you want of her life? She's a provincial after all." She took Binele by the arm and tried to pacify her, "I swear," she said, "that they mean no harm."

The gypsy camp was illuminated with multicolored lanterns and with torches. Large rugs of sackcloth were spread on the ground in front of the gypsy wagons and tents. On top of the spread out rugs were displayed bead necklaces, colorful hand-woven straw baskets, and shoes as well as frying pans, pots, cauldrons, and kettles of various sizes that the gypsies produced out of copper. The gypsy women were dressed in bright rags decorated with many strings of beads. They wore earrings and bracelets and sat beside their wares, each one holding a naked baby either in a sack on her back, or at her breast, or sleeping in her lap. They called to the customers in gypsy Polish, bidding them to come over and pick a bargain. Their shouts accompanied by the jingling of their beads and bracelets, they lured the men with the enticing gleam of their coal-black eyes and the promise lurking in the depths of their partly revealed bosoms. At low tables sat the fortunetellers, foretelling the future from cards or from people's palms at five kopecks a session.

At the center of the camp the gypsy band was playing with so much verve and passion that the musicians themselves were swept off their feet and danced along with the crowd. Some performed acrobatic tricks while playing their accordions or mouth harmonicas as the crowd spun around them. Everything turned in a drunken whirlwind of skirts and ballooning shirts, hair and ribbons flying up in the air to the sound of the music and the yelps, the squeaks, and the deafening whistling. The very ground seemed to be dancing along. The multicolored lights from the lanterns, transformed into a confetti shower of sparks and of beaming threads, enmeshed the entire camp.

The wild rhythm stirred up Binele's restlessness, slithering up and down her limbs. Holding Ziporah by the hand, she began to move with her, to sway and to hop. The 'grooms' and their 'brides' had vanished, carried off by the vertiginous dance. Then someone grabbed Ziporah and danced off with her. Binele stood there, feeling herself like a suddenly uprooted plant in a storm. Around her all was spinning, swimming, and jostling her back and forth, to and fro. A gust of flying dresses swept her along, making her wander about, and she stared, mesmerized by the dancing gypsies. She gasped, enchanted by their men's handsomeness, by their dark laughing faces, their flying black locks, and by the beauty of their women who, in their low-cut blouses with colored beads on their bronzed necks, their white teeth and the whites of their eyes glittering, swirled past her through the darkness. In their umbrella-like skirts, held aloft by the invisible hands of their partners, the women seemed to be suspended in the air. There was a strange magnetic power in their lightness, a fire-charged potency in their men's every movement.

As she strayed about, staring transfixed and bewildered, a gypsy man swept her off her feet, swung her into his arms, and carried her off into the maze of twirling figures. He had a shock of curly black hair and a pair of black eyes which beamed bolts of lightning at her. As if there were a trampoline with firecrackers under his feet, he slung Binele into the air, threw her about in his arms, and whirled her about him in windy circles, so fast that she lost the feel of the ground under her feet and hung on to him for her life, gasping for breath. His arms, his hands were all over her. She felt them with every cell of her body and minded it not the least. On the contrary. She wanted to shout, "Faster! Higher!" That he might again swing her in his arms and make her fly. She began to yell, to squeak, and to giggle just like the other women. The dark gypsy bared his teeth with delight; his black pupils seemed to consume her with their heat.

In the middle of this breathtaking whirling, amidst the sea of dark heads and the glittering navy-blue darkness, Binele was suddenly struck by the sight of a red head that had flashed past her. Only one such crop of red hair had she ever seen on a man. She did not see Yone the Svolotch, but she sensed that it was he, without his skullcap, dancing with a young gypsy woman whose long flying hair fluttered like a black veil in the air. For a moment it seemed to Binele that it was she whom Yone held in his arms, that it was he who threw her into the air and made her gasp for air.

The sky had begun to gray with a new dawn before the crowd started to make its way home from the gypsy fair. Ziporah held Binele by the arm. She glanced enviously at the 'brides.' "Do you have any idea," she whispered in Binele's ear, "how much the 'grooms' spent on them tonight? Look at the strings of beads on their necks." She tried to console herself, "Nothing to envy them for. They'll have to pay back for every single bead."

The 'grooms' could not agree among themselves whether—in order to cool themselves off a little, or perhaps to work themselves up into an even more romantic mood—they should take a walk to Piotrkowska Street in Wilki, or head toward the old cemetery in Baluty, since these were the two most popular places in town where men usually took their dates. As a rule, the Piotrkowska Street served the purpose of showing off one's date, while the cemetery allowed one to enjoy the date in relative privacy. At length, the group split up. A few couples left for Wilki, while Ziporah and Binele, reluctant to quit as yet, and wanting to cool off in the fresh breezy air of dawn, joined those who headed for the old cemetery on Joy Street.

The insane asylum was located near the cemetery. In the gray of dawn, demonic sounds could be heard coming from the building: screams, sobs, and the strangely loud talk of the insane. The 'grooms' were ready to translate their romantic moods into action. Each of them embraced a 'bride,' led her off to a different tomb and vanished with her behind its tombstone. Binele and Ziporah remained sitting on a slab of concrete on top of a grave, and watched whatever fragment of the action became visible to the eye. As soon as the giggling and the laughter of the 'brides' died away, Ziporah whispered in Binele's ear, "Now it's time for us to vanish into thin air, or they may call us over and try to take care of us, too."

They sneaked out of the cemetery.

◕ *3* ◕

YONE THE SVOLOTCH kept his promise and put Binele at one of the first-class *shtoperkes'* tables. She learned to work with the needle and pincer and became so skillful at working in the loose "eyes" or holes, at mending the faulty machine work of the fabrics and at not letting even one damaged spot pass her eyes, that she was rarely given a "beam" to do over. Even the most experienced *shtoperkes* began to admire and envy her. Her only problem was that she could not abide Yone the Svolotch's presence in the hall. He did not bother her, pick on her, or pinch her, but she was afraid that he would, and this made her feel ill-at-ease and restless.

So she decided to find out about Handsome Moshe on her own. He was the chief supervisor of the first floor, the hero of the women's department at Berman's textile factory, with whom all the *shtoperkes* were head over heels in love.

That particular day she dressed for work in her new Sabbath skirt and, when the sirens sounded and work at the factory was over, she placed herself near the exit gate. Although she had been working at the factory for a considerable number of weeks, she had not yet managed to get a glimpse of Handsome Moshe. Ziporah was always in a hurry to go home after work. This time, however, Binele had sent Ziporah ahead. Now she stood at the side of the yard and observed every man who approached the gate. Soon enough—as she traced the glances beaming from all female eyes in one direction, toward the figure of one man—she realized that she was watching Handsome Moshe in person.

She would have recognized him anyway. Her first glance of him confirmed that he deserved his colossal popularity. He was in fact handsome—not only by virtue of the way he looked, but also because of the way he was dressed. He was dressed as if he had just stepped out, or were about to step into, a fancy carriage on his way to a royal wedding.

Here, in this gloomy gray yard, amidst the rushing men in their dark, threadbare jackets, amidst the women in plaids, amidst the sea of lusterless green faces, Handsome Moshe, in his fitted striped suit with paper collar and necktie, wearing polished shoes and holding a walking stick with an ivory knob under his arm, stood out, if not like a prince, then surely like a member of the aristocracy, or like an American who had accidentally strayed into a crowd of paupers. In addition, he had a fine, round, quite young-looking face the color of milk, which sported a barber's mustache in accord with the latest fashion. His small nose was delicately carved, his chin good-humoredly raised, a stiff curl of brown hair peered out dandy-style from under his Panama hat, reaching down to his brown eyebrow. He grinned charmingly as he cracked pumpkin seeds with his teeth. His parted lips, resembling two parts of a juicy raspberry-colored orange, pouted as he spat out the shells. As he did so, the walking stick under his arm rose in the air, as if to ward off the girls who followed him at a distance.

Binele gaped at him in wide-eyed amazement. Her eyes met his for a split second, while she, enraptured and unaware of what she was doing, quickly approached him. As he slowly moved on beside her, he forgot to raise the pumpkin seed that he held in his hand to his mouth. With her figure, her straight back, her fresh skin, and the curious bold glow in her slanted eyes, Binele also stood out in appearance from the surrounding dullness. He blinked at her and, exuding an air of self-satisfaction, asked grinning, "Why are you staring at me like that?"

Upon hearing a normal voice speaking a normal language, Binele immediately regained her composure. She fell into step beside him. "You're Handsome Moshe, aren't you?" she asked.

He raised the pumpkin seed to his mouth and hugged it with his red lips as if he were kissing it. With obvious delight he daintily cracked it with his front teeth, spat out the shell with exquisite delicacy, and asked, "What if I am?" She focused her gaze on his mouth, admiring how deftly and gracefully he cracked the next pumpkin seed, peeling it out of its shell. "Why are you staring at me?" he repeated the question matter-of-factly.

"Is it forbidden?" she asked back matter-of-factly.

"Not if you buy a ticket."

She mimicked his tone of voice. "How much is a ticket?"

He burst out laughing, freely, boyishly, "All sold out!" Sure of himself he took her lightly by the arm and led her out of the gate. "Why did you ask me if I was Handsome Moshe? Doesn't it show on my face?"

She allowed herself another look at him. "It does."

"In that case, be my guest." He reached out the bag of pumpkin seeds to her. She put her hand inside the bag and took out one pumpkin seed. She watched him with a sideways look and tried to crack the seed as daintily as he did. She noticed that his fingernails were neatly trimmed, while hers were long with dark borders. She decided then and there to buy a pair of scissors with her next week's pay and cut her nails.

They stopped on the street where the crowd of workers was thinning out. They cracked pumpkin seeds, smiling at the pumpkin seeds with their mouths, and at each other with their eyes. A question danced around in Binele's head: Should she ask him now to let her work in his hall, or should she wait for another opportunity? They caught themselves, realizing that the street had become deserted and the janitors were locking up the factory gates. He took hold of one of her braids and pulled her lightly ahead.

When they reached the corner, Handsome Moshe, taking his leave of her, raised two fingers to the rim of his Panama hat in a kind of military salute and jumped onto a passing streetcar. Binele wandered on. She had no one to hurry home to. Dreamy and absent-minded, she slowly strolled in the direction of Baluty, going over the conversation with Moshe in her mind. She had no doubt that she would soon be working in his hall. That was what she wanted and what she was sure to accomplish.

She stopped in front of the shop windows on Piotrkowska Street, imagining herself wearing each of the pretty dresses that were displayed inside. She promised herself that when she started working for Handsome Moshe, she would buy herself a dress and treat herself to a ride home in a tram at least once a week. She had known for a long time now that whoever had the necessary kopecks could enjoy the luxurious ride. She repeated to herself the new elegant expression she had heard from Moshe, "Be my guest."

Binele continued to walk at a slow leisurely pace through the squalid, packed streets of Baluty. She still did not feel like going home. She stopped at the stalls in the gates and along the walls of houses. Small mirrors, brushes, and combs were on display on tables in the stalls. She bought herself a bagel and chewed on it as she peered into the huts through the windows. The rhythmical clip-clop of the weavers' looms, a pleasant sound of wood against wood, mingled with the loud rhythmic hum of the sewing and knitting machines that issued from everywhere.

Again the sunken huts of Baluty brought Bociany back to her mind. She saw the shtetl before her mind's eye and recalled the fragrance of its delightful air. Filled to overflowing with homesickness, her heart ached. There were no storks' nests on the rooftops of Baluty, no White and Blue Mountain behind Baluty, no birch wood, nor a lake, nor any poplar roads. Yacov entered her mind. She saw him in his quarter-length pants with his short clumsy gabardine flying in the breeze along with the tassels of his ritual undergarment, as he had run beside her through the Wide Poplar Road during a stormy downpour. She recalled how they had stood against the wall of the horse dealer's stable, glued to one another, holding hands as the storm spread a watery curtain from the narrow roof down to the ground, where it bounced up with columns of drops which looked like fringes made of beads. It was then that she had discovered the magic in the touch of another person's hand.

A black cat passed her as it slithered along a wall. Black cats signified a bad omen to the women of Bociany. But it now occurred to Binele that she would have enjoyed having a kitten to cuddle in her arms, to stroke and caress whenever she felt the same gnawing homesickness that she now felt. She did not take her eyes off the black cat. Impelled by a murky curiosity, she followed the cat, allowing it to lead her on. And so she arrived at a gate where a gypsy woman sat on the ground on a spread-out sack. The cat leaped onto the woman's shoulder.

"Fortune-telling! Card-reading!" the gypsy woman held out her hand, beckoning to the passersby, while with her other hand she stroked the cat's black furry tail.

To her own surprise, Binele took out five kopecks from her new cloth purse, sat down on the ground across from the gypsy woman, and said, "Tell me . . ."

"For five kopecks I read the palm only," the woman answered. She straightened out Binele's palm over her own, directing her gaze to its lines. "Oh, pretty young lady . . ." She gasped, guiding a long black fingernail along the thick line around Binele's thumb. "I see a row of lights. I see . . . one and two and three . . . and I see a big light leading the small ones here in front. A bridegroom. And it's getting brighter and brighter. And I see . . ." The finger with the dark pointy nail jumped over to another line on Binele's palm. "I see my black cat . . . as black as the night . . . dark as Beelzebub . . . and I see black candles burning, pretty young lady." She shook her head sadly. "I can see a wedding. You're walking to church in a black dress."

"Why a black dress?" Binele folded her fingers.

The gypsy woman straightened Binele's hand. "Because this will not be your first wedding but your last. The last fashion will be such."

Binele grabbed her hand back. "Why should I walk into a church? And what kind of fashion is it to wear black for a wedding? For any wedding? And with Gentiles on top of it all!" she cried out, dismayed, on the verge of despair.

The gypsy woman nodded, "I meant a Jewish church. And Moshka will be your bridegroom." She opened her large mouth and displayed two toothless gums and a dark, deep mouth ready to swallow Binele into its fringed red depths.

Binele jumped to her feet and ran away. It took her a while before she recovered from the shock. "And for that I wasted five kopecks!" she could not forgive herself. She recalled the name "Moshka." Had the gypsy woman meant Handsome Moshe? She burst out laughing and shook off the silly fears that had gripped her. Besides, she told herself, she had no faith in fortune telling! The evil creatures that the gypsy woman had mentioned—Beelzebub or the black cat—had simply meant the night of death. It meant that she, Binele, would die the way all people die. And as for the bridegroom, the fortune teller had meant that if it were not one groom, it would be another. By the name "Moshka" she could have implied anybody, since the Gentiles called all the Jews "Moshkas." But that Handsome Moshe had disturbed her mind good and proper, of that Binele had not the slightest doubt.

Somehow Binele was unable to pluck up enough courage to stop Handsome Moshe again on her way home from work. She rather avoided him. "What do I have to bother about him for?" she argued with herself. "What am I missing by working for Yone the Svolotch?" Actually, she ought to have enjoyed working for Yone. She was earning a fortune, three rubles a week! She was a first-class *shtoperke* and was a "'ristocrat among the 'ristocrats of the textile workers." All this was thanks to Yone, who bore her an inexplicable respect. Nowadays when he passed her with a "beam" of faultily repaired material, she could feel his eyes piercing her. But when she turned around to catch his look, he would briskly turn his head away. He never again pinched her on the rear.

She was proud of and much satisfied with herself. She had become a *mentsh* without anyone's help, and she was living on her own. Never in her life had she been so happy or led such a good life. Now she understood what Yacov had meant by saying that in Lodz a person could "sweep up" gold in the streets. She was rich, so rich that she could afford to share her riches with Ziporah and her children. She felt like a real woman of Lodz.

She had completely stopped walking home with Ziporah after work. She took pleasure wandering through the streets. A city was like a human being. When she walked through it, Binele could feel its heart pulsating in rhythm with her own, she could communicate with it, without words, like with a close friend. As she walked home, she made the acquaintance of many young workers, men and women. She had even met a few girls from

Bociany and become friendly with them. Now and then she visited them at their living quarters, eager to hear news from Bociany. Hailing from the same shtetl made Binele feel bound to these girls as if they and she belonged to the same family.

Most of all she loved to walk the Piotrkowska Street. The shop windows attracted her like magnets. She spent hours standing before them, moving from one window to another, pleasing her eyes with the displays of materials, dresses, purses, shoes, and food articles or fruits the likes of which she had never seen before. In the middle of the road clanked the streetcars laden with people and rattled the countless wagons, carts, and droshkys whose wheels pounded noisily against the cobblestones. Mostly the latter were crammed with Gentiles and Jews from the surrounding shtetlekh. At the time of day that Binele went walking, these piece workers from out of town had already delivered their finished work and were heading home with new work. On some wagons Binele could see the cages filled with chickens and geese that these country people had brought along and were now on their way to deliver to their steady customers in town. The sight of the chickens and geese increased the force of Binele's craving for a bite of meat. Every Thursday after work, with her week's pay in her purse, she stepped into a butcher shop. The price of meat had been constantly rising of late, and all that she could afford was half a kilogram of minced meat. She ate a bit of it raw and took the rest home to Ziporah, who kneaded as much bread into the meatballs as she could afford. It lasted them for a sumptuous feast on Friday night and another on the Sabbath.

So life continued in a more or less unvarying routine, until Ziporah's husband showed up. Summer was approaching and Ziporah's husband never considered it worthwhile to spend the summer in prison. And with her mate at home, Ziporah was no longer the same. First, she gave him the largest and best portions of the cooked food. Second, he did not work, but took Ziporah's entire pay from her. Through Ziporah he let Binele know that she too must now give him her pay for rent and upkeep. Yet he never spoke directly to her, as if he refused to acknowledge her presence, but addressed himself aloud to Ziporah with a "Tell her that . . ." Besides all this, husband and wife never stopped fighting; this meant that he beat her up and she cried.

Ziporah's husband was a tiny creature covered all over with hair like a shaggy dog. He had a large belly, a collapsing chest, and a rounded back. His arms were long and his hands were large. He liked to put them into violent motion rather than speak. Or he would throw whatever came into them at his wife. If Binele tried to interfere, he avenged himself doubly on Ziporah. At night these same hands dragged his wife onto his straw mattress.

Binele was now paying him for rent and upkeep, but she still had enough money left to buy herself a pair of scissors and a comb. She also bought a bar of soap that she kept in her rag purse, washing her face and neck every night with it at the water pump in the yard. And she bought herself a "new" secondhand blouse. It was not as pretty as the one with the ruffles that she had been dreaming about, but the blouse had a pretty high collar and was the most elegant piece of clothing on display at the bazaar. In her hair, which she now kept meticulously clean, she would braid in two wide ribbons and tie them into smart-looking bows at the ends. She still clung to the rule that she had formulated for herself right after her arrival in Lodz that "the outer dress covers the inner mess" and that it was not as important who one was as how one looked. Whenever she gazed into the shop windows, she promised herself to buy the pretty dresses, not when she had grown rich, but as soon as she had saved up the money for them. She was convinced that the beautiful dresses would increase her chances of becoming truly prosperous. But in order to save up the money for the dresses she had to move out of Ziporah's room. Although her heart ached for Ziporah, Binele no longer wanted to live with her.

At night, as she lay on the new straw mattress that she had had to buy, since previously, during his absence, she had slept on "his," she thought deeply about Ziporah and her situation. Ziporah could never be a stranger to her. When she heard Ziporah wrestling with her husband at night, she felt as if worms were creeping over her own body. She wanted to block her ears and escape. At the same time she hated herself for the strange jealousy these sounds aroused in her heart.

In the morning, on their way to work, Binele chided Ziporah, "Why don't you send him to the Devil, idiot that you are? He's such a good-for-nothing, and you let him beat you up! Had I not known that he might take it out on you, I would have torn him into pieces."

"Shut up," Ziporah tried to calm her in a voice hoarse with tears. "It's not as bad as you make it look. He and I are such a couple. That's how it is.

Daytime ready for divorce, nighttime ready for the bed. If he didn't love me, he wouldn't beat me up, may he roast in hell."

Binele was familiar with that sort of philosophy. In her childhood, her friend Yadwiga from Bociany had said the same thing about her own parents. But now Binele also recalled a saying by her father, and she quoted it to Ziporah, "If you grind a fool in a mortar, he'll say you didn't grind *him*, but the pepper."

"Yes, I know," Ziporah shook her head sadly. "They say something similar here too. They say, 'If you spit in a whore's face, she'll say it's raining.' But I swear to you, I don't mind. It's not a great tragedy to get knocked about a bit by your own husband, may a calamity knock him out forever. The world won't collapse. He won't kill me, don't worry."

"Of course he won't kill you," Binele continued railing, beside herself with vexation. "He would lose a provider, and a servant, and a woman to bed for free, and a mother for his bastards, if he killed you!" But it was to no effect. She accomplished nothing with her talk.

Binele hid away as much of her earnings as she could, paying less and less for her upkeep and rent, and disregarded "his" growlings and Ziporah's shy reproaches. She was saving, adding one kopeck to another. She kept her "knot" with the savings hidden in her bosom and never parted with it. After work, instead of looking at the shop windows, she now wandered through the streets looking for a room. She inquired of the janitors. There were rooms available, but for even the smallest cubicle in the center of town, a tidy sum of money was asked. She could not afford even half of it.

One day, as she walked through the streets after work, looking for a room, she felt unusually downhearted. In order to cheer herself up, she decided to treat herself to an ice-cream cone. It had been a mild pleasant day, and now, in the early evening, the setting sun's rays reflected in the upper windows of the houses. Binele wandered in the balmy gray light, licking her cone, trying to boost her morale by dreaming great dreams of the happiness that was waiting for her sometime in the near future. She looked in front of her, her eyes buried in the distant haze of the street. Then, without really seeing what was going on around her, she became vaguely aware of the freight wagons laden with furniture, bedding, pots, pans, and various kinds of other household items passing her by one after the other. She remembered that she had seen many such transports recently. Were so many people moving into new lodgings? she asked herself.

Or could these be the belongings of vacationers moving to the country—
but now, so late in the summer?

"Hello, Miss Gold-Braids!" she heard a voice call out behind her.
Someone tugged at her braid. Handsome Moshe appeared beside her.

"My name is not Gold-Braids," she said without losing her composure
and moved her braid to the front. Only then did she become flustered.
From the side, squinting, she took in his elegant beauty with her eyes and
went red in the face.

"What's your name, then?" Moshe's eyes were fixed on her tongue,
which, due to her nervousness, licked at the ice-cream cone with increasing speed.

"Bina's my name," she said.

"You work for Yone the Svolotch, don't you?" he asked as if he had
forgotten their first encounter.

That was an opportune question. It gave her a chance to ask Handsome Moshe to take her on for work in his hall. She finished her ice-cream
quickly and inwardly prepared herself to come out with her plea. But to
her own surprise, she heard herself saying, "He's not really a *svolotch*."

Moshe, just as surprised, puckered his eyebrows. "Then why do the
women call him *svolotch*?"

"Go and ask the women," she shot back, although she hated herself
for talking so impolitely to him.

"Why don't they call me Moshe the Svolotch?"

"Your luck!"

"You know what they call me, don't you?" He blinked at her and pulled
at her braid again. She shook her head angrily, having the impression that
he was poking fun at her. He added, "You told me yourself the other day
that the name Handsome Moshe suits me, remember?"

"And if it does, so what?"

"So I thank you for the compliment."

"For the compliment?"

"For the compliment," he repeated slowly, while she made a note in her
mind of this new foreign word. "Forgive me, but I forgot to ask your family name the other day. So I'm doing it now."

She refused to acknowledge the apology, although she had no idea of
how he had offended her. "My name is Bina Yoskovitch," she flung her
head up proudly.

"Very pleased to meet you, Miss Yoskovitch." He bowed genteelly and clicked his heels together, which amused her greatly and forced her to smile. "My true full name is Moshe Piekarz. And permit me to remark, Miss Yoskovitch, that you have very nice teeth and two very nice golden braids and in general a very charming face, Miss Yoskovitch."

"Thanks for the compliment!" she shot back, making use of the new word, and added, as she usually did when she wanted to amuse someone, "In Bociany everyone called me Marzepa."

"Because to appreciate your beauty one must first know what beauty is, Miss Yoskovitch," he continued in his theatrical voice. "And allow me to correct you, the word is Mazepa, not Marzepa."

"I know," she laughed. "But I was called Marzepa. Can I help that?" laughing, she pointed to the wagons loaded with furniture which passed them. "Look!" she cried. "People are moving out on summer vacation when winter is coming."

The air about Moshe underwent a sudden change. His face took on a serious expression. "Some winter, with a war coming! These people are leaving to settle down in the shtetlekh and villages. As for the rest of us, we may as well put away our teeth into our purses, because we won't need them. I might even be drafted into the army soon, although I was freed from military service. A 'fixer' made me varicose veins on the legs."

She gave him a stealthy glance. Moshe seemed to have become transformed into a different person. The princely happy-go-lucky look had faded from his demeanor. He looked like a bewildered little boy with large frightened eyes. "Did it hurt?" she asked compassionately.

"Child's play in comparison with what awaits me in the army, or, heaven forbid, on the battlefield." Steeped in his morbid thoughts, he walked on silently.

She had no courage to interrupt the silence. She was unable to tear her eyes away from him. Where had boisterous Handsome Moshe gone, Moshe, the famous supervisor of Berman's textile factory? The young man who now walked beside her had suddenly become very familiar and close to her heart. And she so much wanted to see him smile again that, for no reason at all, she burst out laughing as they passed a building where columns of steam, accompanied by the smell of soap, spewed from the exit and billowed into the street. "What do they have in there? A ritual bath or what?" she asked.

He livened up and explained, "It's just a plain bathhouse. I myself take a bath here every Friday. Old-fashioned Jews go to their old-fashioned ritual bathhouses. I consider myself modern and cultured, so I go to a modern bathhouse." He said this partly in jest, partly in earnest.

"I'm also cultured," she immediately made use of the unfamiliar word. "I take a bath . . . permission . . . " she inserted the fancy word 'permission,' which the barber-surgeon's wife in Bociany had frequently used. "Every Monday and Thursday I take a bath." She fingered her braid playfully in front of his eyes, so that he might notice her clipped fingernails and the pretty ribbon in her clean hair. "It's not as important who you are, as how you look. Don't you agree? How much do you pay for taking a bath?"

"If you want to go, I can treat you to one." His face went red as a beet. "It's separate for men and for women, of course. You wouldn't be shy to go in with me, would you?"

She had the impression that it was he who would be shy. "What is there to be shy about?"

"I meant in case you are still a trifle old-fashioned."

"No, I'm completely modern."

"Then we have a date!" he announced. "Friday. And afterwards, we'll go to a movie house." He glanced at her puzzled face. "You don't go to movie houses?"

"Of course I do. Every Monday and Thursday."

"You don't mind going on a Friday, Sabbath Eve?"

"Heavens, no!" She had no idea where they were supposed to be going, nor why she should mind going there on the eve of the Sabbath. But what difference did that make? She would go with him wherever he chose to take her.

"In that case you're really as progressive as I am." He said this respectfully, praising her in a sincere yet somewhat theatrical tone of voice. "In that case do you know what else I would suggest?"

"What else would you suggest?" she asked as if the word "suggest" were familiar to her.

"I would suggest that you come to work in my hall. Yone the Svolotch will fire whomever he pleases as soon as something happens. Berman, the boss, uses him to do all his dirty work for him. And now since Crown Prince Ferdinand was shot in Sarajevo, Russia will enter the war with Austria over Serbia, and . . . and with me you'll at least be sure of work . . . as long as I'm sure."

"It's not necessary," she cut him short, again surprised at herself. "I will stay on with Yone." What foolish devil had made these words come down from her lips? It seemed as if another Binele were sitting inside her, over whom she had no power and who was a constant source of amazement to her.

Moshe looked at her quite hurt. "All the girls are dying to work for me."

"Let them die. I'm not all the girls."

"But he's a ruffian and a bandit."

"He's no bandit to me. He made me become a first-class *shtoperke*."

Moshe leaned over to her ear, "He's a provocateur."

"I'm not so sure about that," she turned up her nose proudly, as if she knew the exact meaning of the word

"What do you mean, you're not so sure?" Moshe was beside himself. "Everyone knows that the Ochrana has placed him at the factory to spy on us, while Berman not only consented but patted himself on his fat belly. You know, don't you, that on the one hand we have the tsar's reactionaries, and on the other, we have the beards and sidelocks to struggle against. May I have as many good years as the number of comrades Yone has sent off to you know where. Their *rov* has given the Ochrana a sign to go by. If they catch a young man who doesn't wear the tasseled undergarment, then he is a revolutionary and should be imprisoned. If he does wear it, he should be left alone."

"Then all the young men should wear the tasseled undergarment," Binele remarked, although she had hardly understood a word of what Moshe was saying. "I'll ask Yone whether all this is true."

"Are you out of your mind?" Moshe cried out. "If you mention my name to him, my life isn't worth a broken kopeck!"

"So I am out of my mind!" Offended and madly indignant, she made a face, waved at him, and left him standing with his mouth open.

She could not understand what was happening to her. She was afraid of the "other" within her, the spiteful one who spoke through her mouth like a *dybbuk,* as if she were not her own master and had no say over her actions at all. How could she have frightened Handsome Moshe and shamed him so, leaving him standing in the middle of the street? And he pleased her so much! Other girls would have been in seventh heaven had he only looked at them the way he looked at her. And why had she refused to work in his hall during these uncertain times? She had so wanted to work for him!

The following day Moshe waited for Binele after work. She could hardly control the outcry of delight surging to her lips at the sight of him.

He accompanied her in the direction of Baluty. "I don't have the slightest intention of saying anything about you to Yone," she assured him straight away.

"I did not expect you to," he smiled faintly. "I suspect he knows about me anyway, but he's afraid of my comrades."

"Are you a Bundist?" she asked.

"Good heavens, no, " he said curtly and changed the subject.

The day was cold and gray. The streets through which Moshe walked with her were steeped in a humid fog that looked like a mass of dirty cotton. The depths of the streets were blotted from sight and seemed to have no end. Moshe and Binele bumped into oncoming passersby. Long rows of women stood along the walls, clad provocatively, stylish hats on their heads, large shiny purses under their arms; they wore shoes with stiletto heels. Moshe looked stiffly ahead, pretending not to see them. He held Binele's arm as if in order to protect her against these women, or to protect himself.

"Look at how dressed up they are," Binele remarked.

"Not my cup of tea," he said curtly.

"Why do they stand here in this weather? They look so rich."

"They're waiting for customers, what else?"

"Why do you say customers, as if they were selling something?"

"Of course they are. They're selling themselves." He drew out a handkerchief from his pocket and blew his nose, as if he were trying to blow away the embarrassment Binele's questions caused him.

"What do you mean they're selling themselves? If you sell something you don't get it back, do you? And they do get their bodies back."

"Quite right. They let their bodies be exploited for money, poor souls."

"What do you mean by exploited?"

"You know what I mean. Used."

"But if they do it for money, they're not . . . exploited, are they? And why do you call them poor souls? They are well dressed, so elegant that I wish it on all Jewish girls. Maybe they're luckier than we the factory girls are. They get a lot of fresh air. And look at their faces. Not as yellow as those of our women. And their eyes aren't puffy. They surely don't have to wake up at five in the morning."

"They only make the impression of looking well. Their faces are painted." He blew his nose repetitiously.

She watched him out of the corner of her eye. She was curious whether he had ever visited such a "house" in Wilki or anywhere else. "Is your nose running so badly that you have to keep blowing it all the time?" she asked compassionately before returning to the subject at hand. "And tell me," she asked, "where . . . I mean, how do they learn this trade?"

He removed the handkerchief from his nose and answered with great solemnity, "This is not a trade that can be learned. A girl has to be born with a character for it. Many a girl would rather die than . . . "

"Don't exaggerate," Binele assumed her friend Ziporah's tone of voice. "Once you've learned it, there's nothing to it. It's like drinking a glass of water. People are just like animals. They have to survive on something."

"Animals don't sell themselves," Moshe put in gravely.

"Of course not. They are being sold by others. If people can sell themselves whenever they want to, that's already an advantage."

"You mean to say . . . that you yourself . . . that you too could . . . "

"I?" She stared at him questioningly. She could not understand how this dandy called Handsome Moshe, the glamorous prince who was so sure of himself, and over whom all the girls at the factory fainted, could increasingly appear to her like a frightened boy who asked stupid questions. Of course she would do anything in the world in order to survive, to have enough food to eat. She would certainly not die rather than . . .

"I?" she repeated.

"Yes, you," he mumbled, looking at her guiltily, as if he had abused her by merely asking the question.

Consequently, she did feel abused and exclaimed, "Are you out of your mind?" Once more she left him standing in the middle of the street and ran off.

Each time she ran away from Handsome Moshe in the middle of their walk, she was certain that she would never see him again. But Moshe took no offense and never asked her why she had run away. He waited for her after work as if nothing had happened and walked her part way home.

The project of going to the bathhouse together never materialized. Moshe never repeated the proposal. But they did go to a movie theater every Friday night. There Binele helped Moshe finish off a bag of pumpkin seeds, while she shed oceans of tears, watching the movies of Ramon Novarro.

At the movie house Moshe and Binele kissed to the accompaniment of the piano music which accompanied the action on the screen. Then they walked arm in arm, maintaining the mock-serious tone of their conversations.

One evening Moshe took Binele to the Yiddish theater for the first time. Moshe had made so much fuss over that particular event and he had infected Binele with so much anticipation and enthusiasm that a week prior to the occasion she had bought herself a "new" secondhand hat. She wore it slanted sideways on her head. It pleased Moshe enormously.

They stood on the top gallery squeezed in among a dense crowd of young people and watched, listening openmouthed to the drama *The Fate of Man*. Binele understood little of the actual dialogue because of the difficult outlandish words that the actors used; nonetheless she grasped everything as far as the tragic life situation taking place on stage was concerned. The people on stage became as familiar to her as her nearest and dearest friends. She felt that she could walk up to them for a talk. And there were, in fact, some spectators in the hall who shouted advice to the characters on stage. Binele felt like doing the same. She would have called out and told them how, in her opinion, they ought to lead their lives in order to solve their tragic problems—if it were not for Moshe, who believed that a cultured person must not shout in the theater.

After that unforgettable performance, which shook them both to the core of their beings, Moshe bared his heart before Binele. He confessed that the theater was his life, that during those evenings when he was unable to see her, he was meeting with the comrades of his illegal party, the Poale-Zion, and that afterwards he met with his artistic friends, four tailor apprentices with whom he had formed a small theater troupe. The troupe did not yet perform in public, but it had already spent three years preparing to do so. When Moshe talked about the Poale-Zion and the theater, his voice trembled with emotion as if he were sharing his innermost secrets with Binele.

From that day on Binele and Moshe went often to the Yiddish theater, most of the time without tickets. They had to sneak themselves in. Moshe rarely had the money even for standing room on the topmost balcony. He supported a large family on his earnings, a father, a mother, and a houseful of brothers and sisters. Sometimes the bag of pumpkin seeds was his only meal of the day. The fancy clothes that he wore, were, like Binele's, all secondhand. He had contacts with the cleaner backstage and could purchase for a real bargain price the outfits that the great actors discarded. Moshe loved to dress well, to enliven the grayness of factory life with his own colorfulness, with his good looks, and his good cheer. He loved to see eyes light up at the sight of him. His pleasure was doubled by the awareness that his elegance gave delight to others beside himself.

The longer Binele went out with Moshe, the clearer it became to her that the entire issue of personal appearance was actually nothing more than a matter of theatrical performance. She gradually arrived at the conclusion that she had to learn rather to "undress" people in her mind, if she wanted to find out who they really were. The same was true with regard to people's manners and behavior. A person could behave as if he or she were very sure of themselves, could pretend that they knew everything, just as she herself pretended, and yet feel just the opposite in his or her heart of hearts.

She slowly discovered that although Moshe enjoyed colossal popularity with the women of the factory and behaved as if he had them by the dozen, he was in fact a shy and withdrawn young man and was just as "green" about many issues as she was. Yet in spite of the fact that Moshe had lost his princely glamour in her eyes, she enjoyed being with him, promenading, going to the theater or to the Train Garden with him and hearing him test himself in the roles for which he was forever getting ready. She quickly learned the lines that he recited aloud before her, as he tried to carve out each word refinedly. She enjoyed serving as his prompter whenever he got stuck in the middle of a monologue or a song, like for instance that funny one that she particularly liked:

> That bride of mine, she is so good,
> she is as sweet as cherry wine.
> She chases me to go on foot,
> straight from Lodz to Palestine.

But the most wonderful thing about Moshe were his kisses. When he kissed her, he was a prince again.

They spent large portions of the nights wandering through the town. Between the kisses that they exchanged while standing in dark corners of gates, Moshe would talk. He told Binele about Lodz, that its center was called Wilki, because wolves—the Polish word for wolves being "wilki"—had once roamed freely through the forests that had stood here not so long ago. That Napoleon, the greatest general that ever lived, when he was on his way to Moscow and was unable to find a passage for his armies through these forests, had chosen for his guide none other than Reb Shmuel Berman, a great grandfather of the owner of the factory where Binele and Moshe worked. Moshe told her how Lodz had sprung into being, how the Germans had appeared and founded the first textile factories, how the Jews had been banned from living in Wilki and had to live in the ghetto of Baluty. He told her how the Jews had anyway learned the weavers' trade and how later many of them became factory owners themselves, like their boss, Berman. Moshe also expounded on the bitter life of the Jewish working class. He said that the Jewish workers were doubly enslaved because they were both workers and Jews, and that when *socialismus* arrived or perhaps even before that, a Jewish homeland would be established in Eretz Israel. Binele again heard the word *Zionismus,* which she had so often heard at Shmulikl the barber-surgeon's home in Bociany. But now the word was not as repulsive to her ears as it had been then.

On the whole, Binele understood very little of what Moshe told her, and she listened without getting overly engrossed in his lectures. They were of no interest to her because they hardly had any connection with her own life. She would often let her attention wander. Even the possibility of a war breaking out between Germany and Russia disturbed her little. For the time being there was no war. For the time being Lodz was Lodz and Moshe was walking beside her. Only on that subject did she consider it worthwhile to concentrate her attention.

Moshe took her to the Luna Park on the other side of town and they rode the carousels. There was an empty field nearby, and Binele took delight in the sight of it. She had not seen a field for so long! She bet with Moshe that she could outrace him across the field. In fact, she did. She was quicker than he. But when they threw themselves down in the grass, she was weaker than he, although he was shy and oh, so clumsy.

On the other hand, however, Moshe was an excellent dancer. He taught Binele the fashionable salon dances and took her often to the dance hall. One evening they even won first price as the best dancing couple.

Every so often, when Binele left the factory yard with Handsome Moshe, she would notice Yone the Svolotch passing by them. He would turn his head, and her eyes would meet his for a split second. In that split second his eyes managed to burn her through with their green fire. She grew disturbed, and she felt herself blushing. She felt guilty about him and did not know why. Yone had been avoiding her in the work hall, yet more than once had she felt his devouring gaze creep all over her. If she quickly turned her head toward him, he fanned his hand at her in a strange manner, adjusted his skullcap, and dashed off.

She slept badly at night, and this was not only on account of Ziporah's husband. Something inexplicable was stirring deep in her heart. There was a kind of fever, a restlessness slithering in her limbs, that she could not calm. Often the sirens would break into a howl in the middle of the night. An epidemic of fires had swept through the town. Moshe had explained it to her. The times were bad, so some factory owners set fire to their factories in the hope of collecting colossal sums of insurance money. She more or less grasped the issue. What she was unable to grasp was why her own heart was racked by strange anxieties at the sight of the red sky at night. As a child in Bociany she would gasp, all afire with curiosity at the sight of a house burning. It used to arouse an almost pleasant excitement in her heart rather than fear.

When the sirens began to howl in the middle of the night, Binele got up from her mattress and walked over to the window. She heard fire wagons rolling through the streets somewhere, pounding their heavy iron wheels against the cobblestones that resounded with the swift pounding of horses' hooves in gallop. Somewhere torches were being carried back and forth in haste. The reflection of their flames hopped along the streets, casting thin dancing shadows between the roofs. The sky was as red as if the sun were setting amidst the darkness of the night, "Oh, Tateshie," Binele, sore in her heart, called her father, "Where are you?"

Back on her mattress, she tried to calm herself with the pleasant images that she called forth from her memory, visions of Bociany, of the Blue Mountain, of her long walks with Yacov along the Wide Poplar Road. She clutched the piece of rag where she kept the two kopecks Yacov had given her as parting money. But she still could not remove her eyes from the windowpane, from the flames reflected in the sky, from the shadows dancing by as if a fiery cauldron were boiling on the other side on the window. She thought she felt the smell of clothes burning, the smell of burning wood . . . burning flesh. "I'm as lonely as a dog," she whispered to herself.

Then the day arrived when the war broke out.

᠗ *4* ᠗

THE SHOT IN SARAJEVO resounded loudly in the shtetl of Bociany.

Bociany considered itself a chosen shtetl where the Messiah would arrive sooner than in any other community in exile. Accordingly, it was singled out in sharing the fate of the chosen people. It was prone to misfortune. And since it was a shtetl of paupers, it had great "luck" in military matters.

Those days when the young men were "recruited" for the army, weeping could be heard in almost every house, with the exception of two or three houses on the market place where the wealthy lived, who could afford to grease the proper hands. Fortunately Bociany was blessed with many storks that had generously supplied the shtetl with many children. Without the children there would have been no means of finding consolation.

Hindele the Scribe's Widow's eyes had seldom been dry during this time of the year, and it was particularly so this year when a war had begun to rage in the world. She could not bring herself to trust her good fortune at having her sons protected from conscription. The army exempted twins from military service and Shalom, her elder son, had been registered in the district officer's books on the date of her younger son Yacov's birth, so that officially the two of them were twins. She did, however, have a reason to fear for their safety. Yacov was approaching the age when he could be recruited by the army, and since the tsar might soon be needing more soldiers on the battlefields, there was a possibility that he might change the law of exemption and might also start drafting younger men.

Yacov worried about these matters much less than his mother. He was satisfied with the fact that he and Shalom had not been drafted that year and refused to give the matter any more thought. He was aware that somewhere young people were dying on the battlefields, but this was a detached form of awareness. On Reb Faivele the Miller's property where Yacov worked, the effect of the war could be felt in so far as Reb Faivele could now only subscribe to papers and magazines from Odessa or Warsaw. During his political discussions with visiting grain merchants, Reb Faivele enjoyed devastating his opponents with an avalanche of statistical facts about the atrocities of the war. Aside from that, life on the Blue Mountain continued in peace and quiet. And the more the news from the battlefields disturbed and dismayed Yacov, the more he relished the sweetness of the days he spent on the miller's homestead.

There were days, weeks even, when Yacov completely forgot what was going on in the world. He gave himself over to vague yearnings for a pair of reddish-blond braids flying in the wind. His longing for Binele had grown into a kind of ongoing accompaniment to his life. She became the form of all that he missed and all that he craved, a symbol of all his wants and deprivations. She was a kind of abstract presence that never left him, not even during the moments when she was absent from his conscious mind.

He played games with the miller's two boys, whom he tutored, Abrashka and his older brother, Shlomele. They greatly enjoyed the theatricals that he organized with them, making them perform on Saturday nights before Reb Faivele, his wife, Zirele, and their guests. The boys acted out the Biblical dramas that Yacov had favored in his own childhood, such as "Saul and David," or "David and Jonathan," or "Joseph and His Brothers." These activities eased the strange burden of responsibility that Yacov had felt ever since he could remember. It was a feeling of responsibility that encompassed more than merely his family, more than merely his people; it was a feeling of responsibility for something indefinable but enormous, a feeling that had always weighed him down and might have been the reason for the sadness that had gnawed at his heart as a young boy. Now, by way of these plays, he regressed for a while into the brightest moments of his childhood. He relived them vicariously through his students and so retrieved, at least partly, the taste for playful abandon that he had so often missed out on as a child.

Sussi, his favorite horse, had become Yacov's constant companion. Whenever he had a couple of hours free from work on Sundays he would ride off as far as he could. Riding Sussi always gave him the lofty, pleasurable feeling of his senses growing and expanding, of his spirit heading toward the mysteries hidden both within himself and in the world.

It was unavoidable that quick-witted Abrashka should sooner or later discover why Yacov vanished from the house for hours every Sunday. He began to insist that Yacov take him along. At first Yacov would not hear of it, but lacking the heart to refuse him for too long, he finally sent him to ask his mother for permission. Long Zirele's answer was of course a firm "no." But Abrashka was not one to be put off easily. He alternately nagged and charmed her, or he exploded into tears, until he got what he wanted. Zirele told him to ask his father, and his father's response was, "By all means. A boy should know how to ride a horse."

When for the first time Abrashka sat in the saddle in front of Yacov, holding on to Sussi's mane, Reb Faivele exclaimed to Yacov, "Watch out! If something happens to the boy . . . " But the warning was given in an altogether different tone from the warning he had once given Yacov in the mill. In Reb Faivele's opinion, exposing a child to needless danger was a crime, but it was another matter when there was an opportunity for a child to learn something. Then a father had to take the risk. Reb Faivele did not want his sons to grow up to become sissies. It bothered him greatly that his older son, Shlomele, whom he called "My Scholar," was devoid of any sense of adventure. Shlomele liked to sit the whole day long with a volume of the Scriptures in front of him and not to leave his mother for a moment.

"Be careful! Watch out!" Reb Faivele kept on calling after Yacov and Abrashka as they slowly rode down the hill.

"Watch out! Be careful!" Abrashka mimicked his father. As soon as they hit the road, he burst out with shouts of delight. "Speed him up, Yacov, hurry! Come on, Sussi, shake a leg!"

To have Abrashka with him was an altogether different pleasure than the pleasure Yacov derived from his solitary rides. The two of them and the horse were like three bodies moving to the rhythm of the same pulse, sharing a common state of mind. Yacov hummed with delight, then intoned a Hasidic song. Abrashka joined in with joyous, boisterous yells, until the singing turned into a melodious cacophony. Sussi's hooves seemed to follow the song's wild beat. He raised and lowered his mane; it seemed that he was not neighing but singing along, contentedly. From that day on, the horseback rides became part of Yacov and Abrashka's Sunday activities.

On one such luminous Sunday in late fall, they decided to let Sussi take them wherever he chose. Sussi suited himself and slowed down, clopping on sedately, with great dignity, while Yacov and Abrashka hummed, or whistled, or rode on in silence. Finally, Abrashka issued a command, "Tell me a story, quickly!" Although Abrashka was now a boy almost ready to study the Gemara, he was still as greedy for stories as he had been as a small child.

So Yacov told him a story. Sussi clopped on and nodded his mane lightly, as though to confirm every word that came out of Yacov's mouth. The stories that Yacov told while riding Sussi differed from the ones he would tell when he and Abrashka went for a stroll. The "riding" stories were about heroism, about the passions of the soul and the powers of the mind. They dealt with heroes who could fearlessly ride into the deepest abyss of suffering and torture and emerge victoriously from it, accomplishing these feats with as much ease as Yacov riding on Sussi's back.

"And now," Yacov intoned in a lilt. "And now we have left the material world altogether and are about to ride into the concealed worlds which have no beginning or end. Look up. Can you see the way the trees are swaying now? They're signaling their transformation into pure spirit. Actually, they are not trees anymore, but the souls of trees."

"And what about the flowers?" Abrashka pointed to a clump of yellow autumn flowers growing alongside the ditch on the Wide Poplar Road. "What's become of them?"

"They too are now pure soul, the souls of flowers," Yacov answered gravely. He remembered Binele's braids, which had a similar color, and he said. "One thing about them I know for sure, namely, that here, in the mystery worlds, they are called *Ahavelekh,* which means Little Loves."

"And what is there for us to do in these hidden worlds?" Abrashka asked.

"Why, I'm surprised you should ask such a question! There are millions of things for us to do here. Our doings are just about to begin. Here, in these worlds, it's not enough to merely have a powerful body. Here we must have a will as strong and taut as a bow's string, so that we can shoot up our thoughts like arrows, so high that they might attach themselves to the Almighty's Chariot and ride with it through the seven heavens."

Abrashka pressed his fists together as firmly as he could. He ground his teeth and tightened his lips with such force that he became red in the face and neck. From under his furrowed brow he looked back at Yacov and pressed his words out through clenched teeth. "Look, Yacov, how taut my will is!" Then he relaxed the muscles of his face and said, "It's done. My thoughts are on that cloud over there. And where are yours?"

"Right beside yours, of course," Yacov answered.

While they were thus engrossed in ruminating over the concealed mysterious worlds and searching the sky with their eyes, Sussi took the initiative into his own four legs and unexpectedly trotted into a ditch, sending Abrashka and Yacov sliding off his back. The withered grass in the ditch was soft and tall but moist at the bottom. Abrashka burst into peals of laughter. "Look, Yacov," he called, "how wet my concealed pants are on my concealed behind!"

Yacov ran after the horse and brought him back onto the road. Sussi had paid for his adventure with a lame leg. Yacov scratched himself under his beard, "What shall we do now?"

"We're not going home, that's for sure," Abrashka decided. "Father might, heaven forbid . . . We'll find a smith and he'll fix Sussi."

Yacov recalled, "There is a smithy on the way to Chwosty."

"So what are we waiting for?"

Yacov took hold of the limping horse's bridle, but almost immediately he began to regret his decision. The smithy of Yoel the Blacksmith was a considerable distance from the Blue Mountain, and then there were frightening rumors going around in Bociany about the blacksmith. While it was true that Yoel the Blacksmith had recently become known as the one who had warned the shtetl of the approaching calamity—the pogrom that had broken out the year before—people had still not stopped gossiping about him. It was wiser to turn back and head for home. But Abrashka was pulling forward, and Yacov himself was worried about Reb Faivele's reaction. So he decided to steel himself for real trouble and prepare himself to meet whatever might come to them, either at the smithy or afterwards, on their return to the Blue Mountain.

Yoel the Blacksmith sat on the doorstep of his small hut, a bottle of *monopolka* cupped in his hand. Sunday afternoons the road was deserted and he had little work to do. So it looked as though he were specifically awaiting his two visitors with the limping horse. At first sight, Yoel's huddled figure blended into the darkness of the hut's interior behind his back. The only bright spots in the gray of dusk were the whites of his eyes and the shine of the bottle in his hand. It was only when he stood up, leaving the bottle on the doorstep, that the two visitors could see the bulk of his full dark figure with the thick black beard that snarled over his black caftan. Apprehensively, they absorbed the towering figure with their eyes and withdrew a few steps as if readying themselves to take to flight.

"Welcome, vagabonds!" Yoel called out. "Are you on your way to Eretz Israel?" He would have frightened them even more as he approached them, if it had not been for the warm gleam of his dark eyes and his deep bass voice, which had a genuinely friendly tone. They relaxed completely when Yoel put his dark stained hand on Sussi's back and said to the horse chummily, "The two rowdies have tired you out, haven't they?" He raised the horse's leg and scrutinized it carefully.

Abrashka told him what had happened and begged, "Fix him well or we can't go home."

"Aren't you on your way to Eretz Israel?" Yoel asked, jesting.

Abrashka was serious, "Not today."

"Why not today?"

"Because today we have been to enough places already."

"Such as?"

"Such as everywhere!"

Yoel guffawed. "Impossible. No one in the world has ever been everywhere."

Abrashka pursed his lips, thought for a while, and said, "For your information, we've even been to the hidden worlds, that's where we've been. That's why we fell off Sussi's back."

Yoel let go of Sussi's leg and straightened himself. He put both hands on Abrashka's shoulders and bent down to him. "Well," he said, "was it worthwhile, in your opinion, to fall off the horse and be hurt, in order to see all those marvels, or wasn't it?"

"I did not hurt myself!" Abrashka exclaimed. "I only wet my pants. Sussi's the only one who hurt himself, and he was not traveling in the hidden worlds."

"You mean to say that you left the horse behind and went there on foot? So how could he have hurt himself?"

Abrashka looked at Yoel thoughtfully. "You might be right, you know. Of course we took him along. We were there, all the three of us, and Sussi took everything on himself. What's wrong with him?"

"Nothing serious, little tramp." Yoel shook Abrashka's chin. "He got dizzy from all the things he saw in the hidden worlds, and his tendon suffered a bit as a result. By the time you reach home he'll be as good as new." Yoel pointed to Yacov who was standing flabbergasted, watching the giant Yoel talking to the dwarf Abrashka. "And what about him?" Yoel asked. "Is he a mute by profession?"

"That's not a mute!" Abrashka laughed. "That's Yacov."

Fascinated, he peered into the smithy. As he was about to enter it, Yoel grasped his arm. "Tell me one more thing," he said. "What did you see in your hidden worlds?"

"Nothing," Abrashka wriggled himself free of Yoel's hand. "I saw the Almighty's Chariot!" He ran into the smithy.

Yacov was ready to call Abrashka back. It was late and they had far to go. But somehow Yoel's presence paralyzed and numbed him. Yoel put his heavy hand on Yacov's shoulder and pushed him lightly in the direction of the smithy, bidding him to enter. "Your little tramp has found the right word for it, hasn't he?" he asked. "But he turned the things upside down. First one sees the Heavenly Chariot then one sees nothing." The sharp smell of alcohol reached Yacov's nostrils. It was so sharp that he had to turn his head away. Yoel panted, "This deep concealed Nothingness, this awesome marvelous mystery! It's been given only to a few to gaze inside it. True, they lost their minds, but what does it matter if the loss is replaced by light?"

"We must go," Yacov muttered.

"Yes, hurry on then." Yoel's voice was both distant and intimate, as he continued, "But first let me tell you one thing. The older a man grows, the harder it becomes to make such expeditions. His eyes cease to serve him well. Only when you're young, and you wet your behind, can you manage to see clearly. But then, when you're young, you're seldom aware of what you're seeing." Yoel motioned in Abrashka's direction. "A fine boy. A relative of yours?"

"No, he's Reb Faivele the Miller's son. I'm his tutor," Yacov explained.

"But he is related to you in a different way, isn't he?"

"Yes, he's a little friend of mine." Yacov smiled faintly. His eyes met Yoel's and they exchanged a sudden quick look of understanding.

Yacov and Abrashka mounted Sussi who did in fact get better on their way back. After a while the boy called out, "Well, let's get on with the story!" But Yacov was not now in the mood for storytelling. He could not abstract himself from the impact of his encounter with Yoel. It had stirred something within him. He could still feel the penetrating heat of

Yoel's gaze and the power of the latter's presence. What a riddle of a man! The black, crude, and fleshy body of a drunkard or a robber, paired with eyes and a voice that seemed to issue directly from the soul, rough and sharp, yet filled with an inexplicable amiability.

Evening was encroaching upon the fields. When Yacov and Abrashka reached the Blue Mountain, they saw it glimmering with lantern lights, as if it were besieged by huge fireflies. The lantern lights bounced downhill, coming closer. Yacov and Abrashka dismounted, and as they started to climb the hill, they suddenly recognized Reb Faivele, Long Zirele, Fredka the Housekeeper, and her husband, as well as a few of the other servants descending downhill to meet them. The dog Bobik was the first to jump on Yacov, licking his face enthusiastically. Then, not at all enthusiastically, came Reb Faivele who grabbed Yacov by the collar and squeezed it tight.

"Where have you been, you good-for-nothing? We almost lost our minds worrying, you ruffian!" he roared, shaking Yacov and crushing the collar so tightly under Yacov's chin that it almost choked him.

"Don't hit him, Tateshie, don't!" Abrashka hung on to Reb Faivele's belt, trying to tear him away from Yacov. "We were at Yoel the Blacksmith's, because Sussi hurt himself."

"I feel faint!" Long Zirele exclaimed and almost collapsed as they made their way uphill. "They've been to Yoel the Blacksmith's!" She spat three times and took Abrashka into her arms as the boy tried to keep a firm grip on his father's belt. She quickly licked his eyes seven times. "Woe is me!" she cried, no longer the reasonable down-to-earth Zirele of every day. "They were at the warlock's place, on a Sunday evening yet! The roads are full of drunkards and werewolves!"

Reb Faivele let go of Yacov so suddenly that Yacov almost fell over backwards. Reb Faivele leaped after him, grabbed his sleeve, and waved his finger in front of his nose. "You're no longer needed here, Yacov, do you hear me? You're no good, devil take you!" He began to shake him again by the lapels, but then calmed down a little. "Oh, no, you're not staying. Tomorrow you pack your things and get out of here!"

"No, he won't!" Abrashka jumped into the air as if he had been burnt. "I'll go with him!" He hit his father with his fists. "Remember, Tateshie! If he goes, I'll kill you!"

Zirele grabbed hold of her head as both Reb Faivele and Yacov joined her in exclaiming, "Kill a father?"

Reb Faivele's anger evaporated during the night. The following day he acted as if nothing had happened.

Yacov and Abrashka continued their Sunday rides on Sussi, but the pleasure of their escapades was overshadowed by apprehension. Suppose something happened again and Reb Faivele did go through with his threat to fire Yacov? Yet, on account of their shared fear, the rides became doubly precious to both of them and they grew even more attached to each other.

Soon Abrashka learned to ride the horse by himself. After he came home from his ride with Yacov he would show off his new skill to his father. He rode around the yard while everyone, young and old, looked on and called admiringly, "Bravo! *Molodiec!*"

Reb Faivele purred into his beard, "That's my lad!" Or he laughed loudly as he waved every time that Abrashka passed him, circling the yard atop of Sussi. Reb Faivele put his hands on his other son Shlomele's shoulders and said, "You see, My Scholar, there's nothing to it. No reason to be afraid."

"I know, Tateshie," Shlomele smiled. "But what's the point of riding a horse when we have a carriage?" He could see no great accomplishment in learning to ride a horse. He was the exact opposite of his brother. Plump and clumsy, he continued to cling to his mother's skirts. He saw the world through her eyes and that world was full of demons and evil spirits that lurked everywhere, even in the blades of the windmill. He saw no sense in seeking adventure in this scary world, when the safest place, the one to which the demons had no access, was near his mother in the kitchen. There he studied with great diligence. He had an exceptionally good mind.

As for Reb Faivele, his main love was for his mill, and after that came his love for his horses. Sussi was his favorite, too, and he would often mount the horse himself and go for a ride through the fields. As he now watched his younger son in Sussi's saddle, his love for the boy grew in his heart. He felt Abrashka, who resembled him so much, to be a new perfected edition of himself. He could not understand why the boy did not feel the same and did not reciprocate his feeling. The more his father was drawn to him, the more Abrashka shunned him. He was always angry with him and his eyes betrayed a hidden fear whenever he saw him.

Later that year, Reb Faivele decided to mate the agile, smart Sussi with a healthy, handsome mare. Abrashka immediately fell in love with the colt that the mating had produced.

Reb Faivele and Zirele were sitting on the verandah, watching Abrashka as he played with the colt in the yard. The lively, mischievous sparkle of his eyes betrayed Reb Faivele's desire to throw himself into the game and play along with his son. Zirele was knitting energetically. Her needles clicked loudly as she reprimanded her husband for his lack of "practicality" in one matter or another. Reb Faivele paid her no heed. It seemed to him that he was indeed running around along with Abrashka, racing after the colt. His heart cried out to jump to his feet, catch Abrashka into his arms, and press him to his chest—his own flesh and blood, his soul. But he was ashamed to do so in front of Zirele, who would immediately guess his "childish" weaknesses and berate him for them. He called out to his son, pointing to the colt, "Do you want to have him as your own, Abrashka?"

Abrashka stopped running. "What if I do?" He looked at his father suspiciously. "What then?"

"If you want him, he's yours."

"Mine?"

"That's what I said. And come over and give your father a kiss and say thank you."

"You mean he will belong to me and to no one else?" Abrashka still did not believe him.

"To no one else. Only to you. Now come here."

Instead of running to his father, Abrashka ran off to find Yacov. "Yacov, Yacov!" he called, "I have a horse!"

Yacov came out from behind the house. Abrashka threw himself into his arms and pulled him to the fence where the colt had stopped to nibble on a clump of grass. "Well, do you see what a good father you have?" Yacov asked the boy as he patted the colt. Reb Faivele had often complained to him about his younger son's lack of affection for him, and Yacov tried to win the boy over to his father. "What will you call him?" Yacov asked.

"What do you mean, what will I call him?" Abrashka beamed. "Sussi Ben Sussi, that's what I will call him!"

Abrashka and Sussi Ben Sussi became inseparable. Abrashka spent hours in the stable, learning from the stable boys how to take care of a horse. He fed Sussi Ben Sussi by himself, washed him, and brushed him. He had horses on his mind to such an extent that even during his studies with Yacov, he would ask questions about horses. Could a horse think? he would ask. Did it have a soul? Could it love a human being? And why would the Messiah arrive riding an ass rather than a horse? When they studied the Rashi commentaries that Abrashka used to like to argue about, inventing commentaries of his own, he suddenly became indifferent to the most exciting of them.

"You're growing a horse's head," Yacov laughed, roughing up the tangled hair that stuck out from under the boy's skullcap.

"Look, I'm growing a mane!" Abrashka grabbed himself by the side-locks. They looked at each other meaningfully, got through the lesson somehow, and Abrashka raced outside to play with Sussi Ben Sussi.

For the Friday evening meal Yacov would go to his mother's house in the shtetl, but the next day he generally came back with Reb Faivele straight from the synagogue, so as not to miss the Sabbath meal at Reb Faivele's. He immensely enjoyed listening to the conversation at the table between Reb Faivele and his guests.

On the table in the dining room would stand the silver candelabra still holding the remainder of the burned candles. The wine in the carafe, surrounded by silver goblets and crystal glasses, shimmered like rubies. The porcelain dishes with gilt-edged borders and the silver cutlery glittered, giving off sparks of light of their own. The family and the guests would be dressed in silk and satin, with black and white frequently the predominant colors. They would sit around the table, their faces pink and fresh and their eyes peaceful, while Zosia, Fredka the Housekeeper's eldest daughter, served the meal. From the plates with gilded borders they ate chopped liver, jelly fricassee, and herring with onions and tomatoes, followed by heads of carp in jellied fish sauce. Then came the Bociany-style *cholnt, yaptzok* with *kishke,* then goose meat and duckling with carrot *tzimes,* and a *kugel* of nuts and raisins. Reb Faivele liked to eat well, especially on the Sabbath, and he continually filled the goblets of his guests with wine. They would smack their lips over the dessert of apple sauce and prunes and, with the meal over, would break into Sabbath song.

Then Reb Faivele always tested his sons. The guests would be generous in their praise. They would compliment Zirele and nod their heads appreciatively at Yacov. Before long the boys would disappear from the table, and Zirele would excuse herself and leave the dining room to take her after-*cholnt* nap. It was then that the guests commonly began to talk about life in their communities. They would speak of the war that had dealt Russia such severe blows. The Germans were reportedly about to occupy the entire west bank of the Vistula. But soon enough Reb Faivele would interrupt them, saying that right after the Sabbath meal they ought to avoid irritating subjects of conversation and he would suggest that they all follow his wife's example and take a nap. Then Yacov usually sought out a guest who was not in the mood for napping but preferred to go for a walk. Yacov would propose that the man accompany him and would offer to show him around. As they slowly moved along the gravel paths, he would ply the stranger with questions about distant places and about the ways of life that were unknown to him.

The main part of the Sabbath always began for Yacov when Reb Faivele emerged from his bedroom and came out on the verandah. Over his shirt he would wear a flower-printed housecoat with velvet lapels; soft leather slippers would hug his feet. The guests would slowly emerge from their rooms. Zosia would then bring out salted chick peas, a basket of fruit, a bowl of raspberries with sugar, cookies, and a sponge cake, and set them all up on a small table on the verandah in a corner sheltered by a thick wall of climbing vines. Lastly she would bring out the samovar and glasses, and while Reb Faivele and his guests made themselves comfortable on the wicker armchairs padded with embroidered pillows, she would fill the glasses with strong dark-red tea and added slices of lemon. So the men would sit around and sip the tea, which was supposed to drive the last vestiges of sleep from their limbs.

That particular Sabbath afternoon, they were all waiting for visitors from Bociany—for Shmulikl the barber-surgeon, whom the citizens of Bociany dubbed The Doctor, and for the landowner's bookkeeper, Pan Faifer, the "writer," whom, on account of his baldness, the citizens of Bociany also called Pumpkinhead. They and their respective spouses were due to arrive on foot by the Wide Poplar Road. For some reason, Reb Faivele would cancel his sons' performance of any of the Biblical plays that they had prepared with Yacov whenever these particular visitors were supposed to arrive from Bociany.

It was not long before the two men appeared on the uphill path; behind them walked the two ladies. The two men carried walking sticks and their wives carried umbrellas, although Jewish Law forbade adults to carry anything on the Sabbath. Shmulikl the Doctor also carried a roll of newspapers under his arm. As soon as he reached the verandah, he dropped the papers into one empty armchair, dropped himself into another armchair, and let out a loud "Ah . . ."

It took the two ladies a longer time to reach the house. Out of breath and wiping the perspiration off their faces with their handkerchiefs, they too finally made it to the top and made themselves comfortable in the armchairs that awaited them on the verandah. Zirele, looking rested and fresh, dressed in a long dress with organdy frills—a dress she had made especially for these Saturday afternoons—made her appearance. She greeted the men with a regal nod and kissed the women. The gathering eventually divided into two groups, one of men and the other of women, but this happened rather gradually. First they all drank tea together, nibbled on the refreshments, and talked about the weather, today's weather, yesterday's weather, and the weather of the day before yesterday, comparing it with the weather at the same time last year, and thus made their prognosis of what kind of weather to expect the next day. While they were thus engaged, Reb Faivele rushed toward his *kantur* and reappeared from it with a pack of newspapers and magazines to replace the pack that Shmulikl had just brought.

Shmulikl took a newspaper from the pile that Reb Faivele had brought out and began to read it aloud. He commented heatedly on the article that had caught his eye and the discussion began. Yacov listened closely. He was sitting outside with his back resting against the enclosure of the verandah. Abrashka knew well that on Saturday afternoon Yacov was lost to him, at least until the lighting of the havdala candle that marked the end of the Sabbath.

Long Zirele rarely spoke to the two ladies who sat on either side of her. Despite her good looks and her towering figure clad in the elegant dress, she felt like an uneducated peasant woman in comparison with them. Swallowing her pride, she reduced her role as hostess to the sole function of refilling the tea cups and serving another slice of cake to the two great ladies who were so intelligent that they could read Russian and German books. Later on, when the air had grown cooler, she brought out a couple of quilts to cover her lady guests' legs.

Shmulikl's wife, the midwife, was dressed in a city dress, long and loose and ash-gray in color. She wore a black jacket on top of it, which was buttoned to the neck like that of a general. She had no sense of style and, although she had a beauty spot on her face and the populace of Bociany considered her to be a ravishing beauty, Zirele as well as the "writer's" wife thought her downright plain.

On the other hand the "writer's" wife was dressed in the latest Paris fashion, which deeply offended Zirele's sense of decency. The "writer's" wife's dress was of a loud beet color. It had tight sleeves and was tight in the waist, with a frilled décolleté neckline. On her head she wore a broad-brimmed hat adorned with practically an entire garden of artificial fruits and flowers. Neither of the two ladies wore a matron's wig and the "writer's" wife's hair was bleached. So Zirele, who did wear a wig, was not envious of her female guests, despite her feelings of inferiority. She was certain that she would not come across them in the hereafter. The gates of hell were wide open waiting for these two grandes dames. Besides, they were not really her guests but "his."

The doctor's wife and the "writer's" wife talked to one another over Zirele who, out of politeness, turned her head alternately to the woman on her right and to the one on her left as she fiddled with her glass of unfinished tea.

The midwife's favorite subject was hygiene. Holding her batiste handkerchief to her temple—she was a long-suffering victim of severe migraines—she complained about the awful state of hygiene in the shtetl. "It has not changed an iota for the last few hundred years," she complained. "The same medieval ignorance, the same superstitions." Then she told her lady listeners how the Jews of Bociany would throw rocks into her house and break her windows just like the Gentiles had done during the recent pogrom.

The "writer's" wife was a coquette who, like the doctor's wife, also had a beauty spot near her nose. She was even more educated than the doctor's wife, since she did not understand a word of Yiddish. Like the doctor's wife, she considered Yiddish a vulgar language, a jargon, the knowledge of which was a sign of inferior education. On the whole she was hardly aware of the fact that she lived in Bociany. Her days were spent in the capitals of *Europa* where she transported herself in her mind. Although she had never ventured any further than the town of Sielce from whence she hailed, she knew from her husband's newspapers and magazines what people wore in *Europa* this season, and what was being shown there at the opera. She was the daughter of one of the elite assimilationists of Sielce. Her father had not only freed himself of his capote and sidelocks, but of the other "shortcomings" of his race as well; he worked very hard to emulate the Gentiles.

The "writer's" wife found the doctor's wife's talk of the dirt and poverty of Bociany a boring topic, and she tried to direct the conversation toward a topic that was more in the sphere of her own interests.

"Of course you're right, dear Pani Doctorova," she ventured. "Take the beards for instance. The men of *Europa* also wear beards. But what a difference! What beards! In *Europa* a beard is the most attractive intellectual feature of a man." She cast a dissatisfied look at her own bald, clean-shaven husband. Like the doctor's wife, she was speaking in an elegant and elaborate Krakow Polish.

But despite the two ladies' attempts at amiability, their conversation lacked luster. Like a flame brought into an airless place, their talk flickered faintly, doomed for extinction. It was obvious that although the two ladies behaved impeccably, they had little in common intellectually and were not overly fond of each other. Finally, the doctor's wife decided to suit herself. She livened up as she concentrated her attention on the discussion that the men were engaged in. She removed the handkerchief from her temple and joined in, displaying her passionate absorption in politics and her expertise in that field. The "writer's" wife minded not a bit. She removed a small mirror from her purse and became deeply absorbed in the reflection of her face as she checked her flawless makeup. She yawned delicately and discretely into the mirror, covering her mouth with her manicured fingers.

Pan Faifer, the bald "writer," was in the middle of proclaiming his solution to the "Jewish problem." In his Germanic Yiddish, he expounded his theory of total assimilation as the only cure for the problem. He upheld the position that the Jews were not a nation but a fanatical religious sect that lived in total darkness, immune to the winds of progress, behaving and thinking the same way as they had behaved and thought for centuries.

"It is inconceivable," he held forth, "that in this day and age, the age of the automobile and the wireless telegraph, when *Europa* has reached the highest level of technology and civilization, a community, living in the very heart of this most progressive continent, should exist on such a low cultural level. And the fault, my dear friends, lies with those Jewish leaders who cling to their outdated notions. It lies in that archaic system of education, introduced ages ago, that makes our people's existence continue on the basis of groundless contradictory ideas gleaned from the Talmud. If you were to ask my opinion, my dear friends, I would have told you frankly that for the sake of total emancipation, I would have demanded what the enlightened amongst us began to demand a hundred years ago, that the study of the Talmud be forbidden. I would also forbid the style of dress which makes Jews look like clowns and causes civilized people to poke fun at them. Furthermore, I would make it obligatory for Jewish parents to send their children to modern schools."

It took much personal courage to voice such views in the house of a man like Reb Faivele who wore a skullcap and who had the blue stripes of his ritual undergarment showing from beneath his housecoat. But the bald "writer" was a bold fighter for his convictions, and Reb Faivele's verandah was the only place where he could display his boldness. Reb Faivele was one of those men who was not afraid to listen patiently to another man's outrageous opinions and then liked to react to them with all the passion he was capable of. Now he was fidgeting in his chair, on the verge of losing his patience.

"And what about conversion?" he finally burst out. "Would you make that obligatory, too, Herr Faifer? Aren't you just as fanatical and intolerant in your ideas of assimilation as the most pious Jew is about his religion?"

"You call me fanatical and intolerant?" the "writer" grinned. "I am the greatest supporter of religious tolerance there ever was. This is precisely the reason why I am against forcing the Jews to convert. The best example I can give is German Jewry. Let people worship whatever god they please, but, for heaven's sake, let them realize that the world has progressed from the times of the Bible and that so has human thought."

"Progressed toward what? Toward wars?" Reb Faivele gesticulated impassioned. "Your civilized countries on this most civilized continent of yours are applying the most civilized means of destroying each other."

"And the tragedy is," Shumlikl the Doctor as well could no longer sit still, "the greatest tragedy is that the children of our nation—for we are a nation, not some kind of religious sect, Herr Faifer—that our children must join the armies fighting against each other. They must kill one another, defending the interests of countries which are corroded by anti-Semitism. And don't you give me Germany as a model, Herr Faifer, because it was the German Junkers who coined the term anti-Semitism in the first place. They hate us with all their civilized refinement. They give us freedoms because it suits their interests and, when it stops suiting them, they'll strangle us again."

One of the visiting merchants, clad in modern dress, moved his chair closer to Shmulikl. "Wait a minute, Herr Doctor!" he called out. "You call us a nation, us, a people without a country, without a decent language or a normal culture of our own?"

The doctor's wife almost jumped out of her chair. "Eretz Israel is our country, and Hebrew, the richest, the most beautiful language in the world, is our language! Moreover, my dear friend, our culture is superior to anyone else's, because it has introduced precepts of ethics and morality into every sphere of daily life. Our ethical laws are the very essence of human progress!"

"Bravo!" Reb Faivele applauded. "But please tell me, Madame, does not Yiddish, the plain Yiddish of Bociany, spoken for hundreds of years, carry the essence of that long moral and cultural past of ours as well?"

"No, I'm sorry," the doctor's wife shook her head adamantly. "Yiddish is not a language but a jargon permeated with the decadent foulness of the diaspora!" She moved her armchair still closer to the men. "When we have a country of our own in Palestine, both the intelligentsia and the people in the market place will speak no other language but Hebrew."

"These are dreams that must never come true!" another merchant guest, dressed in partly traditional clothes, called out. "Hebrew is too sacred a language to be used by the women in the marketplace, by the thieves, or by, excuse the expression, the prostitutes."

"We are all sacred!" the doctor's wife shot back. "Every single Jew, no matter who he is, is sacred. And when we get our country back, as Doctor Herzl said, it will no longer be a dream."

"Doctor Herzl, Doctor Shmerzl!" the irritated merchant exclaimed heatedly. "He himself was an assimilationist, one of Herr Faifer's people."

"But his Jewish heart was in the right place, his Jewish consciousness!" Shmulikl the Doctor, who worshipped Doctor Herzl, was beside himself. "He laid down his health and his life for the Jewish people. Granted, only such an experience as the Dreyfuss Affair had the power to open his eyes, but that made him a Jew in the fullest sense of the word. Alas, that's our tragedy. We need our enemies to make us aware of out nationhood. But that doesn't mean that we aren't a nation, even when we are not aware of it."

Herr Faifer nodded at Shmulikl. "But how can a Jewish state come into being without the approval of the other nations? Doctor Herzl himself negotiated with the Turkish sultan, and England's stand on the matter was influenced by such noble Gentiles as Laurence Alifant and George Eliot with her masterpiece called *Daniel Deronda*. That goes to prove that the people of the world are not all cut from the same cloth, although these noble Gentiles are just as naãve as Doctor Herzl in their belief that Palestine can solve the Jewish problem. Because even if the chimera of Palestine becomes a reality, the majority of Jews would remain in the diaspora. Therefore the Jewish problem must be solved in *Europa,* with a Jewish state or without one. There must be an end to Jewish suffering." He said this with feeling, facing Reb Faivele. "I hope you don't take me for one of those who are indifferent to the plight of our people. And our tragedy is that those young Jews who have moved with the times have been led astray, on the one hand by the chimera of *Zionismus,* and on the other by *socialismus,* which is also, may heaven forgive us, the brain child of a Jewish head. Karl Marx's revolutionaries are a black stain on the face of the modern Jewish intelligentsia."

Reb Faivele, madly indignant, waved his hand at Herr Faifer. "It boggles the mind why you worry so much about this or that stain on our face, Herr Faifer. After all, your only solution is that we should cease to exist. Not enough that our enemies want to wipe us off the face of the earth, you're still ready to give them a helping hand! But I don't want to be wiped out, neither do most of us. We want to live as Jews wherever we are. If only our clerics understood that wordly knowledge is not in collision with our faith, if only they weren't afraid to let in a bit of fresh air! But this is not entirely their fault. The trouble with us is that as soon as we learn to read a foreign newspaper or begin to understand a bit of *poesie,* we turn up our noses at the uneducated riffraff. We begin to hate them worse than the anti-Semites do. That's our tragedy!" He turned to Shmulikl, pointing at Herr Faifer. "You two can shake hands over one thing. You both believe that the world should get what it wants, that is, to be rid of us! So I come and say, no! No matter how strongly I support the idea of a Jewish state, I don't shrug off the diaspora so lightly. We have roots here, we've fought and struggled and survived and done good things for your *Europa ,* Herr Faifer. And pray, don't forget another participant who has some say in this matter." Reb Faivele raised a finger toward the sky.

So the discussion continued for hours, until it was time to light the havdalah candle. Then the guests from Bociany took their leave. Fredka's husband brought the carriage around to the front of the verandah and took the guests home.

Yacov had listened to the conversation with his mouth and ears open. A while ago he had been given permission by Reb Faivele to take whatever books he wanted from the latter's library, and he had been reading a great deal about the movement of the Lovers of Zion and about Zionism. But as a rule he preferred to read novels. This past week he had been absorbed in a book called *Stempeniu,* by a writer with the strange name of Sholem Aleichem. The novel was about a young fiddler who loved many women, but who, for some reason, could never enjoy these loves; his heart remained forever hungry, craving something he could not define. What went on in the heart of one human being fascinated Yacov more than any other subject. He was still seeking the answer to the same questions that had nagged him in his childhood when he had run to Reb Senderl the Cabalist, questioning him about the roots of evil and of human suffering. He still entertained doubts as to whether, without that knowledge, it was at all possible to do anything positive, either for man or for God.

ꙍ 5 ꙍ

ABRASHKA'S TENTH BIRTHDAY fell on a Sabbath the following spring. "You've read Mendele Mocher Sforim, haven't you?" Reb Faivele asked Yacov. "He says somewhere that the only birthday Jews remember to celebrate is a bar mitzvah. Otherwise all they remember are the anniversaries of deaths. But we are going to celebrate in honor of my boy, may he live and be healthy, and not wait until his bar mitzvah."

Yacov volunteered to invite a few heder boys from Bociany so that Abrashka might really enjoy himself. Reb Faivele agreed. He himself however invited no one except his bosom friend, Shmulikl the Doctor, and his wife.

That Sabbath afternoon the backyard was cleaned with particular care. A large honey cake and bottles full of homemade cherry wine were placed on a table on the shady verandah that aproned the house. Another special table with sweets was set up outside for the children. Fredka, her husband, and all their children put on their best clothes, and Kazimierz, the shepherd, brought along a band of musicians from the village. Reb Faivele liked peasant dances. Pretending not to see Zirele's disapproving glances, he took off his capote, rolled up his shirtsleeves, and, in his leather slippers, joined the farmhands and their women in the dance. He danced only for a short while, until Shmulikl and his wife arrived from the shtetl.

Zirele, who was handing out the slices of honey cake and glasses of cherry wine to the farmhands, smoothed out her dress and buttoned it up to her chin. The doctor's wife always made her feel uncomfortable. But today she greeted her with a broader, more generous, and more genuine smile than usual. After all, it had been the doctor's wife, not yet suffering so severely from her migraines, who had assisted at Abrashka's birth ten years earlier.

Zirele kissed her more affectionately than ever and asked her how she felt. The doctor's wife pointed to her head and answered with a groan, "It drives me *verruckt.*" Consequently, Zirele sent away the musicians and warned Abrashka, who was running around with the band of children, to quiet down. However, as far as the youngsters were concerned, her warning accomplished little. The yard reverberated with their boisterous screams and laughter.

Shmulikl and his wife made themselves comfortable in the wicker chairs waiting for them on the verandah. Reb Faivele exchanged a pack of newspapers and magazines with Shmulikl, but today, as there were no visitors present, and as it was Abrashka's birthday, the two friends became engrossed in a serious conversation, not on politics or matters of war, but on the subject of children and modern methods of education. The maid, Zosia, brought out the samovar and served refreshments.

Fredka and her husband sat on the porch of their house. With the musicians silent and the dancing forbidden by Zirele, the farmhands stood idly around, leaning against the fence. Zosia brought out tea and preserves for them as well. The table that had been set with sweets for the children was quickly cleaned down to the last candy. Everyone, except the masters and their guests, watched the children careering wildly around the yard, engrossed in their games.

Yacov sat on the water pump. He chewed on his slice of cake and sipped his tea as his eyes followed the barefoot peasant children and the heder boys whose tasseled ritual undergarments waved like pennants in the breeze. The sight of them all playing together gave him a feeling of comfort and ease. But he was not given to sitting still for too long. Abrashka came running up to him.

"Yacov," he tugged at his sleeve, so that the tea from Yacov's glass spilled on his lap. "Come, Yacov, we're going to play hide-and-seek!"

"Don't you have enough children to play with?" Yacov refused to budge.

"You must play with us. It's no fun without you!"

"Not today."

"Today! Today you must do as I want!"

Yacov had no choice but to cram the last bit of cake into his mouth, leave his unfinished glass of tea on the water pump, and join the band of boys who surrounded him. Before long he was absorbed in their game. The bored, idle, young farmhands who had stood around watching them, livened up. They called to the children, "Hide over here! Hide over there!" At length the young farmhands also became infected with the youngsters' excitement and, no longer able to look on passively, they too rushed to hide themselves somewhere. The game grew more and more interesting and did not stop, even when the sun began its descent beyond the horizon.

The havdalah candle had already been lit, but Shmulikl the Doctor was in no hurry to leave. He and Reb Faivele had long since interrupted their discussion on the subject of education and were now absorbed in a dispute about languages, Hebrew versus Yiddish. Shmulikl was deeply hurt by the fact that for all his worldly knowledge, Reb Faivele clung so doggedly to the market language of the masses; that this same Reb Faivele, who was at home not only with the sacred books, but also with modern Hebrew poetry, should consider Yiddish as sacred a language as Hebrew! Reb Faivele irritated Shmulikl greatly by enumerating the many masterpieces written in Yiddish and by making a fuss over a Yiddish language conference in Chernowitz, as if it were, no more no less, a milestone in Jewish history!

Shmulikl had a great many arguments to prove that Reb Faivele's attitude toward Yiddish was in gross contradiction to the latter's own philosophy of life. But the racket in the yard was aggravating his wife's splitting headache, so he had no choice but to forego his arguments and take leave of the hosts not long after the naphtha lamps had been lit on the verandah. He and his wife climbed into Reb Faivele's carriage, a farmhand climbed into the driver's seat, took the reins in his hands, and off they went. No one but Reb Faivele and Zirele noticed their departure.

Reb Faivele changed his seat. He abandoned his armchair and sat down on the stair nearer to where his wife sat, nibbling on chick peas. He adjusted his skullcap, pushing it back to the tip of his head, and so engaged Zirele in an absorbing, exceptionally serious conversation. When Yacov, who was looking about for a place to hide himself, happened to pass in front of the verandah, Reb Faivele beckoned to him to approach.

"There is something we want to talk over with you," Reb Faivele said to him in a solemn, slightly uncertain tone of voice. He indicated to Yacov that he should sit down on the verandah stair beside him. Yacov wiped the sweat off his face with his sleeve, exhaled loudly a few times, sat down, and looked at Reb Faivele questioningly. Reb Faivele had intended to wait for a while in order to give Yacov a chance to relax completely, but he was not a man of great patience. If he had something to say, he had to say it right away. With his eyes fixed on Zirele, rather than on Yacov, he asked, "How is Abrashka doing in his studies? The mischief has a brilliant head on his shoulders, hasn't he?"

Yacov was trying to catch his breath. His face was flushed, but he had already rid himself of his playful mood. "Abrashka? Oh, he's like fire!" he exclaimed and smiled broadly.

"And My Scholar, Shlomele? He's a genius, isn't he?" Reb Faivele continued.

"Yes, Shlomele will make a great scholar," Yacov nodded.

Reb Faivele braided his hands around his raised knee and rocked himself back and forth. He thought for a minute, then tilted his head closer to Yacov. "You understand," he said with pretended ease, "I was sitting here with my wife, talking. Abrashka is no longer a snotnose, and, before we know it, Shlomele will be ready for his bar mitzvah. We must start thinking about the future." Yacov noticed that Zirele had stopped nibbling on the chick peas and that her eyes had become misty. A sudden sense of foreboding gripped his heart. Reb Faivele coughed a faint artificial cough and continued, "I could send them to Sielce, to the yeshiva. But the Sielce Yeshiva is old-fashioned and we would have to wait for the Germans to take Sielce. In any case, I must see to it that my sons are prepared to deal both with God and with people, do you follow? I want them to know that there exists a world in this world." He shifted his legs, locked his hands around his other knee, and snickered uncomfortably.

Yacov's heart began to toll with alarm. He winced. The yard and the noisy children seemed now distant and unreal. Reb Faivele and his wife appeared to have grown into shadows of themselves. A nightmare had befallen him in the midst of this festive, exhilarating afternoon of playful abandon. Reb Faivele was obviously waiting for him to say something. After a long silence, he prodded Yacov with an elbow, "Why did you make such a sour face, and why don't you say a word? Don't you think I'm right?"

"Why, yes, of course," Yacov mumbled. "The time has come."

"That's it, the time has come," Reb Faivele swayed thoughtfully with his knee clasped between his hands. "The time has come for us to part with the two apples of our eyes, for their own good." He gave Zirele a sidelong glance and leaned closer to Yacov. "You understand our hearts, don't you? You've been like a son to me, so I need not hide it from you. True, there's a war going on, but I'm going to send the boys to Krakow at the beginning of the fall season. Now that the Germans have crossed the Vistula, the road is open . . . Or by that time, who knows, the war might be over. My sons are going to inherit the fruits of my labor, but they must go further than I have gone. And time doesn't stand still. The Germans are about to conquer the world and a new life will begin. Jews will have to know the worldly sciences if they want to succeed. A new life will begin for you, too, you'll see. I have an uncle in Krakow. He'll be glad to have the boys stay with him. I've heard that a new yeshiva has opened there, a modern one, where they teach history, mathematics, and physics, besides the Talmud. So I want . . . " Reb Faivele finally untied his fingers from around his knee and patted Yacov lightly on the shoulder. "I know, I shouldn't have told you this today. But you're not a child. I'll speak to Shlomele myself. What I want from you is to gradually prepare Abrashka, so I had to tell you . . . "

Yacov jumped to his feet. "Don't ask me to do that, Reb Faivele!" he blurted out.

"Why not?" Reb Faivele smiled crookedly.

"Because I can't tell him this."

Reb Faivele grew impatient. "Cut out that nonsense! And take that sour look off your face! You're not at a funeral, Heaven forbid, and I haven't fired you. You can stay on and work at the mill. And as for the boys, if I can bear parting from them, so can you."

In order not to expose himself to Reb Faivele's anger and Zirele's sad reproachful stare any longer, Yacov stood up, slowly crossed the yard, and then broke into a wild run downhill. He slowed down when he hit the road and meandered aimlessly, kicking at pebbles and plucking weeds from the ditch. He chewed on the weeds greedily, hastily as if he were set on chewing up the despair that had attacked him so suddenly.

It was only after the summer had gone by that Reb Faivele could bring himself to reveal to both of his sons his plans for their future—and days of constant lament began for Abrashka. He cried from morning until night, refused to play, refused to eat, refused to study or sleep. It seemed strange that this lively, fun-loving youngster could possess the capacity to reach such a depth of sorrow, and that he should be capable of abandoning himself to it without interruption. It was unlike a normal child's nature. A normal child would have had the ability to forget himself at play and to find moments of respite from the heaviness of his heart. Not so Abrashka.

Meal after meal Reb Faivele and Long Zirele would sit at the table steeped in gloomy silence. Their food lost its savor at the sight of their two downhearted sons. Shlomele, their firstborn, was no more anxious to leave than Abrashka. Shlomele did not want to let go of his mother's skirt and exchange his secure haven in the kitchen for an alien world full of demons and evil spirits. If Fredka entered the room to help her daughter Zosia serve at the table while the family was at dinner, she would gaze at the two boys with such pity in her eyes that one day, during the meal, in order to brighten the mournful atmosphere, Reb Faivele burst into artificially animated talk directed at Zirele. "Krakow!" he exclaimed. "Small thing Krakow! There's nowhere in the entire world to be found a more beautiful city than Krakow, is there, Zirele?"

"That's surely so," Zirele, who had never been to Krakow, confirmed.

"The Vistula is nowhere else as magnificent as in Krakow," Reb Faivele continued to work himself further up in his enthusiasm. "The most beautiful river in the world at its most beautiful place! And there you can also see the monument of Crocus and Wanda. I have, of course, not in mind the peasant girl Wanda whom we all know." He burst into false laughter. "I mean the famous Wanda who lived hundreds of years ago, and whom history calls, 'Wanda who didn't want the German.' Some Wanda she was! Instead of agreeing to marry the German prince who had proposed to her, the stupid goat threw herself into the Vistula!"

Abrashka raised his head from his plate, positioned his fork in his fist with its teeth up, and pierced his father with a look as sharp as the fork. "When I get there, I'll also throw myself into the Vistula!" he exclaimed, thus making it clear to his parents that, as far as he was concerned, the world had come to an end and life no longer had any meaning. Even Fredka had not been able to console him. He would shun her, as he shunned his parents, as though he had resolved that those who loved him were dangerous. Everyone was keen on telling him about the marvels of Krakow, while nobody understood what the Blue Mountain meant to him. "Even before I get there, I'll throw myself into the lake! I'll hang myself from a tree like Vaslav the Fire Chief!" He jumped to his feet and ran out of the room.

Yacov ran after him and caught him in his arms. Abrashka clung to him with all the passion of his despair. "I wish I were an orphan. I wish I didn't have a father!"

"Heaven forbid, Abrashka!" Yacov pressed him to his chest. "A father like yours? You should ask me what it feels like not to have a father."

"It's better not to have a father, than to have a father like mine!"

"But, Abrashka, he doesn't want to rid himself of you. He's going to miss you terribly."

"I want to be rid of *him*! Whenever I have a bit of fun he comes and spoils it. He spoils everything."

"He has your own good at heart. He loves you."

"I don't want him to love me. I don't want you to love me either!" He let go of Yacov. "You side with him!" he exclaimed. "You side with him, because you're just as mean as he is. I never want to see you again! You don't mean a thing to me!" He waved his fist at Yacov and with wild sobs dashed toward Sussi Ben Sussi, who was grazing near the fence. The colt understood that Abrashka wanted to race with him, so he shook his mane and ran off. Abrashka turned to the dog Bobik, buried his head in his fur, and wept bitterly. "Only you are on my side."

In the field beyond the fence, peasants, men and women, were gathering the scythed hay. The scythes attached to their belts glittered in the distance. The scent of cut hay and the autumnal melancholy of the landscape exacerbated the sadness weeping in Yacov's heart.

After a long and heated quarrel, Reb Faivele and Long Zirele decided to postpone the children's departure for half a year. Reb Faivele also hoped that by that time the war would be over. Bociany had long since slipped out of the hands of the tsar and was now German—an historic transition marked merely by the disappearance of the gendarmes from the shtetl. But the battlefront shifted back and forth and the times were still uncertain.

Abrashka's spirits rebounded. He regained his liveliness and his appetite for mischief. To him half a year was an enormous stretch of time, a stretch so long it might never end, and yet it had to be taken advantage of. Nonetheless, the joyful abandon with which he had formerly greeted each day was now subdued. A scar was left in his heart, and he was forever conscious of the threat hanging over his head. His laughter lost the ring of pure delight and of trust in the world. It now sounded as if he were on the verge of tears. He no longer clung to Yacov as he had in the past. Most of the time he spent alone or with the animals, especially Sussi Ben Sussi and the dog Bobik. Sometimes he could be seen alone, racing through fields with ferocious speed.

However, when Yacov went home to spend the Sabbath with his family, Abrashka waited impatiently for his return, tramping back and forth at the foot of the hill. No longer did he run forth to greet Yacov when he noticed him approaching, but would slowly, with halting steps, come over to him.

"Do you know, Yacov," he once said to him. "Whenever you are about to arrive, I hear your voice in my head, telling me, 'Abrashka, I'm on my way. Go outside and soon you'll see me.'" He looked at Yacov with bewilderment in his eyes, the way he now looked at everyone whom he cared for: a long penetrating gaze that seemed to be asking, "Are you going to hurt me because I love you?"

He pursued his studies with more diligence than ever before. Yacov listened to Abrashka's voice with its tearful undertone and his own sadness deepened. He laid his hand on the boy's shoulder and, holding it there, swayed along with him to the appropriate lilt, praying for some kind of balm to soothe their sore hearts.

"Your voice doesn't sound overly cheerful today," he once said to Abrashka. "It sounds like the voice of someone lost in the forest. Do you know, Abrashka, that there exists in everybody's heart such a double feeling: on the one hand, a kind of longing for the day of sheer harmony, sheer perfection, the day in the future when the Messiah will come. And on the other hand, there also exists another longing, a longing in the reverse direction, for the days of the past, the days when we were not yet born. I am myself aware of such yearnings. Everyone experiences them, although not everyone becomes aware of them. It's a sense of being pulled both backward and forward in time, backward toward the perfection that existed during the time when you were in your mother's belly, or even earlier, when you were still in heaven and knew everything. And forward, toward the Garden of Eden in afterlife, when again you will know and understand everything. It's all right to have these cravings but you cannot feed them all the time. As we grow, everything keeps on changing and we must learn to live with the change. Otherwise we lose out on a lot of living, perhaps on all our living."

Yacov was in fact no less confused than Abrashka. But he forced himself not to let the boy notice how powerfully he himself felt the bitter drops in the sweetness of still being together, nor did he want Abrashka to remember, as he did, how near the day was drawing when all would be different.

Abrashka no longer waited for Yacov to finish work in the mill, so Yacov would take a volume of Scripture and sit down in his favorite corner in the back of the house. Just like Abrashka, he nowadays immersed himself in his studies with much more fervor and diligence than ever before. He often opened the Book to the Song of Songs, in the hope that it would help him escape the thoughts which nagged at him.

He wanted to escape from himself altogether, to hide himself in the perfection that emanated from the lines of the Song; he wanted to see his vague yearnings reflected in the reality of utterable words. In the Song he wished to find the sweetness that pertained, perhaps, to the sorrow of parting; he wished to rediscover the riches that all things lost leave in the soul and glean solace from these finds. He believed that life past or present could be perfect and without fault if one were capable of transforming both its lights and its shadows into beauty and song. Then the earth and the sky, despite their discrepancies, could perhaps be likened to a pot with a fitting lid.

But such thoughts did not abide with Yacov for too long. The tear in his heart always let itself be felt. The truth was that God and His world were two separate entities, two solitudes divided by an abyss that could not be bridged. The result was not a harmonious union, but a clash of opposites, of enmities, giving birth to pain. And so Yacov allowed his own torment to surface. He felt himself compelled to tear off the veil of falsehood from the Song of Songs, from the "Beauty of Beauties," whose every letter seemed to kiss and love the other. How could there be talk of love between the Almighty and Man? The Almighty was spirit, the Infinite, while man was trapped by his corporeal form, by dark passions that he did not understand and to which he was driven to yield. And man was finite. From the day of his birth he carried the seed of death within him. And as for the love between male and female, how could such a love be without fault, if it was so difficult for one male to understand another, even if the other were one's own flesh and blood?

His despair nourished by doubts, Yacov recited the verses of the Song, leaving out the commentaries and explanations, so that he might hit directly upon the rifts hiding behind the veils of beauty. Through these rifts, these cracks, he expected Truth to shine forth. He wanted to come face to face with Truth, to confront its dazzling light and discover it to be so repulsive that it would free him forever from his craving for it.

But whenever he tried to tear down one veil after another from the Song of Songs, a sigh would escape his lips, "I am ill with love . . . " The dim image of Shulamit dressed in the form of Binele would come forth from between the lines of the Song to greet him. His mind exploded with visions and smells. He could hardly keep back the tears or control the tremors of his body. His heart yearned and wept. It wept over the breathtaking splendor that he discovered beneath the beauty. "Escape, my beloved," he heard the music of words, "and be like the stag or the young doe on top of the spice mountains." Perhaps a form of escape was possible after all, despite the prison of one's body, of one's self, the prison that a man carried along with him wherever he ran; perhaps an escape was possible through love, imperfect though it might be?

The more deeply he immersed himself in the Song, the more clearly he saw it. Every word grew into an image so vivid that he could touch it, taste it with the tip of his tongue, until he no longer needed to open the Book. Voiceless, the Song recited its lines within him.

Every so often he woke up in the middle of the night and stared at the whitewashed walls of his alcove. He listened to the cats racing over the roof, to the flutter of the sails on the windmill, and to the wind dancing between the trees. An awesome craving swept over him, prompting him to climb out of bed and approach the window. A black yet transparent darkness hung over the foot of the mountain. Below, in the distance, Bociany nestled asleep. There, in a garret filled with the fragrances issuing from the nuns' garden, his mother and sisters were asleep in the large old bed. They were his own flesh and blood. Yet how close were they to him? And that stranger, Binele, whom he now saw swimming through the darkness, her yellow braids lit by the silvery shine of the moon like the braids of light left by a passing comet—what connection did she have to him? What had she taken from him when she had vanished from his sky? What had she left within him?

He heard the wind whisper between the blades of the mill.

> You are beautiful my beloved, and sweet.
> Green is our bed in the storm.
> The narrow strip of a stable roof ceils our heads.
> The wall of a stable is our shelter.
> Behind the wall, the horses are neighing with fear.

The silence thundered in Yacov's ears. Shulamit emerged from the shimmering lake. Or was it Kailele the Bride in her white wedding gown laced with water lilies? Or was it Binele again with her braids undone? He was her slave, a slave of love. He prayed to her, "Your eyes are like black cherries and your hair like the wings of a golden stork . . . " Awe and anxiety overwhelmed him. Somewhere, at some moment in time, love had coupled both his and Binele's births and deaths. He rejoiced in the one, while the other filled him with terror.

Something was happening to him, a tremendous change, a shifting, a transformation. The muscles of his limbs, the physical strength that he felt growing in his body, these were somehow related to the fearful shudders that attacked him so often. At the same time, this inner discomfort also fed his urge to accomplish unusual feats. One moment he felt himself permeated with goodness and generosity of heart, and the next he felt alienated from himself and from everything around him. He either felt at peace with himself or hated and despised himself. Something kept on breaking within him forever, while something else was becoming whole within him for the first time. A question nagged at him, a question as big as the universe. But he was incapable of asking it because he was unable to formulate it in his thoughts, and was left with only a vague question mark.

He came to the conclusion that it was the Song of Songs that had been making him so restless and he decided not to get back to it. But the next minute he had a change of heart and mumbled to himself, "I will go back to it. With teeth and nails I will claw my way out of this pit, of this chaos!"

One late afternoon Abrashka found Yacov in the nook behind the house and sat down beside him. "What are you studying so hard?" he asked.

Yacov closed the Book with a thump. "Nothing," he said curtly. "I'm just glancing through it."

"What is it you're glancing through?"

"Oh, just some passages."

"What passages?"

"The Song of Songs."

"So open it and study with me," Abrashka proposed.

"There are other things that you're supposed to be studying."

"You told me yourself that when you were my age you studied the Song of Songs at the heder before Passover."

"And I understood nothing."

"So I also want to understand nothing. What do you care? Come on."

Yacov flipped through the pages waveringly until he stopped at the right one. "This is a kind of song that King Solomon made up," he explained. "A song about the Creator's love for His people, a kind of parable. It tells of a bride and a groom. The Creator of the World is the groom and the people of Israel are the bride. And they love each other with all their hearts."

"So why did you say it's hard to understand?" Abrashka exclaimed. "Start reading, let me hear!"

They began to chant the words slowly. Abrashka moved closer to Yacov and followed his finger as it moved along the lines. But when the finger halted and Yacov started to explain, Abrashka's smile spread from one ear to the other.

"What's the matter? Why are you smiling?" Yacov asked.

"I'm smiling," Abrashka gestured in a scholarly manner, "because I have no trouble imagining the Almighty as a groom, but when I think of the people of Israel, I see a synagogue full of black capotes and fur-edged hats. So how can the people of Israel look like a girl, a girl with breasts at that?"

"Don't talk like that," Yacov grinned, embarrassed.

"Well, tell me," Abrashka would not give up. "Why can't it be just a story about a bride and a groom?"

"You know very well that there is no such thing as a plain story in the Holy Book. Isn't the way our sages have interpreted it good enough for you?"

"Yes, it's good enough for me!" Abrashka exclaimed. He pulled at Yacov's sleeve. "Come, let's go for a ride and stop over at Yoel the Blacksmith's. Father isn't home and he won't know a thing." Ever since they had first visited the smith, Abrashka had not stopped nagging Yacov about going back to see him, while Yacov kept on refusing. This time too he chased Abrashka away and remained sitting with the Book in his lap.

Abrashka's simple remark about the Song of Songs suited Yacov's mood amazingly well. He could no longer stifle his sinful thoughts. Shulamit was a girl of flesh and blood. She was Binele. In his mind he dressed her in garlands of bluebells and daisies. His imagination played tricks on him. He thought he was seeing her in the dazzle of the sunset, running up the Blue Mountain in the direction of the mill. She hung on to the mill's sails and circled round and round. The wind blew up her dress, filling it with air like a balloon. "I bet you can't catch me!" he heard her call. He saw her bare legs, saw her pink soles beckoning to him. Her disheveled hair fluttered and vibrated like rays of reddish gold. Her face was a sun, a sun that was attached to the mill.

Then he imagined that he saw Binele coming out from under a haystack in the distant field. Blades of hay were entangled in her hair and glittered like bejeweled pins. There were blades of hay in the folds of her ragged dress. They shone like brooches. As the day drew to a close, he saw her running to meet the purple of the dusk that rose from beyond the horizon. The mill began to cast a long shadow. The field through which Binele ran acquired the texture of dark blue velvet; the dew on the tips of the blades of grass sparkled like diamonds. He saw Binele's lover running toward her from the direction of the birch wood. His figure was framed by the glow of the purple lights lingering on the western sky. Yacov's heart was afire with jealousy—even though he himself was the lover. As the two figures drew nearer to each other, the last streaks of light faded below the horizon. Yacov's hand touched Binele's in the darkness. The hand was warm and soft. The darkness mantled them with the holiness of a Sabbath evening. He said to Binele, "My jealousy and my craving for you are one with my desire to know the secret that the Almighty has hidden from us—within us."

Abrashka nagged Yacov so much about visiting Yoel the Blacksmith that one Sunday afternoon he gave in to him and they rode off to the smithy.

Yoel looked as if he were expecting them. Busy at the forge inside the smithy, sparks dancing in a swirl around his head as he clinked his hammer, he greeted them with a boisterous shout as soon as he saw them appear in the entrance, "Welcome vagabonds! Did you land in a ditch again?" Then he became silent, again absorbed in shaping an axle on the anvil. After a while, he nodded at Yacov and smiled when he saw through the open entrance door Abrashka puttering about among the piles of scrap metal in the yard. But he continued hammering as before. It was only when they were about to leave that Yoel left his work and went outside. He lifted Abrashka up, seated him on Sussi, and asked, "So what have you come for, vagabonds?"

Abrashka answered him playfully, "We wanted to come, so we came."

Yacov explained, "From the first time we were here, he's been nagging me to come back."

"And you?" Yoel fixed his eyes on Yacov. Those eyes were so deep, so black and hot, that Yacov had the impression he was both drowning in them and being burnt in their depths. "You were afraid to come, weren't you?"

"I was, but we came anyway."

"That's the main thing. The fact that you came." Yoel helped Yacov mount the horse, gave Sussi a light pat, and turned back to the smithy.

From that day on, Yacov and Abrashka rode off every Sunday afternoon to visit Yoel. Yacov never told any stories on their way to the smithy. He and Abrashka were both too impatient, too apprehensive, due to the fact that they always expected something to happen at the smithy, in the presence of the dark mysterious blacksmith. So they just whistled, chatted, laughed excitedly—a kind of tense laughter—and answered the birds by mimicking their chirping. At the smithy nothing unusual would happen. Yoel would behave as he did during their first meetings. And yet, the moment they left him, they felt like coming back to be with him again.

After each visit at Yoel's, on their way back Yacov and Abrashka knew that they ought to be nervous and worried. They remembered well Reb Faivele's warning never to visit the smithy again. Yet instead of worry and anxiety they experienced a strangely pleasurable feeling of well-being, of freedom. As they rode on, their senses were awake and sharp. They absorbed the landscape with their eyes as it lay spread out on both sides of the road. It was as if every cell in their bodies had acquired a pair of eyes and lips of its own that absorbed every speck of color, every spark of light, and carried it straight into their bloodstreams. Something soulful seemed to have permeated the air about them. They felt this soulfulness almost physically, as if it were tangible. Yacov thought, "I feel such an odd joy. I am happy now, despite the confusion and the bungled thoughts that fill my head. At this very moment I am asking nothing of life, even though my innermost cravings have not been satisfied. The Almighty is as close as a relative, even though He is a stranger, even though He might not even exist."

After a number of such visits to the smithy, Yoel no longer pretended to ignore his guests and began to behave as his heart dictated. As soon as he saw Abrashka dismount, he rushed out into the yard and, with peals of buoyant laughter, snatched the boy into his arms and swung him around like a carousel. Before long, dark traces of his blackened hands appeared on Abrashka's face and clothes.

The next moment Abrashka, his eyes sparkling, stood by the forge in the smithy. Yoel had little work to do on Sunday afternoons after the peasants had returned from church, and the road lay deserted. But for companionship he still kept the fire going in the black furnace, and he kept his hands busy at the anvil. Abrashka attacked him with a thousand questions about iron and other metals, about the fire and the bellows. Once, when he could no longer contain himself in his admiration for the smith, he cried out enthusiastically, "You should have been my father, Yoel!"

Yoel, hiding his satisfied smile in the thickness of his mustache, took Abrashka's shoulders between his hands and said, "You'd better stick with your own father. We two will be like good brothers."

"All right. We, all three of us, will be like good brothers!" Abrashka was delighted. "So be a good brother, Yoel, and forge something for me on the anvil, a bird or an animal, or something like that."

"Don't make a fool of me, little tramp," Yoel pretended offense. "I'm not a bird maker."

"Yes you are, come on!" Abrashka pulled him by the tail of his caftan toward the heap of scrap metal in the yard.

Before long they found the perfect piece of metal. Yoel smelted it in the furnace until it began to glow like a lamp of gold. He then carried it over to the anvil and, following Abrashka's instructions, turned, twisted, and hammered it, until it acquired the shape that Abrashka wanted. He dunked it in a tub of cold water. The metal hissed and steam rose from the water. When Yoel removed it from the water and put it in a dry place to cool off, they could detect the suggestion of a strange animal in its form.

"Such a thing never existed in this world!" Yoel shook his head, pretending astonishment.

Abrashka scrutinized expertly their creation and criticized Yoel for the mistakes he had made. Here he had bent it too much, there he had chopped off too little. To Yacov it seemed that Yoel had only to breathe God's ineffable name into it and the object would come to life; it would rise on its wings and fly off. Then, as if he had read Yacov's thoughts, Yoel began to recite entire passages of the Talmud by heart, as he stood there, scrutinizing the joint result of his handiwork and Abrashka's imagination.

"You're quite a scholar, Yoel." Yacov said in amazement.

"You'd better not ask," Yoel waved his hand dismissively. "With all the scholarship I've acquired, I've only succeeded in digging up the profound meaning of my own humble trade. That suits me fine. Because nothing, my dear fellow, was ever created by mere words, or mere thinking, except fantasies. I suspect that even the Almighty created the world by doing something more than just thinking it up."

Swarthy though Yoel was, with his dark face and sharp features, his skin cracked by fire and wind, his beard, his mustache, and sidelocks one mass of brilliant glittering blackness, it seemed to Yacov that this man's darkness was alight; alight the same way as the blackness of the nights into which Yacov so often peered through the window of his room. The whites of Yoel's eyes, the whiteness of his bared teeth, and the white drops of foam in the corners of his dark swollen lips bore witness to the extent to which he gave himself to whatever he was doing. He inhaled the sweat that wet his mouth and wiped his dripping nose on his sleeve. Other beads of sweat dripped and dropped from his face into the fire and onto the glowing iron that hissed, it seemed, with pleasure.

"Believe me," Yoel added after a long silence. "A piece of work can lift my faith to a higher level of ecstasy than ten glasses of *monopolka* or ten times ten prayers."

In spite of himself, Yacov smiled. In his mind he heard his mother's voice. "Who knows if this is not one of the thirty-six saintly men on whose merit the world exists?" Perhaps Yoel was one of those disguised *tsadikim,* precisely because of his stark earthly appearance, of his rough heavy voice and his hoarse laughter that sounded like thunder; precisely because of his voracious appetite for food and *monopolka;* precisely because of the incredible stories that circulated about him in Bociany. People were saying that he was an Asmodeus, a magician, that he had killed his wife and children, and that he slept with the women in the villages. People would spit three times before they brought his name to their lips.

When he heard that Yacov was a descendant of the Rabbi of Wurke, Yoel gave him a robust pat on the shoulder. "In that case, brother, you're almost one of my kind."

"Why almost?" Yacov asked.

"Because, you understand, I'm neither a Hasid, nor a Misnagind. Surprised? The thing is that I need no *rov* or rabbi to be a ladder between myself and my Maker, nor do I need a synagogue or a quorum to say my prayers. Wherever I stand, there is my synagogue, and whatever surrounds me makes up my quorum. The thing is, when I converse with my Creator, I'm incapable of seeing Him as a king sitting on a glittering throne. If I did, my tongue would tangle up between my teeth and my mouth would go lame. Have you ever heard of a peasant chatting with Tsar Nicholas in his private chambers? I haven't. So when I talk to Him, I make myself comfortable. I see Him as a Jew, a peddler, who wanders from village to village, carrying a heavy sack of troubles slung over His shoulder. When He passes my smithy, I greet him with 'Shalom,' and we chat. It relieves my heart. In the end He feels better and so do I. Understand?"

Yacov felt himself compelled to discuss with Yoel all the questions that had been bothering him. But the moment he was ready to do so, the questions seemed to have lost their importance. Why bring to the surface yesterday's muddled entanglements of mind, when every relationship of one thing with another seemed now clear and acceptable? The main advantage of being in Yoel's smithy was in savoring the comfort of Yoel's presence. Through it alone the perception of one's own self became clearer. It was strange, but for some reason Yacov became more aware of what it meant to be alive. Every aspect of things became its own question and answer, when he was with Yoel.

Yacov had long since harbored the suspicion in his mind that Yoel had been carrying a load of gruesome experiences buried in his memory. Yoel's expressions of joy, his exuberance, his greed for life's delights were not of the light-hearted kind. On the contrary, they were heavy, they were the antitheses of frivolity. His joy and greed for pleasure seemed to come from deep within him, as if they had been forged on the anvil of his suffering. Perhaps for that reason they had the power to touch Yacov so profoundly and to reach the roots of his own suffering. Yoel's hoarse laughter, his sputtered-out words, or his passionate singing were like flames breaking through the cracks in a roaring furnace.

Adjoining the smithy stood Yoel's small moldy and disintegrating hut. It harbored a small room with one small window. Right behind the hut, rows of brick stuck out of the ground. They traced two rectangles in the clumps of wild-growing grass that surrounded and partly covered them. The bricks were the obvious vestiges of a house that had once stood in this place. Its remnants now looked like two tombs. One day Abrashka asked Yoel about it.

"Yes," Yoel muttered. "Years ago I had my house here."

"What happened to it?"

"Nothing. It vanished."

"What do you mean, it vanished?"

"Vanished means that it disappeared."

Much as Abrashka nagged Yoel about the house, he always received the same answer. But Abrashka was not one to give up so easily. "So why do you live here all alone?" He would not let Yoel push him away.

"Because you aren't coming to live with me." Yoel grabbed him by the arms and swung him around.

"If you want me to, I will!" Abrashka yelped. "I'll come!"

Yoel let go of him and the boy eventually settled down to putter and play around inside the smithy. Yoel sat down beside Yacov outside, on the doorstep of the hut. "There is something good about living alone, too." he plucked at his beard and said as if to answer Abrashka's question. "In a way it's healthy. I feel free. Nobody really knows me, no one knows what's cooking in my pot, no one interferes, or gives me advice, or preaches to me, or questions my moral conduct. This way I can really feel myself united with the world. You understand? Man needs the skin of his body to give him shape, set him apart, to isolate him in his singleness. For the same reason he also needs his own private corner. It's like a second skin that divides him from his neighbors. Why do we have one single God, do you think? The answer is obvious. He must have His aloneness. He needs His privacy so that He can engage Himself in the interplay with all of His creation."

"But it's good to live with someone, to be attached . . . to love," Yacov ventured.

Yoel furrowed his thick eyebrows. "To love? It depends what you mean by that. To be attached and to love, are they one and the same thing? I don't think so. Man must be careful to hold the threads of attachment loosely, otherwise they're liable to strangle him. When the threads of attachment are pulled too tight, they break, and all the wells of evil are liable to open. Or sometimes you cling to another human being out of fear both of life and of death. This makes you weak and helpless. You lose your self-respect. And what value is there in a love that turns you into a broken vessel? I don't call that love, that's cowardice."

"But a man wants a wife and children," Yacov did not understand.

Yoel, instead of answering, stood up and went into the smithy to check what Abrashka was doing inside. Yacov remained by himself, trying to digest Yoel's words. He stared at the field across the road. From there he could hear a faint distant voice, as light as a breeze, singing. Yoel came out of the smithy at a run and raced off after a cow that had strayed too far into the pasture. Beside the cow, Yoel owned a few geese and some chickens who pecked about between the heaps of the scrap metal and the boards of broken wagons that littered the yard. Whatever else Yoel needed for his sustenance he acquired in the village across the road beyond the hilly field.

Once he had chased back the cow, Yoel beckoned to Yacov with his finger, and they both watched Abrashka who had come out from the smithy and was now engrossed in playing among the piles of scrap metal and the old wheels that fascinated him. Out of these wheels and the pieces of metal and wood he was constructing an intricate structure.

Abrashka felt himself watched and asked in a preoccupied tone of voice, "Did you hear Wanda singing? I wonder where she lives."

"Not far from here," Yoel answered after a moment. "Across the road, the first house in the village."

Yoel pulled Yacov by the sleeve and led him back to where they had sat before. They gazed at the field opposite them as if they were waiting for Wanda's singing voice to reach their ears again. Then they transferred their gazes to the distant mountains over which the clouds had spread a swimming shadow. But Yoel was incapable of sitting for very long without occupying his hands. He brought out a small black cauldron, in which he had been cooking raisins on the furnace in the smithy, and busied himself in preparing the raisin wine that he drank on the Sabbath; during the rest of the week *monopolka* was his only drink. He arranged a number of empty jars and bottles in front of the hut's doorstep, and sitting down where he had previously sat, he began to strain the cooked raisins through a rag into a large pitcher. He squeezed those raisins left in the rag with his fist and wrung them out with both his callused hands over the pitcher, until there was not a drop left in the rag. He unwound the rag and offered Yacov a few of the squashed raisins, then he heaved himself up from the doorstep, went over to Abrashka, asked him to open his mouth, cast into it the remainder of the raisins left in the rag, and came back to take up his seat beside Yacov.

Yacov sucked on the sweet drops of juice still left in the raisins. He said contentedly, "God's world is glorious in spite of everything, isn't it, Yoel?"

"What do you mean in spite of everything?"

"I mean disregarding . . . "

"If you disregard, then what's left of the glory? Isn't everything tied up together—the raisins with the wine, the wine with you, you with me? And the reverse is also true. Turn it over, put it upside down, mix east with west, mix the bad with the good, and still the reflection of the Eternal Secret is both within you and in the Infinite. Still you and the Infinite are like two concentric circles. If you look at it that way, then it is indeed glorious." Yoel sighed deeply. "Well, you might be right. God's world doesn't look too bad at this very moment, in this very place. But if you had said the same thing to a wounded soldier on the battlefield at this very moment, he would have cursed you. Why do I say this? Because, on the whole, beauty and glory are an odd affair. They're both a yes and a no. Take for example the mountains over there. Beautiful, glorious you'd say. But if you looked well, you would see death hovering between the rocks: one worm eating another, one tree growing on the carcass of another, one rock pressing against another. So how can you know what beauty is, or love for that matter? Only if you look beyond what you see, if you look through it, then do you realize that things are neither beautiful nor ugly, that there is no love or hatred. And therein lies real beauty. That is real love. That is the glory of the world, if you know what I mean."

Yacov's eyes lit up. "If a man is able to think the way you do, the rifts and contradictions are no longer so sharp, are they, Yoel? I wish I could accept them the way you do. But then, where is passion? Such a view of things quenches the flame of passion in one's heart, doesn't it?"

Yoel burst into uproarious laughter. He began to pour the wine from the pitcher into the jars and bottles in front of him. Only after he had covered them with pieces of rag and tied them around the necks with string, did he turn to Yacov, "So, that's what you're worried about? You love your passions too much to let go of them, don't you? And here I am involved in a maddening struggle with myself trying to tame my own flames of passion—let alone the passions of the flesh! But if you only knew, for instance, how passionately I crave a sniff of at least a speck of the secret of creation! Aye, if you only knew how badly my whole being yearns for that!"

"So does mine," Yacov whispered elatedly. "When I was a child, Mother used to tell me about the veils upon veils in which God's world is enwrapped. One world enwrapped within the other. And ever since that time . . . "

His eyes met Yoel's whose gaze went straight through him. No one had ever looked so deeply inside him before. Yoel began to hum a Hasidic tune. He knew countless melodies. Gradually he began to sing. His voice, although a heavy bass, took on a lightness, a softness of tone. Carried away by his sudden enthusiasm, he stood up, stretched his body to its full height, and pulled Yacov up by the sleeve. Sensing fun, Abrashka darted over to them. Yoel pulled them both out onto the empty road. He clapped his hands and snapped his fingers as he sang, while they tried to mimic him and keep time to his rhythm. So they moved in dancing step, round and round, slowly at first, then faster and faster, until their heads began to spin and drops of perspiration rolled down their foreheads and dimmed their eyes. At length all three of them collapsed onto the tall clumps of grass near the ditch.

Once back on his feet, Yoel pinched Abrashka's cheek, "Be a good sport, little tramp, get inside and bring out a volume of the Mishnah, so that your *melamed* here," he indicated Yacov with his chin, "and I can catch our breaths, studying a page or two. Otherwise your *melamed's* head might, Heaven forbid, rust up and who knows what he might do to you."

Yoel's Gemaras and Mishnahs looked much like he himself did. Their pages, like the skin of his face, were full of black blotches, stiff and dry, cracked, creased, and frayed at the edges. Yoel took one look at the book that Abrashka had brought out and pulled his ear, "Didn't you hear what I said? A Mishnah I said."

"I want you to study the Song of Songs," Abrashka entreated winningly.

"Put it back right away, snotnose!"

Abrashka looked at Yoel, astonished. "What's the matter, Yoel?"

Yoel's voce softened immediately. He took the book out of Abrashka's hand. "You must understand, little vagabond," He mussed the boy's hair so that the latter's skullcap fell off. Yoel picked it up, cleaned it on his sleeve, and put it back on Abrashka's head. "You must understand that the Pardes Garden may be entered only by those who have first eaten their share of bread and meat." He slid the volume between his knees. "We'll do the studying another time." He resumed humming a tune. Abrashka moved away, and this time sat down near a pile of clay that Yoel had dug up and moistened for him. With his nimble fingers Abrashka began to knead chunks of clay into small figurines. Yacov, who could sense Abrashka's moods so well, watched him from where he sat. When the boy was with Yoel he was always cheerful and happy, but there was also an air of unusual dreaminess about him.

Yoel's eyes scanned the field across the road and the horizon beyond it. He nudged Yacov with his elbow and said in a hushed voice, "If you only knew how curious I am about how things are over there, in the land of the Song of Songs. I keep on wondering what Jerusalem looks like, what it might feel like to be a Jew in the Holy Land. What it might feel like to read the Holy Scriptures there, or recite the Song of Songs. Strange how generations of a people can long for a country that they have never seen. The blood in our veins must be longing for it. Maybe our blood has a memory of its own."

"I'm sure that a man like you would feel quite at home there, wouldn't you, Yoel?" Yacov asked, a wistful glint in his eyes.

Yoel shook his head. "How can I know here what I'd feel there? A Jew's longing is after all not for a familiar country, but for a country he sees in his mind's eye, in his heart and in his imagination."

"Couldn't it be," Yacov asked, "that once you got there you'd recognize the same country that you had already seen in your head? It sometimes happens to me, when all is calm within me, that everything that is outside of me corresponds to everything that is inside. Often at night, when I look out the window, the world outside seems no more than a figment of my imagination."

"And to me," Yoel rejoined, "everything seems neither material nor imagined, neither something nor nothing."

"I know what you mean."

"You do? But how can you know what I mean, if what I think that I mean is not always what I really mean?" He burst into his loud boisterous laughter. Yacov and Abrashka laughed along with him. He picked up the same tune that he had hummed before. At first there was still a trace of laughter in it, but gradually the tune grew melancholy and drawn out. Abrashka continued shaping his figurines of clay, unaware that he was slowly swaying to the rhythm of the melody. Then the tune weakened, it grew faint and barely audible, until it dissolved into silence. Abrashka raised his head. The three of them let their eyes wander, each over the faces of the other two, until their eyes seemed to become locked into one gaze, their hearts to become enveloped in the same mood at this silent moment of dusk.

It was time to leave for the Blue Mountain. Yacov unhitched Sussi's rein from the tree to which they had tethered him. Abrashka sighed with regret, "Oy, if only we could stay on and on here forever."

Yoel lifted him onto the horse. "When the time comes to leave, little tramp, never say 'Oy,' but get up, go, and be done with it. Have a good ride home!" he called after them.

As they rode off, they looked back and saw Yoel's tall figure standing in the middle of the road, waving at them. "Yoel is like a real brother to us, isn't he, Yacov?" Abrashka asked. "He makes you and me feel like brothers too, doesn't he? And when we are with him, it's as if we lived with him, isn't it?"

Yacov agreed. Yoel and his smithy were a kind of home away from home to them.

◎ 6 ◎

RIGHT AFTER THE OUTBREAK of the war, Lodz had undergone an unbelievable transformation. It was no longer the same city. Its streets were infected by a fever. People walked around dazed by the changes that were occurring in their daily lives, stunned by the threat of losing their fortunes, losing their work places. Their senses were benumbed by the specter of looming starvation and by the threat that they or their dear ones would be sent to the battlefields. Binele was no less bewildered than anyone else.

On that particular day Handsome Moshe had left the factory earlier than usual for some reason. Binele was on her way home and walked by herself in the crowd of nervous and confused workers. No sooner had she come out on Piotrkowska Street than Yone the Svolotch, her supervisor, caught up with her. Before she had time to recover from the shock of his sudden appearance at her side, she heard him whisper in her ear, "I must talk to you. Wait for me at eight o'clock at Church Place beside the Holy Mary statue." A moment later he was gone, having disappeared amidst the throngs of people rushing home from work.

The news of a new series of recruitments was passing from mouth to mouth. The entire city seemed to be plunged into a state of anguish. Binele's heart pounded with alarm, just like those of the people around her. It did not occur to her to keep the appointment with Yone. What could he possibly tell her that he could not have told her at the factory or even in the street when he had stopped her? Had he decided to fire her? Why then didn't he do it right away? Perhaps he had had the crazy idea of having a date with her? But what kind of date was this supposed to be? Hadn't he more than once seen her with Handsome Moshe? Besides, he could surely have found a prettier girl at the factory than she, if he still had a whim for flirtation on such a maddening day.

She was not such a fool as to think that Handsome Moshe had been going out with her because she was attractive or interesting. Moshe was going out with her because basically he was a shy young man, yet he wanted to play the role of a Ramon Novarro in front of the entire world, the role of a conqueror of women's hearts. Having her companionship and being sure of her devotion, he could allow himself the liberty of being bold with other girls. While she felt herself sure of his devotion for as long as he was unsure of himself, she was not one to deceive herself. She knew where she stood in the world.

Instead of heading straight for home, she first went to Church Place, although it still did not enter her mind to meet Yone. She strolled in front of the church along the brick fence that held the statue of the Holy Mary in a niche. She felt neither hunger nor thirst. The fever that had infected the town all around her and the nervous shiver coursing through her limbs gave her the feeling of both being and yet not entirely being there. Of late she had been unable to free herself of that inner uneasiness, of the discomfort within her own skin. Something continually stirred in her veins, something within her heart cried out, she did not know for what.

Church Place was packed with people. Rows of wagons filled with furniture rolled by in long processions, heading out of town. Entire families sat atop the mountains of bedding that filled the wagons, while on all the street corners paperboys yelled at the top of their lungs, "Extra! Extra edition!" Battalions of soldiers and military orchestras, followed by long lines of cannons, marched in the middle of the street, surrounded by throngs of civilians. In their midst marched cohorts of Gentiles and Jews with shovels on their shoulders, on their way to dig trenches. The arriving trams could barely move ahead. They clanked alarmingly, as if announcing their passengers' anxiety to the entire town. Hordes of impatient passengers poured out of them, only to be replaced by other hordes impatient to get in. The church bells tolled with loud, plaintive peals.

On the narrow sidewalks people rushed back and forth, bumping into each other. Many hurried into the shops on Church Place and the neighboring streets, all of which were equally crowded. Empty-handed men and women emerged from other shops, shouting, "They've run out of food!"

The fallen leaves of the chestnut trees in Church Place danced in the autumnal gusts of wind. They seemed to rise in the air to the rhythm of the bells tolling. The wind fluttered the shawls and coattails of the people as they streamed into the church through the open front doors. Through these doors Binele could see hundreds of candles lit inside and people kneeling. She barely remembered that these had been her first living quarters in Lodz.

Then a procession formed in the churchyard behind the presbytery and started marching in the direction of the caserns. Holy pictures and portraits of Tsar Nicholas were borne aloft. People sang "God Save the Tsar." Men with pails and brushes rushed from one gate to another, pasting new, large white posters on top of the posters of an earlier day. The new posters were full of wet print and shiny exclamation marks. "The Germans have broken through the front lines!" Shouts bounced back and forth from one passerby to another.

Carried forward by the hullabaloo, Binele looked up at the clock in the church tower. It was eight o'clock. She noticed the niche in the church's thick brick fence that sheltered the blue wax figure of the Holy Mary with baby Jesus in her arms. She recalled how in the church of Bociany she had once felt very close to the mother of Jesus and how alive and familiar the Holy Mary had seemed to her then. She had even prayed through Mother Mary to her own mother. Now when she looked at the statue, she saw only a wax doll with painted eyes and two glass beads for tears. Binele lived now without having a mother even in the heavens. She was "as lonely as a dog," as they used to say in Bociany. Only at least now she was not really alone in her loneliness. In Lodz, especially during these days of utter confusion, every face she saw was the face of an orphan. Loneliness was written all over the faces of the mothers who ran after their uniformed sons as they marched in military formations. Each of these mothers seemed to be in need of a mother of her own.

As she turned her head the other way she saw Yone walking right beside her. He said not a word. She moved on at his side, unable to open her mouth. Together they waded through the crowd of passersby, at times shoulder to shoulder, at times at a distance from one another, each avoiding looking at the other's face. Binele wondered whether it was the general tension that seemed to thicken the air all around her or whether it was the tension between Yone and herself that so overwhelmed her that she was hardly able to breath. When they reached the corner, Yone took hold of her arm and pulled her in the direction in which he wanted them to go.

"Where are you taking me?" she finally managed to ask. But the minute the question was out of her mouth, she thought she knew the answer. He was taking her to the Ochrana, the Secret Police! Of course! He suspected her of being a member of the Bund. It was because of his fear of the Bund in the first place that he had treated her so well. Now that the war had broken out Yone no longer feared the Bund's vengeance. He was going to denounce her! Yet she could not bring herself to escape. Her cursed curiosity! It was liable to destroy her some day. She could not fight Yone off. Not now. He had cast a spell over her. He mesmerized her. In her confusion, she felt herself impelled to follow him.

She heard him say something. The unexpected sound of his raw voice made a shudder run down her spine. "The boss has begun to evacuate the factory," she heard him say as though casually. "He's about to move it all to some place deep inside Russia. I'm supposed to leave with him. They'll fire you any day now. Handsome Moshe was fired this morning."

She felt as if the ground had caved in under her feet. "I don't understand," she muttered and stopped in the middle of the street. She stared into Yone's green eyes, trying to read an answer in them to all the questions that she was unable to formulate in words.

The catty, biting look that normally pierced her from his eyes was gone. Their green was darker and warmer now. From their depths his answering look beamed at her, devoid of even a trace of hostility. He looked at her rather humbly, rather forlornly. "Don't you see what's going on?" he asked. His voice too had become uncannily soft in its rawness. It made her fear of him dissolve. She regained her self-composure as she resumed walking at his side; he held her by the arm. Her mind regained its ability to function, although her general state of anxiety had increased.

"So what will happen now?" she asked.

"The German occupation of Lodz will happen," he answered.

"I'm not going back to Bociany for anything in the world," she said resolutely.

"Then how are you going to manage if the factories close?"

She resented his question. What business was that of his? She knotted her eyebrows and scrutinized him closely, boldly. All at once she became certain of one thing. He had no intention of taking her to the Ochrana. What then did he want of her? Had he come to meet her in order just to tease her? "I can always find work as a maid," she said, and then asked, irritated, "And what business is that of yours?"

"Who's going to need maids when all the wealthy have run away to the villages?"

"So why did you want a date with me?"

"Because . . . " He let go of her arm and halted for a moment as if to keep her in suspense. Then, as he resumed pacing beside her, he said quickly, "Because I want to run away with you to Eretz Israel."

She blinked. "Are you out of your mind?"

"Maybe I am, but I want you to come with me."

"Why exactly me?"

"You know very well why. That's what I want."

She was beside herself with anger. "And what about what I want?" She was amazed at his chutzpah—to consider her his possession, a kind of thing that he thought himself entitled to manipulate at his whim! Her eyes brimmed over with tears of frustration. "Couldn't you find someone else to make a fool of today of all days? Have you really gone crazy?"

"Maybe I have." He accelerated his pace. She accelerated hers to keep up with him. "I don't want to leave with the boss for that far place inside

Russia," he continued. "And besides, I might be conscripted any day now, and I'm in no mood to die for the tsar."

Only a minute before she had been ready to pound him with her fists in self-protection. Now she no longer feared him. He was not going to take her to the Ochrana and the factory would close soon anyway. She could have left him right then and there and walked off without turning back, never to see him again. But a wave of strange warm feelings surged in her heart. She definitely did not want him to die for the tsar. "Can't you hide somewhere?" She asked with an edge of worry in her voice.

"I want to go to Eretz Israel," he said curtly.

"Perhaps you should."

"With you."

She laughed nervously. "You know what? You don't have to go anywhere. Just take yourself to the madhouse on Joy Street. You're crazy good and proper."

He turned to face her and grabbed hold of both her arms. He squeezed them so hard that she thought he was about to crush her. He sputtered out heatedly, "You're right. I am crazy. I am crazy about you. You know I am, from the day I first saw you. Binele, I swear to you . . . "

She tore herself out of his hands. "The name is not Binele, it's Bina. And leave me alone!"

"Never!" He grabbed her by the waist and pressed her tightly to his chest. "You're mine. You saw me at work. I can't take my eyes off you."

"I belong to no one!" She wrestled with him but realized that she was not using all her strength. If she had really wanted to, she could have extricated herself from his arms and escaped. People stared at them as they rushed by; they would have prevented him from assaulting her. After all, with the factory closing and moving, Yone no longer had a say over her life. But her cursed curiosity, mixed with a compassion hitherto alien to her, made her increasingly weaker as she fought with him. She found herself looking forward to what he would tell her next, to what he would do.

He held her fast by the waist and pulled her forward. His trembling arm transmitted its tremors to her entire body. He buried his face in her hair. She felt the touch of his cheek against her neck and behind her ear. His pockmarked skin was rough. She forgot about the passersby, forgot about the street, forgot about where she was. The church bells tolled in time with the panic of her heart; her heart throbbed with the anguish of the city. She was no longer one being, but an entire city full of people.

And so she allowed Yone to drag her off, convinced that they had both
gone insane. There was a murky taste of joy in that insanity, a taste of victory amidst the confusion of her mind.

They were now deep in the heart of Baluty. Time seemed to have
stopped running at its normal pace. It no longer mattered whether it was
day or night, today or tomorrow. Soon they were walking through sparsely
populated streets where small gardens and lawns divided one house from
the other. The houses became fewer and further apart. Then there were
no more houses, just one open, spacious, hard-soiled field to be marched
through. They came upon a red brick wall. Behind the wall, the dead of
Lodz stared out into the night from the tips of white monuments and
tombstones. Gradually, Binele and Yone drew nearer to the wall, and the
new Jewish cemetery. A narrow carpet of clumpy, dark grass aproned the
cemetery. In the outer field, heaps of swirling leaves were like moveable
graves carried about by the wind. A design of sparse, immobile leaves dotted the dark brick wall that Binele and Yone were approaching.

As they sank down on a heap of leaves gathered at the foot of the wall
and Binele felt herself dissolving under the touch of Yone's hot hands, she
had one clear thought, "I am stronger than he is!" A funny question came
to her mind and made her smile. Why should men be attracted to cemeteries at moments like these? What connection was there between this inner
splitting and falling apart and the craving to be glued to another's body?
And what relation did all this have to the Kingdom of Death?

Yone's lips silenced all further questions. His red mustache, which
looked dark in the dim light, was pricking and burning her. It seemed as if
he were undressing her with his lips. A rain of leaves poured down from
the crown of a tree that protruded over the wall. The dry leaves tickled
her skin, skin that seemed to have become one nerve, sensitive to the
slightest touch. Yone's hands, his rough face, and his beard scratched her
body like brushes made of the autumn leaves. Only his lips were soft and
burning. Yone mumbled incomprehensible words. Binele strained to hear
him, but the blood in her veins roared too loudly. The call of her flesh, for
so long stifled within the narrow confines of her skin, now burst through
her mouth in a scream.

It was quiet and dark all around her. She felt the sticky warmth of
blood between her thighs. The answer to her curiosity was a red and white
flame. Her scream had come from way back. It was her first scream of life
on the day of her mother's death, the day of her own birth. Mother Death

and Daughter Life had joined to explode the womb of mystery and part from each other forever. Now Daughter Life had become Mother Death. Now she would give birth to a life doomed to die. Every human being was an orphan. Everyone's marriage canopy should be spread out in a cemetery, so that Life and Death could dance together, and become one.

Yone's head rested on Binele's breast. With his lips spread in a faint childish smile, he made her think of a baby who had finished suckling. Binele was fully aware of the power she possessed, of the enigmatic force of her femininity. A surge of energy flooded her veins; she wanted to jump to her feet and run off and do something unusual. She could hardly muster the patience to lie there with that napping baby, Yone, at her breast.

"Now I'm happy," she heard Yone whisper. She noticed a warm light in his half-closed eyes. Happy? Was this the meaning of the word that she had for so long wanted to find out? He asked softly, "You will come to Eretz Israel with me, won't you?"

"No, I won't." She rumpled his red hair with maternal tenderness.

"But you'll meet me under the Holy Mary tomorrow, won't you?"

The following day all she could think of was her meeting with Yone that evening under the statue of the Holy Mary. However, before she went to meet him, she decided to stop at the bathhouse that Moshe had once pointed out to her.

She sat in the bathtub, hugged by the soft, foamy water, soaping herself with tenderness and self-admiration. She was astonished at herself and at her delight in the moment to which she was giving herself with such enthusiastic abandon. There was a war going on, and her job was in jeopardy.

A large mirror hung on the opposite wall. She stood up in the tub to admire herself. "I'm not a Marzepa," she muttered as her hands glided over her wet, slippery breasts. How heavy, how giving, how both tender and firm they were! The nipples were turned forward, toward the world, sensitive to every touch, and ready to let all their blessed abundance flow out. She touched her hips, rounded into the shape of a delicate vessel, a form similar to that of her breasts and belly. The belly itself nestled firm and full between her hipbones. Covered with soft, slippery skin, it seemed to undulate in circles around the belly button that held it together. As for her waist, it was there to hold the flesh in place, to discipline and give form to the roundness of her bosom, her belly, and her hips. Like a thin,

tight hoop it prevented the wealth of her body from overflowing its confines and inundating the world.

As for her arms—they were hard. The skin stretched over them tightly,
making it difficult to pinch them. Their strength poured into her hands
and palms. But the hands themselves were molded with softness. The fingers were plump, as if all the work they had done throughout the years
had left not a trace. And then there were her legs. They were like columns.
Straight and smooth as they were on the outside, she could feel the calf
muscles at the touch of her hand—each muscle as hard as a fist, kneaded
into place around the bones. Like springs they balanced the massive
weight of her body. Her feet—whose heels were thick and broad, as were
the entire hard-fibered soles—were unwilling to miss out on the slightest
touch of the ground beneath them. This was her own manner of walking:
with all of her weight pressing down on her soles, while every single toe
faced forward to touch the ground and make it respond like a trampoline.

Her gaze climbed upwards toward her head. She smiled at herself in
the mirror at the sight of her pink cheeks peppered with freckles, at the
reflection of her short, broad "potato" nose, the wings of which trembled
with her smile, at the reflection of the clear slanted eyes above the protruding cheek bones. What color were her eyes? Sometimes she thought
them to be brown, sometimes gray or blue or even black. When she
looked more closely into the mirror she saw a mixture of colors, a mosaic.
All the colors of the world were in her eyes! The colors were woven into
her gaze, which was sharp, appealing, both teasing and questioning. And
as for her mouth—it, in fact, overshadowed the rest of her face. Its moist,
red, and sharply defined lips protruded, ready to offer a kiss to the entire
world, while at the same time they seemed to be attracting the world, absorbing it, and sucking it in.

"I am beautiful," she whispered to herself, reluctant to step out of the
bathtub. Soaking herself in the soft warm water was a pleasure that she
had never experienced before. "I probably felt the same when I was in my
mother's belly," she thought, promising herself that next time she came to
the bathhouse she would stay much longer. But now she had to hurry in
order to meet Yone the Svolotch and his waiting arms. In her imagination,
she saw his arms stretched out toward her through the length of the entire
city, or rather through the length of a large calm sea. For the stormy city
had drowned yesterday. Today only a mirror of water was left. The ribbons of water rolled out from the faucets of the bathhouse and wove

themselves into a soft, fluffy carpet. This magic carpet glided with her through the corridors of streets and took her toward the church with the statue of the Holy Mary, where Yone waited for her, to carry her off toward the new Jewish cemetery.

This time Yone undid her braids. "Your hair lights up the darkness," he said, burying his head in it. Later on he muttered, "Come with me to Eretz Israel. There we'll be lying under a fig tree and winter will never come."

After they had taken leave of each other, Binele could not bring herself to return immediately to Ziporah's dwelling, to witness the quarrels between Ziporah and her husband, or to see the screaming children in the squalor and darkness of the room. She felt instead in a mood for celebration. There was a joyous stirring, an exuberant buzzing going on within her. There were surges of such energy rushing through her limbs that they made her want to break out of the narrow confines of the town whose dark streets she now haunted for hours. The freedom of the luxuriant green pastures, of the roads of Bociany, was what she now needed. She needed the intoxicating fragrances of Bociany's air, the magic of Bociany's nights beneath the enormous sky studded with stars. And she was aching for the beauty of that young man, Yacov. It was for him that she found herself yearning now, a gnawing, stubborn sort of yearning. She was glad that Yacov's face, his curly brown hair, his pipe stem sidelocks, and his honey-colored eyes—his entire figure with its swaying gait—had remained so vividly in her memory.

But if Yacov was whom she wanted, why, she wondered—why her greed for the embrace of Yone's arms? Who was Yone anyway? Who was this green-eyed, submissive Asmodeus with the flaming hair and beard whose hot breath she still felt lingering on her breasts? She was not really curious about him. She had no need to know a thing about him. Yone was her slave. He served her body and helped her find out who she herself was. "Handsome Moshe would have said that Yone is using me, taking advantage of me," she thought. "But in fact it is I who am taking advantage of him."

Nonetheless she ventured one evening to make Yone talk about himself, "Do you know what they say about you at the factory?" she asked as she interrogated him.

"Yes, I know. They say that I'm a stool pigeon," he replied composedly. "I consider this a compliment. You have no idea how we suffer on account of those bastards, those socialists, those revolutionaries, may their names be erased! It's because of them that I lost my father and mother." She observed the same expression of rage and meanness, which she used to read in his face at the factory, disfigure his features. He was silent for a very long time. Only later in the evening did he flare up again. "They work hand in glove with the anti-Semites and with all the enemies of Israel. You should have been here during those years, then you'd have seen for yourself. The Bundists would join up with the strikers and march in demonstrations alongside the goyim who afterwards let themselves loose on Baluty, striking out against the Jews. So who are the traitors, I or they? They've betrayed the People of Israel, that's the truth. It's a sacred duty to seek vengeance on them. Yes, a sacred duty! And if I could, I would have done more, so help me God."

Later the same evening, when he had calmed down, he again pleaded with Binele to leave for Eretz Israel with him. She shrugged, "Stop bothering me with that nonsense."

"We'll be happy there," he assured her. "You'll see, we'll build a Jewish land and we'll live among our own people."

"When the war is over, I will be happy here, too. Here I am also with my own people. And leaving for Eretz Israel, why, it must cost a fortune."

Yone flung his chin up proudly. "Rely on me. I can see you don't know whom you are talking to." He grinned, adding boastfully, "Yossl Tsots is my uncle, did you know that?"

She though he was joking. "My friend Ziporah has a saying, 'He gives himself airs like Yossl Tsots.'"

"Then you should know that my uncle is a great man. It's no small thing to drive the hearse of the first-class corpses. He brings the richest and most famous Jews in town for burial in the cemetery."

"I'm sure you resemble him," she laughed.

"I do. But he's twice as old and twice as fat as I am."

"But his eyes are certainly not twice as devilish as yours."

He guffawed. "What are you talking about? The Angel of Death himself is afraid of Yossl Tsots! Have you ever seen him dressed up in his black livery, wearing his black top hat and black gloves? Have you ever seen his hearse? How handsomely carved it is with silvered reins and the decorated horses! So what do you have to say now?"

"I wish it on all my enemies is what I have to say." Binele looked at Yone and tried to imagine him in Yossl Tsots's outfit, driving the hearse of the rich and famous. A shudder crept down her spine. Perhaps Yone was in fact the devil himself? In Bociany people believed that the devil and his demons could transform themselves into real people and live normal human lives. She had always been curious about the devil and his demons. Perhaps this was why she was attracted to Yone. Perhaps she herself was Lilith the Wanton, who could perform wonders and exercise bewitching charms with the powers of her body?

"You will come with me to Eretz Israel, won't you?" he would not tire of insisting.

She blinked at him mischievously, "Do you want to go there first class, on Yossl Tsots's hearse?"

Yone tugged at a strand of her loose hair. "I'll go on the profits of Yossl Tsots's hearse. Yossl Tsots has made up his mind to transport the whole family to Eretz Israel. He himself is to follow as soon as business slackens. You know how it is. In good times the rich rarely die, while the poor die every day. But now it's first-class season for the rich too. Their fortunes are going aground and so are they."

Binele laughed uproariously, shaking her head. "In Bociany people say that the rich and the poor are all alike when they lie buried in the ground. But that the rich lie more comfortably than the poor when they're above the ground."

Binele met Yone every day and hurried with him toward the Jewish cemetery. She hardly took notice of what was happening around her, nor did she hear what people were saying. Her mind had stopped working. Her body did the talking, and it did so in a language that she was beginning to understand. She felt not a trace of guilt about Handsome Moshe. She owed him nothing. Now that he no longer worked at the factory, she could avoid seeing him except when she wanted to. On Saturdays she did walk in the Train Garden with him. She told Moshe what had been going on at the factory and that weavers and *shtoperkes* were constantly being fired.

"You know," Moshe said to her as they walked in the Train Garden one day, "I suspect that Yone Svolotch saw to it that I should be among the first to be fired from the factory."

She ridiculed him. "And what other silly notions have you got? You're as much on his mind as a speck of dust on his left earlock. Anyway the factory is about to be moved deep inside Russia, so what difference does it make now?"

He conceded, "You're right, it's not important anymore."

He told her that increasingly younger men were being conscripted and that there was an evil decree hovering over the heads of the Jews of Lodz. The tsar had declared that it was because of the Jews that the Russian march on Berlin had had such a catastrophic outcome. A representative of the Russian General Command, the tsar's uncle Nikolay Nikolayevitch, had set up headquarters at the Grand Hotel. There he had received the *rov* of Lodz and had announced to him that all the Jews would be expelled from the city. It was the Jews, he said to the *rov,* who had sided with the Germans and were the enemies of the tsar, and it was the Jews who had purposely cut the wires of the Russian military telegraph. The *rov* suggested to the honorable representative that before the latter put his evil decree into action, he should test the Jews first and allow them to take over the supervision of the telegraph wires. In this manner the expulsion of the Jews from Lodz had been temporarily shelved.

Moshe told Binele that he intended to register with the Jewish militia designated to keep watch over the telegraph wires. "We'll make sure that neither cow nor dog tears up the wires, and in this way we'll bear the responsibility for the fate of the Jews of Lodz on our shoulders."

Handsome Moshe had become a cynic. He was rarely in a cheerful frame of mind, and had lost not only his charms but also his handsomeness. He looked years older. Binele tried to boost his morale and liven him up. He peered at her with his sad, caressing eyes. "You are the only light I have in my life," he whispered in her ear and kissed her gratefully.

She teased him, "And what about your theater and your Poale-Zion?"

"Without the theater and the Poale-Zion, life would have been even worse, but it's you that I want to marry."

She looked at him with wide-eyed amusement. "Can't you find yourself a better match than me? After all you are Handsome Moshe!"

"But you are beautiful Bina."

"I'm a Marzepa."

"Some Mazepa, with a face full of juicy freckles that can drive a man out of his mind. You will marry me, won't you? True, there is a war on, but together we could weather it more easily. A person needs someone to lean on, especially in times of war."

"So you want to lean on me?" Her smile faded.

"You can lean on me, too."

"I don't need anyone to lean on!"

"It only seems so to you." He could not understand why she had become so bitter. He tried to embrace her.

"So you want to marry me and make me a baby," she pushed him away and fumed. "And use me, so that it'll be easier for you to dodge military service!" She gasped, stupefied at what she had said. She did not mean it. A demon was speaking through her mouth in that harsh voice that did not belong to her. She saw a pallor spreading over Moshe's face as the blood receded from it. He bit his lips. His eyes misted over and he turned his head away. Then he took a step backwards, like someone suddenly stabbed in the heart. In the blink of an eye she threw herself at him, braided her arms around his neck, and kissed him passionately on the lips. They were standing in the very middle of the Train Garden, in full daylight, and in full view of the many people who stood around talking heatedly. For the first time in her life she uttered words of apology, words that had never fallen from her lips before. "Forgive me," she said. "You made me so dizzy with that . . . that marriage proposal that I didn't know what I was saying."

She forgot that she had taken an oath never to marry. She remembered Yone—and yet she gave in. A couple of days later Handsome Moshe bought her a fake platinum ring and gave her a silken scarf with a design of forget-me-nots as an engagement gift, and Binele became his bride.

The same week that Handsome Moshe had showered Binele with gifts, he proposed that, as bride and groom, they both attend an antiwar demonstration that the workers' parties had organized for the next day. He already belonged to the Jewish militia and guarded the tsar's wire installations against an invasion of cows or dogs, thus protecting the Jews of Lodz and preventing their being exiled. But he loathed the tsar with all his heart and he loved his party, the Poale-Zion, which hoped to build *socialismus* in the Jewish homeland.

"You understand," he tried to explain to Binele. "Throughout the hundreds and hundreds of years of Jewish history, the Jews have traveled to Eretz Israel in wagons and small boats, disregarding all obstacles such as attacks by robbers or pirates, all in order to reach the holy earth and be buried in it. I don't call that *Zionismus* but *idiotismus*. Because *Zionismus* means going to live in Eretz Israel, not going there to die." He noticed that she had abstracted herself, as if his words had not reached her. He pressed her arm more tightly and whispered with a nervous tremor in his voice. "The Poale-Zion marches under its own banners, and I'll be in the front row, carrying one. You will march with the masses somewhere behind me, so that if the Cossacks attack, you won't get hit because of me."

Binele refused to hear of *Zionismus*, nor did she want Moshe to go to the demonstration. In her opinion, such demonstrations were the greatest madness one could imagine. It was like putting one's healthy body into a sickbed. What did they expect to accomplish, those Poale-Zionists, those workers' parties? Did they think that by marching in a demonstration against the tsar, just as the pious Gentiles marched in processions for the tsar, they would stop the war? She had not the slightest intention of exposing herself to the Cossacks' knouts, just because of a stupid idea. So she almost quarreled with her fiancé the very week of their engagement. Only the fact that she saw Moshe so enlivened, so enthusiastic and determined, impressed her. It boosted her respect for him. So at length she agreed that Moshe should go to the demonstration in good health, while she would, in good health, do as she pleased, namely not go.

As she lay on her straw pallet in Ziporah's room, she could not stop thinking about Moshe, Moshe the dandy, the charmer, the actor, the dancer, Moshe the timorous and delicate, and Moshe the stubborn, the enthusiastic Poale-Zionist who feared not the prospect of being beaten up by the Cossacks—Moshe, her future husband. She ought to listen to him more attentively, she told herself. She should learn from him the things that he knew and she did not. She was so ignorant, unable even to read or write. Granted, she had the ability to adjust to any situation and to find out about things on her own; she could quickly learn the unfamiliar and new that she encountered at every step, and she knew how to use her own reason. But so often she said and did silly things. Perhaps her reason made her blunder because it was not polished or sharpened. Knowledge and understanding could help to improve it. She wanted to understand and to learn, but not particularly the things that Moshe had been talking about. First of all she wanted to understand her own strange self, then to understand life and people in general. She wanted to be able to easily discern the difference between what people said and what they meant, between what they did and who they were.

In the morning she still had no intention of going to the demonstration, yet she set out in the direction of Piotrkowska Street. Moshe had mentioned the approximate time when he would be passing the first corner of Piotrkowska Street with the flag in his hands. It was a cold rainy day. The clouds sagged over the roofs and a dark grayness enveloped the city. Clusters of humped, huddled-up people with caps or plaids drawn down over their heads, so that only their watery blinking eyes were visible, streamed by her. She wrapped her plaid more snugly around her.

She was not thinking of the demonstration. She was still thinking of Moshe and herself. Now that she was his bride, she felt that she owed him an explanation, although what had happened between Yone and herself had been Moshe's own fault. Why was it that all he would do was kiss her tenderly, holding her in his arms as delicately as if she were made of porcelain? Why had he never taken her forcefully into is arms and pressed her to his chest so tightly that her bones cracked and a fire ignited in her body? Why was he such a milksop? But then, how could such a milksop not be afraid of the Cossacks, and march, flag in hand, in today's demonstration?

Perhaps Moshe did not really love her or want her enough? Was it not, in fact, possible that he wanted to marry her for the sake of convenience? But what kind of convenience could there be in marrying her? He would be getting not a penny in dowry. And then, such devious calculations did not sit well with the character of the Moshe she knew. Her heart refused to suspect an ulterior motive on his part. Wasn't she rather aware of his respect for her and for her body? Yet she wished that Moshe would treat her with at least some of Yone's reckless passion, his wild enthusiasm.

She had to tell Moshe about Yone. There was no other choice. But first she had to break with Yone. Anyway something had begun to frazzle in her relationship with him. Their encounters had grown increasingly frustrating; they seemed to mix with the frosty raindrops dripping on her skin and penetrating her heart. Yone had still not given up hope that she would leave with him for Palestine. He had promised that before he arranged for the provision of papers and transportation, he would find a place for the two of them in Baluty, now that the weather was turning wet and cold. In fact, she badly wanted to have a place of her own, if only for a short time. But she wanted to live there without Yone, even without Moshe.

As she entered a side street, approaching the Piotrkowska, a black mass of people seemed to burst forth from the distance, surging toward her. Tens, hundreds of people at a run blocked her way, shouting, "Back! Turn back! The Cossacks are coming!" A stranger grabbed hold of Binele's arm and pulled her back.

The mass of people escaping through the side streets swept her along. She was worried sick about Moshe. Where could he have run to with the flag in his hands? She had to find him. She scoured one side of the street and the other, scanning the faces in the passing crowd. In the distance she could see the Cossacks as they swished their knouts through the air and chased the marchers, who scattered in all directions. She pressed herself against a wall as she continued to search for the sight of Moshe's face. Her eyes were tearing from the cold, the tension, and the worry.

Suddenly her heart stopped. She saw a face: her brother Hershele's!

The next moment she found herself in Hershele's arms. A spasmodic sob escaped from her bosom. He carried her with him so that her feet barely touched the ground. Strong Hershele! He turned into the Promenade, which was also packed with fleeing demonstrators. For a moment the two of them, hemmed in by the crowd, were forced to stop as they clung to one another, arms entwined, face glued to face. Then he pulled her further along. Carried by the mob, they were pushed into a narrow street, all the while keeping their heads turned toward each other. Binele's eyes overflowed. Hershele's were aglow with the fury of a madman. He would not let go of her hand. The grip of his fingers was like that of a vise. Then he grabbed hold of her waist again, since her trembling legs refused to move fast enough. She hung on to him for dear life, letting him drag her further and further away from the hullabaloo. Finally, he pulled her into a gateway and pressed her against its arched wall so they could catch their breath for a moment. Then they entered the yard, found a stairwell, and collapsed on the stairs. Clinging to each other, they tried to shove themselves even closer. Hershele stroked Binele's wet hair with both hands. She held his face in the palms of hers.

"Don't cry, Binele," he said, still panting, as he tried to calm her. Dear and familiar though his voice sounded, there was a strangely alien ring to it.

She was unable to control her tears. "Hershele . . . dear Hershele . . . " she repeated in a mumble. She could hardly believe her eyes. It seemed impossible that she should be sitting beside this young man, who looked so unlike the Hershele she remembered, and yet that it should still be he in person. "What are you doing in Lodz? And you look so big and strong, Hershele!" She kissed his wet face, moistening his glasses with her tears.

"And you wear glasses!" She removed the glasses from his eyes. "I'm going out of my mind, so glad am I to see you!"

"I inherited Father's weak eyes," Hershele explained hoarsely. He took the glasses out of her hands, wiped them with the inside of his coattail, and put them back on. "You've also changed. I never knew you to cry before. And look at those braids! How long they are! And how pretty you are!"

She laughed through her tears. "Do you remember how everyone used to call me Marzepa?"

"I never did," he shook his head emphatically. "But I was jealous of you. You weren't afraid of Father or of anybody else. You were a born revolutionary."

Their conversation was chaotic, full of questions and incomplete answers. "And Father . . . " Binele gave a painful sigh. A fresh wave of tears washed down her face. "Does he know that you are in Lodz?"

"I wrote to him," Hershele answered as the expression of his face changed. There was something hard and unpleasant about it now. The face reminded her less of the Hershele whom she had known and more of Yossele, their father. Like their father, Hershele had straight blond hair and thick blond eyebrows. Deeply hidden beneath them, his eyes had a metallic sheen that spoke of stubbornness and determination. His gaze, too, was like that of their father, sharp and direct. Hershele was not as tall as their father, but like him he was heavyset and had broad shoulders. And his gestures were like those of his father. "I wrote to him," Hershele repeated. "My comrades informed me that he sat the seven days of shiva in mourning for me."

"He probably did the same for me," Binele nodded. "I ran away from home. But I met two girls from Bociany who were there for the holidays, so they must have told him about me. Oh, Hershele, if you only knew . . . " She burst into tears again.

He pressed her hands together. "If you never cried in olden times, why should you cry now?"

"I'm so happy to see you. We'll stay together, won't we?"

"And fight together . . . "

"Yes, fight together for . . . "

"Against all those who want to turn us into worms, who want to make us servile and teach us to crawl on all fours. Against the tsar and the rich and the clergy . . . and against Father, too."

"Against Father?"

"Of course, against him too. He's my greatest . . . he almost destroyed me as a person, as a human being."

"But you loved him so much!" She wrinkled her forehead in amazement. "You obeyed him so."

"Because I was a child. I needed him to love me. Now I am a man and can do without his love and without my love for him. I hate the harness of obedience he forced on me. I hate everything he wanted to impose on me. Imagine! He sat down to mourn for me, his only son, as if I were dead! Can you fathom that? Oh, no, I don't mourn for having lost him. I fight him. Do you understand?"

"No, I don't," Binele mumbled.

He moved his face closer to hers. His eyes lit up with that metallic glow that made her think of her father when he was angry. "I have a new religion, Binele," he blurted out, "a religion that worships man, not God. And I have a leader who is more than a father to me. His name is Lenin. He gives meaning to my life, gives me back a feeling of my own worth. He has straightened my back. He means more than God ever meant to me." Hershele talked with so much passion that the corners of his mouth grew white and foamy. "As you see me here, Binele, I'm ready to give my life for my ideal. Yes, to sacrifice it with a song on my lips." He stroked her head. "Do you remember how you used to run out onto the Wide Poplar Road to check whether the Messiah was on his way? It is dangerous to go on living in a never-ending wait for something that no one but yourself can bring you. We, Binele, you and I, and all those who have gathered in the streets today, we the abused, the spat upon, must break our chains and become our own liberators, Jews and Gentiles alike." He caressed her face and grew silent, as if he were waiting for Binele to echo his words. At length he took out an old onion-shaped watch from the pocket of his threadbare coat, glanced at it, and pulled at Binele's hand. "Come, I'll take you home, so that I can see where you live. And don't worry, from now on I'll take care of you."

She stared at him dismayed. "You haven't told me a thing about yourself. How do you live? Where do you work? What has happened to you during all this time?" He stood up from the stair they had been sitting on. She reluctantly heaved herself up as well and walked out into the street with him. Suddenly she remembered. Moshe! The worry about his safety began to prey on her mind again. How could she have forgotten him so completely? She had to rush off and find him. Quickly she gave Hershele her address. "*Vitish* people live on the Faiferovka, too," she added to reassure him.

"That's the right street to live on." He grinned and nodded his head approvingly. "Those are the streets where the blaze will start and set fire to this cursed world of ours." He squeezed her hand so hard that it hurt.

She stared at him. "I want to move out of there. Perhaps we could find a place for the two of us? I could live with you. It would be fun. And I will take care of you, not you of me. I can see how you're walking around with buttons missing!" She tugged at the treads left by the missing buttons of his coat. "Where do you live, Hershele?"

He let her wait for a reply. "I don't have a permanent address," he finally said, "for reasons of conspiracy, do you understand?"

She did not understand. "What do you mean by that?"

"I'll tell you another time. One doesn't become a seasoned revolutionary overnight. We must both be patient."

"I don't want to be patient, for heaven's sake! Oh, Hershele, I must run now, but I never want to part with you again, do you hear me?"

He gave her a brief smile. "We may have to. For the cause. One day you'll understand. The main thing is that I found you in the right place. You'll learn fast and become my true sister."

"And what am I now, a fake one?"

"Now you are my blood sister. You're the sister of my heart, and this may be an obstacle. There is no time these days for weaknesses."

"I am not weak." She grew irritated. "I'm as healthy as a horse." She threw her arms around him and kissed him loudly on the cheek. "You are saying stupid things because you've gone crazy just like me. We met so suddenly. What kind of obstacle-shmobstacle can I be to you? I would do anything for you!" She kissed him on the other cheek. "You must come and see me tonight. Don't forget the address. I'll be waiting for you at the window. If the women in the street accost you," she blinked meaningfully at him, "tell them that I am your sister. They all know me." She giggled nervously. "I must run. I'll be home at ten. Will you come?"

"Not today," He shook his head sharply, "nor tomorrow. After tomorrow at ten in the evening. Where are you running to now?"

"I cannot tell you in such a hurry. The 'spiracy . . . " She blinked at him.

"Conspiracy? Good. I won't ask any more. We shall talk then."

"Yes, we shall talk and talk. Take care!" She gave him a last hug and ran off.

The streets were more or less back to normal, except for the gendarmes on horseback who slowly circulated parallel to the sidewalks. Binele remembered that she had agreed to meet Moshe at the Train Garden after the demonstration. The garden was muddy and deserted, drops of rain dripped from the trees. She paced back and forth along the gravel paths, waiting. Her head swam. She was worried about Moshe and was overjoyed about having met Hershele. She could hardly believe that she had seen him, her Hershele, who was hidden somewhere within the young man whom she had just met, a young man so close to her heart and yet so much like a stranger. He had spoken to her in such an alien and yet familiar language about things that were hardly of any interest to her. What was it that all these young men wanted? What meaning was there in the madness that possessed them? She had easily made peace with Hershele's shaven cheeks and his wearing modern dress. It was a new skin, a new mask. But his words were no mask. Nor were Moshe's words, nor were Yone's for that matter. One day she would force herself to concentrate and listen more attentively to what they all had to say. One day she would force herself to be more patient with them and be less preoccupied with her own curiosity about other matters.

It was strange that what they all tried to tell her not only bored her to tears, but frightened her as well. And most frightening of all was what Hershele, the brother whom she had just met in this confused and confusing city, had said to her. What was it that he had said? That she was not his real sister. No more nor less! He had practically washed his hands off her, for the time being, until he changed her, until he made her over into a more suitable kind of sister. Then he would take care of her as if she were some weakling. Otherwise she was an obstacle.

What had happened to him? What devilish power held him in its spell? Held them all in its spell? It was such an obvious delusion that they could change this world into a better place. How would they do it? Were they God? And God Himself—would He be able to undo what He had done? Wasn't that why she had no faith in Him? And certainly she had no faith in people. Then where were they, all those young men, heading to with that dark demonic force expressed in their words, in their slogans and songs?

Oh, she did not give a hoot for their words! Her heart longed to see Hershele again. It was such a long wait until after tomorrow. When she sat with him, held his hand, and looked at him, she knew the closeness between them would come to the fore and speak its own language. To hell with words! She would disregard them, shrug them off. But in the meantime all that Hershele had left her with were just those terrifying words. And where was Moshe with the red banner, which he had most probably not been given to unfurl in the grayness of that day?

The time they had agreed to meet had long since passed when Binele finally saw Moshe approaching from the distance. She ran toward him. Distraught, looking haggard and downhearted, he took her into his arms and passionately pressed her to his chest—just as she had always wished him to do. She avidly surrendered to his embrace.

"Thank heaven nothing happened to you," she whispered, ready to confide to him the news about Hershele. Yet the expression on his face made her check herself. She would have to let him speak first.

"The Ochrana knew about everything and mobilized the Cossacks." Moshe clipped his words and cut his sentences short. "There are victims. Hundreds arrested. Demonstrations during wartime are paid for more dearly than during peace."

"Of course," she groaned. The news did not surprise her.

Moshe led her into the arch of a gate and drew an envelope from his pocket. "Here, I brought you a present." Exhaustion had disfigured his features and could be detected in the hoarseness of his voice. A sad light shone on her from his eyes. He brushed aside the strand of hair that fell on his forehead. "Well, why do you stare at me like that? Open it."

She drew a card out of the envelope. It was a photograph of a foreign-looking man. "Who is this?" She looked at Moshe questioningly.

"It's Jean Jaurés," Moshe explained. "A great man. A great hero. He was shot in a coffee house in Paris because he was a pacifist."

Two days later, a couple of hours before she was to meet Hershele, Binele set out to meet Yone and break up with him. She intended their meeting to last no longer than a split second. Then she would be free to prepare herself for the meeting with her brother. Yone brought an embroidered coat lined with sheepskin as a present for her. Her mouth watered at the sight of it, so overwhelmed was she by its beauty.

"Try it on, go ahead," he said and helped her into the coat. "Now you won't be freezing in the cold. And see, I guessed your size just right. You look like a real 'ristocrat in it."

"How did you come by it?" she asked distraughtly.

"That's none of your business. And this will keep you warm, when I'm not with you, until we leave for Eretz Israel."

"I've told you a thousand times that I don't want to go to Eretz Israel!" she cried out, desperation in her voice. An ache gnawed away at her heart.

"Rely on me. When the time comes, you'll want to go." He laughed his familiar hollow half-laugh. He never seemed capable of broad open-mouthed laughter, and Binele loathed the hoarse coughing sound that he emitted instead.

She took off the coat. "Here, I don't need it." She pushed it into his hands.

She hated his laughter, while he loved her resistance. He threw the coat back onto her shoulders and embraced her. "You do need it, just as you need me. And you are mine."

"I am no one's!" She tried to free herself from his grasp.

She was his—in the fur coat, surrendering to him on the cold ground covered with wet, dead grass and leaves, beside the wall of the Jewish cemetery. She did not tell him that she would no longer come to meet him. She took leave of him as usual, walking off in her sheepskin coat.

When she had burst breathlessly into the room, Ziporah told her that a young man had been to see her. He had asked Ziporah to tell Binele that he would not be able to make it that evening at ten. He had to leave town, he knew not for how long. He would see her as soon as he returned. "How on earth did you get yourself involved with such an intelligent young man with glasses? And, goodness alive, it takes my breath away to look at you in this elegant fur coat that you came so suddenly home in. Handsome Moshe might take it back if he found out about that fellow in the glasses," Ziporah chattered on enviously, pretending to tease Binele.

"It was my brother, Hershele," Binele explained forlornly.

At the factory Binele did all she could to avoid meeting Yone's eyes. He would wait for her in the stairway or on the street as she walked home.

Each time she was forced to face him, she had another excuse for not being able to meet him "under the Holy Mary." Each time she hissed out to him, "Do you want your fur coat back?"

"I want *you* back!" The light of his green eyes pierced right through her.

Soon the factory was completely shut down. There was no Yone. There was no work. Her gratitude to Ziporah and her feelings of responsibility obligated Binele to abide with Ziporah and not move out and leave her to struggle on alone during the oncoming winter in wartime. But Binele found an excuse. She told Ziporah about Yone. She told her that she wanted to erase every trace of herself so that he would not be able to find her. And Ziporah approved of her decision.

"This *svolotch* may really do something horrible to you, God forbid," she said.

Binele left Ziporah some money from the "knot" of her savings and moved into a loft in Wilki that she had found for herself. With so many people having left town, lodgings were now easy to find, and they were affordable. Now she had a corner of her own, just as she had longed for, for so long. Her dream had become reality—yet the reality had a different taste about it than the dream.

Three months later, Ziporah took Binele to Gaiger's hospital for horses to have an abortion. Ziporah provided Binele with all the details of what Gaiger usually did before he performed an abortion. Binele hid a sharpened pocketknife in her bosom and inserted a few long hairpins into her hair. She had no intention of letting Geiger take advantage of her. She took along a large part of her savings and was prepared to pay with her last kopeck, but she would by no means allow herself to be abused by Gaiger.

Ziporah was barely able to walk—she had been running a high fever all of that past week—but she waited for Binele in the street. Binele entered the stable. When they caught sight of her, one of the horses' attendants called out, "Gaiger, a 'bride's' here to see you!"

A few minutes passed, each as long as an eternity, before Gaiger made his appearance, stepping out of the neighboring room. He wore a blood-stained *roubashka,* the sleeves rolled up over the elbows, and knee-high boots with heels that were supposed to add to his height. He paced among the sick horses and embraced them, asking each one of them, "How are you, lover?" Then he sized Binele up from a distance with his expressionless stone-gray eyes. "How long have you been pregnant?" he asked dryly from where he stood.

The sight of him filled her with dread. Yet she answered, trying to keep her nervousness at bay and make her voice sound calm. She had to muster all her will power, all of her courage, in order to face what awaited her. "How much does it cost?" she asked.

Gaiger did not answer but indicated the neighboring room with a nod of his shaven head.

The room was large, it had a wet cement floor, the walls were inlaid with floor tiles. A large, wet table stood in the middle of the room. "This is where he operates on the horses," Binele thought. One of the stable hands entered the room after Gaiger and proceeded to wipe the table with a long rag of sackcloth. Gaiger went over to a shelf and with his back turned toward the room, busied himself doing something. The attendant looked at Binele meaningfully. She turned her head away from him and stared at Gaiger's fleshy neck and at the shaven skull that stuck out from the collar of his black *roubashka*.

"Why are you standing there like a golem of clay?" the attendant finally asked, as he kept on wiping the table. "Get undressed."

"I'll wait," Binele replied.

"There is nothing to wait for," she heard Gaiger say. He still had his back turned to her. "These men are my assistants."

Slowly she began to undress. The attendant pointed to a nail on the wall where she was supposed to hang up her things. The pocketknife fell out from under her dress. The attendant picked it up and gave it back to her. "Here, put it into your purse and take out the money." He snatched the purse from her hand and opened it. He waited for her to put the knife inside. Then he thrust his hand into the purse. Not finding what he was looking for inside, he stared at her questioningly.

"How much?" she asked, reaching into her brassiere for the "knot" with her savings. Her teeth chattered. The cold in the room penetrated every cell of her body.

"All of it." The man grabbed the "knot" from her hand and threw it into the air as if he were playing with a rag ball. "You'll pay the rest later," he added, putting the "knot" on the shelf in front of Gaiger. "And take off your shoes. You'll be more comfortable." He turned and walked out.

Binele, naked and barefoot, stood on the wet floor, hugging her hunched shivering body and rubbing at her rough, goose-pimpled skin with trembling hands. Her eyes were fixed on her purse, which the man had hung on a nail close to Gaiger. "I still have the hairpins," she thought, trying to calm herself as she riveted her eyes on Gaiger's back. Gaiger untied the rag-knot and counted the few rubles wrapped inside it. "Get onto the table and spread your legs," she heard him say.

She lay on the cold moist table with her legs spread apart. She looked at her bosom as it jumped up and down to the rhythm of her heart. She was shaking violently and had to bite her lips to keep from moaning. "I will not die. I will not die," she repeated to herself.

Gaiger turned around, approached the table, and placed himself at Binele's feet. As before, his stony face with its cold eyes was expressionless. But his large ears were turning red. His lower lip curled down to his chin. Slowly a grimace akin to a grin began to play in the corners of his mouth. In his hand he held a short stick with a black cotton tip resembling a small burned-out torch. He stood there motionless for a few moments. His small gray eyes grew increasingly darker and warmer as his gaze wandered over Binele's shuddering body. At length he laid the stick with the cotton on the edge of the table. He slapped Binele's knees lightly so that they half bent and he pulled her toward him on the slippery table. The lower part of her legs dropped and dangled over the table's edge.

"That's a girl," he panted, lifting her legs and bending them. He placed her heels against the two corners of the table as if he wanted to fasten them there. With both hands he felt the nipples of her breasts, then slid his hands, fingers spread apart, down along her belly. "No screaming is allowed," he told her quietly. "The gendarmes are running around like poisoned rats." He was silent for a moment, then added, grinning, "I have a method to calm your nerves so that it won't hurt you so much." He reached for the clasp of his thick leather belt.

"Mister Gaiger," Binele tried to sit up, holding one hand over the pins in her hair. Gaiger grabbed a firm hold of her heels. With her knees raised, she could only partly lift herself. "If . . . if you dare . . . I'll kill you!" And she fell backward.

"Don't make a fool of yourself," Gaiger said casually, composedly, letting go of one of her heels to unbutton his pants. "All the 'brides' go by me that way."

"I'm not a 'bride'!" she screamed and again raised herself onto her elbow.

"What are you then, a groom?" He quickly pulled her closer to him. She fell back, hitting her head against the table. She raised her head with the help of her elbows. Straining the muscles of her neck and back , she tried to sit up. There was a hairpin between her fingers. She aimed it at Gaiger's eyes. "Don't you dare!" she howled.

He grabbed her wrist, tore the pin from her fingers and threw it on the floor. His short, hard hands smacked her first on one cheek, then on the other. His face was now as beet red as if all of its shiny skin had been peeled off. "I like you," he panted loudly. "So help me God, I like you! What did you expect? That I would risk my life aborting you for nothing? What are you jumping out of your skin for? You're already pregnant anyway, and *vitish* you aren't, not on your life!"

"I am too! I am!" She tried to tear herself out of his hands. She, who had never known what fear was, now found herself at the bottom of the most terrifying abyss. "I am *vitish!*" she roared.

Gaiger was amused. "You are?" he guffawed loudly. The muscles of his red face loosened. His entire face seemed larger, more puffy. "Then why don't you want to have the bastard, tell me?"

"I do! I do! But not this one!"

Gaiger jerked at her legs. She lost control and fell back with a thud. How weak and drained of energy fear could make one! All her strength escaped with her screams. "I do want . . . " she heard herself howling. Her body shook with such violent convulsions that it bounced up and down on the table. She barely heard Gaiger shouting something in the direction of the door. His two assistants burst into the room and grabbed Binele's hands from either side of the table. Gaiger came inside her, then the assistants took their turns. Her mind grew dim as she felt something invade her flesh and drill in her insides. A torch pierced a boil within her body, setting it aflame in a vast explosion of pain. A thick river of blood cascaded out of her, a sea of thick red darkness.

It was all over. One of the men stuck a fistful of cotton between her legs and lifted her up. The other poured a glass of *monopolka* down her throat. The assistants left. Gaiger too was gone.

She somehow managed to get herself off the table. Doubled up with pain, clutching at her belly with both hands, she dragged herself over to the wall where her clothes hung. It took an eternity before her shaking hands could hold each piece of clothing still enough for her to put it on.

She slid her feet into her shoes and, pressing her thighs together, she shuffled over to where her purse hung suspended from a nail. She took it down and made her way to the exit. Dragging her feet, legs pressed together, shrunken, she groped for her way into the stable, patting the walls with her hands as if she were blind. The two attendants were busy with the horses. They smiled chummily at her. *"Molodiec!"* one of them called out. "You didn't even let out a peep!"

The other saluted her in mock military fashion. "Just like a soldier," he sneered. "She ought to be sent to the battlefront."

"Yeah," the first one also saluted. "She could cheer up a battalion of soldiers!"

It seemed incredible to Binele that these two men could watch her nearly collapse and not move away from the horses to at least help her into the street. "Monsters!" she sobbed. "You're less human than the horses are!"

It was snowing outside. Binele collapsed into Ziporah's arms, so limp and powerless that Ziporah slipped and they both almost toppled over. Holding on to each other, they somehow managed to drag themselves to Ziporah's room. Binele slumped down on the straw pallet. As during peacetime, Ziporah's husband was already vacationing in prison. Her children lay on the other straw mattress, all running high fevers. Ziporah made a pot of watery soup and tried to feed them. They could swallow no more than a spoonful or two. She gave Binele a bowl of soup and then stretched herself out on her own straw pallet. There they all lay on the straw pallets on the floor of the cold room.

The following day Ziporah was unable to raise herself from her mattress. One of her neighbors, a "bride," brought in a pot of chicory coffee and a few slices of bread. In the evening, another one came by with a bowl containing a few boiled potatoes.

Binele lay for four days on her straw mattress, barely aware of what was going on around her. On the fifth day she started to feel better, and, gradually, she recovered. But Ziporah and her children were very ill. Typhus was raging in Baluty and spreading to infect the rest of the town.

Along with typhus came the winter and its snowstorms. Bundled up in Ziporah's rags, which she wore over her coat, Binele began once again to visit the Church of the Holy Virgin Mary. Nowadays the church was packed all day long with anxiety-ridden people, and the old canon collected generous donations in his plate. Binele contributed her share and took as much "change" as she could. If she had a chance, she also took a few candles and hid them under her coat. Then she went to the bazaar where she sold them to buy food.

She had no desire to see Handsome Moshe and certainly none to see Yone the Svolotch. She had come to hate men with a fierce hatred. They were beasts, worse than animals. They were cruel warmongers. The only love they were capable of was the love of destruction. She was no longer anyone's bride. She belonged to no one, not even to herself. She was a stranger, a body without a person inside, an automaton mechanically doing what it had to do. She nursed Ziporah and her children. They swallowed almost nothing solid, but they drank a lot. Never had she seen anyone, especially a child, capable of filling itself with so much water. She put cold compresses on their heads and watched over them at night. Then, one day, as gusts of sleety rain swept across the street and the windowpanes chattered along with the teeth of the sick in their fever—the ambulance wagon arrived and took away Ziporah and her children, as well as a few "brides" from the house.

Binele sat in Ziporah's empty, dingy room. She did not feel in the least like going back to her own neat little room. She felt herself more at home at Ziporah's. The dull gray light of the wet wintry day floated in through the window, wafting in its icy breaths. She listened to the frost cracking on the windowpanes, and could hear the distant rumble of artillery fire. The front was approaching Lodz. The earth shuddered.

The battle over Lodz lasted from the eighteenth of November to the fifth of December 1914, and it ended with the defeat of the Russian army. By the time the Germans entered Lodz, Binele was in the hospital with typhoid fever.

෨ 7 ෨

BOCIANY BECAME DEEPLY INVOLVED in the war: many of Bociany's sons had been taken into captivity and many were killed on the battlefield. The front itself was never too far away, although it moved from one side of the Vistula to the other. Mercifully, it was remote enough not to further disturb Bociany's inhabitants with its ferocious thunder. Life on the Blue Mountain, at Reb Faivele the Miller's farm, continued, proceeding in its normal rhythm. The only noticeable change was the change in the weather. Fall had passed and winter had arrived.

During the winter there could be no talk of Yacov and Abrashka riding off to visit Yoel the Blacksmith. The frost burned fiercely, the world lay buried under mountainous featherbeds of snow, and Long Zirele did not allow her sons outdoors for long—unless Reb Faivele took them to Bociany in his sleigh. Then the boys were covered with quilts and furs so that only their eyes were visible.

Abrashka missed Yoel the Blacksmith and could not stop talking about him to Yacov. He complained that he dreamed about Yoel at night and heard his voice in his sleep, urging him to come to the smithy. Finally he could no longer bear his separation from the blacksmith and began to search his mind for an excuse to get himself out of the house and head off to visit Yoel. He broached the subject that preyed on his mind, not directly, but in a circumspect manner, first by flattering and cajoling his parents. When he had sufficiently warmed their hearts and they had showered him with praise for being such a fine obedient son, he considered it opportune to came out with his plea to be allowed to go for a ride in the sleigh with Yacov. "We won't go far," he begged. "And you can dress me so that I look like a bear, if you want to. I promise I won't catch cold." He nagged and charmed and insisted until he ended up winning his father over to his side. His father usually gave in to him more easily than his mother, since Reb Faivele was always intent on ingratiating himself with his son. Reb Faivele then embarked on applying a verbal strategy designed to make Zirele yield, but the strategy did result in a small quarrel between himself and his wife. Eventually, however, Reb Faivele became sufficiently master of the situation to be able to tell Abrashka that, weather permitting, he might go for a sleigh ride with Yacov, but only on a Sunday afternoon when the road was empty and he stressed that they had to be back before sunset, before the drunkards appeared on the road.

Sunday afternoon was exactly when Yacov and Abrashka wanted to leave. They only had to wait for a sunny Sunday to comply with Long Zirele's wishes. When such an afternoon finally arrived, Yacov harnessed

Sussi to the sleigh and climbed into it next to Abrashka. They covered themselves with furs and quilts and rode off.

Abrashka was so excited that he trembled and saw nothing of the surrounding countryside. Yacov, however, did look around. He inhaled deeply the sharp air through his nostrils. The frost pinching his cheeks and the tips of his fingers had no bearing on his delight in the mild caresses of the sun. Fluffy beds of snow covered the ditches on both sides of the road. The boughs of the poplars that skirted the ditches were weighed down with heavy clumps of snow, while the road itself was smooth and white. The whiteness sparkled as if it were strewn with diamonds, each one of them fringed by the pink rays of the afternoon sun. As if he were a reflection of the white world around him, Yacov felt white and clean within himself.

The sleigh slid quietly and lightly over the snow. The clip-clop of Sussi's hooves was muffled as if the hooves themselves were wrapped in rags. The subdued stamping was reminiscent of a heartthrob. Steam billowed from Sussi's mouth with his outbursts of lively neighing. The steam wafted toward the field where the snow lay untouched, stretching smoothly toward the horizon until it dissolved into the expanse of sky. It gave Yacov the feeling of being enclosed in a crystal dish covered with a cavernous crystal lid, a dish inserted into an oven kept hot by the burning frost. Inside the dish everything was intimately white, intimately warm, as the sun itself was trapped in the tightly covered crystal dish. Only the sun's reflection was outside of the crystal lid. High and distant, it sent down its rays to glide on silver skates in front of Sussi. Yacov and Abrashka exchange not a single word throughout the entire ride.

They arrived at the smithy to find the doors of the hut and those of the forge shut and bolted. The snow that had fallen during the night lay on the hut's threshold heaped up like fluffed pillows. There was not a trace of life anywhere.

"He isn't home!" Abrashka moaned.

"We'll wait a while," Yacov decided, and he moved up closer to Abrashka in order to cover both their heads with a fur, so that only their eyes could be seen. Their steamy breath wet their faces. Abrashka was not really sure whether it was the steam from his mouth that moistened his face or whether it was damp from the tears of his brimming eyes.

"We're not moving away from here until he comes," he whispered.

At length they noticed a dark figure looming far in the distance across the road. The figure as it rapidly came down the field plowed through the whiteness, surfacing and disappearing, like a boat hitting against rocks or sinking behind swells. "Here he comes!" Yacov cried.

"Yoel! Yoel!" Abrashka tore himself out of the furs, jumped down from the sleigh, and began to hop around in the snow, shouting Yoel's name at the top of his lungs.

Yoel emerged from the field and clumsily scrambled through the deep snow in the ditch. His coattails were all covered with snow as he rushed toward Abrashka and gave him a slap on the rear, as if they had seen each other only the day before. Panting and puffing, he inquired, "How are you, vagabond? Did you sleep well?" From inside his caftan he drew out a round loaf of black bread and pushed it into Abrashka's arms. Then he went over to the sleigh and helped Yacov cover Sussi with a large blanket of heavy sackcloth and unharness him. All three of them led Sussi into the shed near the smithy, beckoned him into a stall, and hung a sack of oats over his neck.

They entered Yoel's hut. Yoel flung open the shutters of the tiny window and the blinding white light of the outdoors poured in through the frozen panes, bringing into view the sunken cot covered with a blanket of sackcloth. There Yoel seated his visitors. As for himself, he rolled up his sleeves and embarked on lighting the black stove that stood a few steps away from the cot. Finished with that, he threw off his coat, unbuttoned his vest, and moved the small crooked table over to the cot. He sat down on a chair to pull off his boots, which were stuffed with paper and rags. Having unwound the foot-clouts from around his legs and feet, he then hung them up on a cord, next to his ragged shirts, underwear, and other tattered pieces of clothing that had long since lost any resemblance to any recognizable garment.

He seemed to have forgotten his visitors who quietly sat watching him. They saw him put a black pot of chicory coffee on the stove. He washed his hands over a barrel in the corner, then returned to the table to cut the loaf of bread into thick slices. Still appearing to disregard them, he handed the slices of bread to Yacov and Abrashka. When the coffee came to a boil, he poured it into three tin cups, brought them over to the table, and seated himself on a chair. They blessed the bread, bit into the soft still-warm dough, and tried to warm their red frozen fingers on the prickling heat of the tin cups. The steam rising from the coffee cups warmed their faces.

Yacov had a vague idea of where Yoel had just come from. His suspicion, however, diminished not in the least his respect for the man. The more clearly he had come to see Yoel in his mind during the weeks of separation, the more he felt in awe of him, an awe that was mixed with an odd kind of envy. He wished he could be like Yoel, and yet at the same time he became dimly aware of a barrier within himself that would forever prevent him from becoming such a man. Abrashka, Yacov thought, could overcome such a barrier. Abrashka and Yoel had much in common.

As they sat there, silently chewing on the bread and sipping their coffee, the faces of two young peasants appeared in the thawing window panes.

Yoel put his cup down on the table and jumped to his feet. "Stay here!" he cried out and, looking somewhat disturbed, he ran out of the hut. Yacov and Abrashka put down their cups and dashed toward the window. They wiped the melting frost off the panes and peered out. A noise was heard coming from the smithy. They could make out the sound of loud hoarse voices punctuated by Yoel's rancorous laughter, laughter that sounded altogether different from Yoel's normal laughter. They saw the two young peasants rushing out of the smithy, jointly carrying a heavy wooden box that they loaded onto their sleigh. They returned twice more into the smithy, each time coming out with a similar box. At length they covered the boxes in the rear of their sleigh with layers of sackcloth, climbed onto it, seated themselves in the front, and quickly rode away.

Abrashka rushed to the door. "Yoel!" he called. "I want to come into the smithy!"

"No!" Yoel shouted back angrily and vanished from sight. After what seemed a very long wait, Yoel appeared in the door. His face wore an unusually serious expression. "Well," he said to Abrashka. "What are you waiting for? Come out."

The smithy looked different but it was difficult to tell why. Yoel shut the door and busied himself with the bellows, pulling at them as he lighted a fire in the forge. Yacov and Abrashka moved into a corner, closer to Yoel and the fire. They watched the hissing and cracking tongues of flame in the furnace and listened to the clinking and hammering sound of iron hitting against iron as Yoel got himself busy shaping a shaft on the anvil. The sight of the silent Yoel with sparks swirling around his head as he hammered and pulled at the bellows made them think of a sorcerer conjuring up various shapes and forms in the flames inside the furnace, shapes and forms for which their hearts longed.

"Oh, Yacov, look inside!" Abrashka whispered, pointing at the flames. "I see a golden bird in the fire! Can you see it? Look how it dances about! Oh, if only I could snatch it from the fire, give it a pair of very thin wings and a beautiful head with a beak!" No longer able to restrain himself, he dashed over to Yoel. "Yoel!" he cried heatedly, pulling at his caftan. "I beg of you, Yoel, put this away for a minute. I saw a golden bird in the fire. Take a piece of iron, and do me a favor, make me a bird from it."

"Make me a bird . . . " Yacov smiled and repeated Abrashka's plea to himself. He badly wanted that Yoel the sorcerer should today, in his silence, perform a feat of magic beauty. A powerful yearning for some kind of wonder took hold of him. He too saw a golden bird dancing in the fire. It was none other than Binele. He saw the reddish golden strands of her hair flutter inside the furnace. She was like a flame, flickering before his eyes, teasing him, phantom-like, unattainable—Lilith. If he touched her, she would burn him, set him on fire, devour him.

Yoel put aside the shaft that he had been working on and picked up a piece of scrap iron that he found in a corner. He thrust it into the fire, then, still white and aglow from the heat as it was, he transferred it to the anvil. Abrashka shouted commands, ordering Yoel where to bend, to fold, and to cut the pliable glowing piece of iron. "I know it will come out black," Abrashka chattered heatedly, "but never mind. It will be a bird of black gold, and it will be able to fly, even though it will seem to be standing in the same place."

Yacov's wistful smile broadened. Binele was the golden bird that had flown away while she was still standing in the same place in his heart. Would she also turn into black gold? There was so much of the dark, of the unknown and unfamiliar about her. But this was exactly what attracted him, what pulled him toward her, and what burned him.

Abrashka, preoccupied to oblivion with his creation, had caught his hand on a nail that stuck out from the box against which he was leaning. He hastily sucked on the bleeding cut. Yoel glanced at him sideways and laughed his warm rich laughter. Abrashka joined him, laughing softy, warmly. Yoel and Abrashka were now joined in a union from which Yacov felt himself excluded. "Maybe this is because there is something in me, in my nature, that although it allows me to be playful, prevents me from losing myself completely, heart and soul, in any game," he thought. "I cannot give myself to anything to the point of forgetfulness, to the point of becoming oblivious of the past or the present, not even when I am telling a story."

Yoel dipped the still glowing "bird" in a tub of ice water, and the "bird" hissed and steamed. Then he put it back onto the anvil to dry. Abrashka bent over it and squeezed his finger, making the blood in ruby-red droplets drip from his cut onto the hissing, bubbling bird. "Yacov!" he shouted excitedly. "Look! Can you see it? The bird is alive! It drinks my blood and it likes it." He pressed more droplets of blood from his finger and let them drip onto the bird.

"Breathe the Ineffable Name into it, Yoel!" Yacov repeated a childhood prayer in his heart.

As if he had heard Yacov's thoughts, Yoel raised his dark hands toward the roof, and cried, "Hallelujah! The bird has accepted Abrashka's soul!"

"Yes!" Abrashka copied him and also raised his hands. "Hallelujah! My bird will fly to the Seventh Heaven! Eh, Yoel, what do you say? It will fly as high as the Throne of Glory, won't it?"

Yoel pulled Abrashka into his arms and looked intently at him. Yoel's eagerness to communicate with the boy twisted his features as if he were in pain. His thick black eyebrows were knotted together and his forehead was wrinkled. He sat down with Abrashka on an overturned barrel and held him on his knees, brushing the boy's burning cheeks with his beard. "Exactly what will become of the bird, I can't tell," he said in his deep, warm bass voice. "It's enough that it will fly. That's no small thing. As for making it pass through the seven heavens and reach the Almighty's Throne of Glory, that, my friend, is even a harder task than we are capable of imagining. Do you have any idea how difficult it is for even the purest and lightest soul to reach the very First Heaven? The powers of evil wait for you everywhere to prevent you from climbing any further. Then, if you succeed in spite of those horrendous obstacles in reaching the Heavenly Palace, these same evil powers will try to trip you at the very entrance to the Heavenly Chambers, and you're liable to get yourself trapped in the fiery storm that rages inside. You will have to manage to keep your head on your shoulders so as not to go out of your mind or to be burnt by never-ending bolts of lightning. Then, right in the middle of your struggle, when you think yourself about to succeed, flames of fire will burst from your own body, and you will burn like a torch, but you will have to try to remain in an upright position, even though your arms and legs are on fire and you find yourself suspended in a bottomless void."

"Oh, my goodness!" Abrashka raised his hands to his cheeks. "I don't know if I'll be able to do all that."

"So you see," Yoel concluded. "That's why I say that I really don't know whether you'll arrive at your destination with your bird. But in the end, is it really a question of arriving?"

"Of course it is! I must give it a try!" Abrashka cried. "If you send a bird out into the skies, you want it to arrive somewhere, don't you? My bird must reach the Throne of Glory. My bird must see Him, see how He looks."

"Oh, for that you needn't give yourself the trouble of sending the bird up to investigate. I can give you the facts myself." Yoel smiled. "The Creator of the World sits on an extremely high throne. His holy crown is the color of electrum and His Ineffable Name is written on His forehead. His footstool is made of fire and hail, it constantly emits lightning and thunder and constantly creates light and shadow. As for the Almighty Himself, His eyes move from east to west and from north to south. He sees everything, down to the slightest speck. And He Himself is also made half of fire and half of ice. On His right hand hovers Life and on His left, Death. He holds a fiery scepter in His right hand, and the Sacred Scripture with His plan of the universe in His left. A curtain is spread out before Him that shows everything that has happened and everything that will happen. The seven principal angels, His ministers, stand on the other side of this curtain awaiting His command. So, there it is, and I've saved you a trip full of hardships and headaches." Yoel shook Abrashka's arm. "That's what you wanted to know, isn't it?"

"No!" Abrashka called out. He thought for a while, then asked, "And what about the Messiah? He has to make the trip in the opposite direction, from the Heavenly Palace, through the seven heavens, down to earth, doesn't He? Do you think He'll make it?"

"Of course He will. But it's more important to *believe* that He will, than whether, in fact, He will. His actual arrival plays only the part of a signature on a promissory note."

The "bird" was cool now and fixed into a permanent form. Abrashka picked it up and slipped away into a secluded corner behind a box to play with it in private. Yacov took the opportunity to move closer to Yoel. "Tell me," he whispered close to him, "What about *Zionismus*? I'm sure you've heard about this completely new movement. The Zionists want to recover Eretz Israel without the help of the Messiah and so put and end to the exile. What do you say to that?"

Yoel waved his hand dismissively. "What's so new about it? We've always been torn between the love of Zion and the diaspora, between the wish to save ourselves and to save the world. Didn't Ari Hakodesh say that the Almighty did the right thing to spread us among the peoples of the world so that we might save the sacred sparks hiding in the darkness all over the earth? But at the same time, we are exhausted from dragging ourselves around with the load of our mission upon our shoulders and, in our straits, we long for Zion. As for the Messiah, how can a human being strive for something without having Him in mind? He is the striving. You can deny His name, but not Him." Yoel snatched at Yacov's sleeve with sudden urgency and looked around to make sure that Abrashka was not within listening distance. "Listen," he whispered, a note of urgency in his tone of voice. "There's no one in this world as close to me as you are. So I've decided to tell you something . . . to tell you this . . . it's important to me."

Before Yoel had time to start saying what he wanted to say, he was interrupted by the sound of a powerful pounding of fists on the door of the smithy. The door was thrown open from the outside and there entered, along with the gust of icy air, two men in green uniforms with helmets on their heads. Outside, two massive horses—such as were never seen in Bociany—stood tied to a tree. Nearby stood a freight wagon with another horse harnessed to it. The two strangers wandered around the smithy, rummaging in its corners and peering into all the boxes. They ordered Yoel and Yacov to stand up. Finally one of them asked in German, "Where do you keep the copper and the brass?"

Yoel shrugged. "We don't make horseshoes out of copper or brass here," he replied in Yiddish.

The German grasped the answer more from Yoel's shrug than from his words. "Don't you have any copper and brass at all?"

Again Yoel shrugged. "May I have as much knowledge of evil as . . . "

The Germans went outside. Yoel, wearing only his vest, went out after the Germans, who were now rummaging about in the yard. One of them entered the hut. Within a minute he reappeared, holding his nose with one hand and raising Yoel's wine goblet in the air with the other. "You must never lie to a German officer!" he shouted triumphantly at Yoel, and then grinned with satisfaction. His companion beckoned to him, and they untied their horses and mounted them. Sitting in the saddle, the German threw Yoel's Sabbath beaker into the freight wagon in front of him. He motioned to the driver to move on and the horsemen and the wagon rode off in the direction of Bociany.

"Those were Germans, weren't they, Yoel?" Abrashka came toward him excitedly. "If you ask me, they look exactly like those Riders of Evil who came down from the Heavens. And what do they need your wine beaker for? They surely don't need it to celebrate the Sabbath."

"No, they need it to make balls for their cannons." Yoel wiped his face with both hands. He seemed relieved.

Again they heard the sound of a strange rumbling clatter coming from the distance. All three of them went further out down the road to try and see what was making that formidable noise. At first all they could see was a blizzard of snow rolling along the road toward them from the direction of Chwosty. After a while they could make out the belly of a four-wheeled monster that was moving swiftly toward them. Two helmeted heads and two pairs of green epauletted shoulders protruded from the monster's trunk.

"It's an automobile!" Yacov exclaimed. "Look, Abrashka, it moves by itself, without horses!"

"Are you sure they're not pedaling with their feet?" Abrashka asked.

"Heavens, no. They use a motor."

Abrashka lurched forward in surprise and then set off at a gallop after the machine. Yacov followed him with his eyes, then he glanced at Yoel and moved closer to him. "Yoel, you were about to tell me something."

"So I was." Yoel sounded more relaxed. He looked back to see how far Abrashka had run in pursuit of the automobile, then he led Yacov up the road in the opposite direction. "I'll make it short," he began. "A year or so ago I got myself involved in helping the young Poles who had decided to organize themselves in order to fight for their fatherland. At first the landlord's son was their leader, but then he left to join Pilsudski's legion. There were some Jewish boys amongst them, too. Idiot that I was, I thought to myself that a free Poland might be a good thing for us Jews, too. I also thought that it is their slavery that makes the goyim look at us the way they do, and that we in our own bondage reciprocate their hatred. To them, every Jew is a cunning crook on the one hand, and a nincompoop on the other. On the one hand we are the killers who crucified the son of their God and are being punished for it now; on the other, we are invincible sorcerers tied in a mysterious way to the Lord of the Universe, from whom we have wheedled the Holy Bible and the power to lord it over the world through our underhanded tricks."

"It's the priest who makes them believe all that," Yacov remarked.

"We, on our side," Yoel continued as if he had not heard him, "also consider a goy as being both something more and something less than a human being. We see him as a cabbage head, a pork-eater, someone who can't even count on his fingers, someone whose reason is on the same level as that of the animals with whom he lives. At the same time we see him as Asmodeus, the mouthpiece and the fist of the Evil One. We tremble a mighty trembling before him, knowing that while our lives are first of all in the hands of God, they are secondly in the hands of the goyim. Or perhaps it's even the reverse. And as you see me here alive, Yacov, I can't help myself. There is something in me that cries out against such short-sightedness. Our sages are right. Man is a sacred vessel. That's why he can't bear the whip on his back forever. He's born with no real talent for being a slave. Even the person who sees himself as the Almighty's slave is not a complete *mentsh*. Because the truth is that slaves don't care about anything. A slave relies on his master. He doesn't consider himself responsible for anything. A free man is different. He takes a part of the Almighty's responsibility upon himself. So, you understand, having these thoughts in mind, I helped the young Poles in whichever way I could. I even forged weapons for them and hid them in the smithy. I've even cut myself off from the few people who once in a while came to greet me. It was safer that way. Then came the pogrom, and it dawned on me that my boys did not so much want their freedom as they wanted the adventure of wielding an ax. They thirsted for blood, and our blood is the easiest and cheapest to come by. So they bled us white. I said nothing, but from then on I found all sorts of excuses to get myself out of doing anything for them. The sight of them made me want to puke." Yoel grew silent, walking on with his head bent, his hands clasped behind his back.

A long while passed before he resumed talking. "This morning the boys heard that the Germans were going to search Bociany and set up an administration. So they came for the boxes of the weapons that I had hidden for them in the smithy. I told them then and there that they should never again ask me for anything. This worked them up into a fury good and proper. They said my saying that meant that I was going to betray them, dirty Jew that I am, that I prefer Germany to a free Poland. I laughed in their faces. Woe to that laughter! Because, you see, they might want to get rid of me. I know too much. So . . . " Yoel who had been talking quickly, slowed the flow of his words. "So, Yacov, bear this in mind, and that's all I wanted you to know." He turned back and Yacov followed him.

"But why don't you run away?" Yacov felt his throat stiffen. "They might kill you."

"I'm not the running type. And where should I run to?" Yoel grinned. "This place is sacred ground to me. This is where I want to die. But never mind, I'm not going to let myself be done in so easily. I know I'm dumping a load of worry on your head. But keep it under your hat and keep your mouth shut. Just bear witness, and if necessary, say the kaddish after me. I ask for nothing more."

Abrashka was hastily approaching them. "Yacov!" he shouted, "let's take the bird and chase after the machine! Quickly!" He ran into the smithy, grabbed his "golden bird," and waited impatiently for Yacov to harness Sussi to the sleigh. He tried to mount the sleigh by himself but slipped and was caught by Yoel. "Yoel, we'll come to see you next week, God willing!" he promised, as Yoel seated him in the sleigh. "Well, get in, Yacov!" He stamped his feet impatiently. "We've got to catch up with the automobile!" Laughing excitedly, he waved at Yoel, and they drove away.

That Sunday the Germans searched all the houses in Bociany. They carried off all the utensils made of copper and brass, the samovars, the brass doorknobs from the houses of the wealthy, and the brass from the tips of the church's steeples. They disbanded the town's militia and assigned an Oberst and a few Ordnungsdienst men to take charge of the premises adjoining the prison. The county officer retained his post, but he had nothing to do and had almost no say in the shtetl's affairs. Instead, it was the Jewish "writer"—who now called himself Herr Pfeifer, although people persisted in calling him Pumpkinhead—who now became the most important official in Bociany. He was so elevated because now all the official books and documents were required to be written in German. Herr Pfeifer was also obliged to participate in many public functions.

The Sunday following their visit to Yoel, Abrashka had had the opportunity to see quite a number of machines without horses when an entire convoy had driven into the shtetl. On that Sunday Reb Faivele's family had dressed warmly and climbed into the sleigh for a ride to Bociany. Reb

Faivele was eager to see the changes that had occurred in the shtetl with his own eyes.

After the family had departed, Yacov provided himself with a walking stick and set out on foot for the smithy. What Yoel had told him during his previous visit had not left his mind for a second. Yoel's decision not to escape from danger overwhelmed him with worry, but he was too much in awe of Yoel not to respect his wish. So Yacov now headed for the smithy with the sole purpose in mind of checking on Yoel and making sure he was still safe. That was all that he could do. Upon reaching the vicinity of the smithy, he hid himself behind a poplar tree, observing the yard from a distance, until he saw Yoel emerge from the shack to chop wood in front of it. Yacov felt himself impelled to hurry over to him and take advantage of the opportunity to converse with him freely and spend some time with him. He badly needed such an eye-to-eye encounter. But he feared that Yoel would immediately guess the reason for his coming and would not have liked it. So he checked himself and turned back.

The next day life in Bociany and on the Blue Mountain returned to its every day routine. The political and administrative changes in the region had little real bearing on people's daily lives. But one change was made. Reb Faivele and Zirele decided that Yacov and Abrashka had caused them too much worry when they had gone off for their ride in the sleigh that Sunday, and they decided it was wiser to forbid any similar escapades in the future. So, for the rest of the winter Yacov sneaked out of the house every Sunday afternoon and, alone, set off on foot to the smithy to check on Yoel and turn back. During his long walks in the cold, he would carry on such lenghty imaginary conversations with Yoel that on his way back he had the feeling that he had actually talked with the man. And so, gradually, he grew accustomed to hearing Yoel's voice in his mind, a voice that eventually so merged with his own that he no longer knew which thoughts were genuinely Yoel's and which were his own. In his imagination, the barriers dividing their minds seemed to have vanished.

On a warm pre-spring Sunday, the last week of the month of Adar, Yacov and Abrashka finally got permission to go for a ride with Sussi. The snow on the road had completely melted and the ground had begun to dry. The two of them immediately set off for the smithy.

It was strange that Yoel remembered how suddenly they had left him the last time they had visited him. When he found himself alone with Yacov for a minute, he chuckled ruefully and said, "You know, the moment I saw you two before my eyes for the first time, I immediately saw you leaving me again, forever."

Yacov gaped at him stupefied. "We, leave you forever? But why? You are our rabbi, Yoel, our brother."

"Am I? So what? Even so I am but a station post in your growth, a kind of milestone on your roads."

"But from wherever we are, from Bociany or elsewhere, we will always come to see you."

"Why do you say 'we?' The roads of the two of you are about to part as well, aren't they?"

"To lead us where, Yoel?"

"How should I know? I'm no prophet. But you must not despair on this account. After all, each dear person is but a milestone on the other's road. I don't mind it, as long as you're not leaving today." Yoel was in a pensive mood. It was as if an old wound had opened within him. But eventually he grew weary of his depression. He called to Abrashka, who as usual was busying himself with broken wheels and scraps of metal in the yard, "Come here, little tramp. I've got this bright idea of taking a walk to the birch wood today and seeing what's new there now that the winter is gone." He bolted up the smithy, brought out a small bottle of *monopolka* from his hut, and thrust the bottle into his pocket.

The birch wood was awakening to spring. The trees stood in pools of mud that mirrored their trunks and crowns. It looked as if the earth had disappeared and everything was growing out of the sky, a sky reflected in the water that spread beneath one's feet. The tree trunks, cracked and peeling, looked as white as if they were still dipped in snow, but their crowns and branches were covered with tiny leaves of a bright delicate green.

"Look at them, vagabonds!" Yoel exclaimed, pointing to the small leaves fluttering on the boughs. "Have you ever seen such a green? The Almighty tinted it with a most tender hand. No wonder it's so good to pray here. I've been waiting for months for the day I could come here for my morning prayers."

"Does Reb Senderl the Cabalist still join you for the morning prayers?" Yacov inquired.

Yoel nodded. "He does. Although, mind you, he does the praying in his own way."

"What's his way?"

"His way is that of being his own man, just as I am my own man. He prays in a sweet voice, just as a man should pray in a forest. But I heat up; I sip and slurp the words as if they were a boiling pot of peas. I'm too busy with myself, mind you, to leave room for the Almighty, while Reb Senderl is full of Him. He practices solitude while living among people, whereas I practice solitude by being alone. So my solitude cannot compare to his. He studies too much and lives too little. He fasts more than he eats, spends days and nights in the cold antechamber of the synagogue, and doesn't miss out on even one midnight service. And that, you see, is not my cup of tea. Our Maker wants a man to live in his body as in a bright healthy house, so as not to have a weak schlemiel to worship Him. There is enough misery in life as it is, and it's sinful to inflict additional suffering upon ourselves. Therefore I like to serve the Creator by eating and drinking." He bent over to Yacov's ear, and whispered, "and by sleeping with a woman, too." He continued in a loud voice, "Moreover, as far as the forest is concerned, Reb Senderl believes that when he comes here, he brings to life the plant part of his own soul. He believes that every human being possesses a plant part and an animal part within him. He believes that the trees are incarnated souls and therefore he can become one with them on a very deep level. As for me, I respect the tree because it is a tree, the dog because it is a dog, and my relatedness to them lies in the fact that though we are different, the same infinite is reflected in each of us. And now we have to meet a friend of mine."

Walking more deeply into the forest, they approached the cluster of thick trunked oaks fringing the border of the lake. Among the oaks lay a large birch tree with its trunk split down the middle. Its crown, made up of a few thick dry boughs, brushed the earth, forming a low arch. But from the very middle of the split trunk there grew two large healthy branches covered with clusters of budding leaves.

"Is this your friend?" Abrashka asked Yoel as they stopped in front of the tree.

"Right you are!" Yoel nodded. "You can sit piggyback on him. He doesn't mind." He leaned against the tree and took the bottle of *monopolka* out of his pocket.

"What happened to it?" Abrashka asked.

Yacov sat down on the tree's trunk. Yoel picked up Abrashka with one arm and seated him between himself and Yacov. "Can't you see, little vagabond?" Yoel patted the tree's trunk. "He's been hit by lightning. The same day as I was. That's why he is my friend."

"You were hit by lightning?" Abrashka asked in disbelief. Instead of replying, Yoel tapped the bottle with his palm and the cork popped out. He took a long sip. "And the other trees are not your friends?" Abrashka asked.

"Of course they are," Yoel wiped his mouth with his sleeve. "I treat them all as equals and they treat me the same way. But this one," Yoel again patted the tree, "this one is my rabbi friend. It teaches me how to live."

"You mean it speaks to you?" Abrashka suprised, blinked at him.

"It speaks to you, too. It says, 'Never give up, little vagabond, because you are stronger than you think.' This reminds me . . . " Yoel turned to Yacov, "of the words of a great rabbi who once said that the real bondage of the Hebrews in Egypt lay in the fact that they got themselves accustomed to it. You must never get accustomed to what you're able change, do you hear me, little tramp?" He pulled Abrashka's ear. "Only when you cannot bring about a change for the better, should you resign yourself, make the best of it, and keep on struggling with your last breath to survive. Because you, little tramp, you are just like a tree. Your legs are planted on the ground and your head in the sky. One pulls downward, the other pulls upward. So when a tree is trapped in a storm, when the earth and the sky join forces to war on its life and to test its strength, when they smite it and burn it, then there are two possibilities: either the tree is crushed and it breaks or, with all the blowing and throwing, it grows as submissive as a twig, pretending to give in to every gust sent against it. But precisely then it becomes resistant like a cedar. Yes, soft and pliable like a twig, yet proud and strong like a cedar. The oaks here," Yoel pointed his chin toward the broad trunked oaks, "when they fall, they fall straight and stiff and that is perhaps why fire chief Vaslav Spokojny chose an oak from which to hang himself. That's their nature. You will rarely see an oak behaving like a birch. But a birch is capable of behaving like an oak, too."

As Yoel continued talking to Abrashka, some traits of his personality seemed to be revealing themselves with more clarity to Yacov. As much as it was humanly possible, Yoel was trying to be the master of his life. He tried to dominate it, but not by force. He lived for the moment, sucking every drop of enjoyment that it had to offer out of it. In his pursuit of the gifts of the present he was persistent and stiff-necked, disregarding public opinion or any laws imposed on him from outside. Yet he seemed to recognize the limits of his resistance or rebelliousness. "I wish I could reach your level of wisdom," Yacov said to Yoel in his heart, although he was fully aware that despite the things about Yoel that had begun to clarify in his mind, the man himself remained as much a mystery to him as ever.

Yoel, while he talked on, seemed to be reading Yacov's mind, as had happened many times before. Still patting the tree's trunk, he said, "But even closer than this friend here is to me, are you, the two of you." His voice grew hoarse. There was a substantial amount of *monopolka* already circulating in his veins. "Believe it or not, but you have become a sort of family to me." He appeared embarrassed when he said this. He squinted into the neck of the near empty bottle and replaced the cork. "Yes, you are strangers," he went on, "and yet . . . your appearance at my doorstep means a great deal to me." He was silent for a moment, weighing the bottle in his palm, then he added, "But I won't cling to you. I will take all that you have to offer and you will take all that I have to offer. And we must do it with ease, without tugging and pulling, without greed. Because . . . " he addressed himself to the bottle, "if you chance to receive something good, you must not be arrogant and must never demand from Mother Fate more than she's willing to give you. Such demands irritate her. She's a spiteful, capricious mistress. The more you try to wheedle something out of her, the more she'll play her tricks on you. You can stand on your head and it wouldn't help. So why stand on your head?"

"Yoel," Abrashka had digested Yoel's words in his own way. "When I grow up, I'm going to become a smith and move in with you. We'll both be blacksmiths, won't we, Yacov?" He pulled Yacov by the sleeve, "You'll come and live here with me, won't you?"

Yacov did not answer. The eyes of both Yoel and Abrashka were fixed on him. Abrashka's were full of excitement, Yoel's were searching and knowing at the same time. "Well, why don't you answer him?" Yoel shook Yacov's knee. "What will you do when the little vagabond becomes a smith like me?"

"Then I will become a rebel like you," Yacov said wistfully.

Yoel stared at him with pretended sternness. "In that case you must remember two things. First, that only live fish can swim against the current; and second, that you must not follow any false Messiahs, and a false Messiah is precisely the one who doesn't permit rebellion against himself." Yoel jumped to his feet. He shook himself as if he were trying to shake off his seriousness and cried out, "Now, if it's really true that one of you wants to become a smith like me, and the other a rebel like me, then you leave me no choice but to offer you both a swig from the bottle." He raised the flask in the air. "To seal the bargain!" He rubbed the bottom of the bottle against the tree, patted it vigorously until the cork popped out, and caught the cork in midair. He offered the bottle to Yacov. "Here, be a man, take a swig and fill your heart with boldness." He watched as Yacov gulped down a few mouthfuls of *monopolka,* his face turning red and blue as he choked and coughed. Yoel burst into peals of hearty laughter. He stepped away from the tree, his belly protruding, and grabbed hold of his waist as he laughed. He snatched the bottle from Yacov's hands and pushed it into those of Abrashka. "Your turn now, little tramp!" he shouted. "Take a swig and be a man! A man must taste everything the world has to offer. Well, take a sip and swallow, one and two!" Abrashka jumped off the tree, held his throat with his hand and quickly swallowed a mouthful of vodka. "That's a boy!" Yoel beamed.

Abrashka broke into screams. He hopped around in the mud puddles surrounding the trees, holding his neck with both hands. "Help! Help!" he yelped. "It burns!" He jumped up into the air and down, splashing mud all over himself. "Oy, I can't catch my breath! Oy, my throat! Oy my stomach!" He ran out of the wood.

Yoel's gasping laughter sounded as though he were seized by an attack of whooping cough. Tears filled his eyes. He sucked the bottle's last droplet of vodka into his mouth, thrust the empty bottle into a mud puddle, and took off at a run after Abrashka. Yacov followed them. Abrashka was hopping along the road when Yoel caught up with him and embraced him. When Yacov joined them, Yoel put his hand on Yacov's shoulder and called out, "Come on, vagabonds, shake a leg!" and he made them join him in a kind of hopping dance. They could not follow him for too long. The poplars on the road seemed to be dancing; the smithy, the shack, the road itself twirled before their eyes. The ground grew as soft as butter and their knees buckled. The three of them were seized by a wild attack of laughter.

"Look, Yacov, the earth is shaking!" Abrashka squealed, tears of laughter pouring down his face. "Soon they'll all fall down, look, look!" He collapsed into the ditch and rolled over the clumps of thin wet grass at the bottom.

Yacov fell down beside the ditch and lay prostrate with his arms spread out like a toppled scarecrow. Yoel pulled off his caftan and cast it aside.

With his torn shirt ballooning out around him and his tasseled ritual garment flying, he danced a wild *kozatchok* by himself. His arms spread, he
hummed a tune in a deep bass voice and kept rhythm by snapping his fingers. He danced off far down the road. It seemed to Yacov, who had
raised his head not to lose sight of him, that he saw not one Yoel, but ten,
a hundred, an entire band of gigantic Yoels. Yoel turned back, still dancing, squatting, throwing out one foot, then the other as he executed a *hop-
sak*. He danced on and on without a minute's pause. Yacov saw everything
swaying around Yoel and wondered how Yoel could manage to keep himself on his feet. Yoel's head no longer seemed his own as it wobbled to the
right or to the left. When he finally could no longer dance with full vigor,
he clapped his hands and hummed as he struggled to keep his shaky feet
from getting entangled in one another.

Abrashka had long since stopped laughing. Yacov, suddenly becoming
aware of his silence, stood up and looked into the ditch. He saw Abrashka
lying comfortably on his side, his cheek pillowed in the palm of his hand
as he snored loudly. Yacov tried to get himself down to the boy. He fell,
heaved himself up again, and made an effort to pick up Abrashka, but at
every try he ended up collapsing on the grass. He laughed at his own
strange clumsiness.

Yoel, who was still making an effort to continue dancing, approached
the ditch. He stopped short, leaped into the ditch, lifted Abrashka into his
arms, climbed up out of the ditch, and carried the sleeping Abrashka into
the hut. He laid him down on the sackcloth that covered the sunken straw
pallet on his cot. With swift deft movements, as if he were performing a
habitual chore, he divested Abrashka of his soaking clothes. He took his
cotton-stuffed winter coat off a nail in the wall, covered Abrashka with it,
and busied himself lighting the stove. Then he and Yacov removed their
own wet clothes and Yoel spread some of them out on the tin pipe and
some he hung up to dry on the cord above the stove. His eyes met
Yacov's. He said in a whisper so as not to wake Abrashka, "You understand me, don't you? I'm not the type who eats and drinks today for fear
that he'll die tomorrow. But we must be afraid neither of life nor of
death."

"For that, a man needs to have your strength, Yoel," Yacov whispered
back.

"Or my weaknesses," Yoel grinned into his beard. He took out a loaf of bread from the oven where he kept it as a protection against mice and, partly dressed, they sat down at the table. Their knees touched as they pulled chunks of bread from the still warm loaf and wiped the sweat from their faces. It was growing very warm in the hut. "We'll have to roast ourselves in this heat until our things dry. And the boy mustn't catch cold." Yoel turned toward the sleeping Abrashka. "He's some character, this little vagabond of yours," he said with his mouth full. "Ask me and I'll tell you exactly what goes on in his head. He has this craving, you see, to touch everything with his hands. How do I know it? Because I'm like that, too. I need to relate to objects through touch. But he goes further than I do. Have you ever seen his eyes when I make the playthings for him? You can read the craving in them, the need to transform the things he sees in his imagination into something tangible. I must confess that I too enjoy the smelting and forging of those scraps of metal for him. Child's play? Yes, but a man remains a child forever."

Yacov smiled. "Perhaps the Almighty is also no more than a child, what do you think?"

"Perhaps," Yoel nodded. "Can you imagine His delight in creating this toy called the world for Himself? I figure His fingers bled just like Abrashka's and the hurt, too, must have given Him delight. As you see me here, I can imagine Him, the Eternal One, the Infinite Nothingness, involved in His play. I can see Him withdrawing into Himself, contracting so as to make room for His creation, then thrusting forth His original thought by the power of His will, thus giving rise to the first differentiation between Himself and His work. Can you fathom that, tell me?" Yoel grew excited and sucked in the spittle that, along with crusts of half-eaten bread, had popped out of his mouth onto his lips. "Through this enormous will of His, the force of which we shall never be able to measure, He shoots out from Himself the ten Sefirot, His vessels of light. He contracts again and again expels His radiance. He does this all the time, forever and ever, eternally toying with this plaything of His, the world. A contraction, an expulsion, pulsating like the human heart, like the lungs breathing in and out, or like a woman in labor. And even when He withdraws from the things that He creates, His trace remains within them like oil or wine in an empty flask. The result is that in every one of us there lingers on the aroma of our Maker. And that, brother, is what gives us our pride."

"Or arrogance," Yacov muttered.

"No, brother, only an idiot can be arrogant. We have only to remember that we come into this world between the outlets of urine and excrement and that we leave it as garbage to fertilize the soil. In truth, it is surprising that we don't go out of our minds with wonder that such specks of garbage as we are carry each an entire world within ourselves and that a drop of the Creator's oil dwells within us. But we mustn't be humble, either. False humility is a sin against the Almighty. So our pride must attain its proper balance. That's why I keep on telling you that man cannot tolerate slavery forever. Sooner or later he breaks his chains." Yoel, drunk now on his words, was elated, beside himself with enthusiasm. "No use denying it," he continued. "He has created us in His own image. For example, take Him and the *Shkhina,* His emanation, His wife. He carries her within Him and yet they are separated. Still they desire each other with the greatest passion. This passion vibrates like electricity through all His worlds. And that's what is reflected in miniature in the vibrations between man and woman. We express all this business in rough awkward words because we are ill equipped to encompass things that we can grasp only with our senses. Yea, how can we grasp, how can we form an idea for ourselves . . . "

In his enthusiasm, Yoel did not notice that his voice had risen to a shout. It woke Abrashka, who for a while remained lying on the cot with his eyes open, looking around and seeming to try and recall where he was. Then he saw Yoel and Yacov sitting half-dressed at the table. He smiled broadly at them and sat up. Wrapping Yoel's coat around himself, he cried out, jesting, "You're discussing the Holy Scriptures without me?" Ready to invest "his own two kopecks" in the conversation, he turned to Yoel, and said, "Yacov insists that the Song of Songs is a parable about the Almighty and the Jews, so I want to ask you, Yoel . . . "

"Welcome, welcome, my vagabond and scholar!" Yoel gestured at him gaily and stood up. He went over to the window, picked up a jug from the sill and brought it over to the table. "Now that you've become a *mentsh* again," He said to Abrashka, "let's refresh ourselves with a bit of sour cream." He filled a clay bowl with the cream and handed them each a wooden spoon, then he pushed the table closer to the cot. Abrashka sat up on his knees, and the three of them ate with gusto from the same bowl. "And what is your expert opinion of the Song of Songs?" Yoel asked Abrashka and licked the cream off his whitened mustache.

"I say," Abrashka mimicked him and also licked at the white foam around his mouth and then wiped his face dry with his arm. "I say that Yacov's pulling hairs, that's what I say."

"So, that's what you say, eh?" Yoel continued sipping at the cream. Soon all three of them were scratching at the bottom of the bowl. Yoel stretched his body and spread his hands apart, palms open to the ceiling, as if he intended to raise himself from the chair to restart his dancing. He bent so far backwards, balancing on the chair's hind legs, that the chair began to creak and he almost toppled over. He began to hum, "How beautiful thou art and how sweet thou art . . . bim-bom . . . in pleasures. Thy form is like the date tree and thy breasts like clusters of grapes . . . "

Yacov, alarmed, pulled at Yoel's sleeve, indicating Abrashka with his eyes, "He's not even eleven yet."

"So what?" Yoel waved his hand. "He'll eventually get there, won't he?" Still he checked himself, straightened up and pulled at Abrashka's ear in mock anger. "And who are you, little pepper grain, to judge when someone is pulling hairs and when he isn't? What do you know, you little ignoramus? Perhaps you're going to tell me that you've been present at the writing of the Holy Book, eh? Or perhaps you've had the opportunity to look straight into King Solomon's heart, have you?"

Abrashka was not intimidated by Yoel's ridicule. "No, I've not. But I know that King Solomon was the smartest man in the world and that he had a thousand wives, so he surely knew that a wife can't be compared to the People of Israel because the People of Israel are many men and such a comparison is for the birds."

"Thus have you judged!" Yoel said with pretended anger, but could barely contain his laughter. "And what our sages have decided is of no importance to you, is it? Perhaps you'd better be patient and wait until you're taller by a head than you are now and your mind gets filled with a bit more knowledge before you give your definite expert opinion?"

"You talk just like my father!" Abrashka burst out, finally feeling himself offended. He clambered out of Yoel's cotton-padded coat, scrambled down from the cot, and pulled his clothes down from the cord. Dressing quickly, he shouted, "Everyone tells me to wait until I'm a head taller than I am now! And what am I supposed to do in the meantime? Stuff my head with sawdust? You want me to study the Toyre, don't you? So should I use my head to do it, or should I use my . . . " He jammed his hat on top of his skullcap and ran out of the room.

"He's mad at me," Yoel shrugged guiltily. He sized Yacov up with a curious glance. "You too entertain doubts, don't you?"

"I do, yes," Yacov conceded.

"So keep on entertaining them in good health. In any case, the whole business of both seeking the truth and doubting is nothing but a brain game. It's worth not even the hole in the bagel, believe me. Each man sees the world and the Toyre through the prism of his own soul, and no one can see them or the Creator as they really are. That's that. That's why when you call Him from the profundity of your own being, you get back only your own echo. You call your own roots forth within Him."

"But Yoel," Yacov rejoined. There was something that he wanted to say, but that something loomed so very vaguely and murkily in his mind that all he could do was ask in return, "don't you ever feel at a loss, I mean feel lost, Yoel?"

Yoel nodded, "I do."

"What do you do then?"

"I go to my woman," Yoel answered casually. But Yacov blushed and turned his head. "Hey, don't turn your eyes away from me," Yoel seized Yacov's chin and forced him to turn back his head. "If I can look you straight in the eye, then you must be able to do the same. You're a friend, so I can tell you . . . "

"If you want to," Yacov whispered.

"Yes, I want to. There is no use denying it. The more strongly a man desires a woman, you understand, the stronger is his craving to make the broken vessels whole, yes, those vessels that broke at the moment of creation, after the third *Sefira* burst from an overflow of light, when the Creator had cut His fingers as Abrashka did, so that they bled. When I go to my woman . . . a woman whose heart is filled with sweetness and whose voice is like a flute, I feel that I am making the vessels whole, that I'm rescuing the sparks of the *Shkhina,* if only for a moment." He would have continued, but he saw the reflection of something akin to pity in Yacov's eyes and could not bear it. He stood up, opened the door and called Abrashka who was wandering about outside, kicking pebbles. "Hey, little tramp, come over here!" Abrashka, his head hanging, kicked one of the pebbles in the direction of the hut and approached hesitatingly. He looked at Yoel from under his lowered head, reproach in his eyes. "Why do you walk around with your nose down?" Yoel asked in his deep warm voice.

"That's none of your business." Abrashka pouted.

"It's my most important business. Come here!"

Abrashka came to the door, his lower lip protruding over his chin. He stopped on the threshold and raised his head to Yoel. "I thought that you were different from everybody else."

"I am different." Yoel pulled the boy into the hut toward his chair and seated him on his lap. He tried to tickle him under his chin. "Do you still remember my name?" he asked with a chuckle. "Yoel is my name. But my true name is Yehoel. And do you have any idea what that name means and who I really am?"

"I know very well who you really are," Abrashka's voice grew warmer.

"No, you don't. You see me sitting here, but in the blink of an eye I can become an angel, and not just any angel, but the principal angel, the one called Yehoel-Mittatron. The fact that I am tall and fat and speak in a bass voice is just to confuse you, because angels don't like to be treated like angels. Nonetheless I'm the greatest and most important angel of all the angels. If I sneeze, it thunders. If I laugh, the sun shines. If I cry, the entire earth is flooded. So you'd better not make me cry."

"And what if I do?" Abrashka began to giggle.

"I just told you what would happen. And, on top of it all, the Almighty would get angry with you because I am His favorite. I alone stand on the Almighty's side of the curtain, that curtain that separates Him from the other angels, so that they might not see His face. Moreover since I'm the angel Mittatron, I also direct the heavenly yeshivas where the Messiah in person comes in now and then to study. So, I am on personal terms with Him, too."

"Then why don't you ask Him when He will come?"

"I asked Him, may I live so long! A thousand times I've asked Him. But He is so indolent and answers in such a quiet slow voice that even an angel can't hear or understand."

"But if you are an angel, what are you doing here on earth?"

"Because I'm also a fallen angel." With unexpected tenderness, Yoel pressed Abrashka to his bosom. But, as if he were ashamed of his show of emotion, he immediately let go of him. He lightly pushed Abrashka off his lap. "Go and open the bottom drawer of the water bench and take out a deck of cards. I'll teach you to play a sixty-six." Abrashka, stunned by the quick transition from the heavens to a deck of cards, nonetheless rushed over to the water bench. The next moment a sticky much-handled deck of playing cards lay on the table. "A man must try his hand at everything at least once, so long as he doesn't hurt any one else." Yoel's voice took on a didactic tone as he explained the rules of the game to Abrashka and Yacov.

Yoel was in a strange mood, and that day was filled with his monologues, explanations, and card-playing, as well as with long silences and misunderstandings. There were moments when they each felt ill-at-ease and shy with the others.

As Yacov and Abrashka were about to leave, they heard a noise coming from the direction of Bociany. The three of them waited at the roadside and listened. "No, it's not an automobile," Abrashka shook his head.

"It certainly isn't," Yoel said and stepped forth to meet the approaching cloud of dust. A covered wagon came into view and then another. A band of chanting Hasidim surrounded the wagons. "They're on their way to visit the Rabbi," Yoel declared.

The Hasidim were dressed in ankle-length dusty coats, wore threadbare felt hats on their heads, and had red handkerchiefs tied around their necks. Their long coats were unbuttoned, and from under their fluttering gabardines the fringed undergarments stuck out unevenly. Their voices were hoarse, and they gesticulated wildly. The misty sparkle of their eyes and the purple blotches on their cheeks betrayed the fact that they had made a stopover at the inn.

Abrashka waded into the crowd with Yacov close behind him. One of the wagons carried a small barrel of liquor. While Yoel checked their horses, one of the Hasidim handed out thimblefuls of vodka. Their arms looped around each other's waists, the Hasidim took hold of each other's belts. They roused themselves into song and started to hop around in circles. When Yoel finished his work, he drank some of the offered vodka and, fishing Abrashka out of the dancing crowd, took hold of his shoulder and explained warmly, "Bear in mind, little vagabond, that dancing is a formidable form of prayer. When you dance, you pray not just with your mouth but with your entire being, not just with your soul but with every spark of life within you."

"But why do they always dance in circles, round and round and round?" Abrashka asked.

"Oh, that they do for the same reason that they eat bagels. A circle is the most perfect shape, the Almighty's favorite shape. The earth, for instance, is round like a circle, and in a circle everyone and everything is equal. There is no first and no last." Abrashka pulled Yoel through the maze of flying capotes to where Yacov was conversing with a young Hasid. The next moment all three of them hopped along with the Hasidim. Then Yoel let go of their hands and broke into such a wild acrobatic *kozatchok* that even the Hasidim stopped dancing. They gathered in a circle around him, clapping their hands, singing, and yelling at the top of their lungs. By the time Yoel stopped dancing, it was time for the *Minkha* prayers. "Come," Yoel proposed. "Let's go and pray in the birch wood."

The Hasidim were reluctant to lose so much time, so each of them placed himself to pray facing a poplar tree. The road began to look like a double of itself. Every few steps there stood a tree and a man in prayer.

When the wagons finally moved on, Yoel, Yacov, and Abrashka accompanied them partway down the road. "I'm sure," Yoel called out to the Hasidim as he took leave of them, "that the Rabbi will come out on the road to greet you with song and dance!" On the way back to the smithy, he threw one arm around Yacov's shoulder and the other around Abrashka's. "Aye," he sighed with satisfaction. "It's good to have a break from seclusion every now and then." He turned to Yacov, "Do you remember that we once talked about the difference between being alone and loneliness? I like to be alone. But too much of it for too long leads to attacks of loneliness, which in turn lead to self-pity. And self-pity is the worst kind of company. So once in a while, I find it necessary to unlock the door of seclusion and throw it wide open."

Back at the smithy, Yoel seated Abrashka on top of Sussi and helped Yacov mount the horse. He put his hand on Yacov's knee as if he wanted to keep him from leaving for another instant. "Don't misunderstand me," he said. "A man must have the strength to face himself. The Almighty said to Abraham, *'Lech lecho,'* go and get yourself out into the world. But He could also have meant, 'Get yourself out into yourself'. We speak of Egypt, of our bondage, our exodus. The truth is that here, in the heart, there is our real Egypt." He pounded his chest with his fist. "Only when you free yourself of your inner bondage, only then does the freedom from slavery to others make any sense." Yoel slapped Sussi on the rear and the horse set off at a gallop.

There happened another odd day many weeks later, when Yacov and Abrashka visited Yoel in the middle of the summer. It was a sultry, overcast day. Rain seemed to be gathering in the clouds but never fell. Few words passed among the three companions. The visitors, just like their host, were overcome by a mood of languorous indolence and lay stretched out on the grass by the ditch, in their pants and ritual undergarments, but with their shirts and shoes removed. Yoel seemed to have dozed off. Yacov and Abrashka stared at the sky with sleepy eyes.

Wanda's voice was heard singing somewhere in the distance. Yoel sat up as if he were awoken by the voice. Yacov noticed that Yoel's face glistened moistly and wondered whether it was perspiration or the trace of tears. Yoel, weeping? Yoel wiped his face with the palms of his hands and moved closer to Abrashka. From where they were lying by the roadside, they could make out the slim silhouette of a woman gliding along the line of the horizon like a tightrope walker.

Yoel rose to his feet and went into the hut. When he reappeared, he was carrying a basin full of cherries and leaves. Yacov and Abrashka sat up and let their legs dangle over the ditch. Yoel, basin in hands, squeezed himself in between them. They ate the cherries in silence punctuated by their spitting out the pits. In the oppressive grayness and heaviness of the air, the sparkling red of the cherries seemed to enliven and refresh the surroundings. The sweet-tasting juice cooled their mouths pleasantly. The three companions, having regained a quickened sense of enjoyment, continued to consume the cherries, unable to stop. Yoel held up two cherries that were linked by their stems. "Look at them, children, just look at them!" he marveled. His eyes, though sad and misty, reflected his wonderment and admiration for the perfect beauty of the cherries. He transferred the same gaze toward the horizon and let his eyes glide over it as though seeking for Wanda's vanished figure. He shoved the two cherries into his mouth and spat out the pits so that they landed far across the ditch.

Abrashka tried to copy him and to spit out his pits as far and as high as Yoel's. Before long, Yacov, too, joined in the game. "You know what?" Abrashka burst into giggles. "We, all the three of us, are crazy!"

Yoel nearly choked on a pit as he burst into laughter. "You're as wise as the devil, my crazy little vagabond." He embarked on decorating Abrashka's ears with double cherries, making them dangle at the boy's lobes like earrings. "But there is a difference between your craziness and Yacov's or mine."

"What's the difference?" Abrashka hung linked cherries on both Yacov's and Yoel's ears.

"The difference is that I'm a madman who talks too much. Yacov is one who talks too little. But you are just right. The most perfect madman in the world!" The basin was empty. Yoel turned it bottom up and put it on Abrashka's head.

Before his visitors left to return to the Blue Mountain, Yoel put two rubles in Yacov's palm. "When you come next time, God willing," he said, "stop at the inn and buy me a bottle of *monopolka*. You'll save me a trip." He spoke cheerfully, almost gaily, although there was still an air of sadness about him as he looked at Abrashka and seated him on the horse. "If you happen to run into any demons on the road, you crazy little vagabond," he waved a finger at him, "don't forget to say the abracadabra."

"What's abracadabra?" Abrashka asked, bursting into uproarious laughter.

"It's serious business, so don't laugh!" Yoel twisted his face into a fearsome expression. "And you'd better beware! Remember to call out the name of the demon Shabriri. Each time you repeat it, you must cut off one letter of the name, one after the other. Like this: Shabriri-habriri-abriri-briri . . . "

Inspired by Yoel's chatter, Yacov leaned down from the horse's back and whispered in his ear, "Yoel, could you spare a bit of time to study some cabala with me, on a Sabbath afternoon let's say?" Yoel smacked the horse's rear and shook his head in a such a manner that his response could be understood as both a yes and a no.

On their ride home Abrashka went on repeating, "Shabriri-habriri-abriri-briri . . . "

⊚⊚ *8* ⊚⊚

REB FAIVELE AND ZIRELE had decided to keep their boys at home for the summer. But now the summer was drawing to an end, and to Abrashka and Yacov there remained only a few Sundays left to be spent with Yoel. In order to be together with him as much time as possible, Yacov and Abrashka set out for the smithy immediately after the midday meal on the

Sunday following their last visit, but they did remember to stop at the inn first and buy *monopolka* for Yoel.

The inn was packed with peasants and Jews, with wagon drivers and wholesalers all of whom, due to some unfinished business with the shop-keepers on the Potcheyov, lodged there over the Sabbath. Here, Gentile and Jew spent the whole afternoon in each other's company. They occupied tables together, occasionally drank together, and all kept account of whose turn it was to pay. They made quite a racket, as the Yiddish language mixed quite spontaneously with the peasant Polish. There was much singing, there were arguments, and every so often a scuffle broke out among the Jews or the Poles themselves, or between one group and the other. Despite the noise, the absence of one of the inn's most important customers was felt acutely. It was Vaslav Spokojny, the late fire chief who in former times had sat there every Sunday with his vest unbuttoned and his face hot. Drunk and boisterous, he had made everyone gather around him to listen to the incredible tales of his heroic deeds at putting out this or that fire. Now he himself and his incredible suicide had become the subject of tales told by others. As for the new fire chief, he was neither a great talker nor a great drinker, but was a pious Christian who stayed home on Sundays.

Yacov left Abrashka to watch the horse, entered the tavern, and bought the bottle of *monopolka* for Yoel. From the snatches of conversation at the counter and the buzz of chatter all around him he gathered that there had been a fire in a village during the night. It made no impression on him and he walked out to where Abrashka was waiting.

The major part of the road lay already far behind them, when a strong smell of smoke reached their nostrils. At first they paid little attention to it. It was common for the peasants to burn their fields at this time of year and the wind was evidently spreading the smell of these fires. But the closer they came to the smithy, the stronger was the smell. The air grew dense and sooty. A transparent cloud of smoke sagged low over the field to the right. Yacov presumed that the fire he had heard mentioned at the inn had probably happened in the village across the field.

Yoel was not at the smithy. Yacov and Abrashka sat down to wait for him. An hour or so passed, then another. The air was somewhat easier to breathe. The cloud of smoke hanging over the field was dissolving. Yacov and Abrashka wandered about the silent smithy and among the heaps of broken wagon parts and wheels in the yard. A couple of chickens and geese were going about their business. The cow in the shed started to moo and would not stop. As a reminder, occasional bits of soot were wafted into the yard by the breeze. Abrashka stooped over a heap of scrap metal and lazily inspected its pieces. He raised his eyes to Yacov, "Maybe he's in the village? Let's go and have a look."

"We'll wait here," Yacov answered firmly. Yoel would not have approved their coming to the village in search of him, he thought. He leaned against the fence and gazed across the field in the direction of the distant village huts. The hours passed. At length, when the sun was beginning its descent in the western firmament, a silhouette appeared on the horizon and advanced across the field. Yacov strained his eyes as he watched the silhouette grow."Here he comes!" he called to Abrashka, pointing at the dark figure approaching from the distance.

"You're right," Abrashka confirmed and now allowed himself to become fully engrossed in playing with the pieces of scrap metal.

Yacov crossed the road and set out across the field in the direction of the approaching figure that, as it drew nearer, increasingly lost its resemblance to Yoel. Suddenly Yacov found himself face to face with a panting, distraught peasant.

"Jesus Maria! A Jew!" the peasant cried out with a note of relief in is voice. He wiped the sweat and soot off his face with his sleeve. "You must have fallen from the sky!"

Even before the peasant had managed to catch his breath and tell Yacov why he was so pleased to see him, Yacov knew. His head began to reel and the figure of the peasant multiplied and danced before his eyes. The ground seemed to be rising under his feet. "Yoel!" a voice burst out roaring in his head.

"I was on my way to Bociany, to see my Jewish acquaintance," the peasant said as he beckoned to Yacov to follow him. He turned around and headed uphill beside Yacov. "The blacksmith was like one of ours, you understand, he was like a brother to us all. We'll bury him in the village. But we want to bury him the Jewish way, as he would have wanted to be buried, may God our Lord have mercy on his soul. So I was on my way to my Jewish acquaintance to find out how to conduct a Jewish funeral. You'll tell us, my boy, won't you? And you'll bring your *rov*, too."

Yacov never remembered how he got himself to the village, nor when it was that Abrashka had joined him. He had the impression that he must have crawled there on all fours or crept there on his belly because he did remember how his legs had refused to obey, how they had turned into lumps of clay, and how he had felt impelled to prostrate himself on the ground and never get up.

The peasant brought him to a collapsed house that was still smoldering, its jagged, broken beams still glowing and hissing. It looked as if the entire village had gathered around Yacov, staring at him with bewildered eyes. They made a lane for him to pass through. A dark-faced woman came rushing toward him, giving forth an uncanny shriek. She threw her arms around his neck and dropped to her knees at his feet. Her body shook spasmodically.

"Jesus Maria, dear little Jew . . . " She bowed over Yacov's muddy shoes. "He saved my swallows, the saint. He pulled my children out of the flames, the poor, poor saint!" She let go of Yacov, scrambled to her feet, and with the plaid on her shoulders flapping in the wind like the wings of a black bird, she ran down the narrow path that led to the village shrine. The peasants followed her.

The peasant who had met Yacov in the field pointed his chin in the same direction and pushed Yacov ahead. "May the Lord our Father press him to His heart." The peasant crossed himself.

Yacov, totally drained of energy or will, allowed the peasant to push him toward the shrine. Abrashka was at his side. They tightly clasped each other's hands. The only parts of their bodies that they were aware of were the palms of their hands, the larger hand holding the smaller. A wooden Jesus peered down on a heap of kilim quilts and peasant plaids that lay on the ground at the foot of the cross.

"He was still alive when he saved the smallest," a peasant woman, rocking a baby in her arms, whispered sobbing in Yacov's ear. "But then he collapsed and we could not revive him." The woman made the sign of the cross over herself and her baby. The others, the village children included, followed suit. The crowd, young and old, wept softly and fell to its knees. The woman with the baby in her arms also went down on her knees.

Only Yacov and Abrashka remained standing amid the sea of bent, swaying backs. Like two wooden poles they stood face to face with the wooden figure suspended from the pole of the cross.

"Get me a wagon!" Yacov cried out in a voice not his own.

A ripple went through the bowed backs. The peasants scrambled to their feet and turned their grief-stricken faces covered with tears and soot toward Yacov. "When he was alive you refused to have anything to do with him," a woman said scornfully.

"He's ours," others in the crowd nodded.

"Get me a wagon!" Yacov repeated in his commanding strange voice.

"Tell us how you Jews conduct the ritual . . . " the peasant who had first met Yacov, a robust, middle-aged man with the withered face of someone much older, demanded of Yacov with barely controlled anger. "We'll give him the honors he deserves. We'll bury him here, beside the shrine, because he is a hero. The women will take care of the grave."

"If you want to honor him," Yacov shouted in the same dry, firm tone of voice, "then you must let him be buried in the Jewish cemetery. There is no other honor for a dead Jew."

The silence that followed his pronouncement was so deep that the wind could be heard raising the dust on the sandy path. The cry of the babies left in the huts was heard. A few women hurried home. Some men also withdrew from the crowd and conferred in whispers among themselves. They were joined by the peasant who had accompanied Yacov. After a while the group vanished behind the huts. The others stood, surrounding Yacov and Abrashka with a wall of silence, as if they expected Yacov to shout another command.

Yacov hardly noticed them. Although they barred his view of the heap lying on the ground near the cross, he could hear Yoel's voice in his mind's ear, "I am but a milestone on your road." The voice pierced a deep hole in his heart. He had the feeling that he was waiting for something but could not remember what. The women began to whisper among themselves. One of them started to explain something, while another tried to tell him how it had all happened. Another few kissed Yacov and Abrashka's hands as if in this manner they wanted to transmit their blessings to Yoel. Despair swelled in Yacov's heart, turning into violent rage. But he kept himself in check. He had to keep his mouth shut at any cost.

The group of conferring peasants reappeared heading toward a barn. They brought out a wagon. One of them came out leading a horse from a stable. A murmur of dissatisfaction passed through the crowd surrounding Yacov, but no one moved or said a word aloud. Yacov took a step forward toward the wagon and waved his hand at the men. "I have a horse. Just get me a harness."

Yoel was laid out on the wagon and covered with a red and green plaid. Yacov and some of the peasants harnessed themselves to the wagon and, accompanied by the entire village, they made their way down a circuitous path through the fields. Abrashka shuffled along far behind. Thin and lonely tolled the bell of the small shrine in the rear. The peasants began to talk among themselves in increasingly louder voices. They crossed themselves frequently and sighed noisily.

When Yacov arrived at the smithy, he untied Sussi from the tree. He caught a glimpse of Abrashka, who stood in front of Yoel's hut. The boy was so pale that the skin of his face seemed blue and his lips looked black. His eyes were dry but dark with bewilderment, fear, and pain. His chin trembled slightly. Yacov left the harnessing of Sussi to the peasants, and approached the boy. At the same instant both his and Abrashka's eyes focused on the bottle of *monopolka* that they had left in the doorway of the hut. Yacov picked it up and put it in his pocket. For a moment they stood facing the closed door of the hut. Yoel's cow was still mooing. A peasant woman opened the shed and sat down to milk the cow.

Sussi stood harnessed to the wagon. "Stay near me," Yacov whispered to Abrashka and put his hand on his shoulder as they came back to the wagon. "Come up front," Yacov pulled at the boy's sleeve. "Let's walk beside Sussi. Or do you want to hold the reins on the other side and I'll stay here?" Abrashka walked around to the other side of Sussi.

The wagon moved. Some of the peasants pushed it from the back while the rest followed, scattering through the fields. They looked like puppets walking on the string of the horizon. Their vanishing and reappearing from behind the sheaves of harvested rye, accelerated the whirl of memories spinning in Yacov's head. The sheaves of rye also resembled puppets holding on to each other by the shoulders. Heads hanging, they were puppets of mourners, of Hasidim frozen in dance.

The peasants pushing the wagon from the rear continued to do so for another stretch of the road. Then they too scattered into the field. Peasant boys ran ahead of the wagon along the ditches, stopped, waved their hands, and chewed on blades of grass as they watched the wagon go by.

Finally there was no one left. Far behind, the sun in the sky was completing its descent. Beams of reddish gold wove through the web of the poplar boughs. The road itself was striped like the back of a zebra by the shadows of the trees on both sides. Yacov walked beside the horse. His mind was now blank, empty, frozen. He was aware of nothing except the fact that he was too far from Abrashka, whose face he could not see. At length he could no longer restrain himself and called out, "Wouldn't you like to come over to my side?"

"I want to stay where I am," Abrashka replied.

The way was very long on foot. An eternity seemed to have gone by from the moment when Yacov and Abrashka had passed the same spots on the road on their way to the smithy. Yacov measured the expanse of the fields with his eyes. Every patch was familiar to him. He and Abrashka had ridden past them so often. He knew from looking at them how much road there was still to cover, and yet he was confused. The road seemed to be leading nowhere but toward Yoel, Yoel whose presence he felt beside him, within an arm's reach—although Yoel had gone up the field and had not returned yet, would never return.

Yacov did not so much see as sense that someone was coming down through the side of the field. He did not turn his head or change the rhythm of his steps until the sound of weeping behind his back jerked him out of his stupor. He turned his head. There, holding on to the rear of the wagon, walked a barefoot woman in a loose, sloppy blouse that stuck out unevenly from her skirt. Her long blond hair dangled in tousled clumps around her bowed head, like a thick flaxen veil. The muffled sobs escaping from under the veil of hair seemed to roll along with the pebbles under the wagon, splitting into squeaky pieces under the weight of the wheels. Yacov cast the woman a passing glance and then again stared straight ahead of him. Sweat poured down his forehead and burned his eyes. The woman's lament grated on his ears.

Suddenly she was at his side. Now he could see a pair of red swimming eyes, a creased mask of a face, and two swollen lips. However, this was not the older woman he had first thought her to be. She was young. Her form was familiar.

"Where are you taking him?" she asked, her voice sounding an eerie pitch. Hadn't he seen this face and heard this voice before?

"To the Jewish cemetery," he replied curtly.

"Why are you taking him away? He's mine."

"He's neither yours nor mine. He's his own," Yacov said this more to himself than to her. He added aloud, "Because he is a Jew."

"I'm coming with you," she announced and moved back to the rear of the wagon.

Yacov began to recite the psalms loudly, so that Abrashka could hear him. He moved back a bit to get a glimpse of the boy. Then he turned his head around further and saw that the young woman was walking so that the knotted mass of her hair hung over Yoel's uncovered face. His heart stirred violently. He had to tell her to cover Yoel's face. He had to say it aloud so that she could hear him through the unbearable noise raised by her sobs and the churning of the wheels. But then he felt himself overcome by an urge to have a glimpse of Yoel's face also, to see it for the last time at this sunset hour of this last Sunday spent in Yoel's proximity.

In order not to be noticed by Abrashka, Yacov let Sussi maintain the same pace. He himself proceeded with his loud recitation of the psalms while he stopped and let the front of the wagon pass him. The young woman straightened herself. Her mane of hair flew back like a curtain to reveal Yoel's face—a dark, raw knot of flesh. The brush of hair on Yoel's face, his beard, his mustache and sidelocks were all partly burned and the pelt of hair on his head looked like a net of copper wires. Yacov walked on, moving ahead alongside the wagon, still reciting the psalms, his eyes wide open. He stared at Yoel's face—a mask with no lips, no eyebrows or eyelashes, a sliver of white beneath the closed eyelids, a black pointy nose. A stranger. A pile of earth, of dry mud. A scarecrow. It cast a dread upon Yacov.

He tugged at the fringes of the plaid shawl and pulled it up to cover Yoel's face. He walked ahead to resume his place beside Sussi and took hold of the horse's bridle. His mother's words came to mind. He heard her whisper, "All this is only a mask, a veil superimposed on the hidden worlds . . . " He was struck by the thought that one day he would be accompanying his own mother in the same manner, walking next to her dead body, feeling himself desperately abandoned. "If all that is only a veil, Mother, then why does it cut so deeply into my heart? Why such unbearable hurt?" It was at this moment that his grief had begun to melt. The blankness and dullness of his mind was replaced by the burning awareness of the truth, by the needle-sharp sting of finality. Unable to control himself, he burst into sobs. All the previously desensitized emotions awoke inside him, surged to his mouth, and poured out from it in a lament, in the howl of an abandoned lost child.

"Yoel! Yoel!" he heard, through his own loud sobs, the sound of Abrashka's voice sobbing. As he listened to it, it seemed to Yacov that from the depths of the Wide Poplar Road, from all the points on the horizon beyond the fields, beyond the marshes, beyond the hills and the mountains, beyond the patches of forestland and the lake, Yoel's voice was coming back, reverberating with a booming echo, "Yehoel!"

At first he thought that the young woman walking behind him was saying something or that she was chanting exorcisms in her own language. But then he realized that in her broken voice she had joined him and Abrashka in their lament. She was repeating Yoel's name in a crippled, alien pronunciation. The broken syllables of Yoel's mispronounced name deepened the sense of Yacov's loneliness in a world that seemed to be falling apart forever.

When they finally reached the Blue Mountain, Yacov stopped the wagon. He walked around it toward Abrashka, took his hand, and climbed part of the hill with him. There they halted. "Now we will say our own good-bye to Yoel," he said to the boy softly, still holding his hand. They both turned to face the wagon that stood, small and peaceful, amidst the poplars down on the road. "This is how we'll do it. We'll hold each other close and speak not a word, not a word. We'll listen to him in his silence and then I will say kaddish. So let's not cry now." He put his arm around Abrashka's shoulders, and so they stood, in a silence filled with the whispering of blades of grass, with the buzzing of wasps, the twitter of birds, and the quiet hum coming from the shtetl and the villages. Although they were staring at the wagon, it seemed to have vanished from sight. Yoel hovered around and about the two them. The surrounding silence roared with his words, with his songs and his laughter—and with their own joy of having known him and with their grief of having lost him. Abrashka struggled to hold back his tears. He sniffled and finally surrendered to his need to weep. Tears coursed undammed down his face. Yacov recited the kaddish as he stood behind Abrashka, his hands on Abrashka's shoulders. After he had finished reciting, he made the boy turn around and said to him, "Go home now. You can tell your parents everything, if it helps you. It no longer matters. And here . . . " He pulled the bottle of *monopolka* out of his pocket. "Put this under my bed."

Abrashka embraced him. "What will happen now, Yacov?"

"Now we'll have to live without Yoel."

Abrashka's overflowing eyes looked up at him. "He wanted to save the sparks of holiness, didn't he, Yacov? And he was burned."

"But he did save them. He saved you and me, too. Now go." Yacov freed himself from the boy's arms and ran down the hill.

Abrashka did not move. Whenever Yacov looked back at the Blue

Mountain after he had descended the incline, he could see the boy's thin frame between the poplars growing smaller and smaller. He remembered how he and Abrashka had looked back at Yoel standing in the middle of the road as they had left him after a visit, seeing him grow smaller and smaller with the distance. He also remembered himself standing in the middle of that same road, as he had followed another wagon with his eyes, the one that had taken Binele away from him. Indeed each parting was a kind of dying, but parting in death was unlike any other parting, a thing beyond hope.

The sun had set. Soft rays of light permeated the air along the road. A serene stillness hovered over the landscape. The barefoot young woman was noiselessly following the wagon, holding on to its rear boards with both hands. She was so quiet now that she seemed like an apparition. Yacov looked back at her every now and again to make sure that she had not vanished. They were passing the horse dealer's stables. The sight of them brought Binele's face again before his mind's eye. He took comfort from the image. He was so exhausted that he felt he would never arrive in Bociany. He tried to dwell on the memory of himself standing hand in hand with Binele under the narrow roof of the stable where they had taken shelter during a thunder storm. In his yearning for the support of her touch, he once again remembered the presence of the young woman and, looking back, he saw her walking only a step behind him. Her hoarse voice broke through his thoughts of Binele, disturbing the image in his mind.

"He was my first one, you know," he heard the woman say.

Despite its huskiness, the voice startled him now with its familiar sound. He knew it well. He looked more closely at her and was not surprised to recognize Wanda. He had known it all along. He had known but had refused to acknowledge it. He did not want to hear her speak. He wanted her to keep quiet, to be blotted out of sight, to become nonexistent. Slurring the words, he quickly began to recite whatever psalm came first to his mind, as if each psalm were an exorcism. But the power of Wanda's voice overwhelmed them. It penetrated him, stirring up his torment, storming every fortress of safety within him.

"I was a little girl when . . . " Her voice broke, each word that she uttered was but a moan, "when the fire broke out in his house near the smithy . . . in the middle of the day. There was not even a storm. Just a hot sticky day. A black cloud passed by. He was working at the forge. A single thunderclap. It hit the house. His wife and all three children were inside. The whole place just burst into flames. The fire swallowed everything. The people in the village didn't even know there had been a fire. The firemen never arrived. There was a curse hanging over his head. He teased the Lord and he teased the Devil." A fit of crying stopped her from talking. She tried but was unable to continue for a long while. At length she recovered herself, swallowed her tears and forced the words out from her mouth. "And then . . . today . . . at dawn . . . In his sleep he smelled the fire. In a second he was over at the Wojciechovas' house. By the time the firemen came, it was all over. If my father, the fool, were still alive, it wouldn't have come to that . . . "

Aghast at her words, Yacov wished he could prevent them from penetrating his mind, wished her to stop talking. At the same time he was greedy for her words, wanting her to tell him more and more. He found himself oddly jealous of what she knew about Yoel. But soon her voice sank into silence again. She abandoned herself to tears that did not stop even when the wagon reached Bociany.

He made a deal with her that she would borrow a horse from a peasant who lived in the shtetl and would by herself drive back to her village in the empty wagon. They arrived at the poorhouse that was located in the vicinity of the Jewish cemetery. In front of it there stood the wooden stretcher on which dead bodies were laid out for the ritual cleansing before burial. Yacov, with the help of two other Jewish men, put Yoel's body on it. He unharnessed Sussi, tossed the harness into the empty wagon, and without so much as nodding at Wanda, he left her then and there. Leading the horse by the bridle, he headed toward the Potcheyov to buy a candle to be lit for the soul of the deceased. He decided against stopping at his mother's shop.

Several times during that night, as he lay on his bed in his alcove at Reb Faivele the Miller's, Yacov took out the bottle of *monopolka* from under his bed. He was overcome by a desire to savor the tastes that Yoel had savored. It was as if the *monopolka* could help him satisfy his thirst for Yoel's presence, could help make the latter's being become a part of his own, so that he could carry it within him to the end of his own days. But he did not uncork the bottle. The main taste of Yoel's life had, after all, been the taste of suffering. In that suffering had been rooted Yoel's love of life. The *monopolka* might have made the real taste disappear, even if only for a short while. Yacov did not want this to happen.

◎◎

Finally, the day arrived when the intertwined course of Yacov and Abrashka's days drew to an end.

Abrashka neither wept with frustration nor rebelled. Nonetheless, Reb Faivele's house took on the aspect of Tisha B'Av, the day of fasting and mourning for the destruction of the Temple. Fredka's husband seated both boys in the carriage and Reb Faivele climbed up to seat himself between them. Long Zirele cried real tears and Fredka could not be consoled. She would not stop heaping blessings on the boys' heads in both languages, Yiddish and Volinian. Her husband climbed onto the front seat and swished his whip through the air. The mill workers and farmhands, the peasant children and the dog Bobik, all ran after the carriage until they reached the foot of the hill. There they shouted good-bye and waved. Once on the Wide Poplar Road, the carriage turned in the direction of Chwosty from where the train left for Krakow.

The same evening, Yacov took the bottle of *monopolka* out from under his bed and, thrusting it into the pocket of his caftan, set off downhill, heading in the direction of Yoel's hut. It was a cold evening in late autumn. Wanton gusts of wind careered across the fields. The moon and the stars were obliterated by swiftly scudding tatters of heavy cloud. It seemed as if there were no sky at all and, in the increasing darkness, the road rolled out like a black carpet for Yacov's feet.

He marched quickly, arms swinging. His heart hammered in his chest and his breath escaped in heavy whistles through his nostrils. He felt as if his head were not his own, as if someone had unscrewed it from his body. It was rolling somewhere in a sea of rocks, colliding against them, yet causing him no pain. He recalled having read somewhere that a man's desire can grow to become so overpowering that he can actually cease to feel it. That must have been the reason why he, Yacov, felt no pain. So powerful was his compulsion that his head had itself turned into rock.

Now and then his head stopped reeling and he felt it on his shoulders again. Filled with distaste, he scoffed at himself, "Am I going out of my mind? Am I to remain a Soft Mirl, a sissy, forever? True, I feel like a double mourner. Yoel is gone and, without Abrashka, life at the mill is hell. But what happened to Yoel was a tragedy. And tragedy is Fate. I must accept it. But Abrashka's departure? Well, after all, it's for his own good. And then, Abrashka is neither my brother nor even a relative. He's the son of a stranger. I was merely his tutor. That's all. It's crazy for a man in his twenties, whose mother is constantly bothered by the matchmaker with marriage proposals for him, to feel so heartbroken. Almost all my friends in Bociany are already married with children of their own and adult worries on their heads. And here my head, like that of a child, is still full of butterflies! I should be content that I've done my job and can now concentrate on my own future."

But all these wise thoughts seemed banal and not really his own. His future? Was it not premature to worry about it now? How could a person who saw himself as he, Yacov, now saw himself, as a bird with broken wings, strive for anything in the future? Yet looking at himself in this manner was also wrong, very wrong. His wings broken? That was false. Why, at this very moment he was actually soaring through the darkness on two enormous wings. What he now felt was probably the discomfort of maturing. He had just begun to spread his wings. That was it! They were carrying him away from the petty and the commonplace. Not that he was giving himself airs, thinking himself to be God knows who. He was a worm crawling on the ground, but a worm with two widespread wings! He would not surrender and become a genteel pauper, a meek family man of Bociany, like his brother Shalom had become. He did not yet know what would become of him, but he would raise himself on his wings, he would seek for the light hiding behind the clouds.

But in that case, what was he doing here, in the darkness of the night? He knew well what he was doing. He was out, looking for Yoel. That was what he was doing. He was out in search of the residue of Yoel's humanity, of his manliness. He was on a pilgrimage for Yoel's soul, for his power. Dark and uncanny as that power was, it glowed and radiated a love that burned and caressed, that hurt and consoled. Yoel's soul could never have gone the way of his flesh and have vanished without a trace. Its strong aroma, like the aroma of wine in an empty wine bottle, would linger on forever in all that Yoel had touched with his hands and his feelings.

"Ye-ho-el!" he called out in the darkness. "Yoel!" Was he calling the all-knowing angel Mittatron, or the earthly human friend, to come and help him find what he was out to seek? He checked himself. Would calling out

Yoel's name summon him from the darkness? In what form? After all, it was not the physical Yoel that he, Yacov, was after. Although he longed for the man, he had already made peace with the finality of his disappearance. What he craved was Yoel's innermost being; he craved the air about Yoel, so that he could breathe it in and absorb it with all his senses. But what shape could that ethereal Yoel take on to become graspable by one's senses?

The darkness responded to this question with a vision. Yacov had often talked with Yoel about visions. Imagination and thought created a man's visions, which in a certain way consisted of matter, the matter of dreams that took on their own conceivable physicality. Dreams were the rays of awareness that broke through the barrier of the mind's limitations. Presently Yacov, as he rushed headlong down the Wide Poplar Road, saw an apparition. A female form came soaring toward him through the darkness. She stopped, looming in the distance, in the middle of the road, arms spread wide, as if she were preventing him from going any further. "No entry," she warned him. But as he drew nearer, she receded. "Enter!" she seemed to entice him.

It was not the first time that he had seen this particular vision after Yoel's death. It had flashed past his inner eye when, in his alcove, he had reached under the bed for the bottle of *monopolka*. Like a germinating seed it had been growing within his mind until it now appeared before him in its full size. The woman had a long slim waist, swaying hips, long legs with bare feet, and streams of cascading blond hair. Her name was not Binele, but the craving for a touch of her, which was tearing him apart, had some relation to his feelings for Binele. But this new vision was opening a path in the dark that he felt would bring him as close to Yoel as he could ever come. He knew full well where he was racing to.

His gaze sharpened. He was at the point in the road where the smithy should have come into sight. In fact, he saw patches of dark shadow rise against the blackness of the night. Should he head in their direction? When he left his room, he had had enough presence of mind to take along a few matches and a small piece of kindling wood. With such sureness had he lied to himself, telling himself that he was on his way to Yoel's hut. So should he in fact enter Yoel's hut now, light the kindling wood, and look around? Perhaps he would go over to the water bench and remove the greasy deck of playing cards from the drawer to keep as a souvenir? He had not been to the smithy since Yoel's death. Perhaps he would indeed have the sensation of being in Yoel's presence when he stood between the walls of the hut; there he would inhale the smell of the living Yoel as one inhales the smell of wine from an empty wine bottle.

No. Yoel had never lived in that hut. He had only sheltered himself there. His real home, his dwelling, was located inside himself. There he had carried all his treasures, all the reproductive seeds of his humanity, and had shared them with whomever he met, spreading them over the slices of peasant bread, sprinkling them onto the bowls of sour cream and scattering them on the basins full of cherries. And, while doing this, he had grown increasingly richer. Yoel's relationship with the Almighty and with other human beings was one and the same. Even trees and inanimate objects were his friends, if he invested his emotions in them. But not walls. Walls were empty shells, dead skin that Yoel had shed, leaving it to join the pieces of junk in his junkyard. So if Yoel lived on in some way, it was in the objects of his passion. He lived on in the village across the field, in the existence of the children whose lives he had saved, and even more tangibly he could be found in that one particular human form . . .

Instead of making for the smithy, Yacov turned in the opposite direction, in the direction of the field across which he had walked—or rather crawled on all fours—to claim Yoel's body. Now it was Yoel's soul that he was coming to claim.

He remembered well. Yoel had once told Abrashka how to find it. It was the first hut in the village. There was a light still burning in the window just as in some other windows of the village. The wisest thing to do would be to first peer inside through the windowpane. But he had no patience. He dashed toward the door, rapped on it, and waited for what seemed an eternity.

"Please open, Wanda," he called in an odd-sounding, controlled voice.

Was it she or someone else who had opened the door? He did not stop to look. He lurched forward, halted in the middle of the room, and took out the bottle of *monopolka* from his pocket. He reached it out to the shadowy female figure who stood in the interior of the room at a distance from him. "I came so that we can drink Yoel's bottle of *monopolka* together." He said this calmly in his strangely controlled voice, but inwardly he felt himself trembling.

Wanda was wearing her usual long, pleated skirt fastened tightly at the waist over a loose unbuttoned blouse. The tiny embroidered flowers on the blouse's sleeves and neck were covered by waves of her heavy hair. Combed and shiny, the waves of hair were draped like curtains all around her shoulders, opening like a gate in the front to expose a triangle of forehead, a pair of shadowy eyes, a thin, short nose that looked almost transparent, and her face's most distinguished feature—her mouth—open, large, and moist. It was with her mouth that she seemed to be looking at him, as well as with the exposed part of her neck and the part of her bosom that was both hidden and uncovered by the unbuttoned blouse.

He could see her no better when she came closer. It was as if her shadowed figure had dazzled him. Yet he noticed her long eyelashes flutter and the nostrils of her thin, sculpted nose tremble. Her mouth seemed to have lit up. Moist and red, it looked as if it had just been kissed. She was saying something but he could not grasp what it was. He did not understand. He did not listen. Her protruding bosom, the uncovered flesh that peeked out from the unbuttoned blouse, her neck, her hips under the dark folds of her skirt screamed so loudly at him that he could hear nothing else. It was Yoel who called him though that body, and it was he, Yacov, who craved to answer him through it. He put the bottle down on the table. He trembled so that he had to hide his hands and take care not to collapse. Nonchalantly, he thrust his hands into his pockets and spread his legs apart.

"Bring two glasses. We'll drink," he ordered gruffly.

Their eyes met. "I know what you've come for . . ." the stinging little flame that lit up in her eyes seemed to be telling him. She turned and covered the window with a torn kilim. With a teasing, peacock-like sway of her hips she crossed the room toward the corner where a bed covered with mountains of pillows and kilims seemed to be waiting. She dropped to her knees, rested her elbows on the edge of the sheet, folded her hands, and raised her head toward the framed picture of the Virgin Mary and Baby Jesus that hung on the wall. On a small shelf beneath the picture stood the candle that illuminated the dark room. The whisper of Wanda's prayer reached Yacov's ears; it seemed to be calling him to approach. It was not in her voice alone that he heard this whispering call. He also heard the call coming to him from the soft whiteness of her neck. Her neck shone from between the strands of her hair that now flowed down in front of her, tracing curly question marks on the sheet.

Still trembling, he came close and sat down on the floor beside her, his arm, his torso, his thigh pressed against hers. He felt the warmth of her body pouring into him. The chills running through him increased. He drew up his legs, wrapped his arms around them, and leaned his chin on his knees. When her voice stopped whispering, he said quietly. "I was his friend."

"I know. He told me," she answered.

"I bought the bottle of *monopolka* with the money he had given me the last time I saw him. I brought it with me now so that we could drink it together. Go and bring two glasses."

"Yoel drank straight from the bottle," she remarked.

Yacov heard Yoel's name pronounced in the different, alien accent that conjured up a strange, alien Yoel, a Yoel of whom he was jealous and on whose account he envied Wanda. He wanted her to repeat Yoel's name over and over again, so that he could familiarize himself with it. But of course! How could he have forgotten so soon? Yoel had used to drink straight from the bottle.

"Then we'll also drink straight from the bottle," he replied and started to get up.

She stopped him, grabbing at his sleeve, and reaching for his hand. It felt good to be thus restrained by her, to be pulled back toward her, yet he quickly freed his hand from hers. He did not want her to become aware of its tremor.

She smiled abstractedly. "I don't drink. Nor do I sing anymore. When you drink or sing, you dampen the memories. They grow blurred. I don't want this to happen. I pray to the Holy Mary and her son every night, asking that she should bring Yoel to me, and you see, ever since my grandmother and her son—my father, the fool—died, I have two sets of mothers and sons in the heavens to answer my prayers. And they all bring him back to me whenever I wish. Perhaps they've sent you to me for the same purpose."

"I . . . I . . . " Yacov stammered, glaring at her. He wanted to tell her that, on the contrary, he had come so that she should bring Yoel back to *him;* that now it was he who was praying to her all the while as she was pulling him down beside her near the bed. "I beg of you . . . " he muttered hoarsely. "Let's drink this one time, let us . . . "

She swayed. He let his gaze drown in the sea of her hair as she moved her face closer to his. "Taking even one sip would also be a sin. We must not allow it to blur . . . " Startled, he nodded his agreement. He had been thinking the very same thoughts the day before, and the day before that. But now he found it difficult, all but impossible, to stay sober for fear of the shudders that had taken hold of him. "I didn't expect . . . " he heard her continue, "that you would ever come. But since you're here, tell me . . . "

He watched his hands fall on her shoulders, watched his hands clasp her neck covered with the silk of her hair. He attacked her hips and tied her to himself with his arms looped around her waist. The touch of her burned his hands as though she were a piece of glowing white coal, as if she were a sculpture of glowing iron forged by Yoel in his smithy. She too trembled and shuddered.

"You tell *me.*" He heard his own voice rustle hoarsely in his ears. He longed to consume this sculpted, glowing flame, to let it burn in his insides, or rather to be devoured by it—and to know. Her mouth was still on his lips. Their breath mingled. Her hands and his were a part of the same body. The opening in her blouse grew larger. Her body seemed to be falling out of its clothes; his body fell out of his.

Clutching each other, they lay on the floor, mouths locked, skin glued together, arms and legs entangled, each the prisoner of the other. His hand caught on a cool, thin thread between her breasts, and a cool, toothed object struck his fingers. A small metal cross.

"I had to take it off when I was with him. But this time I must wear it because I'm frightened." She mumbled with her mouth on his ear. "You . . . you kiss me here, through the cross."

He kissed her through the cross while he imagined himself carrying it on his back—running through a desert—through a field, while a crowd of children, of peasants, men and women, old and young, were all chasing after him. The Tree of Knowledge was the Tree of Death. God had taken the shirt of innocence off Adam-Yacov's body and dressed him in the garb of sinful manhood—a double-sided black gabardine. One side shone even brighter than his former shirt of light; the other dazzled him and made his blindness grow deeper and darker than ever.

The gray of the new day was slowly brightening the sky when Yacov left Wanda's hut and made his way downhill toward the road. He did not notice when he passed Yoel's smithy and the hut. Once back at the miller's house, he sneaked into his alcove and lay awake on his bed until morning.

In the morning a distraught and saddened Reb Faivele came into the kitchen where Yacov sat, eating his breakfast bowl of kasha and buttered bread, and pleaded with him to continue working at the mill. Long Zirele came in to add her plea to her husband's. Yacov understood that both Reb Faivele and Zirele were clinging to him, as though he had the power to make them feel closer to their sons, whom they already missed badly.

He agreed to stay. Days and weeks passed. His employers were kind to him. He was doing what he had always wanted to do. He was helping out his family. Every week he brought his mother a few pounds of flour as well as potatoes and a chicken for the Sabbath. Reb Faivele paid him a few rubles weekly, which he also brought home to his mother. And besides, there were the interesting visitors, the discussions on Sabbath afternoons, the pleasant evenings when he devoured books from Reb Faivele's library or talked or played chess with Reb Faivele. At the same time his compulsion to leave was so strong that it grew into an obsession. It was just as strong a force as the one that had driven him to Wanda's door that memorable night.

Hindele the Scribe's Widow could read her son's heart like an open book. She was not clear in her own mind exactly what she wanted for Yacov, but of one thing she was certain. Although he was helping to ease her worries about the family's daily needs, she did not want him to remain a mill worker forever. The matchmaker, Reb Menashele, had been paying her visits for a very long time with all kinds of attractive marriage proposals for Yacov. Yet not even marriage seemed a satisfactory answer to what she wanted for this particular son of hers—although she reproached herself for her attitude. Was not a successful marriage for her children the dream of every Jewish mother? Was this not the crowning glory of her achievements? But what bothered Hindele was the feeling that Yacov would not be happy.

One day, a couple of years ago, she had seen Yacov from a distance in conversation with a girl with reddish braids. Even from afar Hindele could perceive the presence of a particular tension between the two. But who was the girl? Where was she? Hindele knew that she would have to wait for Yacov to come on his own and tell her about the girl. The new fashion of the young, that of finding mates of their own choice, was not to

Hindele's liking at all. Marriage was such a decisive and responsible step! It involved not only the partners themselves, but their progeny as well. How could a young, hot-headed, inexperienced person be fit to make such a vital decision? There was a reason for the proverb that said love is blind. However, it was true that her elder son, Shalom, lived in great harmony with the wife whom he had picked for himself.

Still, she could not help it. It was not the issue of Yacov's finding a wife for himself that was her major concern. She was well aware of his innate restlessness, his undefined cravings, and the contradictory impulses of his heart. She discerned them in the secretive flicker breaking through the soft calm light of his eyes. Never mind, there was no need for him to spell it all out for her. True, she badly wanted to understand him. To figure out the nature of the powers that drove him, and grasp what he was after. But more than that she wanted to know how to help him take delight in being alive and in savoring the wonders of God's world. Dimly she understood that Yacov himself was ignorant of what he wanted to do with himself.

Of late Yacov visited his mother's home frequently. Every morning he went to the synagogue to say the kaddish for Yoel and would often hang around in the shtetl for hours. He also looked up his friend Ariele, Fishele the Butcher's son, who now worked at the plush factory of his own free will, in accordance with his political principles and his belief that the proletariat was the salt of the earth. Ariele was not married yet to Rivkele, Zelig the Tailor's daughter, with whom he had been in love for a couple of years. There was no time for such things in the life of a revolutionary, he told Yacov. It saddened Yacov profoundly that, despite their affection for each other, he and Ariele had drifted so far apart, as if each of them were living in an entirely different world.

He much preferred to visit Reb Senderl the Cabalist. He talked a great deal with him about Yoel and about the things that Yoel had taught him. So on the day that he had made up his mind to leave Bociany, Yacov as usual entered the familiar dingy shop. A pair of bright childish eyes lit up in the shop's interior. Reb Senderl seemed to possess not much more than this pair of luminous eyes. Ever since the pogrom, he had grown into a shadow of himself. Even his rich silver beard had thinned out and grown sparse. Perhaps that was the reason why his eyes, contrasting so sharply with the pallor of his sunken face, seemed to shine clearer and brighter than ever. The lit, soot-covered naphtha lamp on the table faintly illuminated the yellow bricks of soap and the book that lay open in front of the old man. A ray of light coming from the lamp streaked his neckerchief. His mouth, no more than a dash of blue above the silver-haired chin, broadened into a smile as soon as Yacov entered the store.

"There he sits, old Reb Senderl, my childhood mentor," Yacov said to himself as if he were fixing the image before his eyes in his memory. He registered in his mind the smells that he inhaled: the smell of soap, the rancid odor of the humid walls, and the smell of the grimy naphtha lamp. He also registered the sounds that he absorbed with his ears: the hushed lilt of Reb Senderl's voice, as he greeted him. The voice seemed to be devoid of any physicality, as if the many years of reciting, humming, and whispering lofty words had transformed it into an echo of his spirit.

The words of the greeting were the same as of old. "Welcome, Reb Yacov! What questions have you brought along today to disturb my peace of mind?" Reb Senderl stretched out his transparent hand to shake Yacov's and immediately noticed the tormented expression on his visitor's face. He knotted his eyebrows and began packing his pipe with coarse tobacco. "Has anything, God forbid, happened?" he asked.

Yacov inhaled deeply the soothing stillness that permeated the air about Reb Senderl. "It may yet happen," he answered, "to me. I'm thinking of leaving Bociany."

Reb Senderl lighted his pipe, but the light in his eyes was quenched. He spread his hand in a gesture of dejection. "Now? When there is a war raging? How can you hurt your mother so? Do you insist on making her join the crowd of weeping women? And do you have any idea, my boy, what's been going on in Bociany?"

"What do you mean, what's been going on?" Yacov asked.

"The world's coming to an end, that's what's going on." The timbre of Reb Senderl's soft voice grew tremorous. "Not enough that the war has dealt us such cruel blows, we now have to deal with that other tragedy. It has surfaced like oil to float on top of the water. The young men from the *besmedresh* have turned into heretics, apostates, and unbelievers. They've abandoned the fold and escaped straight into the arms of the Evil One. They're breaking their parents' hearts. Oh, how they're shredding them! We've become a people mourning its living sons. And what's worse, our very existence as God's people is hanging by a hair. Even the most devout and God-trusting parents are, in their despair, beginning to believe that the Evil One has finally achieved the sowing of the seeds of our destruction. And there is nothing to console them in their grief." Reb Senderl wept. Tears poured down his parchment cheeks and dripped onto the page of the open Book in front of him. In the light of the naphtha lamp his tear-stained face looked like a lantern of sorrow.

"Don't despair, Reb Senderl," Yacov put his hand on the old man's shoulder. "It isn't as bad as you think. Be it as it may, the core of Jewishness in our hearts is indestructible. We are only searching . . . "

"Searching for what?" Reb Senderl raised his woeful eyes to Yacov. "Everything you search for can be found right here." He pounded on the open Book with his small fist. "And as for that core of Jewishness, it will become fragile and perishable if we don't protect and safeguard it with the greatest care. How much time can it take before it too is lost? Perhaps even you . . . "

"All I know, Reb Senderl, is that I feel myself stifled. I'm choking. Something has gone awry."

"Why has nothing gone awry for generations? But now, suddenly . . . Perhaps you, too, are beginning to lose faith."

" All I want is to find a new path for myself."

"There is no new path, silly child. There is only one path, one road, and it is neither old nor new. It is The Road."

"But I am drawn to . . . "

"So you are. There is always that outward pull within us. Do you think that I've never been troubled by murky drives? So what if you are? The inward pull is always a million times more powerful for a true law-abiding Jew."

"I want to be captain of my own ship, as Reb Faivele the Miller puts it."

"Nonsense!" Reb Senderl waved a dismissive hand. "Are you so foolish, too, as to delude yourself into thinking that you have the power to steer your ship? Don't you know who is at the helm?"

"So I am foolish, so I want to at least have the illusion . . . " Yacov gazed affectionately at the old man. "Perhaps, Reb Senderl, after having cruised around the world, I will return to these shores and you will be waiting for me here." He stroked Reb Senderl's arm and smiled encouragingly.

Reb Senderl sniffled while trying to puff at his pipe, then he removed it from his mouth. He wiped his eyes with the palm of his small dry hand and opened the drawer of his table. He took out a tin badge thickly covered with crookedly engraved letters. "Here . . . " He choked back his tears. "Take this amulet. May it protect you . . . " He could not finish the sentence and held out his trembling hand with the amulet to Yacov. Yacov took it, mumbled a word of thanks, and bent down to kiss the old man's hand.

He left Reb Senderl's shop with a slow halting step; his heart ached with the old man's grief. In fact, he wished for nothing more than to be able to return some day to these shores, to the serenity and peace of Reb Senderl's presence, to the warmth and security of his mother's garret and her embrace, and to the beauty and simplicity of Bociany. But stronger still than all his conscious wishes was his compulsion to savor everything he was capable of savoring, just as Yoel had taught him. The concrete tangible world was of primary importance. Without it the world of the spirit had no meaning. He needed to touch this tangible world with his own hands, to see it with his own eyes, not just through books and commentaries. And in fact he nourished the desire to impress his own seal upon it, to be active in it, to achieve something, even if it were something small, of little significance, but something that was meaningful to him. The question was only whether, despite this core of his Jewishness, he would be strong enough to hold on to the thread that, like an umbilical cord, kept him tied to his origins. Or would he be severed from it and never again be able to find his way back?

The thought of his mother preyed on his mind. He knew that she differed from other mothers, that she would not sit down on a low stool to mourn him for seven days as if he were dead, no matter what sinful acts he committed. After all, she had allowed his youngest sister, Shaindele, to attend the worldly elementary school that the Germans had opened on the Narrow Poplar Road. And his mother was herself an avid reader of profane books, not just the books that she borrowed from the book peddler, but also those that Yacov had brought her to read from Reb Faivele's library. He had no doubt that she would understand him. But would that help soothe her heart?

How could he possibly weigh his mother's worries and fears for him, reasonable or not, against his own desire to see the world and live his own life? Could he help it that the world was at war precisely at the time when those needs had sprung to life within him? Yet he felt dejected and guilt ridden. And what exacerbated his guilt even further was that he had not prepared her, that he had had so little time for her during these last few years, and had kept her in the dark as to his most important thoughts and emotions. Only after Yoel's death, in order to find solace, had he begun to pay her frequent visits. Was he not teasing her by offering her that short-lived joy of renewed, though illusory, closeness?

Shalom's wife had given birth to her second son, and the day of cir-cumcision was at hand. Hindele decided to organize a small celebration in her garret. Yacov brought up a few benches from the *besmedresh* as well as a table, which was placed on the landing. Hindele's friend, Nechele the Pockmarked, the widow of the late Reb Laibele the Sexton, helped in the preparation of the refreshments, and Hindele also provided a few bottles of cherry wine.

During the celebration she let the invited Hasidim sing and dance on the tables and benches to their hearts' content. The Hasidim were so car-ried away with their singing and dancing, and Hindele and Nechele had grown so intoxicated with the merriment, that they completely forgot the fact that they all found themselves in the loft of a house so decrepit that only a miracle prevented it from collapsing. And indeed it was Yossele Abedale who sounded the alarm when he heard the floor beams emitting threatening cracking sounds. The Hasidim waited impatiently for a few minutes and when they heard nothing, resumed their merrymaking with renewed enthusiasm.

The day before, Hindele had approached Yossele Abedale with her in-vitation to the festivities. She insisted that he not shame her, heaven for-bid, by shunning her celebration. Was he not a neighbor of many years' standing? Had they not shared each other's joys and sorrows? Was he not the friend who knew more about her than anyone else in the world? And had they not danced together that memorable night of his daughters' weddings?

Yossele had been standing in front of his shop, leaning against the doorpost. He was having increasingly more trouble with his eyes. Often his eyesight was completely blurred for long frightening moments during which he nearly felt himself losing his balance. He spoke of it to no one, but he felt himself safer being on the Potcheyov than walking the roads and passing through the villages, peddling his merchandise. So he could not hide his irritation when Hindele had issued her invitation, although he had rarely been angry with her during these past few years. But this time he lashed out with vehemence, shouting at her and telling her to leave him alone with her nagging. He, go to a celebration? She wanted him to honor her table and brighten it with his presence? How? With those failing eyes of his? With his bitterness and grief at having lost his three favorite children one way or another? It was clear as day that the woman was inviting him out of pity. Never mind, he could do without her pity. He could still stand erect, proud and sturdy as an oak tree.

However, as it happened of late more often than he wished, he finally gave in to her. And when he did so, his mood changed. He knew not how it came to pass, but the grateful look in Hindele's black, plum-shaped eyes—dark, deep, and both warm and sad—and the sound of her soft caressing voice filled his heart with a soothing sweetness and rekindled his optimism. For some strange reason he even grew as cheerful as someone conquered by the charms of a nagging child.

Presently, Yossele leaned against the frame of Hindele's garret door, the way he usually stood in the door of his shop, and as soon as he heard the floor beams groan again, he again called out, "Have God in your hearts, people, the floor is giving in!"

This time there came the sound of a very loud crack. The floor shook and a few of the Hasidim fell from the benches on top of which they had been dancing. Yossele tried to save whomever he could. The men rubbed their heads, their backs, and their limbs, laughing and moaning. Hindele, relieved that there were no serious injuries, urged her guests to sit down. They did so and, squeezing themselves together, made room on the benches so that everyone found a place at one table or the other. Hindele covered the tables with white tablecloths and she, her daughters, and Nechele served the men the prepared dishes and filled the glasses, which she had borrowed from Nechele and some of her neighbors, with red cherry wine.

Reb Senderl the Cabalist, who sat at the head of his table, next to Shalom, the proud father of the new member of the congregation, drew the men into a discussion on the passages of the Talmud concerning the birth of a son. Yacov sat at the other table, listening to another pilpulistic dispute on matters of The Law. He could not take his eyes off Yossele

Abedale who sat squeezed in among the Hasidim at the same table, towering over them with his massive torso and proudly raised head. A stranger.
Yet Yacov felt himself related to him somehow. He admired Yossele's majestic presence, the broad shoulders, the rich yellow-gray beard, the stern
serious face, and he could not help thinking, "Binele sprang to life from
his seed." He scrutinized Yossele's face, trying to find a trace of her in her
father's features.

Yossele's face was full of grooves and creases, dry and hard, yet it expressed an inner composure and peace. He was definitely glad to be here.
His gladness derived from a feeling much deeper than the mere satisfaction of having given in to Hindele and thus given her pleasure. It was the
gladness of having done the right thing. It was his duty to be here. It was
his duty not to remain aloof, but to join the community in its joys and sorrows and thereby strengthen its spirit. It was important to cling devotedly
to the army of the faithful, to those who were ready to carry the burden
and the glory of Judaism no matter what. It was petty and unbecoming
for a Jew during these times to isolate himself for whatever reason or to
be bothered by whether or not one or another of his fellow Jews was to
his liking. Tragedy had struck not only him, but almost everyone of the
older Hasidim sitting at these tables. They all suffered the worst kind of
pain, inflicted not by any strangers, but by their own flesh and blood, by
those whom they loved most in the world—their children. Every drop of
wine, every bite of food shared together contributed to healing the scars
of the community's wounded spirit.

While the Hasidim ate and chatted, Hindele stood at the window behind the row of men who sat with their backs turned to her. She felt
somewhat faint and the humid air coming in through the open window refreshed her. She inhaled deeply the sharp scent of the wilting autumn
flowers wafting in from the nuns' garden, the fragrance of the fallen
leaves, the odors of the faded grass and the muddy soil. Their smells
mixed with the smell of the food and the aroma of the cherry wine. Dizzy
from both her joy and the strange sadness that had overcome her, she
could barely hold back her tears. That sadness disturbed her greatly. She
could find no tangible reason for it.

Her eyes accidentally met with Yacov's across the room. They stared at
each other with such intensity as if despite themselves they were reading
each other's most secret thoughts. Yacov found himself wilting under the
hint of adoration that he discerned in her look. He realized that he was in-

capable of finding the strength within himself to hurt her. He smiled back at her, a filial boyish smile.

⊚ 9 ⊚

THE DAY ARRIVED when Hindele saw the confirmation of something she had suspected all her life, that there was no such thing as pure joy, that as a rule life alloyed joy with bitter drops to make it bearable. She also knew that the bitterest drops, just like the sweetest ones, were often provided by those closest to one's heart, as, for instance, by one's son.

She had grown more and more aware that Yacov was not his usual self. He walked around as if he were not really there. He was absent-minded and irritable. And so Hindele had gradually come to suspect that he was thinking of going away. With trepidation she awaited the moment when he would make up his mind, and she was certain that soon he would.

In fact, he did so, in spite of himself. One day at the beginning of winter, as soon as he had sat down beside Hindele the way he had used to sit down with her in the past, she knew, before he even opened his mouth, what he was about to tell her. Still she listened to him attentively as he embarked on telling her in detail about Yoel and Abrashka and his present-day lonely life at the mill. As he talked, his eyes met hers. The anguish he read in her gaze made him realize that she knew much more about him than he could possibly tell her, and also that notwithstanding her worry, he was so much a part of her that she wanted what he wanted, whatever that might be.

"So you want to leave for Lodz," she finally said it for him, helping him broach the subject that he obviously found difficult to introduce into their conversation.

He took advantage of her question. "It's better to be gone to Lodz than be gone into the tsar's army, isn't it?" He smiled faintly. "The Germans are in Bociany and they are in Lodz too. So at least you are now free from the worry that Shalom or I might be conscripted."

"Thank Heaven for that," she nodded, thinking that he was throwing himself "with a healthy head into a sickbed." People were running away from Lodz to the small shtetlekh. There was the threat in Lodz of hunger and epidemics. Yet she had to find courage within herself to accept his decision. He was the master of his life, not she. And what would she be gaining by opposing him? "That means," she muttered, "that you think of leaving—when?"

"Tomorrow," he said.

She stood up and began to busy herself about the room. She opened the drawers of the cupboards and thrust her hands inside so that he would not notice how they trembled. She was looking for things that she could give him to take along on the trip. The winter had begun with piti-less ferocity that year. Stealthily, she glanced at Yacov, already missing him in her heart. Certainly she wanted whatever he wanted. She respected him and respected his decisions. She knew that he could not learn from her ex-periences or trials. She only prayed that he would have the wisdom and strength to learn from his own experiences and trials. However, no one could deprive her of the right and the privilege of abandoning herself to suffering, to the feeling that her heart had been cut into pieces. Of course she would postpone her tears until later, until tomorrow or after tomor-row, when he was gone. She would have a lot of time to weep and tremble and pray for him—for the rest of her life. But now she had to see to it that her eyes remained dry. Her boy, the magnificent young man who sat at the table, was following her every move with his eyes, those eyes that she likened to two tiny dishes filled with honey. She forced herself to meet his gaze, a gaze she could hardly bear, yet had to bear and wanted to bear.

"Why don't you say something, Mameshie?" she heard him ask.

"What is there to say, Yacov?" She collected herself and walked over to him, keeping herself as straight as her stooped back permitted. She put her small work-worn hand on his head, covering it like a second skullcap. She kissed his forehead. "You know well what I have to say." Again she sat down beside him, taking both his hands in hers. "You know that being away from home is like being doubly exiled. But it would be selfish of me to try and convince you to stay. No human being, not even a mother, should jealously guard her treasure. It must be shared, it must be offered to the world. So I must allow you to become a wanderer. It is written that the Almighty said to our father Abraham, '*Lech Lecho*,' 'get thee out into the world.' The *medresh* says that Abraham our father was like a bottle of perfume whose fragrance can be savored only when in motion." She swallowed hard. "There's little in the cupboards that I can give you to take along."

She gave him to take along her tearful half-smile hidden in the corners of her mouth.

When Yacov arrived in Lodz, the rigors of the German occupation were already firmly established. Starvation raged. The factories were closed. The sirens howled no more. The tension and excitement of production and industrialization had been silenced by the war as if by the blow of an ax. Like a body drained of energy, the city had collapsed into impotence.

The new rulers plundered the city, carrying off anything that might be of use to their *Heimat*'s war machine: food, raw materials, machinery, and able-bodied workers. Members of the militia went from house to house looking for copper pots, brass mortars, samovars, and doorknobs and requisitioned them for the production of ammunition.

The Russian ruble had lost its value. The hordes of unemployed who aimlessly roamed the snow-covered sidewalks looked like vagabonds and beggars dressed in rags. The typhoid epidemic had passed. Now it was the turn for tuberculosis. Funeral corteges of both Gentiles and Jews followed one another in somber processions through the streets. The wealthy as well as the poor and unemployed—anyone who had the slightest opportunity—left for the villages and shtetlekh where food was more easily available.

As soon as Yacov had arrived in Lodz, he asked to be directed to a Hassidic *shtibl*. Someone indicated a *shtibl* located on Piotrkowska Street. It was a cold, windy evening. He was frozen and exhausted from the long trip in an open peasant wagon. Sleepy, frostbitten, he felt the icy desolation of the town spreading over his heart. But the moment he stepped over the threshold of the smoke-filled dingy *shtibl*, a pleasant warmth embraced him. A "cannon" oven, the fire inside it lively hissing, greeted his eye. The room was packed with Hasidim. An old gray-bearded man stood at the pulpit reciting the evening prayer. There was so much noise around the reciting man that he could hardly be heard.

Yacov plowed his way through to the oven, put his bundle of belongings on the floor, and then sat down on it, turning his hands and face toward the heat coming from the oven. He scanned the room with his eyes.

Lights and shadows played on the frozen windowpanes. The cracked peeling walls were illuminated by a sooty lamp that flickered, dangling from a cord in the center of the grimy ceiling. A crooked grandfather clock leaned against the wall, supported by a crooked bookcase. The books looked worn, their covers twisted and bent, the pages rolled and frayed at the edges. In the depths of the room stood an old cupboard that served as a receptacle for the Torah Scroll. The table in front of it, where the men reciting the prayer stood, was covered by a sheet of dirty paper.

Yacov examined the faces of the Hasidim, some of whom sat on the benches along the two rows of tables on top of which heavy open tomes were scattered. The rest stood around the room in knots and clusters. He was looking for a face inviting enough to be approached and asked for advice.

A teakettle was passing from hand to hand. The Hasidim poured boiling chicory coffee into tin cups from it. Holding the cups in their hands, they continued talking, switching the cups from one hand to the other, depending on which hand they needed to punctuate their speech with an animated gesture. Their heads were in continuous motion as their lips avidly sipped and slurped and spilled both words and coffee. They were discussing politics and the Jew-hatred rampant on both sides of the battle lines, among the Prussian officers as well as the Russian gendarmes and officials. The Russians were in the process of displacing Jews from all the territories close to the lines of battle for the sole reason that the Jews knew the German language. That was enough to consider them a dangerous, treacherous element. Those Hasidim who were not discussing war, discussed their day-to-day worries, mainly those concerning health and food.

"Here, this will help you warm up faster," Yacov heard someone say to him. He raised his head. A tall, fairly corpulent, young man, neatly-dressed and looking older than himself, held out a cup of coffee to him. "I saw you come in with your bundle. Where are you from?" the young man asked.

Yacov thanked him for the coffee and told him where he had come from. Without ceremony the young man seated himself on the edge of the bench across from Yacov. His round full face with its prominent, finely shaped eagle nose had an air of openness and amiability about it. A pair of bright, slightly protruding eyes shone at Yacov with the warm gleam of comradeship.

"First I need a place to sleep," Yacov told him. "and then I want to find work."

The young man shook his head in disbelief, "You must have been crazy to have undertaken a voyage to this dead town in order to find work. If I were you, brother, I'd get up straight away and return to where I came from. Or perhaps you came here rather to atone for your sins?"

"Not quite," Yacov rejoined and looked the young man over more closely. There was an air of refinement and nobility about him, despite his unassuming comportment and attractive directness of manner. "What about you?" Yacov asked. "Why didn't *you* escape from this dead town as you call it, although I can see that there are quite a few Jews still around." He indicated the crowded *shtibl* with his chin.

"Not everyone can afford to get away," the young man shrugged. "And as for me, I am rather the exception than the rule. In fact, my entire family is on forced winter vacation in the country. I've come back to escape from the boredom and also to take care of my father's house. In Lodz, you understand, I personally can find the means to keep me from going insane more easily than in the country. But as I told you, not everyone can compare himself to me. It's only when I've nothing better to do that I drop in to this *shtibl*. It's lively and homey here, as you can see. Here the rich and the poor are treated alike; that pleases the poor and in a way also the rich, in particular the has-beens like myself. This *shtibl* is known by the name of Reb Mayer Weiskop, the great ex-industrialist who is its founder and supporter. And you've the honor of talking to his son. So now you can, I suppose, understand my exceptional situation. My name is Baruch. What's yours?"

"Yacov Polin," Yacov replied. They shook hands.

Baruch pointed to the opposite corner of the room. "Can you see the man who's sitting there? He is the main reason for my coming here so often. He's the only one who never talks about the war or about matters of livelihood. Because what do you think is going on here? Nothing but hollow chatter, regurgitation of the same issues over and over again. But that man there, in his corner . . . At least he studies the Zohar day and night. So I sit myself down next to him, ask him my favorite set of questions, and this prevents my mind from freezing over."

Yacov was not in the least inclined to discuss any spiritual matters at the moment, yet he could not refrain from asking, "What's your favorite set of questions about?"

Baruch waved his hand dismissively. "Oh, that depends on my whims at the moment, on the time of the day, and on the day of the week. Today, for instance, Rabbi Akiva's saying, 'All is predestined, yet the choice is given,' has been rattling about in my brain nonstop. The older I grow the more I see the contradiction in terms and the less I can find anything to bridge it. Even the nonbelievers are nonplussed on the issue. They replace the Almighty with fashionable words like 'nature' or 'economic conditions' or 'environment' or 'the historic imperative' or some other inflated word. The truth of the matter is, brother, that the entire issue of freedom, about which there is such a ballyhoo going on in the world, is nothing but a pie in the sky."

Baruch interrupted himself. A man at the pulpit was intoning the prayer for the mortally ill. Baruch leaned over to Yacov and whispered, "If you wait here a little while longer, you'll be able to accompany the crowd to Baluty, to a celebration for a newborn male. The newly rich of Baluty, mind you, entertain with a lavish hand."

"Who are the newly rich of Baluty?" Yacov asked. He had heard that Baluty was the slum district of Lodz where only paupers lived.

Baruch raised a finger into the air. "They are yesterday's rag collectors, the thieves, the riffraff, that's who they are. They have embraced the noble and lucrative profession of smuggling. A hungry city, emptied of food and clothing, pays with gold for a bite of food, a piece of clothing, or for anything usable. And such people, you understand, are afraid of nothing. So the most cunning and agile amongst them are feathering their nests. It has taken my father a lifetime to make his fortune, to build up a business, and to lay the foundations of a trade. Nights he did not sleep, days he did not see the light of the sun, so enslaved was he by his goal. But with this scum it happened overnight. In a storm the garbage rises to the top."

Yacov stood up. "I must ask if anyone here knows of a place where I can find lodgings or where a good pair of hands is needed," he said. "I've worked in a mill."

Baruch also stood up. He pulled at Yacov's sleeve. "There is the *gabe*," he said as they began to plow their way through the clusters of Hasidim. "The *gabe* knows everyone and everything. He's a kind of job-and-quarters broker."

When he saw the two young men approach him, the attendant of the *shtibl* called the *gabe*, drew a red kerchief from the pocket of his shabby gabardine, and blew his nose loudly as if in order to hear them better. He was a short but agile man. With his small reddish hands he shook two of Yacov's fingers and then began to quiz him on where he came from, what his name and lineage were, and whether he knew one or another of the followers of the Alexander Rabbi in Bociany or Chwosty. When he heard that Yacov was a descendant in direct line of the Rabbi of Wurke, the *gabe* blew his nose again, this time with an air of great reverence, and said in a hoarse voice, "Wait here." He vanished into the crowd and returned a few minutes later, dragging by the arm another man of similar height but twice as fat.

"Reb Saivel Malkes!" the *gabe* introduced the man with much respect and pompously blew his nose again.

Reb Saivel Malkes gave Yacov his small plump hand to shake. "A weaver in my workshop has come down with consumption. So now I've got two looms standing idle," he said hurriedly. "I don't have to tell you that there's no rush in the business, but a grandchild of the Wurker Rabbi must have a place to rest his head and a crust of bread to eat." The *gabe* had obviously briefed him on the important details of Yacov's biography and lineage. Reb Saivel Malkes sized Yacov up with a skeptical eye. "You haven't got a clue about weaving, have you? You haven't studied it at the *besmedresh,* eh? Never mind. There's plenty of time these days to introduce a young man to the secrets of the trade. Wait for me. We'll go to the celebration and then you'll come home with me. I'm giving you a place to stay."

Yacov thanked him, thanked the *gabe,* and thanked Baruch. Baruch pressed his hand, taking his leave. "You're leaving?" Yacov asked regretfully. "Too bad. Now we could have talked. I mean, the problem of freedom . . . it interests me very much."

"My problem is that I'm not free right now," Baruch answered, smiling. He tilted his head toward Yacov and whispered in his ear, "Remember one thing. There is a difference between what goes on in the *shtibl* and what goes on at this particular Hasid's home. Here you two are equals. There, he is the boss. So don't be overly delicate with him, because surely he won't be delicate with you."

"What do you mean by that?" Yacov stared at him.

"You'll see for yourself. I'm not a gossip." With that Baruch left the *shtibl.*

Yacov signed a contract to work at Reb Saivel Malkes's workshop as a weaver's apprentice for two years. The workshop was located in the heart of Baluty, in an enormous backyard surrounded by grimy tenement houses. The workshop itself occupied a one-storied wooden structure at the front. Some of its windows faced the street, others the backyard. The workshop consisted of a few rooms on the ground floor, each of which harbored two or three dark weaving looms, whose aspect brought to Yacov's mind the skeletons of nondescript monsters. The space along the walls was taken up by the straw mattresses on which the weavers and their apprentices slept. Reb Saivel, his wife and five children lived on the upper floor.

Although Reb Saivel was short and fat, he possessed the energy of ten giants. He was never still and his crafty head was always filled with colossal ideas about how to keep himself on the surface and stay there despite the storms raging on the sea of life. It was, in fact, true that two looms stood idle in Reb Saivel's workshop. It was, however, untrue that there was a slack in his business. Reb Saivel worked hand in glove with the greatest smugglers of Baluty who provided him with his raw materials, that is, wools of the best quality. Reb Saivel could afford to eat meat and hallah in the middle of the week, but he preferred to pass as one of those work-shop owners whose luck had fallen, like bread with the buttered side down, due to the vicissitudes of the war. He was forever sighing and complaining that he had come down in the world and how bitter the times were. The two idle looms at his workshop were for public show, to ward off an evil eye, so that the "the world" should not envy him or betray him to the police.

Work at Reb Saivel's started at six in the morning and continued until long after the boss and his family had gone to sleep. Breakfast and supper consisted of chicory coffee and a slice of black buttered bread. At lunch time, the workers were given a sour water-soup, which however had a meaty smell, and a chunk of black unbuttered bread to be consumed in haste while sitting at the looms. If Reb Saivel allowed a half an hour's break in the afternoon, the workers leaned their folded arms against their looms and napped. As a result, the workers felt themselves to be nothing but extensions of the wooden monsters at the sides of which they spent their days.

Yacov was taught the trade by a middle-aged, sickly looking man whose mane of gray, unkempt hair was larger than his green wrinkled face. The man had small, watery eyes whose pupils nestled in a net of red veins. He wore a pair of eye glasses that sat precariously on the tip of his bumpy nose. The glasses were attached to his ears by a piece of wire on one side, and a piece of string on the other. He was called Laibel the Hump not because he had a real hump—that is, he had not come into the world with one—but because he had this professional deformation from having spent his entire life hunched over a loom. His back and drooping shoulders formed a kind of basin, round in the back, hollow in the front. Even when he walked he looked as if he were attached to an invisible loom.

Yacov was taught the trade after Laibel the Hump was finished with his own work. That was what Reb Saivel had ordered. Yacov himself had more important things to do during the day. He had to earn his board by helping the boss's wife. She could of course afford a maid, but she was afraid to "tease people's eyes." And why should she feed another mouth and waste food during these bad times when some of her neighbors were living on five pfennigs a day, if Yacov could do for her all the chores that a maid could? He swept and scrubbed the floors, took her children to the latrine, chopped wood, carried water, peeled potatoes, and went on errands. At the sight of him the neighbors in the yard commented on what a "Jewish heart" Reb Saivel and his wife had, taking in another mouth to feed during such bitter times.

Laibel the Hump was a good and patient teacher and Yacov could have quickly learned the trade from him. However, Laibel had the habit of keeping his bumpy nose, with the glasses on its tip, close to Yacov's face and talking to him about matters that had no direct connection with what Yacov was doing with his hands. An indirect connection they did have, because Laibel's monologues had only one topic, namely, the working class. When Laibel warmed to this topic, it was as if he were pulling strings that had neither knots nor ends. His voice flowed smoothly, with subdued passion. It poured into Yacov's heart with a *Gemara* lilt and stirred it so that Yacov soon forgot to move his hands. Fortunately the boss was asleep.

As Laibel talked, Yacov visualized the working class in the form of one of the enormous golems that his mother had told him about when he was a child—a golem who served his boss, the *tsadik* who had created him, with humility and servility, while it never entered anyone's mind to ask the golem what he himself wanted. When Laibel spoke of the Jewish Workers' Bund, Yacov saw the golem straighten his back, growing increasingly taller, until his master was unable to erase the word *emes,* truth, from his forehead. The breath of God penetrated the golem's chest and expanded it, filling it with pride and self-respect. When Laibel recounted what had happened in 1905, in this town, which was so ugly and yet so fascinating,

Yacov could vividly visualize the street fights and the battles on the barricades. He could see the golem breaking his chains in rebellion, could see
him spilling his blood in order to save the sanctity of life. The lost revolution of 1905 had wounded the golem but had not destroyed him. Unlike
the golem of his mother's stories, the golem of Laibel the Hump's stories
was indestructible, since the need for justice and freedom was indestructible. When Laibel described how the Cossacks had attacked demonstrators, when he described in gruesome detail the executions and pogroms,
Yacov's heart pounded as if he were personally present during those
scenes, seeing himself as the victim of the brutalities.

At times he thought that the hand of fate had, for better or worse,
brought him together with this fragile man in glasses, whose voice
sounded both so powerful and so intimate that it seemed to spring from a
source hidden within Yacov himself. In his mind he saluted his childhood
friend Ariele and felt closer to him than ever before.

Laibel's continuous talking sessions disturbed Yacov to such an extent
that they deprived him of his sleep. He was mystified by the power that
Laibel had over him merely by the magnetic force of his words. He would
never have believed that words, spoken words, could posses the means of
actually becoming deeds, becoming almost acts of violence. Yoel the
Blacksmith and his teachings had of course left an indelible mark on
Yacov's mind and heart. Yet Yoel's words had never dimmed the independence of Yacov's own thoughts or so at least he believed. But he felt that
in some way Laibel's words deprived him of independence, that they vio-
lated his soul in a strange manner, and that he, Yacov, was so mesmerized
by these words that he allowed Laibel to dominate him.

Alone at night, on his straw pallet, Yacov tried to regain control over
his thoughts by translating Laibel's words into his own language. As he lay
with his eyes open, he saw the line of prisoners marching through the
marketplace of Bociany on their way to Siberia. He could clearly hear the
clank of the chains on the men's arms and legs. In his mind he saw those
men stumbling through snow-covered taigas, through the empty white
plains of homelessness. He also saw himself on that Passover eve when
the Gentile boys had chased after him, set on making him perform the
role of their Jesus. And he saw himself at an even more distant time in his
life, on the very first day of grief he could remember, when his father and
his brother Itchele were still alive. His mother had not earned a penny on

the Potcheyov that day. The family went to bed hungry, and for the first time he had heard his mother weep in secret on her bed.

The young man, Baruch Weiskop whom Yacov had met at the *shtibl,* believed that freedom was a pie in the sky. Perhaps he was right, because man was in fact chained to the narrowness of his limitations; man found himself confined in the cage of his destiny, unable to grasp what lay beyond. Yet inside that cage man was free to chose between good and evil. Within that cage brotherhood was possible. But while Yacov thought all these thoughts and relived the painful images of his past, he had the strange feeling that the magic of Laibel's words had conjured them up. His heart pined more than ever for Yoel the Blacksmith's words, but he felt that Laibel's words in their overwhelming immediacy had obliterated them.

During the course of that long winter Yacov saw little of the streets outside. It was very cold and his clothes barely kept him warm, even indoors. Only the upstairs rooms of the boss's flat were heated. And then he had not got the time to see the town. The only parts of it that he had managed to acquaint himself with were the streets of Baluty through which he ran on errands for his mistress. And on the Sabbath he badly needed to rest. Spending the whole day within the confines of the house, sitting for increasingly longer hours at the loom, exhausted him. His back felt as if it had been cut in two. It deprived him of the energy or the will to go out.

Spring sneaked slowly into the town. In Lodz the arrival of spring was heralded not by trees bursting into bloom, nor by the twitter of birds, nor by the smell of plowed fields. Here its arrival was announced by the stench of the thawing gutters and latrines. Yet the sun blinked softy through the window of the workshop and the snatches of blue sky that he could see through it began to entice Yacov to get himself out of the house. Whenever he took the boss's children to the outhouse, or chopped wood in the backyard, or pumped the water pump, he kept his head turned toward the sky and thought of the storks that by now would have arrived in Bociany. He missed his mother and he missed something else, something that he was unable to formulate in words.

He asked himself over and over again what he was doing in this bitter exile and was amazed at himself for having given up Reb Faivele's Blue Mountain, and the expanse of landscape surrounding the windmill, in exchange for such a miserable existence. He wondered at himself. Why on earth had he, of his own free will, sold himself into this slavery? Perhaps Baruch Weiskop was right to have asked him if he, Yacov, had come to Lodz to atone for his sins. But Yacov knew, knew with the kind of knowledge that was beyond any rational explanation, that he had to be where he was, that his road, whether he wanted it or not, led precisely through here.

He was glad to have to carry the many pails of water demanded by Reb Saivel's wife every day. There was no canalization or water plumbing in Lodz. True, there was a faucet in the boss's house, since there was a water reservoir in the garret that the janitor would pump full of water every day. But during the warm days the heder boys would sneak into the loft and stealthily bathe themselves in the reservoir. So Reb Saivel's wife, in fear of epidemics, refused to use the water from the faucet. After all, she had a skilled water carrier in Yacov.

Yacov turned the wheel of the water pump, drank himself full of fresh cold water, washed his face, wet his hair, and took delight in the images that the water evoked in his mind: a stormy downpour; a race, barefoot, through the Wide Poplar Road in Bociany; two reddish-yellow braids; a wreath of bluebells on a girl's head; the smell of sun-baked heather all about the girl—a girl whose presence he could feel in the radiance of the spring day embracing this very town. As he crossed the yard with the two pails in his hands, he inhaled deeply. The air smelled sweetly, despite its stench. It smelled of Binele.

One warm Sabbath afternoon Reb Saivel asked Yacov to accompany him to the Hasidic *shtibl* on Piotrkowska Street. As soon as they entered the *shtibl,* Yacov realized how much Reb Saivel enjoyed being seen with him. Everyone at the *shtibl* seemed to know that Reb Saivel was treating the young provincial like his own son. People praised Reb Saivel to his face, while Yacov's face burned with shame. He was Reb Saivel's possession, a convenient tool used by Reb Saivel to gain prestige for himself. Yacov pretended not to mind his role. It was worthwhile to pay this price for the chance it gave him of meeting Baruch Weiskop. In fact, that day Baruch happened to drop in at the *shtibl.*

The moment he saw him, Baruch called out across the crowded room, "Yacov Polin! *Sholem Aleykhem!*" He got himself over to Yacov, snatched him by the sleeve and pulled him out of the room. "You see, I remembered your name," He beamed.

Yacov smiled back at him. "I remembered yours too. I hoped to find you here."

"Come, lets go down into the yard for a breath of fresh air."

Talking in hurried broken sentences, each curious about the other, they rushed down the stairs.

Yacov said candidly, "I consider myself lucky to have met you. Somehow my life has arranged itself in such a way that if I don't have a least one close friend, I can't breath with both nostrils."

"So you picked me to fulfill that function?" The gaze of Baruch's slightly bulging eyes beamed at Yacov with their intense heat. "Then let me warn you, brother, that I'm not good at these things. If someone takes one step toward me, I take two steps away from him."

Yacov smiled. "Yet it was you who took the first step toward me, remember?"

They walked over to the outer sill of a downstairs window and leaned against it. Groups of young men who had also come out of the *shtibl* stood around in the yard. Hands locked behind their backs, they swayed, shook their heads, and whispered heatedly among themselves. Yacov asked, indicating the young men with a flicker of a glance. "Haven't you got any friends among them?"

Baruch shook his head. "No, I haven't. First of all, they don't trust me. They know me too well, understand? And besides, I remind them myself that I am still an upper-class man, even though my father has come down in the world. I told them that I consider all their heated talk as being nothing but child's play, and play that is dangerous to boot. Even the war hasn't opened their eyes. On the contrary. They expect the Messiah to come riding out from the battlefields. They want to change human nature, no more no less. Do you see that fellow there, pushing a leaflet into the other's pocket? It's not a question of fearing the Secret Police nowadays. They are hiding their secrets from the other Hasidim or from their parents."

"What kind of leaflets are these?" Yacov asked.

"They call it 'literature,' woe to us! Some literature!"

Yacov thought of Ariele and the young men of the *besmedresh* in Bociany and of the pamphlets that Laibel the Hump had given him to read. One of the pamphlets was called, *What Every Worker Should Know and Remember,* another was called, *The Passover Haggadah in a New Version,* in which Laibel's ideas were set down in a simple Yiddish, although the thoughts that they had awoken in Yacov were not simple at all. His curiosity aroused, he pulled at Baruch's sleeve. "Come, let's join them,"

Baruch brushed off his hand, "Not me!"

"What are you afraid of? They won't kill you."

"Don't be so sure. For their ideals, as they call them, they're ready to kill their fathers and mothers. They're very fluent in strong words."

"The Bundists?"

"The Bundists, the Bolsheviks, the Anarchists, the Zionists, devil take them all! With the same zest that they used to dance a Hasidic dance, they're now dancing the revolutionary dance, the dance of death. How the yeshiva and the *besmedresh* have led to all this, kill me if I know."

Yacov was about to say that he did know how, but he checked himself and gave in to Baruch. He did not approach the young men that day. Talking with Baruch was more important. There was something appealing in Baruch's face, in his direct warm gaze, in which a craving for joy seemed to alternate with shadows of despair. Despite Baruch's reserve and his "warnings," Yacov felt that the two of them were linked by a thread of inner relatedness, that like in himself, there was a spirit of rebelliousness in Baruch, a rebelliousness of a particular nature. It was a rebelliousness that was vague and indefinable, yet it seemed to have taken on a more tangible aspect now that it was juxtaposed against the rebelliousness of the young men who were gathered in the yard. It did not matter that Baruch's attitude toward these young men and Yacov's own attitude were in such sharp contrast. But for that reason he still restrained himself from openly sharing his thoughts with Baruch.

On the way home Yacov walked at Reb Saivel's side, oblivious to the latter's conversation with the other Hasidim. Instead, he observed the people in the street. Weariness and hunger were written on their faces. The entire town in its monstrosity seemed fatally ill. Oddly enough Yacov had the impression that thanks to his short conversation with Baruch, the son of a wealthy man, the suffering of the town penetrated him even more deeply than it had on other occasions. He repeated to himself more firmly than ever, "This is my destiny. Here, in this valley of tears, I must find my way. Here I must come to understand myself and take hold of my life."

He thought that this dreadful town was sublime in its own way, sublime in the vastness of its grayness, of its bleakness and of its depths of suffering. In its broken rhythms, in its stifled tempo a powerful outcry was struggling to be heard—the silent scream of never-satisfied human cravings, of never-satisfied wants and needs.

During the ensuing summer months Yacov, one way or another, managed to get himself out of the house for an hour or so every day. On Sabbath afternoons he walked the littered streets of Baluty. Doors and windows stood open. The sounds of babies crying reached his ears from inside the moldy huts. So did the sounds of Sabbath song, the sounds of heder boys being tested by their fathers, and the sounds of wistful Yiddish songs that in their simplicity went straight to his heart. As he walked, he scanned the faces of the girls who strolled by, looking for one with reddish-yellow braids, prominent cheek bones, a skin dotted with tiny freckles, and a pair of slanted piercing eyes.

One Sabbath evening he let himself be swept along by a an excited crowd that headed for one of the grimy backyards where a wedding was being celebrated. He observed the people's faces as they watched the four-pronged bridal canopy being set up near the water pump. There was a mingling of festive capotes, fur-edged hats, and shabby gabardines. The candles in the people's hands flickered with their longing for the great light, for the eternal Sabbath, the day of complete perfection, the day of serenity and peace. Tears the size of beads cascaded down green-looking female cheeks as the *dian* read the marriage contract to the bride and groom, whom the weeping women had probably never seen before. "How near this is to my heart," Yacov thought. "This pitiful, woeful joy. How loudly it resounds within me with the longing of Bociany for the coming of the Messiah."

The Hasidim sang and danced in a circle, while the women danced a *patcher*. When the rhythms started to sweep him along, Yacov joined the circle of dancing Hasidim, shut his eyes, and saw himself arm in arm with Yoel and Abrashka dancing on the Wide Poplar Road in front of the smithy.

It was not an easy task to make Reb Saivel Malkes yield and allow Yacov to leave for Bociany to visit his mother. When Reb Saivel finally gave in to Yacov's pleas, a year had gone by. It was wintertime and the holiday of Hanukkah was approaching.

Dressed in an old gabardine that he had brought from Bociany and that was falling apart, Yacov set out on the road, and before he even arrived in Bociany, he was already there in his mind. Wrapped up in kilims, he sat huddled in the wagon on which he had hitched a ride, shivering with cold, while his heart was full of summer. In his mind's eye he could already see Bociany's magnificent wooden synagogue as it looked on the arrival of the Sabbath, basking in the mildest colors of the Almighty's pallet. He saw the gauzy veil of lights and shadows peeling away from the sky to enwrap the shtetl in a kind of otherworldly beauty. He longed for the sights and sounds of those hours when the profane dress of Bociany had vanished and the translucent Sabbath air filled every corner with serenity and loftiness. He saw his mother in his mind's eye, standing in the fragrant loft, blessing the Sabbath candles; he saw the expanse of fields, the birch wood, the lake, the poplar roads, the Blue and White Mountains. He saw Abrashka and Yoel; he heard the sound of a Hasidic tune carried by a female voice; and he saw the body of a woman, smelling of heather, straw, rain, and earth. He saw Wanda . . . He saw Binele . . .

On the first Hanukkah eve he sat next to his mother, in the loft. His sisters, his brother Shalom with his wife and children all sat around the table. It was odd to compare one's longing for a place with the reality of seeing it before one's eyes. The garret appeared smaller and shabbier than Yacov remembered it, his mother looked older, his sisters and brother were more distant.

The first lit Hanukkah candle flickered on the window sill. Yacov held Shalom's little girl, Liebele, on his lap. He was telling the family of the wonders of the great city of Lodz, a city too big to be walked through on foot. As he talked, he grew aware that the words that he used sounded awkward and out of place between these walls, as if he were speaking in a foreign language. A surge of great love rose in his heart for everybody and everything that surrounded him, and yet, at the same time, he felt himself alienated from it all—except his mother.

The potato pancakes that Hindele continued to serve vanished from the plate even before she had managed to put it down on the table. Never before had Yacov known how exquisite crusty potato pancakes sprinkled with sugar could taste. He could not get enough of them. Hindele goaded him, "Eat, eat in good health. We're in no danger of running out."

The sight of Yacov made Hindele's heart sore. He had come home with yellowish caved-in cheeks, his body as thin and emaciated as if he were suffering from consumption. She bit her lips, making an effort not to utter a word about his looks. What would she accomplish by letting him know that her tears were not only on account of her joy at seeing him, but were also due to her worry about his health? She was determined to feed him so well during the few days of his visit that it would provide him with energy at least for a while. She did not stop cooking and baking, and placing bowls brimful with food before him on the table.

Night after night she sat up with Yacov, talking with him for long hours. His sisters, Gitele and Shaindele, both of whom now helped Hindele earn a living as well as they could, were already fast asleep. So Hindele and Yacov, their voices hushed, sat by the light of the flickering Hanukkah candles. He munched on poppy-seed cookies and sipped chicory coffee from a mug, his eyes focused on Hindele's creased, worn face. He told her of all the people he had met, of all the happenings that had imprinted themselves on his memory. His voice rasped somewhat waveringly when he started to tell her about Laibel the Hump, the nonbeliever, who was teaching him the weaver's trade.

She noticed his discomfort and said to reassure him, "Believe me, Yacovshie, the Almighty prefers nonbelievers with warm hearts to the pious with hearts of stone. But on the other hand, I don't envy the nonbelievers. They are neither Jews nor Gentiles. And then, this nonbeliever of yours preaches nothing new. You should know that for every old song, a new melody can be found."

Put at ease and grateful for her words, he moved closer to her. "The thing is," he avowed, "that the Bundists support the idea of revolution. They are not against shedding blood if necessary, of using Asmodeus's own weapons in their fight against him."

Hindele chewed on her underlip thoughtfully, then she rejoined, "That's because they cannot rid themselves of the evil in their own hearts."

"They are ready to sacrifice their lives."

"In order to bring the Messiah by force?"

"They say that our blind belief in the coming of the Messiah is a hindrance on the road to redemption. They believe in man, Mameshie. Man must take his fate in his own hands."

"Are they such nonbelievers?" Hindele was startled. "Don't they believe in the existence of God at all?" She fixed her astonished eyes on Yacov. "I thought that your nonbelievers merely absent themselves from prayer, that they walk around with their heads bared, and that they nourish the notion that traditional dress brings them no closer into the presence of the Almighty. But to deny Him? What then do those poor souls know of life if they live in such darkness? You see, Yacov dear, how poverty and misery can throw people into the straits of purgatory? Can you imagine how much suffering such a person must have borne before he arrived at such conclusions? Job also blubbered like a madman when he was struck by one blow after another."

"But what solution is there?" Yacov tried to bring her back to the level of approval that she had previously expressed. "It's wrong for one man to create a hell for another or for one man to thrive at the expense of another man's labor. And Mameshie, if it's a question of relationship between one man and another, the choice is free. And for all you know," he galloped ahead, using words recklessly, "the Almighty may be waiting for man's rebellion against Him, that is, if in fact He exists at all."

Hindele quickly covered her mouth with her hands as if she herself had uttered these words and wanted to take them back. "Yacov dear," she muttered. "What do you mean if He exists at all? Don't tell me that you too don't know . . . "

Yacov said no more. For a while he sat beside her in silence, then changed the subject. "How is business at the shop?" he asked.

She understood. What point was there in pursuing the subject any further? It was clear as day that Yacov had been swept off his feet by the same epidemic that had attacked the children of even the best and the most pious in Bociany. She would have to make peace with the fact that Yacov had left her in more ways than one. She was powerless, incapable of leading him back onto the right path. But not all was yet lost. After all, what were a man's thoughts, what were his fancies and speculations against the reality that permeated his soul, against the reflection of the eternal light that he carried within him? That reflection, untarnished, was still alight in Yacov's heart. Actually, it shone now brighter than ever; it beamed at her from his pale face. A person's face was the mirror of his soul. Both the good and the bad of his nature were inscribed on his face. It was merely a question of being able to read it correctly, and she could read her son's face. It was like an open book to her.

She held Yacov's hands in the palms of her own in the same way as she had held them when as a child he had come home with frozen fingertips. "Thank Heaven," she answered casually. "The shop is doing well. The shtetl has been flourishing ever since the people from the big cities have arrived. And did you see the town hall that the Germans have built? They've also expanded the school, and there are rumors spreading that they're going to put down rails so that the train from Chwosty can reach Bociany. And as you know, Reb Senderl is no more, may he rest in peace. It happened only three months ago and already no one remembers him. It's as if there had never been a Reb Senderl in the world. I miss him badly." Her voice breaking, she continued. "All of Bociany goes now to Shmulikl the Doctor for cures and medication. Who knows? Perhaps it's for the better, but Bociany is no longer the same. On the surface all appears to be the way it was, but in reality it isn't."

Yacov slept in his old place on the mattress beneath the window. It gave him a taste of melancholy sweetness to wrap the old feather quilt around himself. It brought back the flavor of his oblivious innocence, the flavor of his childhood, at the same time as it made him acutely aware that he had lost it forever. For long hours he lay awake, listening to the silence. Before he drifted off into sleep, he remembered the nights when as a little boy he had grown frightened and had plunged into his mother's bed.

In the morning he set out for the mill to visit Reb Faivele. As he strode along the snow-covered Wide Poplar Road lugubrious memories preyed on his mind.

Reb Faivele the Miller received him with open arms and boisterous exclamations. He pressed him to his chest and kissed him on both cheeks. But otherwise he had little time for him. Reb Faivele's business had undergone an enormous expansion during the war years. Smugglers arriving from starving towns near and far were gathered in front of his *kantur,* warming themselves by the large fire cauldron on the verandah as they waited for Reb Faivele to see them and strike a deal. Peasants swamped the mill with sacks of rye and wheat that needed to be ground. The peasants were more impatient and more arrogant than they had ever been. So Reb Faivele soon broke away from Yacov and, panting and perspiring, his caftan tails flying, rushed back to the *kantur* and the mill, to come back to Yacov for a another while, pick up the thread of their awkward conversation, and then rush off again.

In this manner Reb Faivele managed to throw in a few bitter words on the subject of his two sons. "How does the saying go, Yacov?" he grinned dejectedly. "All children are smart when they're small and that's how they remain when they grow up, as smart as children are. My son Shlomele, may he be protected from an evil eye, is growing up a pious wizard, while Abrashka, the monster, thinks that he has studied enough and already knows everything. He carouses about in the streets of Krakow and has gone crazy to boot. All he does when he sits down on his behind is carve idiotic baubles out of wood." He shook Yacov's shoulders and then pushed him away, "Go, go into the house and say hello to my wife."

Yacov went into the house to see Long Zirele. She offered him a glass of tea and preserves and asked him in her dry matter-of-fact tone of voice about Lodz and its people. He had nothing to talk to her about. When he had finished his tea, he sat with her a while longer out of politeness, and then went out to see Fredka.

Fredka embraced him with her warm strong arms. She could not get over her amazement at how tall and manly Yacov had become, nor how lank and pale he was. She talked a little about Abrashka, then her talk turned in circles as she added bits of news from the village, gossiped about the farmhands, and listed who in the villages had gotten married to whom. She told him that the cow had calved and that the dog Bobik was aging. Then she walked out to the yard with him and they entered the stable. Sussi and Sussi Ben Sussi had their heads buried in sacks of oats.

"Perhaps you'd like to go for a horse ride?" she proposed in an uncertain tone of voice. "True, you can drown in the slush . . . " She tilted her head toward him and added in a whisper. "And you must watch out for the drunkards. They've begun to grumble against the Jews again. The yokels want a free Poland, so the bloody fools are going to claim it from the Jews. Those who are really serious about a free Poland have joined the legions, but the riffraff does nothing but grumble."

Yacov embraced Sussi's neck, patted Sussi Ben Sussi, and took his leave of Fredka. On his way home he found himself thinking about Wanda. Fredka had mentioned that Wanda had gotten married and was now the mother of a little boy. She was a wanton no longer, nor had anybody heard her sing again. Yacov thought that the finality of things past was more striking when faced in places that had served as a background for that past, places that in themselves had barely altered. The image of Wanda as he saw her in his mind's eye was final, a happening frozen in memory. Never again would it have anything to do with his life.

He felt uncomfortable with the sentimentality that had taken possession of him and also with his worries. Was it possible that a new attack by the Gentiles awaited the shtetl while he would be far away? Bociany had lived with such dreadful expectations for years and years. He had grown up with them. Fear, anguish, distrust of the Gentiles. The specter of the Gentile boys who had chased after him in his childhood had haunted him all his life. He thought of the Gentile boys who were passing him now on the road. He thought about the heder boys who cavorted in the market-place in Bociany, thought of the children of Baluty, those who ate dirt, breathed dust, and never saw fruits grow or fields ripen. Yet the children of Baluty, like the children of Bociany, were capable of enjoyment, of play, and of laughter. Little was needed to make a child smile. There was simplicity and directness in a child's manner of expressing its love of life. Then what happened to the same children as they grew? At what moment in their development did the devil sneak into their hearts? How did bitter-ness and hatred come to nestle in their bosoms, confusing their minds and disfiguring their smiles? Every human being had his day, his moment when he had lost his innocence. Every man was an Adam who had fallen from God's grace.

He was surprised at how little his thoughts had to do with faith and the devotion to God's laws. "If this is so," he thought to himself, "then I won-der whether I can still call myself a religious Jew, no matter whether or not I've reached a conclusion concerning the existence of God. Conse-quently, I am a hypocrite to continue and accept the six hundred and thir-teen commandments as the framework for my life. It's high time that I formulate my own commandments for myself. What should they be? For the time being I know of the foremost one: Try not to harm anyone, not to wrong anyone. Try to be a *mentsh*." He questioned himself, "But does this alone entitle me to consider myself a Jew? After all, I can be nothing else but a Jew. Being a Jew is part of me, of my total self. Even this nonre-ligion of mine is Jewish in its essence. Actually all that I am looking for is, as Mother says, a new vessel for the old wine, since, as far as I am con-cerned, the wine in the old vessel has gone sour."

He was passing the inn. A few drunken peasants stood in the open door, waving their bottles of *monopolka* at him. Had they recognized him? Perhaps his childhood friend, Bornek, Manka the Washerwoman's son, was amongst them? Gratefully, he waved back at them. It occurred to him that he looked at them with Jewish eyes. By waving back at them, he thanked them for not attacking him. Fear and distrust stood like a wall between them and himself, preventing him from greeting them in true brotherhood.

Before he returned to Lodz, Yacov visited his friend Ariele, who was presently the chairman of the Bund Organization in Bociany. Ariele had finally married Rivkele, Selig the Tailor's youngest daughter, his bride of long standing. Rivkele wore no matron's wig but had her own long black hair, which was a revolutionary act in itself. Such an open break with tradition exposed her to the hostility of public opinion, to which she as well as Ariele responded with nonchalant bravado. Ariele's reception of Yacov was a mixture of friendliness and reserve. But at leave-taking, Ariele could not restrain himself and came out, bitterly reproaching Yacov for not having found the time during his stay to feel the pulse of the other Bociany, the young, the new, and the enlightened.

"I'm sorry to have disappointed you," Yacov said to him, as they shook hands. "But I'm not ready for it yet."

"I've heard this song before," Ariele grinned.

"I cannot help it."

"Will you ever be ready?"

Yacov shrugged, "I don't know."

10

ON HIS RETURN TO LODZ Yacov did not immediately discard his traditional clothes for modern ones. Nor did he cut off his sidelocks or shave off his beard as he had decided to do on his way back from Bociany. He postponed the step from one week to the other and from one month to the next. He chided himself for his wavering. However, this was a step of great importance, and he had to prepare himself inwardly for it.

At the same time his visit to Bociany had intensified his longing for Binele, a longing that had grown so powerful that it made him wander the streets of Lodz and look for her in every female face. She seemed to have grown and expanded within him, to have stepped out far beyond her image and the memories of her that he cherished in his heart. He was not surprised that his love for her had flourished or that it possessed him so tenaciously even though it was based on so little. It could have grown even on much less. As from a single seed fallen on receptive soil an oak tree grows, so his love for her could have grown in his soul from a single gaze of her eyes. He repetitiously heard her ask him, "When you come to Lodz, will you look me up?" He heard the answer that he had given her in his heart, "Even if I am never to find you, I will still go on looking for you. I miss you so much that it hurts." He had not the slightest notion of how to go about finding her in this town, this sea of wretched humanity. He chided himself for his hopes. Yet walking the streets had come to mean seeing nothing and no one, but only looking for her.

He tried to distract himself from his obsessive thoughts about Binele by escaping into reading, or into making order in his confusing ruminations concerning his new outlook on life.

Laibel the Hump's comrade, Vove Cederbaum, the young weaver who worked at a loom in the next room at the workshop, appeared at Yacov's side one late evening after work as Yacov sat talking with Laibel. Vove tugged at one of Yacov's sidelocks. "Should I cut them for you?" he asked good-naturedly.

Yacov pushed him away. "Leave that to me." Laibel the Hump also looked sternly at Vove, telling him to leave them alone.

Vove had no intention of leaving them alone. "Catching flies and cutting sidelocks has to be done quickly. The rest doesn't go so fast."

Yacov took the opportunity to explain himself to his two workmates. He told them candidly, "I have to let it all boil over inside me. That's my nature." He turned to Vove, "I'm not one of those who are in a haste to Germanize themselves and follow the fashion. Furthermore, I wouldn't consider cutting the earlocks a sign of my breaking with the past. If you want to know, I can still see my mother and father, and also the heder and the *besmedresh* as having brought me to this point in my life. I can see myself still bound to my entire ancestry. Because, whether you want it or not, we carry all of Jewish history on our shoulders."

"Holy God of the Feather-Pluckers!" Vove exclaimed, smirking. "We've carried enough of history on our shoulders up to now. Now is the time to make history. And, brother," he pounded his fist against Yacov's shoulder, "there are moments in history, just as there are moments in a man's life, when a radical operation, like the cut of a knife, is the only means of salvation."

"I'm not mad about operations or cutting with knives." Yacov shrugged.

"Neither am I. But the time has come for us to become our own doctors." Vove replied with a chuckle.

"And what if you're a quack? Give me one example when such an operation has been successful, when a man who has cut with his past has managed to redress himself. How? By stopping the life-giving flow of blood to his heart? Yes, and tell me when a revolution has ever succeeded in bringing about a people's true redemption."

"There is no other choice but to try."

"I don't dare to take the risk."

Laibel the Hump sat quietly, listening to the verbal duel between Yacov and Vove. Only after Vove had gone home did Laibel come to sit down beside Yacov and start to talk to him, seriously and frankly. He showed a deep understanding of Yacov's sentiments. He also knew Jewish history extremely well. He knew how to enmesh Yacov's mind with his words and ever so slightly divert the train of Yacov's thought in the direction of his own convictions.

That night, as he lay on his mattress, Yacov mulled over in his mind what he had said to Vove and what Laibel the Hump had told him. Again he thought of the long breath of generations that kept him bound to the past. He was convinced that only that past could give him a long breath into the future. Yet he was, in fact, on the brink of becoming the first in a chain of generations to break with the traditional way of life, with the code of laws governing a Jew's prayers, his daily behavior, and his dress. The longer he thought of it, the more daring the deviating step he intended to take appeared to him, the more he felt himself weighed down by the burden of responsibility.

The next Sabbath, after havdalah, he set out for the Hasidic *shtibl* on Piotrkowska Street to test himself. He felt at home at the *shtibl*. Everybody knew him and greeted him with friendliness. The Hasidim liked to engage him in cheerful argument, and he was quite capable of holding his own during their merry get-togethers.

Baruch Weiskop was there. The *shtibl* was still the only place where he and Yacov met and chatted with one another. It was here that their odd friendship had taken root. Beside Baruch, Yacov met the Zohar scholar, the cabalist, who sat in a corner oblivious to his surroundings. Yacov and Baruch conversed with the old man who reminded Yacov of Reb Senderl the Cabalist of Bociany. Yacov was still attracted to the cabala. He relished the air of its unearthly spirituality. It gave wing to his imagination. Its abstract speculations allowed his mind to freely roam the realms of the unknown. They made his dreamlike musings sing out with the joy of discovery; a joy that could be triggered by a mere paragraph, or a combination of words, letters, numbers, or sounds.

Yacov felt himself refreshed and stimulated after his conversation with the old man. The taste of something pleasant yet long-forgotten lingered on within him, as if he had listened for hours on end to a sweet, suddenly remembered melody, the words to which were gone forever.

He talked little with Baruch this time, afraid to betray his innermost thoughts to him. Before he left, his eyes took in the *shtibl* at a glance and he said to himself, "I feel at home here. I am leaving this place as one leaves a home."

Finally he did what he had resolved to do. He cut off his sidelocks and beard. As soon as he did it, he was overcome by a powerful need to see his mother. Had she at that very moment felt the cut in her heart? What would she say at the sight of him? How badly would she be poisoned by the cup of grief that he had prepared for her this time?

His boss, Reb Saivel Malkes, made no fuss about the change in Yacov's appearance. His other workers had begun to dress in the Deutsch fashion a long time ago. Reb Saivel himself had begun, in secret, to trim his beard, as was the fashion among the newly rich. After all, the country belonged now to Germany, and it was difficult to resist the winds of modernity that had started to blow away the old way of life. No longer was Lodz part of old-fashioned, backward Russia. The whole wide world now stood open. Even the most orthodox members of the Jewish community in town understood this and, accordingly, had begun to modernize the heder schooling and their own appearances, some to a greater extent, some to a lesser. A man with a practical sense like Reb Saivel considered it his duty to follow the new trend, if only slightly.

Yacov began to notice things that, on account of his preoccupation with himself, had previously escaped his attention. Even at the Hasidic *shtibl* young men would come in wearing modern hats. When he had first met him, Baruch Weiskop had worn a fur hat and a winter coat styled in gentile fashion. Baruch walked the streets with a walking stick suspended from his arm, looking more like a Polish aristocrat than a Hasidic young man.

Reb Saivel Malkes could not understand why Yacov was in such a hurry to leave for Bociany again and break his mother's heart. "The longer you put off your visit, the easier you'll have it later on," he reasoned with Yacov. "After all, you are a descendant of the Wurker dynasty. Why offend people? Bociany is a hick town. It will take some time before the Deutsch epidemic arrives there. But it will. It's spreading like wildfire. Soon no one will notice a thing."

Yacov was by now a full-fledged weaver, although as long as his contract had not expired, he was still considered an apprentice. He was still doing chores and running errands for his mistress, who was full of praise for him. Presently, the last weeks before Passover were at hand and there was much to do around the house. His mistress, like her husband, was reluctant to let Yacov leave.

Yacov had no intention of explaining to Reb Saivel why he so badly wanted to see his mother. He could hardly explain it to himself. There was no need to convince him that he would break his mother's heart with his appearance. Yet he felt that she must see him as he now looked. So he braced himself with determination, stood up to Reb Saivel, and finally got what he wanted.

He went out on the highway to hitch a ride in a wagon. It was a long trip and he had plenty of time to think. The sight of flowering orchards, blooming fields, and blossoming gardens made him think of the distant battlefields where young men his age were the fodder for enemy guns and lay wounded or dead on similarly green pastures. There, the chirping of the birds was accompanied by the moans of men in agony. There, human blood was as cheap as water. A wave of oppressive gloom swept over him. It cast a dread upon him, a fear for his life, for his inner safety, a fear of the unknown, of the boundlessness of the world, of the brutality of life where he would have to manage without the supporting faith in God. He tried to talk himself out of his anxieties. He exerted himself to find pride in standing on his own two feet, find pride in daring to face life and the world without the supporting faith in God.

His heart stirred uncomfortably when he finally jumped off the wagon on his arrival in Bociany. Peasant women, carrying baskets full of the first fruits and vegetables to be blessed by the priest, crossed his path in the marketplace. Mass was being observed in the church where the peasants prayed for a good harvest. As he walked through the marketplace, Yacov felt the eyes of the town Jews riveted on him. Of course he could have dressed in his old clothes and pretended that his sidelocks were hidden under his traditional cap, and thus walked through the shtetl. But he had rejected that idea. He wore a loose, stained suit that Vove Cederbaum had lent him. Vove was taller and more broad-shouldered than he, and Yacov had to strap his belt tightly over his rib cage so as not to trip over the cuffs. He had also rolled up the sleeve cuffs so as not to appear to have no hands. On his head he wore a creased peasant cap that clearly revealed the spots where he had cut his sidelocks. Let the shtetl inhabitants pierce him with a thousand eyes and point their fingers at him, he thought, but between his mother and himself the truth had to prevail.

When he entered the garret, Hindele and his sisters turned their heads toward him. They stared at him with strange expressions on their faces. They had not expected him and now could not believe their eyes at the sight of him. However the moment they recovered, the girls clapped their hands with delight. Hindele, numbed for a moment, rushed over to him with outstretched arms.

Hindele's joy at seeing him, the radiant smile that lit up her face seemed no different to Yacov than during his previous visit. She said not a word about his appearance, as if it had escaped her notice. Confused and grateful, he kissed her, nearly hoisting her into the air. It was almost indecent. But his sense of relief at not having upset her was so powerful that he was beside himself with exultation.

In reality, the absence of Yacov's sidelocks and beard had hit Hindele like a bolt from the blue. It had made her heart sink. The shock that she felt was to last much longer than the first split second of recognition, only right afterward, the joy of seeing him made her spirit rebound. She could not help it. She was overcome by a compassionate tenderness at the sight of this new transformed son of hers, decked out in a suit that made him look like a Purim player. He was still skinny and pale, and his honey eyes were shot through with a network of red veins from lack of sleep. Yet she also sensed a spring-like awakening in him. He looked healthier somehow, more zestful and more sure of himself. In every one of his gestures she discerned a willfulness and strength that she had always been certain that he possessed.

Despite that gnawing ache deep in her heart, she knew only that she could not take her eyes off him. Of course it was important that he dress like a Jew—she reasoned with herself, trying to soothe her heart—but, after all, a human being came naked into the world and naked would he leave it. Again and again she assured herself that Yacov's true dress was not what he wore on the outside but what he wore within him. Of course his new appearance and the missing beard and earlocks went hand in hand with the heretical thoughts that he had expressed during his previous visit. But wasn't it silly to allow this to hurt her so? His words, like his new dress, belonged to the domain of the misleading and illusory. Let the entire world consider her mad, she thought, yet she knew beyond any doubt that Yacov was just as good a Jew as his father and his forefathers had been. And on top of it all he looked so princely. Even through this baggy outfit of a Purim player, his princeliness shone through. She had the feeling that she was going out of her mind with adoration. She could barely get over the fact that this big marvelous creature had come out of her small thin body. Her Yacov was a "heart thief." Looking at his face—which seemed much smaller without the beard, yet expressed both a boyish innocence and manly strength—no one, she thought, could resist opening his heart and feeling love for him.

"When will you finally tell me," she beamed, "that you want to become a groom and settle down?"

"I am a groom," he smiled back at her, "but I have no bride."

Hindele felt rejuvenated and girlish. During the rest of the holidays she busied herself about him, never taking her eyes off him for a second. It was a waste to miss the slightest moment of his presence. She placed the Passover pancakes and matzo dishes before him, purring, "Eat, eat in good health."

Saturday afternoon Yacov went to see Reb Faivele the Miller to inquire about Abrashka. The more prosperous his business and the more frequent his sons' refusals to come home for the holidays, the more irritable and bitter Reb Faivele had grown. He had lost all of his zest and his relish for life. When he was not yelling at his workers or quarreling with his wife, he walked around cursing and groaning, ordering everyone around in order to vent his frustrations. Or he exerted himself, carrying heavy sacks of flour, or repairing the blades of the mill. He still observed the Jewish rituals in detail, but his religious fervor had evaporated. His conversations with his close friend, Shmulikl the Doctor, on the one hand, and with Herr Pfeifer, the bald "writer," on the other, had finally brought him to the conclusion that only a Jewish homeland could salvage the Jewish soul. But what Reb Faivele wanted was a Jewish country where Yiddish, the tongue of the people, would be raised to the distinction of a national language.

A long holiday like Passover without his two sons, the apples of his eyes, was torture to Reb Faivele. He knew not what to do with himself, and he received Yacov like a restless lion exhausted from his own restlessness. He embraced the visitor, cuffed him affectionately, and launched into a heated monologue about politics, Jews and Judaism and his theories on how to solve the Jewish problem. Dressed in a robe of a flowery design with velvet lapels, his hands laced behind his back, he paced in his slippers back and forth on the verandah. He avoided any mention of his sons. Finally, after Yacov had repeatedly questioned him about them, Reb Faivele stopped pacing and burst out, "What do you want of my life? Besides the fact that he has turned into a good-for-nothing, Abrashka has taken it into his head to study cabala. Have you ever heard of such idiocy? I ask you, how could such a crazy notion enter his head in such a modern place as Krakow?"

"So he's studying cabala?" Yacov gasped surprised, inwardly satisfied with the news. He knew where Abrashka's interest in the cabala had originated.

Reb Faivele fumed. "So you can see how crazy he is already! And do you think that's all? He's also nagging me to register him at the Krakow Academy of Art-shmart. The apple of my eye wants to become a sculptor! He's making me a hole in the head with his nagging."

"And Shlomele?" Yacov asked.

"Shlomele, the other apple of my eye?" Reb Faivele sneered bitterly. "He's crazy too, don't worry. When the Almighty sends a man good fortune, he does it in pairs. These new times have thrown some into one extreme and others into the other extreme, because if all were thrown into the same corner, the world would topple over, wouldn't it? So my firstborn, Shlomele, you see, is just the opposite of Abrashka. He keeps his nose buried in the Talmud. If the world would have turned ten times upside down, he wouldn't have noticed. Don't worry, no farm, no mill, no business is on his mind. As far as he's concerned, the inheritance that his father has worked his fingers to the bone to build, can go to hell. He wants to become a snotnosed *rov*, is what he wants to become. You'd say it's all my fault, because I sent them away from home? No, brother! Whatever I did, it would have helped me as much as cupping glasses would help a corpse. If a man has two heirs, of whom one fears the slightest breeze and the other goes looking for the wildest storm, they will each find what they're looking for!" Reb Faivele sighed heavily and put his hand on Yacov's shoulder "Oh, Yacov, who knows as well as you the dreams I've dreamt for my sons. But as people say, dumplings in a dream are not dumplings but a dream."

On his way home, Yacov thought of Reb Faivele with a mixture of compassion and revulsion. There was a great deal of self-love in Reb Faivele's generous love for his sons, he thought. Meaningful to Reb Faivele were only the dreams that he had dreamed for them, not their own dreams. Yacov's gratitude to his mother increased a thousand fold.

The same Saturday after sundown, Yacov, his heart filled to overflowing with tenderness for his mother, sat in the loft, listening to her murmuring the prayer, "God of Abraham." As he lay at night on his straw mattress under the window and inhaled the fragrance of the flowers in the nuns' garden, he whispered into the dark, out of the fullness of his heart, "I love you, Mameshie."

Hindele heard him. "I love you too, my son," she answered from her bed.

Yacov thought that her generous love for him, which sometimes weighed on him so heavily, was the wisest and most selfless kind of loving. He did not consider himself capable of such a love.

This time during his stay in Bociany he avoided meeting Ariele. In his mind he linked him with Laibel the Hump and Vove. He wanted a respite from the power that they wielded over him.

Yacov returned to Lodz with a sensation of renewal. True, he was still at a loss, but now he had the support of his home in his blunderings. He had brought back a new sense of ease and openheartedness from Bociany, a rekindled curiosity about people, and a willingness to step out of his shell in order to learn and gather experience. He somehow could not rid himself of his closeness with Laibel the Hump, but he refused to have anything to do with Vove Cederbaum, whom he disliked and feared. Vove was a total stranger to his soul. The roughness and ruthlessness of his speech, his coarse jokes, his dry rationality, his matter-of-factness and his lack of imagination, all irritated him beyond words.

Vove Cederbaum was a few years older than Yacov. A bony young man, he was tall and broad-shouldered with a shock of unkempt hair and a strong pointed nose that attracted attention to his hollow cheeks. His chin was prominent and upturned, with a cleft in the middle, which gave it the shape of a pear. The name Cederbaum suited him. He had the straight proud bearing of a cedar, despite the fact that he had practically been brought up at a loom. He was a heavy smoker and around the edges of his loom lay rows of cigarette butts. Sometimes he lit two butts at once and his head was always surrounded by a cloud of smoke. Vove loved small talk and could discuss the trivia of daily life with great seriousness. But when it came to the topic of his "movement," he would become not just serious but tempestuous. He burned like a furnace and his every word seemed to be wrought in the flames of his passion. He worshipped Laibel the Hump. When the boss was not around, Yacov often observed Vove and Laibel whispering to each other in a corner. At such moments Vove's hard face took on an expression of unusual deference and affection.

The atmosphere in Reb Saivel Malkes's workshop had changed beyond recognition from the days when Yacov had started to work there. Reb Saivel had grown more approachable and the workers had become less careful about not aggravating him. One day at lunch time, Vove, his bowl of soup and his portion of black bread in hand, came to sit down next to Laibel and Yacov who were eating their lunch together that day.

"Whatever Vove does, he does it with his whole heart," Laibel remarked. "When he smokes, the entire room drowns in smoke. When he chews his bread the whole town of Lodz and its environs shake on their foundations. When he slurps his soup, it thunders through heaven and earth."

"The proletariat is starved," Vove said with his mouth full. His small metallic eyes, framed by protruding eyebrows, twinkled. He had the habit, which annoyed Yacov, of saying "the proletariat" when he meant "I." He bent closer to Yacov and, working his mouth energetically, said in a nasal twang, as he pointed at Laibel with his spoon, "Laibel the Hump, the jealous enemy of the people, told me that you're busy reading about the Spartacus uprising."

"I was," Yacov answered. "But now I'm reading *The Shtetl* by Shalom Asch. My ex-boss in Bociany gave it to me as a gift."

"So you've put away Spartacus in order to creep back into the shtetl?" Vove snickered and loudly scraped the bowl with his spoon.

Yacov, in good spirits, aped Vove's tone of voice, "I'm not creeping, I'm walking with a poetical literary step, after having finished with Spartacus."

"What do you mean you've finished with Spartacus?" Vove shook his mane of stiff disheveled hair.

"I finished reading the book."

"Then why don't you say so?" Vove wiped his mouth on his sleeve. He went back to check the collection of cigarette butts on his loom, picked one up, returned to his companions, and lit it. "So how do you like Comrade Spartacus?" He puffed at his cigarette, enveloping himself and the other two men in a cloud of smoke.

"I like him quite well, but not everyone's born to become a Spartacus," Yacov rejoined.

"But everyone can belong to Spartacus's army, and it's high time for you to enlist."

"I told you, I haven't got the makings of a soldier."

"Holy God of the Feather-Pluckers! You're pulling out! Coward!"

"Pulling out of what? Did I sign a contract with you?"

Vove's eyes met Laibel's stern glance. He was silent for a moment, then added, "How many times do I have to tell you that catching flies and making the revolution have to be done fast?"

"First I have to wait for the revolution in my head to die down." Yacov shrugged.

"But you mustn't play around with the revolution in your head for too long, brother. If you do, you'll end up like Hamlet, sitting around and chewing cold *cholnt,* which is fatal to the digestion."

"I'm in no hurry to say yes to bloodshed."

"Do you have a better solution, my saintly *tsadik?*"

"I'm still looking for one."

Vove lived with a woman comrade "from the movement," whose name was Baltche. She was a plump young woman with a broad open face and warmth and directness in her manner. She was a hosiery maker and lived with Vove in a room not far from the workshop. Saturday mornings she would send a piece of strudel over to the workshop with Vove for Laibel the Hump and Yacov.

One Sabbath morning, while Yacov was still half asleep, Vove, dressed in a black *roubashka* and neatly ironed pants, appeared by Yacov's mattress at the workshop. He put down the piece of strudel for Yacov on the work bench and boomed in his raw voice, "Good Sabbath to you, enemy of the people! Raise your lazy reactionary behind and get up. The proletariat wants to take you for a walk."

Yacov knew that Vove would not leave him alone. So he reluctantly gave in to him, got up from his mattress, washed, and shaved. He ate his piece of strudel and washed it down with a mugful of cold chicory coffee. Vove, a cigarette in his mouth, followed him around, commenting on Laibel the Hump's article that he had just read in the recent issue of the party publication, the *Awakening*.

Soon they were outside, walking through the streets of Baluty. Before long, it began to dawn on Yacov that the purpose of Vove's strolling with him was to convince him that the revolution was not to be postponed. By showing him the woeful sights that, despite Baluty's neat Sabbath appearance, greeted their eyes on every side, Vove wanted Yacov to see that the noose was already around humanity's neck and the waters had already risen to engulf the world. Vove was a child of Baluty. His ancestors had lived here for many a generation. He knew every grimy house, every dirty yard, every smelly alleyway, and he knew all of their countless inhabitants. He spoke about human lives that were worse than those of animals and of fates that screamed to the skies for justice.

Vove said, "Your creator of the World is a pursuer of justice, isn't He? Yet it's written in black and white about all the wars that He has waged. And, brother, when He goes to war, He certainly doesn't wear any silk gloves."

"You want to compare yourself to Him?" Yacov smiled. "He is supposed to see everything before Him. While man sees only what's in front of his nose and even that he sees badly."

"But he feels very well!" Vove burst out, madly indignant. "Man knows when something hurts him. Take Hersh Lekert, for example. He was a cobbler, a quiet soul who would not hurt a fly on the wall. But when he heard that Von Vahl, the Governor of Vilna, had ordered the flogging of Jewish demonstrators, the news lifted him off his cobbler stool. Without saying a word to anybody, he went and shot the bastard. But Hersh Lekert, the schlemiel, the milksop, the ignoramus, was no sharpshooter by profession. So he missed the target and lost his head for it anyway. Believe me, Lekert was just as peace loving a fellow as you are, but the human spark within this miserable nothing of a man had jerked him out of his complacency and made him burn with indignation. This happened in 1902, and the same thing happened in 1905, when hundreds and thousands took to the streets. Ask Laibel, he was our commander. When the jug is full to bursting, its ear breaks by itself. When you are so hurt that you can bear it no more, you don't philosophize, you scream. The same is about to happen now. Great things are going on on the other side of the border, underground, but soon they'll explode. And here too. The Poles are fed up with being in continual bondage. True, the yokels are a blind herd. They see in us the cause of their misery, devil take them, but they are just as much in exile as we are. They must open their eyes and see who their real enemies are."

Vove had sharp arguments. He knew a great deal on his subject. At times he sounded as if he were reciting entire pamphlets by heart. He did so, using the language of Baluty, peppered with his own wisecracks and a fair amount of foul words. Yacov disliked him less. Vove easily became excited, yet in a way, he projected an inner equilibrium that Yacov envied. Vove seemed to be walking a straight clear path, which, despite his vulgarity, created an air of nobility about him. Yacov also envied Vove's attitude toward people. Vove was straightforward, bluntly direct, while he, Yacov, would always feel himself facing a wall when he came in contact with another person. When he talked to another person, he felt himself talking through that wall, failing to grasp the essential message transmitted to him, failing to transmit his own essential message. Only with his mother, or with Yoel and Abrashka, had there been moments when souls touched.

Yacov allowed Vove to talk on and on. He questioned Vove's more sweeping statements, and they argued. Yet Yacov was already aware that he must not wait until all his doubts had vanished, that part of his reluctance to take a decisive step was caused by fear, fear of responsibility, fear for his safety. Anyway, he knew that the times of absolute faith either in God or in an ideal were liable never to happen again in his life. They were gone as his childhood was gone. He could not forever remain an onlooker. He had to act. Only through action could he assert himself and test his courage. Even if his actions had only a minimal objective significance, they were of great importance to him.

The following week Yacov allowed Vove to take him to the workers' meeting places, some of which were located in the yards of synagogues or *besmedresh*s, places that were holdovers from the tsarist times of illegality.

"Under the tsar," Vove explained, "our situation was crystal clear. But with the Germans around we never know where we stand. Officially we are legal these days. But since we support the idea of an independent Poland, our legality is only skin deep."

One of the meetings to which Vove had taken Yacov took place at a coffeehouse. There hung a red banner on a wall with two inscriptions: *Allgemainer Yiddisher Arbeter Bund* and *Workers of the World, Unite!* The room was packed with young men and women who sat next to each other, smoking. Yacov's face flushed at the sight of them. It was a Sabbath day. The young men sat with their heads uncovered and the girls wore blouses with short sleeves. The air was difficult to breathe. The smoke was so thick that Yacov could hardly distinguish people's faces. His head swam.

Before they even managed to seat themselves properly, Vove was asking the chairman, a bearded middle-aged man who wore thick glasses and looked like a school teacher, for permission to speak. Before long Vove towered over the gathering as he stood against the wall, tall and threatening. He was criticizing and, in a thunderous voice, bawling out his comrades for their "work done." The crowd stirred and flared up. Some nodded their heads in approval and called, "Bravo! That's right!" while others shook their heads in protest and yelled, "Boo! Wrong! Wrong!" Some stormed against Vove, others encouraged him. Some waved at him, others shrugged at him. Vove, oblivious to what went on around him, continued speaking his mind in his bellowing voice.

On their way home, Vove, satisfied with himself, prodded Yacov cheerfully with his elbow. "Did you hear how I told them off? That's called democracy, brother. These days, when you talk, you talk. Not like in the tsarist times when we gathered in lofts or in the cemetery, or in the Konstantine Forest. Then, when I happened to heat up about something, I had to hold a handkerchief against my mouth to muffle the sound of my voice. Today it's a pleasure."

Yacov hardly listened to him. He had no idea what Vove and his comrades had quarreled about, and he did not care. He wondered whether he himself would ever be able to fit into such a crowd, into a life of technical, practical squabblings about "work done," about "tactics," and about what Vove called, "organizational matters." These topics were too mundane and dry to kindle his interest. They seemed to narrow a mind's horizons. Yet every time Vove proposed that Yacov accompany him to a meeting, something stirred within him and he went along. It seemed to him that he heard Yoel's voice inside him, saying, "In order to accomplish something tangible, you must diminish your horizons. You must place yourself on a single, narrow path and forget the wide road to which it leads. You must pursue that narrow path doggedly and look only at what's in front of your nose. Amidst the narrow-mindedness of those people's atheism, amidst their desecration of the Sabbath, amidst the cloud of smoke and trivial talk, you may yet discover sparks of sacredness."

Finally Vove and his girlfriend, Balcie, took Yacov to the workers' culture club known as The Harp, which served as a decoy for the party headquarters. There Yacov felt as much at home as he had at the Hasidic *shtibl.* The club was ten times as spacious as the *shtibl* and much cleaner. But the brightness and warmth that embraced him had nothing to do with the bright paint on the walls or the large size of the rooms.

One of the rooms served as a soup kitchen. Young people sat together with the middle-aged, smoking, passionately discussing political news, and gesticulating. Some read books or newspapers; some whispered among themselves and laughed. A group at one of the tables broke into song. Those sitting at other tables joined in. Yacov heard these Yiddish songs for the first time. Falsetto male voices and squeaky female voices abounded, yet somehow the singing sounded fresh and youthful, full of verve and vitality, even more so than the Hasidic singalongs familiar to him. He thought that the added female element in the choir of voices had something to do with it.

After a while the crowd rose and went into the neighboring larger room, which soon became so densely packed with people that they overflowed into the other rooms. At a table on a raised platform there appeared a medium-sized man dressed in a black velour jacket. His black hair was streaked with gray as was the thick mustache that framed his prominent, sensuous mouth. The gaze of his large burning eyes seemed to caress his listeners, while their glow reached the most distant faces in the room.

The man spoke about the Jewish people and the Yiddish language. He spoke about the sources of Jewish folklore, about a people's soul as the spring of creative beauty, all expressed in the speech of the simple man in the street, in the language of the artisan, the maid, and the woman in the marketplace. He spoke of the Jewish mothers rocking their children to sleep with songs or tales. He spoke of the language of the weavers of Baluty, of the shopkeepers, the tradesmen and factory workers. But mostly he talked about the founding of a secular Yiddish school designed to raise a new generation of proud, modern, freedom-loving Jews.

The man's words moved Yacov deeply. He asked himself the question that had not stopped nagging at him ever since he had changed and modernized his appearance: How could he remain a complete Jew without carrying the yoke of religious law? The speaker at the table seemed to have understood the struggle that went on in his, in Yacov's, soul and in the soul of every modern Jew—the struggle with the traditional way of life, with a generations-old code of customs and rituals. Being a *mentsh* in the sense of the Yiddish language, meant being an ideal, ethical human being. A Jew who meticulously followed the religious laws affirmed his existence as both a *mentsh* and a Jew. The question was: If a man rejected his faith in God and held on only to the moral and ethical laws, could he still be a Jew in the full sense of the word? The speaker seemed to have found the answer to this question. The national identity of a modern people, the speaker held forth, is expressed in its culture, in its language. The modern Jewish national identity is expressed in the Yiddish language and in all the cultural and folkloric riches it contains.

Vove, suddenly as playful as a child, poked Yacov with his elbow and gazed at him with laughing eyes. "The proletariat has surprised you, eh?" Yacov stared at him distractedly. "You haven't got a clue who the speaker is, have you? It's I. L. Peretz, you nincompoop!"

So that was I. L. Peretz, the author whose works had so deeply impressed Yacov. Yacov absorbed the stillness in the room through which the speaker's warm voice flowed forth from the distant platform. When the voice went silent, a storm of applause broke out in the room. Yacov clapped his hands so hard that his palms hurt.

I. L. Peretz was carried from the room on people's shoulders, but the crowd did not disperse after he had left. The meeting was to be continued. Vove's comrades loved meetings. They lived and breathed meetings. As if they all were limbs of one agitated body, they could not tear themselves away from each other. A meeting was this crowd's substitute for going to a house of prayer.

Four young men in Russian blouses and corded belts appeared on the platform, carrying red banners. They were followed by a woman in a white blouse that was severely buttoned up to her chin. She wore a long black skirt and high-heeled boots. Behind her came a small but sturdy looking man wearing knee-high boots and then another short man, fragile and familiar looking. The latter busied himself adjusting the glasses that were attached to his ears by pieces of wire and string. The young men with the banners placed themselves along the back wall of the platform. The others seated themselves at the table that was covered by a red table-cloth. Only the sturdy-looking short man in knee-high boots remained standing. He drew a wad of papers from his pocket and began reading a long poem dedicated to the children of Baluty.

"That's Moshe Socrates," Vove explained delightedly. "He's our propa-gandist among the pimps and whores of the Faiferovka. He's been at it since 1905. Since that time he has also been sweating to become a great poet, and he hasn't sweated it out of his system yet. Such an old bones making such a fool of himself! He's a first class agitator and a veteran of all the prisons of Lodz and the districts, but that's not good enough for him. He insists on wearing the crown of a rhyme-maker created in Peretz's image. He may work at it until doomsday and he still won't reach Peretz's ankles. But mind you, we need such trash producers too, to touch the primitive hearts of those who know not any better. And believe me or not, this Moshe Socrates sometimes moves me good and proper with some of those trashy poems of his. He hits the nail on the head unwit-tingly, you understand, because he knows life in Baluty better than any of the most talented writers we have."

When Moshe Socrates finished, the woman in the white blouse stood up and sang Peretz's song about the three seamstresses, "The Eyes Red, the Lips Blue." The crowd hummed along and gave her an ovation when she finished. Then the short man in the crooked glasses stood up, raised his fists in the air, and began his speech. Yacov could not believe his eyes.

"It's Laibel the Hump!" he cried out.

"What did you think?" Vove replied with pride in his tone of voice. "He's the chairman of the school committee."

Yacov's heart also filled with pride. Laibel the Hump, his teacher of weaving and his personal agitator was now standing on the platform in front of a mass of people. It grew very quiet in the hall as Laibel talked on, impassioned in his gesticulation. His voice sounded like a bell. It had an altogether different timbre from the voice he used for the monologues he whispered in Yacov's ear when they sat at the weaving loom. Laibel looked different too, straighter. As he talked on, he strolled out from behind the table where he had begun his speech and paced back and forth in front of the platform, raising his fists in the air. He would have resembled a prophet, had he not been forced to constantly adjust the wires of his eyeglasses. Laibel used different expressions from the ones he would use in conversations with Yacov. Now his sentences were full of long, difficult, outlandish words. Despite them, however, Yacov understood Laibel's speech perfectly well.

In fact, Laibel's speech brought home to Yacov for the first time the realization that Laibel was just as much a dreamer as he himself was. Within Laibel, just as within himself, there was a yearning for an earthly paradise that would embrace everything alive, everything that existed in this world. And just like Laibel, who wanted Jewish children to take over that dream and transform it into reality, Yacov was enthusiastic about the idea of a free Yiddish school where teachers and children would meet joyfully, where the thirst for knowledge would not be blocked by the dogmatic barriers of The Law, where acquiring knowledge would not be accompanied by a whipping on the behind, and where love, not fear, would flourish.

Yacov tried to bring himself back to reality and shake off the state of strange euphoria that had overcome him. "All I know," he thought, trying to cool his enthusiasm, "is that ideals are just like the horizon. Man walks in its direction while the horizon keeps receding. Therefore I must dedicate my hope, as Yoel would say, not to paradise itself but to the road leading toward it."

Still the meeting had not drawn to a close. After Laibel the Hump, a neatly dressed man, fattish, with a goatee, appeared on the platform. "He's the secretary of the party," Vove whispered in Yacov's ear.

The secretary of the party looked gloomy and when he began his speech his voice trembled with outrage and bitterness. "What a senseless, cowardly act, comrades!" he called out. "The German Social Democrats have voted for military credits for Kaiser Wilhelm's government! And are the Russian Social Democrats, led by Plekhanov and Kropotkin, any better? Didn't they come out with their Russian patriotism against Germany? This *Burgfrieden,* comrades, this going hand in hand with our class enemy, this patriotic-nationalistic fraternizing with the bourgeoisie, comrades, is a black stain on the conscience of us all!"

Yacov turned to Vove, "I don't understand," he whispered. "If this is a meeting about the new Yiddish schools, then what do his words have to do with it?"

"What do they have to do with it?" Vove repeated his question heatedly. "They have everything to do with it. Do you think that we are going to build a school suspended in the air? Our school must be rooted in life. We are realists, that is what we are, and one thing is related to the other. Wait and you'll see how he ties it all in."

Yacov smiled to himself. Wasn't he after all at a Jewish gathering? Wasn't the pilpulistic roundabout way of reasoning ingrained in Jewish thinking? In fact, as if he had heard what Vove had just said, the secretary drew some papers from his pocket. His face lit up and his voice took on a lilting pitch as he began to quote from articles by the late Jean Jaurés, by Romain Rolland, and by Stefan Zweig. "These noble thinkers, comrades," the secretary exclaimed, "these great spirits, these prophets from both sides of the battlefield speak the language of a different Europe. They speak the language of humanity and of brotherhood among men. It is to that Europe that we belong, we, the unemployed weavers, hosiery makers, knitters, tailors, and cobblers, we, the Jewish working class, the Jewish toilers! And it is in that spirit that we shall raise our children, so that they may strive with us for a more beautiful, a happier future. We want it, comrades, and we shall attain it! Long live international brotherhood! Long live socialism! Long live the Bund!"

As the speaker sat down, peals of "Bravo!" shook the walls of the hall. The crowd rose to its feet and, deeply moved, began to sing, "Brothers and sisters of work and of want, / all those in need dispersed through the world." Yacov listened to the words. When the refrain, "We swear devotion for life unto death," was repeated for the last time, he joined in, knowing that his fate was sealed. He had taken an oath for life unto death.

A few days later Yacov enrolled as a member of The Harp. He began to borrow books from The Harp's lending library and did not miss a single meeting or lecture. Coming to these gatherings and spending long hours with a crowd of people of the same mind was contagious. Although at first Yacov did fear that Reb Saivel Malkes would fire him for leaving the workshop so many evenings during the week, but Vove put his mind at rest.

"Reb Saivel knows as well as we do," Vove said, "that things in the world are coming to the boiling point. What do you think? Let Reb Saivel just utter a peep. You may have hired yourself out to him, but you're not his slave."

Reb Saivel Malkes was well aware that something was cooking in the world, something was aiming to undermine the very foundations of his existence. Distressing news was arriving from Russia and Germany. In Lodz the working class was beginning to raise its head again. A new epidemic was spreading in the form of Workers' Professional Unions to which Jews and Gentiles together could, and did, belong. This foretold nothing good. It was therefore important to be on good terms with one's own workers in case the dreadful situation indeed ended in the tragedy of revolution.

So, like a pious Jew hurrying daily to the synagogue, Yacov continued running to meetings at coffeehouses, at the union quarters, in the backyards of the *shtiblekh* or at The Harp. He became an expert at distributing leaflets. He would go from one house to another, climb to the top floor of each stairway, place a leaflet under every door, and continue until he reached the ground floor. In this manner he would cover an entire block, an entire street, an entire district. Before long he was voted a delegate of the weaver apprentices to an inter-union conference.

He became the proud bearer of a Bundist membership booklet and stopped wondering whether or not he was in complete agreement with the principles of the movement. In his heart he felt comfortable. His life acquired a new rhythm, a new coloration. He was, of course, aware that he was living what he called "on the surface," and that although he had taken the decision to join the party on his own, he somehow had been drawn into joining it. But he hardly had any time to sort out his thoughts. He told himself that this was the form that he wanted his life to assume. Only at night, when he lay on his straw mattress, would he ask his inner voice for comments. Then he allowed himself to wander off in his mind into the regions that he had roamed in Yoel the Blacksmith's company. "I indulge in these reveries so as not to become like a piece of glass," he put it to himself, "so that I not only reflect my surroundings, but retain a color of my own."

When Yacov put on his first new suit, which he had bought secondhand at the bazaar in Baluty, it occurred to him to celebrate the occasion by paying a visit to the Hasidic *shtibl,* in the hope that he would find Baruch Weiskop there.

It was a wintry Sabbath night after the havdalah candles had been lit. In the *shtibl* a large crowd of Hasidim had gathered. They gesticulated feverishly as they discussed the news from the front. Baruch Weiskop was not there.

Later on, Yacov noticed a skinny, shabby-looking man enter the *shtibl.* The man pushed his way through to the stove to warm himself, and drew out a small fiddle from under his coat. He was quickly surrounded by a group of young Hasidim who insisted that he play something. The musician did not need much coaxing. He blew on his fingers a few times, held his hands for a while over the stove, and then put the fiddle under his chin. He thumbed the strings of his fiddle, made a circle in the air with the bow, and, ever so softly, let the bow down to perch and sway on the strings. The crowd fell silent as the grayness of the room became suffused with heavy melancholy notes. The sounds of the music seemed to be winding their way along the cracks of the grimy walls, seemed to be slipping down the ice-covered window, to be climbing over the paint peelings dangling from the ceiling, and sliding down the cord of the sooty, hanging lamp. The sounds seemed to be hugging the cupboard that served as a repository for the Holy Scroll, to be stroking the shelves full of swollen books, books bent with age and usage and covered with the imprints of the hands that had flipped through their pages. His longings stirred by the plaintive melody, Yacov knew that, although he no longer belonged there, he would never be free of the image that he beheld before him; he knew that the musician's fiddle would continue to weep in his heart and that he would forever cherish this tune in his heart as in a nest.

On his way back to the workshop he ran into Baruch. They stared at one another for a moment and then burst into laughter. "I somehow knew I'd meet you today!" Baruch exclaimed. He was clad in a dress coat with a fur collar, a hard hat perched awry on his brown curls. In his hand he held a stick with an ivory knob. He took hold of Yacov's arm, "Come up to my place, and let's warm our bones with a schnapps." They climbed up to a spacious, almost empty flat. A mouse scuttled from under a sofa as they entered. "It makes no sense to heat the whole flat," Baruch said as he steered Yacov through a maze of corridors and rooms.

They entered a large, warm chamber that was heated by a tall tile oven. In contrast to the other rooms, this one was so crowded with furniture that there was barely any room left to move around in. It contained a bed, a desk, a sofa, cupboards, shelves of books, boxes of books, books on the floor, and books on the windowsills. Baruch came over to the bookcase that Yacov, impelled by curiosity, had immediately approached to peruse.

"You'll laugh at me," Baruch said, "but I've begun to study Latin and philosophy. I've four teachers. These days you can get the best professors to tutor you for a pittance. You see," he pointed to one of the shelves. "The best of German literature. And I'm studying French, too."

Yacov nodded. "The same's happening to me. I've become wild with curiosity about everything. It's like an attack of hunger, I would say . . . a greed for knowledge. I read everything I can lay my hands on. But you have teachers, so you probably study systematically."

"That's what you think!" Baruch waved his hand. "Every day I feel like drinking from a different barrel. What would you say if I told you that I'm going to move a piano into this room and study music? And yes, between you and me, there's also a greed for women. A morbid greed. Because suddenly I feel myself free to chose . . . to explore. It's dangerous. How do you manage in that domain?" He did not wait for Yacov's answer but burst into laughter, "Well, why do we stand around in our coats?" Yacov removed his coat and put it down on a chair, while Baruch took his off and threw it recklessly on the bed. He was dressed in a fitted, German-style suit. When he removed his hat, two long sidelocks came dangling down to reach his shoulders. He pulled at one of them and hastened to ask, "It looks ridiculous, eh? You did the job more thoroughly than I. Well, I have my reasons. When I go to see my father, for instance, I still put on my Hasidic clothes. So what? Must the kind of hat I wear let everyone know what's going on in my head?"

"You don't have to justify yourself." Yacov assured him. "Actually, I've been looking for you, in order to justify myself before you. Most likely these guilt feelings will stay with us forever. So we must learn to live with them. I'm sure that sooner or later you'll do as I did."

Baruch shook his head. "Maybe I will and maybe I won't. I'm a nihilist, to use the fashionable word. So it makes no difference to me one way or the other. I just like to blend into the surroundings like a chameleon, in order to avoid complications. And you? Don't tell me you've become a full-fledged atheist."

Yacov smiled thoughtfully. "Yes, but I'm one who is not entirely devoid of faith. God lives on in me in mortal agony. He doesn't die but keeps on dying. This doesn't mean that I've ceased to think of myself as being a full-fledged Jew. On the contrary. I rather feel myself as a more proud, a more expansive Jew. I take up more space in my own eyes and that makes me feel more of a Jew."

Baruch gave him a glass of schnapps, pulled him over to the sofa, and made him sit down. Yacov, warmed, felt himself ready to open his heart to Baruch more than ever before. He clinked glasses with him and quickly gulped down the schnapps. Baruch reached for his coat pocket, drew out a bag from it, and from the bag a greasy paper with knockwurst. He pushed a piece of the knockwurst into Yacov's hand and refilled both their glasses.

"The glass of schnapps has become part of my lifestyle," he said. "It loosens me up inside. I feel lighter, I see better, hear better, and don't withdraw into my shell if a person like you approaches me."

Yacov, slightly intoxicated, shook his head. "That's no good. The two of us should be able to talk when we are sober."

"But how can you deny the role of alcohol as a great leveler? What better means is there than alcohol to bridge the irremediable antagonisms between those who are worlds apart? For instance, I am a capitalist, you are a pauper. I a believer, you a nonbeliever."

Yacov shook his head tipsily. "I told you, I'm not a total nonbeliever. I'm still God's fool, so help me God."

"No matter whose fool you are, the epidemic of secularism has caught up with you good and proper."

"So it has. In the past, my thoughts of Him," Yacov pointed to the ceiling. "used to overshadow my thoughts about man. Now the opposite is true. Now I crave for the expanse of the entire earth and for all the people on it. And if you ask me about anti-Semitism, I'll say this to you, Baruch: If the Gentiles don't free themselves of their Jew hatred, I foresee nothing good either for the Jews or for the Gentiles. The Jewish tear and the Gentile tear must both be mixed into the drink of brotherhood." He raised his empty glass to Baruch.

Baruch shook his head, amused and amazed. "I can see why you have no need for alcohol. You can get drunk on hollow phraseology."

Yacov was not hurt by Baruch's sarcasm. "Hollow phraseology becomes less hollow when it's being acted upon."

"And how do you accomplish that feat?"

"I've become a member of the Bund."

"What of it? Don Quixote also fulfilled his fantasies by taking so-called action. He fought windmills."

"And tell me, you yourself don't fight with windmills? Who doesn't? Don Quixote at least was . . . was not indifferent. This made him more of a *mentsh*."

Baruch laughed. "You think that I don't go to listen to your Bundist speakers? Of course I do. To amuse myself. I go to the Zionists too, and to the Territorialists, and to the Anarchists. They all support my faith in my own party, the party of the Pessimists-Nihilists."

"Woe to you."

"Woe to *you*."

"I have faith. I believe. It is you who have lost it."

"Trash!" Baruch waved his hand "In my eyes you are as blind as any Hasid at the *shtibl*. The Hasid deludes himself that he's happy because he holds on to a tassel of the Almighty's undergarment, while you delude yourself that you're happy because you hold on to the undergarment of His substitute: man! What a substitute! I prefer the Hasid's faith. At least his God sits on a throne of glory, while yours is the lice-infested neighbor on your pillow." Baruch's gaze lit on Yacov's wooden clogs. He stared at them for a while and then stood up and rushed over to a cupboard. A pile of shoes fell from it onto the floor. He held out a pair to Yacov. "Here, try them on."

The shoes did not fit Yacov. Baruch made him try on another pair, then still another one, until finally Yacov slipped his feet into a pair of comfortable, shiny, black patent leather shoes. He knew that the shoes did not match his "new" secondhand suit nor the rest of his shabby attire, still he thanked Baruch and drank another glass of schnapps with him to "wet" his new shoes. Baruch wiped his mouth and exclaimed, "In that case, take off your pants and jacket, too!" He opened the cupboard doors wider and looked through the suits that hung inside.

Yacov felt offended on behalf of his "new" suit which Baruch seemed not to have noticed. He protested, "Leave it be. I don't feel well in someone else's clothes. Shoes are a different story. I was cold in the clogs."

Baruch dangled a hanger with a suit on it before Yacov's eyes. "What are you calling 'someone else's clothes'? Weren't you preaching brotherhood a minute ago?"

Yacov leaned forward to him, "I want you to meet my friend Vove Cederbaum."

"If you take the suit, I'll come to meet him."

"I won't take it, but you will come anyway, won't you?"

Baruch put the suit back into the cupboard and spread his hands. "For the life of me, I cannot make you out. You want to bring about a revolution, you want to take their wealth away from the rich and give it to the poor. And here I give you a suit out of my own free will and you refuse to take it."

Yacov refused to discuss the subject of the suit any further. "I'll take you to see Vove, all right?"

Baruch shut the cupboard doors. He sat down next to Yacov and looked at him, as it seemed to Yacov, with envy. "You have many friends now, don't you?" he asked.

Yacov nodded proudly. "We are all like one big family." He pretended not to remember that his only close friend was actually Vove, and that even with Vove the closeness was of a superficial nature; his feelings for Vove were a mixture of distaste and affection. It was in fact only to Baruch that Yacov felt himself drawn. He conceded, "Basically I'm not a sociable person. I fear becoming dissolved in the crowd. I like to keep to myself too much. So this whole thing is still new to me."

Baruch spread his hands. "And I live completely without friends. Not because I'm afraid of losing myself in the crowd. My personal foibles are too many and too powerful for that ever to happen. With me it's rather a fear of people as such. I don't trust them. There is no room for comradeship in my movement."

"To experience comradeship you need to share a common ideal with others. This creates a bond that is sometimes stronger than blood kinship. In a way Vove is closer to me than my own brother."

"Is he closer to you than I am, too?" Baruch half pretended to be jealous.

"Oh, you!" Yacov regarded him affectionately. "You're a different story altogether. You are like me. You are me, but in another edition, in another dress. Even our digging inside ourselves, our heavyheartedness, and our somberness are almost identical."

"Says who?" Baruch protested. "I'm not somber!"

"Oh, you are, but you refuse to admit it. Take me for instance. I've never been as full of life, never have I felt myself being as free and satisfied as I am now. Yet, I can't deny that beneath this cheerful and optimistic facade there is something grieving, something gnawing at me that never lets go. I know that I'll never be rid of it. Neither will you."

Baruch was silent for a long while, then he changed the subject. "Guess what I've been doing of late." he said. "I go around buying up stocks and shares, telling myself that they might regain their value some day. If you insist that you and I are so much alike, how about the two of us going into partnership?"

Yacov shrugged, "I've got no talent for business."

Baruch refilled their glasses. "I know. You've got the talent for remaining a pauper and forever complaining about it. *Lechaim!*"

Yacov clinked glasses with him. "I've also got another talent—one which you lack—namely, that of finding myself good bedfellows. Their bodies may well be lice-infested, but at least their hearts aren't."

When Yacov left Baruch's apartment it was late in the evening. As he walked through the snow-covered streets in the cold, he was all of a sudden gripped by a great longing for Binele. Through fogged-up eyes he stared into the faces of the women who passed him. Perhaps one of them was Binele? The alcohol circulating in his veins made every female who passed him possess something of her, a similar gait, a similar hair color, similar eyes. Yet each one of them painfully denied her existence.

It so happened that the following evening he went to the library at The Harp. There, at one of the reading tables, he suddenly saw a head of reddish-yellow hair, saw a plaid shawl on a pair of shoulders that had a familiar outline. The plaid was folded on the woman's back in such a manner that it seemed to be concealing a pair of braids. His heart skipped a beat. His limbs felt weak as he approached the figure sitting bent over a book. He put his hand on a shoulder covered with the shawl. "Bi . . ." he uttered.

The shoulder moved. The woman's back straightened. A head turned toward him. He saw the sallow, creased face of a young woman, who had not the faintest resemblance to Binele. She had no braids. Her hair reached to her shoulders.

"Yes?" A pair of very sad brown eyes stared at him questioningly.

It took a while before Yacov recovered. "Oh, excuse me. I thought . . . "

She smiled faintly, "Are you looking for someone?"

"Yes . . . no . . . ." he stuttered.

"You must be new. I never saw you around here before." She heaved herself up from the chair and held out her hand to him. "Nice to meet you, comrade. My name is Bronia." She picked up her book from the table and made it vanish under her arm covered with the shawl. Having noticed the lost expression on his face, she asked. "Is this the first time you're returning a book? Come, I'll show you which librarian to approach." She beckoned to him with a gesture of her head, took him protectively by the arm, and pulled him along in the direction of the counter. "Let us pass, please, comrades," she whispered solemnly to the people standing around, indicating Yacov with a flicker of a glance. "A new member . . . "

As they waited for the librarian, Yacov finally took possession of himself. "I am not new," he said to the woman. "I can manage. Thank you very much."

"You are not new?" she was surprised. "What union do you belong to?"

"The weavers' union."

"I'm in the needle trade. A seamstress."

They had nothing more to say to each other. Yacov thought that she would leave him then and there. But she did not move from her place. He observed her from the corner of his eye. There was something about her that still reminded him of Binele. Perhaps it was the color of her hair, although now, at close range, it looked lusterless and straw-like. There was perhaps something of Binele also in the shape of her shoulders and the way her head sat on her short neck.

The librarian was free to take care of him. Yacov forgot about the woman and became involved in conversation with the librarian whom he asked for advice concerning the book he wanted to take out. When he finally got a book and turned around, he saw the yellow-haired woman standing right beside him.

"Did you get what you wanted?" she smiled at him.

"No, it's out. It doesn't matter. There is so much to read."

"To me it matters a lot." she nodded. "When I have a job I have little time left for reading, with all the party work in the evenings. Now, like many others, I've got no job. That's why the library is so crowded. But in general, I like to read with a system, so that I can progress in my socialist education. I, too, rarely get hold of the book I want. Our library is not sufficiently equipped for the growing number of readers."

Her sad eyes seemed to be at variance with her terse matter-of-fact words. She followed him to the door. He was glad. He took pleasure in the fact that she reminded him of Binele. They went down into the street and sauntered back and forth along the Piotrkowska. She spoke of her union and her party activities. He only partly listened to her, yet enjoyed immensely her presence at his side. Finally she invited him to her room for a cup of chicory coffee.

◎◎ *11* ◎◎

A DAY BEFORE THE DEMONSTRATION for workers' solidarity, Yacov was canvasing the streets of Baluty with a packet of leaflets in his hand. He went from one gate to another, rushing up flights of stairs and putting leaflets in front of every door. In spite of the biting frost he was hot.

As he hurried from one gate to the next, he caught sight of a sky-blue beret and a face in the crowd of passersby. A pair of braids flashed past his eyes. He looked back. The face turned toward him. His heart began to pound, his feet froze in place, his mind stopped. The two braids drew closer. The slanted eyes swam toward him. It was impossible to take in the whole figure before him with his eyes.

"You are Yacov, aren't you?" he heard Binele ask.

He blinked, trying to look at her. The familiar, the dreamed-about, was standing before him, peering out from a new form, a new electrifying appearance. She was and was not the same girl whom he had known in Bociany, the one for whom he had longed. His joy at seeing her was and was not the joy he had envisaged at their first encounter in Lodz. Yet the sight of her overwhelmed him. It took his breath away. He wanted to cry out "How beautiful you are!" but was unable to utter a sound. Her face dazzled his eyes; he stood there gaping, struggling to absorb her presence. Her newly acquired beauty had little to do with her face or with her physical appearance, although it was precisely her physical aspect that surprised him, stunned him, and made him speechless. He saw her high cheekbones, the slanted Mongolian eyes with their hot, biting light, saw the freckles on her pale face, saw her slender yet sturdy body and the full protruding bosom. But the beauty that overwhelmed him and deprived him of strength radiated not from her body but rather from some source within her, the same source that had drawn him to her years ago.

"Well, say something, for heaven's sake," she murmured, looking as if she too were dazed. Her cheeks, flushed by the frost, shone through the veil of steam coming from her breath.

"You look different," he mumbled.

She tossed her braids back. "You too. We're getting old." She smiled faintly.

"How has life been treating you?" he asked.

"Like a sinner in hell." She tried to control her voice. "I worked at Berman's factory as a *shtoperke*. Then the war broke out. I was sick with typhus. Now I work at plaids in a workshop, there, across the street. I twist the fringes. Here, look." She showed him her red fingers, which were bruised and callused.

He had the impression that she was entrusting him with her wounded hands because she wanted him to take them and hold them between his palms. But the tenderness that came over him made him place a leaflet on her palms to cover their bruises.

"Read it," he said hurriedly. "Come to the demonstration tomorrow. The time and place are marked in the leaflet. We'll see each other there. Now I must run." He forced himself to turn away from her.

Binele, confused, was left standing with the leaflet in her hand. After a moment she recovered and ran after him. She grabbed his arm. "I can't read!" she pointed to the leaflet.

He was grateful to her for letting him see her face once more. The sudden sight of her had been too overwhelming. Or perhaps there was something in him that made him reject what he had most yearned for, what he most wanted—just as he had done in Bociany, when he had run to her with the news that there was an opportunity for her to leave for Lodz, to escape from him. Now his eyes were again full of her. He wanted to touch her, to convince himself that she was tangible. He took the leaflet from her hand and quickly read it to her in a hoarse voice. "Tomorrow morning at nine. The textile workers meet on the Promenade. I'll be there too. I'm a weaver." He pushed the leaflet back into her hand, nodded his head, and ran through the arch of the gate where they had stopped. Fixed in place, she followed him with her eyes. He felt her gaze on him as he ran through the yard and turned his head back a few times.

"Wait, Yacov!" She came up beside him. "I didn't understand a word you said."

He burst out laughing loud and free. "I'm an idiot!" She grinned and nodded in agreement. He said, "I must have been out of my mind. You could have gone away and I would have lost you again. Wait for me outside the gate." He ran into the stairwell of the house next to them.

Binele waited in the archway of the gate. Fear seized her by the throat. How little it would take to lose Yacov again in this sea of houses, streets, and people, in this town that had hidden him from her for who knew how long. What had happened to him since she had seen him last? There was so much she wanted to ask him. She would not let him go now, would not let things happen as they had with her brother Hershele who had vanished without a trace. She did not take her eyes off the yard for a moment; she stood and watched Yacov running from one stairwell to the next, each time waving at her. She scanned the area with her eyes, making sure that there was no other exit from the yard. He had to pass through this gate. She would not lose him. When he had entered the last staircase it seemed to her that he was taking too long. An eternity had passed since the moment when she had first laid eyes on him.

He came out of the stairway and quickly walked up to her. They left the gate together, glancing at each other out of the corners of their eyes. "His eyes look like two warm chestnuts," she thought to herself. Slowly, with uneven steps, they moved ahead. She sensed his tension and impatience. He turned to her and motioned at the pack of leaflets, "I must distribute these first. Tell me where we can meet in an hour."

"What do you mean meet in an hour?" She looked fearfully at him. She was loath to lose sight of him for a whole hour. He might forget or mistake the place where they had agreed to meet. "I'll come with you until you finish. I'll help you. I know a lot about politics," she boasted.

"No, I must do it by myself. We'll meet in an hour. It'll be easier."

She was trembling. The reddish-yellow braids moved up and down on her bosom. Short, feather-thin tendrils of hair fluttered like a veil on her forehead while others swayed like sidelocks, dangling from under the sky-blue woolen beret that covered her ears. Her entire face seemed to be swimming before his eyes, as if it were about to dissolve into the air and vanish.

He caught himself, realizing that she was asking him something. He was too distraught, too intoxicated to absorb her words. She insisted that he take her along, that much he understood. So he gave in and nodded. He let her wait for him in front of every gate. As they walked together from gate to gate, he heard her tell him that she knew what he was doing, that she was well informed about *socialismus* and *Poale-Zionismus*. But she twisted the words around and mixed up one thing with the other. Every one of her expressions was a knot over a bag of riddles. Who was she, this Binele of today? What was she trying so feverishly to convince him of? And why did she look so disturbed, so lost, so desperate in her excitement, when there was something so powerful in the air all around her?

At length he was finished with distributing the leaflets. He and Binele began to walk slowly along the streets. They bought bagels, nervously chewed on them, and talked, each not hearing what the other was saying, or rather not understanding. Long silences fell between them. Then each grew frightened that the other might take the silence as a sign that they had nothing else to say to each other and should part. They resumed their conversation, continuing to pour out sentences that missed one another or ran into each other; they each cut off the other's flow of words, finally allowing only single ones, clumsy and lame, to stumble on disjointedly. Binele knew only one thing, that she would not let Yacov go. She would not move away from him. Looking at him was a cure for everything sore and sick within her. Her heart pounded like that of a robber afraid of capture. She did not know how to handle this strange new fear of losing Yacov. Then, all at once, she saw him stop at a street corner. He reached out for her hand and shook it. She froze. "You are not leaving already?"

"I must," he grinned ill at ease.

"Take me with you!"

"I can't."

"Why can't you? I will follow you."

"Binele . . ."

No one had ever called her Binele that way. Her name on his lips sounded like a song. She had had no idea that she possessed such a flowing, caressing name. She noticed the wistful expression of his pale, sad face. His yearning eyes, moist with emotion, seemed to be calling her. They stroked her face with a tenderness that took her apart as they lingered on her cheeks, eyebrows, and hair. She could hardly bear that gaze; she could not peer into the depths of his eyes for too long. She felt herself devoured by them. Those eyes made her feel weak in her knees, in her entire body.

He let go of her hand and took a step away. She grabbed his arm. "You know," she whispered as if, with the tears that filled her eyes, she could keep him from leaving, "I had a friend here. Ziporah was her name. Her three children died at the hospital, and she herself has vanished. Maybe she killed herself."

He stood a step away from her and did not come closer. "I know how you feel," he said from that distance. "I've also lost a friend. Yoel the Blacksmith from Bociany. He ran into a burning house in the village to save a child, and his heart gave out. It was a great grief to me, too. You knew him, didn't you?" She nodded. He watched her wipe her eyes with the palms of her hands. "It's getting late," he muttered. "I must run. If we don't see each other tomorrow morning, then come to The Harp in the evening. You know where The Harp is, don't you?" She nodded. He turned sharply and walked off.

An oppressive wave of anxiety swept over Binele. Yacov was indifferent to her grief. He had a mild, handsome face, but in reality he was a cold fish. Or perhaps he was married now, perhaps he was a father of children? A powerful, uncontrollable, bitter-sweet feeling of humility took hold of her, and she raced after him again. She snatched him by a sleeve. "Yacov," she panted. "Just tell me one thing. Are you going home to your wife?"

He bit his lips. What obstructive force was it that kept him from taking her into his arms and forgetting about everything? He felt a need to go down on his knees before her, to stretch himself out before her feet, and to let her step over him. Her humility reflected in his face. "I'm not going home to a wife," he answered, grabbed hold of her hand, shook it again, and ran off. She did not run after him this time.

Slowly Binele walked away in the direction of the snow-covered Train Garden, where she was to meet Handsome Moshe. When she had recovered from her illness and had been unable to find Ziporah, she had looked Moshe up. He had also fallen ill when Lodz still belonged to the Russians. He had caught cold while keeping guard at the telegraph poles, and it had developed into pneumonia. His life had been in danger for many weeks.

Moshe had changed beyond recognition. He had completely given up his dandyish mannerisms and had become a serious young man, too serious as far as Binele was concerned. He read books and missed not a single performance at the theater, where he and Binele saw serious dramas together. They also saw comedies at the revue theater. But if Binele burst into laughter during the performance of a serious drama, or if she suddenly felt like weeping during a comedy, Moshe rebuked her. He made her understand that a cultured person must refrain from loud laughter during a dramatic performance because the characters on stage were doomed to defeat in a drama, whereas to cry during a comedy performance was simply a waste of money—even if he and Binele had sneaked themselves into the theater through the back door, without tickets.

At present, Moshe nourished two ambitions: to become an orator for the Poale-Zion and to become a professional actor. He took Binele along to the lectures of all the famous speakers who visited Lodz, in the hope that he would learn the art of oratory from them. As far as Binele was concerned, Moshe's two great ambitions were in fact one. She observed how much of an actor each great orator was, how, by modulating his voice to make it sound thunderous or soft, he copied the great performers of the stage. It seemed to her that the more a speaker tried to behave like an actor in a serious drama, the more he sounded like the clown in a burlesque. But some great speakers impressed her as much as the great dramatic actors. She could not forget them or their speeches for a long time afterwards. So she went along and joined Moshe in making his great plans and dreaming his beautiful dreams.

Handsome Moshe was strolling in the frozen snow-covered Train Garden, waiting for her. She threw herself into his arms and pressed the leaflet that Yacov had given her into his hand, saying hurriedly, "Read this to me slowly."

He glanced at the leaflet, crumbled it into a ball, threw it into the gutter, and said resolutely, "We'll march in the demonstration under the banners of the Poale-Zion."

"Of course, of the Poale-Zion," she agreed. She cared not the least for anyone's demonstrations. In her opinion, demonstrations differed very little from Catholic processions on Sundays or holidays. The only difference between them was that instead of church banners with pictures of Jesus and the saints, the demonstrators carried red flags with large pictures of their leaders, who, like the saints, had serious noble faces. But she had one more thing to ask Handsome Moshe, "Do you know the address of The Harp?"

Moshe looked at her searchingly. "You met someone from The Harp who gave you the leaflet, didn't you?"

"What if I did?"

"So you could have asked him for the address of The Harp." The flame of jealousy was kindled in Moshe's eyes. Ever since Binele had vanished so suddenly from his life, he had grown suspicious of her. He could not understand the riddles posed by her enigmatic behavior and moods. By no means could he explain them. Although his reason told him that his suspicions made no sense, he allowed them to carry him away into a tangle of anxieties. The more he grew attached to her, the more eager he was to marry her, the more insecure he felt. Now he looked at her with distrust, his face twisted into a grimace in the vain effort to disguise his feelings. When it came to Binele he was not a good actor at all. The more he cared for her, the worse he acted. Sometimes he thought that it was from her that he should learn the art of acting. He leaned over to her and asked, "Are you playing games behind my back?"

"What games?" She grew angry as usual when he came out with his wild suspicions and made a fool of himself as if he had lost his reason. But at the same time his sensitivity amazed her. It was as if he could see what was going on in her heart. "Do you want your ring back?" she asked.

"I don't want the ring back, but you could have told me."

"Told you what?"

"That you want to become a member of The Harp. I told you from the start that I'm a member of the Poale-Zion. There can be no secrets between bride and groom because husband and wife share the same life."

"We aren't husband and wife yet."

"But we shall soon be, won't we?"

"Of course."

"Then don't you agree that there should be no secrets between us?"

"Of course." She said "of course" in such a way that he was not certain whether she meant yes or no. She went on, "Then why are you making such a big secret about The Harp? Can't you tell me where it is, if I ask you?"

"You really don't know?"

"Moshe!" she cried out beside herself. She did not have much patience for him that day.

"The Harp is the name of the Bundist club. When I take you home, I'll show you the house. You can join whatever club you like, but I want you to be honest with me. And, for your information, the Bundists are no better than the Bolsheviks."

"Leave the Bundists and the Bolsheviks alone. My brother is a Bolshevik. You said so yourself when I told you about him. So watch out! And don't you dare tell me that I'm not honest with you!"

"Binele," he said softly and looked at her with such imploring eyes, the expression on his face so tortured, that it made her heart melt. She smiled, embraced him, and kissed him on the cheek. Moshe, soothed, slowly began to talk to her about *Zionismus* and Eretz Israel. Binele thought of Yone Svolotch, who had been conscripted into the Russian Army, or so her girlfriends from the factory had told her, and had not been heard of ever since. She was certain that he was in Eretz Israel. It occurred to her that it would be all right with her if Moshe also decided to leave for Eretz Israel. Then she would have peace of mind.

Moshe's talk was full of outlandish words, and he repeatedly mentioned the words "the left" or "the right," which made her automatically turn her head either to the left or to the right. He meant of course the "wings" of his movement, the left wing or the right wing of the Poale-Zion, which she began to visualize like some gigantic bird. But when he embarked on describing the life of the *halutzim* on the kibbutz, she felt herself drawn into his monologue, and his words began to register in her mind. Life in a kibbutz made her think of everything beautiful in the life of Bociany, a Bociany where she would be neither hungry nor lonely. A thought entered her mind that perhaps she should allow Moshe to talk her into becoming a member of the Poale-Zion. He was, after all, her fiancé, the closest person she had in this world, and she knew how to appreciate him—if only The Harp had not begun to play in her head that day.

Moshe embraced her. He pulled her under the arch of a muddy gate. He kissed her mouth and eyes and stroked her hair. "I love you, Binele," he whispered. "Whatever you did, to whatever party you belonged, I still would have loved you."

"I love you too," she said with an air of genuine candor. At the same time she wanted to burst out and tell him that she did not know what love was, that she loved no one and did not know if she would ever learn to love him, just as she did not know if she would ever learn many other things. But to the surprise of both of them, her eyes filled with tears. This made Moshe even more romantic. More than her words, her tears reassured him of her feelings for him. The more affectionate and tender he grew, the guiltier she felt.

Binele told Moshe that she would not take part in the demonstration because she did not believe in demonstrations, as he well knew. After a restless night, she got up the next day and, although she dressed hurriedly, she spent quite a while in front of her little mirror, trying to arrange the blue beret on her head with more flare than usual. She ran down into the street and rushed toward that part of the Promenade where the Bundist marchers were supposed to gather for the demonstration. She waded into the crowd, scanning the faces, until she found Yacov.

His face lit up, and he flushed when he saw her. "Binele!" He spoke her name so lovingly that her heart ached. "Come, march with me."

Her heartbeat sounded in her ears like a drum. Handsome Moshe was marching with the Poale-Zion, while she marched here, beside Yacov. Since the day before, when she had first seen Yacov, she had been marching beside him. She wished that Yacov would take her arm and not allow her to run back to Handsome Moshe. She gazed enviously at the young men and women all around her, who marched in lockstep, their arms linked. But Yacov, radiant, his head raised high, his gait strong and firm, marched at a slight distance from her. He sang loudly with the crowd and moved his arms to the rhythm of the march music played by an orchestra. She began to march like he did, falling into the rhythm of his steps.

Never before in her life had she found herself among such an enthusiastic crowd of people, who yet all seemed connected, moving together as if they were parts of one enormous body. They were workers. She was one of them. As she marched on, head high, bosom forward, steps light and rhythmic, arms loose and swaying, it suddenly became clear to her what Handsome Moshe and so many of her girlfriends at the factory and the workshop, and what even Ziporah had tried to explain to her. She belonged here, along with all these pale, worn-out, shabbily dressed men and women, who looked so powerful and festive this day. These were her real brothers and sisters, just as Ziporah had been closer to her than a sister. It was Ziporah's presence that she felt the most as she marched. All of them, she thought as she looked around, wanted to achieve a better life, to create a paradise on earth. True, she could not quite figure out how they would go about reaching that goal, but she knew that her place was with them. Her place was next to Yacov. It seemed to her that she and Yacov were both walking down the Wide Poplar Road, surrounded on all sides by a boisterous singing crowd that had come to join them in celebrating their walk together.

She stared intently at Yacov, and said to herself, "I never had a home. Now The Harp will be my home. If he who walks now beside me belongs there, then this is my place as well." A painful question pierced through her mind. "And Moshe, Handsome Moshe who loves me so much, I don't know how to repay him for all that he gives me of himself, what can I do about him?" Her eyes filled. Since the day before when she had run into Yacov, she constantly felt like weeping. Now as the mass of people burst into a new song and she clearly heard the words, "In the salty sea of human tears," the tears ran so profusely from her eyes that she could barely see where to put her foot down.

Yacov finally reached out for her hand. He stared at her in astonishment and tilted his head close to her. "Why are you crying, Binele?"

"Because . . . " she stammered, "because I'm happy."

When Yacov took Binele to The Harp for the first time, the rooms were packed full. In the large assembly room of the club, people stood tightly pressed together. Fantastic news had arrived from Russia. The Russian people were waking up, determined to take their fate into their own hands. Unrest was stirring in Germany as well. The humiliated, the downtrodden, the workers, the peasants, the women, and the soldiers refused to carry the chains of oppression any longer. The yokes on their backs were cracking apart with thunderous threats.

A small man wearing a pair of thin glasses fastened to his ears with a piece of wire on one end and with a string on the other, paced so close to the edge of the platform that it seemed that at any moment he would stumble and plunge into the hall. He raised his fists and shook his grizzled mane of hair until it stood upright. His voice had started out sounding as clear as a bell but grew increasingly hoarse. The hoarser it became, the more his listeners were enraptured, carried away by the fire of his impassioned words.

"That's Laibel the Hump," Yacov whispered in Binele's ear. "He taught me the weaver's trade and helped me to become a Bundist."

"Such an educated weaver!" Binele wondered.

"He educated himself at night after work," Yacov explained. "What you learn on your own, you know better than what you learn from a teacher."

When they walked out into the street after the meeting, Binele confessed to Yacov, "Do you know, I don't really believe in the revolution in which you all believe. I mean, perhaps it's true that it's almost here, but I don't believe that it'll do anything to change the world."

"Why not?" he asked.

"Because that's how the world is made. God loves the good pauper, but He helps the rich villain. A question of luck. My friend Ziporah used to say, 'One person doesn't have the appetite for the food, while the other doesn't have the food for the appetite.'"

"You mean that one is born to be rich, while the other is born to be poor?" Yacov asked, upset. "We are all born naked, equal, and everyone deserves an equal share in the good things of this world. Otherwise nothing makes sense."

"But the masses, they are like brothers and sisters when they suffer from hunger and want, or when they march in a demonstration. They will make the revolution just as the speaker in The Harp said they would. They will even sacrifice their lives for the revolution. But after the revolution is won, and they can get themselves to the cauldron of food and to all the good things, the stronger will push away the weaker, and there will be a new class of rich and poor. That's how the world works. Everyone likes to fend for himself, and what you need is luck, only luck. If you have a mother, that's your good luck. If I never had a mother, that is my bad luck."

"And maybe you have no mother because your father didn't call for a doctor? Maybe she could have been saved?" Yacov said softly. "But I won't say that there aren't things over which we have no control. There are. But there are other things that we are capable of changing. Even if it only seems to us that we can change things, we must try. We must try to change even our own nature. We must realize that our selfish, evil deeds destroy us. If we don't, there will never be an end to wars, to revolutions, and to killings of any sort. But people, even if they are evil, want to be good. That's why we have religion. We thought that God and religious laws could help us be good people. But they don't. We must learn to change on our own, inside ourselves. The world has stood for too long on foundations of hatred. Perhaps now is the time to put it on a foundation of love." The word "love" made him flush. His eyes were covered with a warm mist as they met Binele's. In order to disguise the uneasiness that the word "love" had caused him, he quickly changed the direction of his words. "It is said," he smiled faintly, "that when Moses raised his hand over the Red Sea, it refused to divide and let the Israelites pass. Only when one of the Israelites jumped into the water, did the miracle happen and the sea split in two. So we must be the first to jump into the water."

Yacov and Binele talked on and on as they walked. Yacov's talk made a noise in Binele's head. Of course what he said seemed unreasonable and impossible. Yet she badly wanted to believe that the unreasonable and impossible could happen. She began to think that Ziporah and her children did not have to die, that her own mother did not have to die, that trying to do something good for the world together with the brothers and sisters was perhaps worthwhile.

"You are rearranging the furniture in my head," she said to Yacov, nervously braiding and unbraiding her hair over her bosom. Inwardly she added, "And also the furniture in my heart." Because while they talked about these "political matters," there was another, a continuous and unspoken conversation going on between them. Something inexplicable was flowing back and forth between them. She could feel it clearly as they walked on and on.

The lantern man, dressed all in black, appeared on the street. He lit one lantern after another with a long hooked pole that resembled the pole that the firemen of Bociany were meant to use in order to save the storks from burning roofs. In the yellow-green light of the gas lanterns the street took on the look of a long deep corridor, a tunnel with faintly blinking lights that both Yacov and Binele had entered. In the dark Yacov's face also resembled a lit lantern. It grew increasingly brighter, lighting up everything within Binele. And the brighter it grew within her, the more she felt the tears surging toward her eyes.

Yacov took leave of her in front of the house where she lived. Although it was a night in February, it seemed to him that he smelled the flowers in the nuns' garden in Bociany.

Spring was finally announcing its arrival. Yacov decided to take Binele for an excursion to the Konstantine Forest on the outskirts of Lodz. It was a forest of pine trees, secretive and dark, unlike the twittering birch wood of Bociany where blueberries and blackberries grew. Here the ground was dry, full of brown needles that cracked under every step like the dry bones of a skeleton. In the summertime blueberries and raspberries grew here too, but they had not the same taste as those in Bociany. In order to arrive at the Konstantine Forest, one had to walk down the entire long Konstantine Street, facing the constant danger of being attacked by thieves and drunkards. Binele began to feel uneasy even before she had entered the forest with Yacov.

Yet the Konstantine Forest was a Jewish domain, in particular on the Sabbath. And this was a fine warm Sabbath afternoon at the beginning of March. Entire families were seated on boxes and tree stumps, the children gamboling around with their undergarments flying. The women busied themselves with bags of food and bottles of drinking water. They raced after the children with slices of bread that they wanted them to eat, or they spoon-fed the younger ones. The infirm sat on deck chairs, enjoying the air. Bearded old men sat crouched on low stools with open volumes of Scripture on their knees.

Everywhere between the trees there strolled groups of young men and women, who paraded, holding big fat books under their arms, the more "weighty" and visible the book, the more impressive the sight of the person who carried it. The names of Tolstoy, Dostoyevsky, Heine, Marx, and Engels and the titles of their works sounded in the air, as they were tossed back and forth by the strollers. Some, as they strolled, recited long poems aloud, poems learned by heart—thus indulging in the only dignified form of flirtation admissible during these progressive times. Nature in its state of awakening had the power to inspire these poetry lovers and fill their recitations with additional depths and meaning. Those young couples who had already advanced beyond the level of discussing great works of prose, or reciting poetry in a group, and preferred to do it alone, broke away from the others and proceeded deeper into the forest.

There were also groups of young men and women who had not come to the forest merely to waste time on flirtations and chatter. They sat on rocks and tree stumps, conducting their political meetings under the trees. There were others who studied the sciences together. At the center of one such group stood a long-haired man leaning against a tree, loudly discussing the new trends in modern Yiddish literature with his companions. Not far from there another group sat gathered around another tree, and a woman in a black sweater was teaching her listeners the words and melody of a newly composed Yiddish song.

Binele and Yacov wandered among the trees, all the while seeing to it that there should be a barrier of bushes and branches to fill the space between them. Binele was overcome by a feeling of regret and sadness. She missed Bociany badly. She had not gone back there since the day when she had run away. Now she pressed Yacov to give her news of Bociany, but he was not in the right mood. He was silent and withdrawn. When he did begin to talk, he spoke of the events happening in Russia. Then he told her of the Konstantine Forest, that it was here that the first illegal meetings of the Bund had taken place. It was here, in the year 1905, that the workers who had fought in Lodz atop barricades of overturned trams, furniture, and broken lanterns, had been executed. During the victims' funerals the Cossacks had attacked the processions, and again people were brought to this forest to be shot. Yacov's words depressed Binele even more.

Yet in order to keep their conversation going, she asked him, "Would you be ready to fight on a barricade and let yourself be killed?"

He shrugged. "I figure that in the heat of battle there is no time to ask oneself such questions."

She got not the slightest pleasure out of their walk. Every time that there was no shrub or a bush to come between her and Yacov, her heart began to pound so violently that it hurt. When she caught sight of his warm brown eyes, so strangely overcast that day, she felt herself drowning in the depths of their wistful sadness. She was furious with herself. "What's the matter with me?" she chided herself. "Haven't I had enough to do with men? Don't I hate them all, all except Handsome Moshe?"

She could not forgive herself for considering Yacov's words to be more beautiful than Moshe's, even though Yacov, too, spoke of things that hardly interested her. Handsome Moshe was more talented than Yacov. He would become a great actor one day. Moshe had a fine flowing voice, whereas Yacov spoke with long silences between his sentences, as if it were hard for him to bring them out. His words fluttered in the air, they seemed uncertain and trembling. Yet they made their way to her heart and stirred it. She absorbed the yearning sweetness of their sound along with the warmth that radiated from him.

At last Yacov stopped talking about those cold insignificant issues that had so little to do with what was happening between the two of them. He indulged in unfolding a string of memories. He recalled the time when she had charmed him as a little girl, and the evening when for the first time he had taken her home from the Blue Mountain. She had been crying then. He livened up and asked, "Do you know the meaning of your name,

'Bina'? It's the name of the third *Sefira*. It means wisdom." It also meant fertility, but this he did not tell her.

She was thrilled, and exclaimed, "So now you know why I'm such a stupid cow!"

Her self-deprecation annoyed him. "Don't say that. I know that you are wise even without thinking."

"Thank you for the compliment!" she laughed. She could not understand how a person could be wise without thinking. "If I am so wise that I don't need to think," she said playfully, "then let me tell you that my name comes from the word 'bee.' I can sting and give honey, just like a bee. Anyway my name is Yiddish not Hebrew. It means *Ich bin*, I am—Bina."

"You are Bina," he echoed her.

"And you?" she asked. "Tell me about yourself."

"About my name?"

"About everything." She wanted to know everything about him, down to the slightest detail. "Tell me, for instance what has made you come to Lodz."

"I was drawn to come."

"Do you remember that you promised to look me up as soon as you came to Lodz?"

"I've been looking for you ever since I got here," he conceded, "but Lodz is not Bociany. Lodz is like a stormy sea."

"Yes, it is like a stormy sea," she agreed. She was surprised that she could feel so well and at the same time be so sad.

"And you see that we did find each other in this great sea, but the waves carry you off in one direction and me in another."

"What do you mean by that?"

He waited a while without looking at her before he answered her grimly. "Do you remember the demonstration for workers' solidarity? Last week a young man came up to me in the street. He told me that he had seen you and me marching together. He said he was your fiancé, that you two are about to be married and that I should leave you alone. A fine, polite young man. I told him that we, you and I, are from the same shtetl, that we only recently ran into each other. Are you really going to marry him?"

She was struck dumb. Finally she forced herself to confirm it, "Yes, so I am."

They left the forest. Binele knew that this was the most important moment in her life. She was losing Yacov, perhaps she would never see him again. Or perhaps she would. After all, he had taken her to the Konstantine Forest and he had advised her to become a member of The Harp and to learn to read and write. But if she met him again, he would continue indulging himself in these "cold" conversations, and she would never discover the finer things about him that she longed to know. Yacov and she would never become any closer than they were. This meant death, the death of that "something" between them that had flourished for so long in the secret nooks of their hearts.

Suddenly, her walking home with him, this fraction of time that they could still enjoy together, became impossible to bear. Without another word, not giving Yacov another look, Binele tore herself away from his side and almost lurching forward, she raced away from him. She could hear him call after her, could hear his footsteps running behind her, but she was determined not to let him catch up with her. She had once won a race with him. He would probably muster all his strength to overtake her. She would do the same to escape him. But her heart raced too fast, her heart begged her legs to give in, to wait for him. She lost trust in herself. Yacov's steps came closer. She had not appreciated the strength of his determination.

She rounded the corner of a house, rushed through a gate, and ran up a flight of stairs. She heard the thump of Yacov's feet running past the gate. After a while she walked out into the street. There was no trace of Yacov. The street was dark. There were drunkards lying in the corners of the gates. One of them lay on the sidewalk with his feet in the gutter. He called after her. The street was a dark tunnel with no light.

On her bed that night, she could not rid herself of the image of Yacov's face. It floated down toward her from the windowpane, from the ceiling, from the corners of the room, and then vanished as it approached her.

The next day she could not keep still at the workshop. The minute the boss went out of the room, she dashed to the window and peered out into the street. Perhaps Yacov was standing outside? Perhaps he would walk past the building? At lunch she ran outside and scanned the faces of the noisy crowd that passed her. Something had happened. She knew what it was. The revolution was sweeping through Russia. It was silly to expect Yacov to think of her today. "I never want to see him again," she assured herself, and yet she rushed over to Reb Saivel Malkes's workshop, where

Yacov worked. She stood across the street with her eyes glued to the gate for the entire lunch break. Perhaps he would come out. It was a glorious sunny day. The air was full of hope and promise.

After work, the moment she stepped out into the street, Binele looked about her. Perhaps Yacov was waiting for her? She felt a hand on her arm. "Have you heard the news?" She was confronted by Moshe, who pulled her with him, talking about the wonderful things that were happening in Russia. He led her into a soup kitchen. They shared a bread soup. Binele ate rapaciously, as if she wanted the soup to fill a void within her. Moshe was talking nonstop. "The soldiers have refused to shoot at the demonstrators in Petrograd." He slurped both the soup and his words. "They established a soviet of both workers and soldiers. A delegation of the interim government went to Pskov to meet with the tsar and he abdicated along with his son! Can you imagine? No more tsar! The Romanov dynasty and all the other dynasties are gone forever!" Moshe talked on and on, his mouth wet, dripping with soup. He seemed possessed, beside himself, feverish in his excitement. His entire body shook and his face was twisted into one knot of tension. To Binele he had never seemed more distant. Diligently, she polished her plate clean with a piece of bread.

Exhausted, weighed down by the discomfort of her heart, she slowly dragged herself up the stairs to her loft. There was still half a flight of stairs to climb when she leaned against the banister and raised her head. A small, dirty light bulb faintly illuminated the staircase. She was about to start counting the number of stairs that she still had to climb, when she saw an apparition looming high above, on the landing. She saw a tall, stooped masculine figure like that of a gigantic prophet, with a gray, unkempt beard and the facial pallor of a corpse. His gaze dark, his forehead overcast like the sky during a storm, he stood there, holding a cane raised in the air, looking like Moses about to hit the rock to make the water gush from it.

Binele gasped for air. Her heart swelled with maddening joy. She spread out her arms and exclaimed, "Tateshie!" Arms extended, she rushed up to Yossele Abedale, taking two stairs at a time. She reached for his gabardine. As she took another step, the cane in Yossele's hand came down on her head as if her head were a rock.

"Take that! And that!" Yossele panted, bringing the cane down on her again and again. "Working on the Sabbath! Running around with pimps, you whore! Come home with me this minute! You scum! You scabby-head!" A sob, heavy, Job-like, issued from his mouth along with an avalanche of curses. The whacks from the cane continued to beat down on Binele. Yossele almost fell down the stairs.

She flung up her arms to shield her face, and so she stood, frozen in her movement, bent under the torrent of blows. She was possessed by an ice-cold curiosity to see how far he would go with his blows. A stream of blood ran down her neck. An uncanny shriek finally escaped from her chest. She made an about-face and rushed down the stairs. She heard him call after her, "Come here! Come back right away!"

Out in the street, she ran ahead, holding on to her head with both hands. When the blood began to dribble through her fingers, she entered a gate, knocked at a janitor's door, and asked the woman who answered the door of the dark dwelling to give her a rag to cover her wound.

The woman crossed herself. "Jesus Maria!" she exclaimed. "Has the revolution broken out in Lodz, too?" Binele told her that she had fallen in the street. The woman crossed herself again and mumbled, "A bad omen. Blood will flow in the streets of Lodz any day now."

The woman washed Binele's wound and wept. Her youngest son was in the Polish battalion that was supposed to be returning from Russia. Her oldest son had joined Josef Pilsudski's legion in Austria. "When Pilsudski was imprisoned in the Magdeburg Fortress," she told Binele, sobbing, "the legions fell apart. Now that the Chief has been freed, the boys flock to him to form a new legion. And who will wipe the blood off their wounds, dear Jesus?" She dabbed the cut in Binele's head with a piece of towel. "Dear Mother of God!" she moaned. "Your head is really split open!" She would not let Binele leave until the bleeding had stopped, and the entire time she kept on talking of her sons who had left to fight for a free Poland.

Once out in the street, Binele let herself be carried forward by the crowd. People—their faces either somber or jubilant, twisted by either smiles or by weeping, and looking like masks in an enormous masquerade—pushed against her. Newspaper vendors raced through the streets, calling hoarsely, "Special edition! Extra! Extra! Revolution spreading throughout Russia! War coming to an end!"

Binele stared at the confused crowds of passersby through the thick heavy veil of her numbness. Nothing hurt her. It was late in the evening when, dulled and stunned, she finally turned in the direction of her house. Slowly she climbed the four flights of stairs, peering up from under her eyebrows to check whether the figure of the fearsome avenger was still waiting for her. The landing was empty. She staggered into her room, locked the door, and in her muddy, blood-stained coat, threw herself on her bed. Only now did the wound in her head begin to throb. A thousand hammers seemed to be pounding in her skull. Yet the fierceness of the wound burning in her heart was still harder to bear.

The next day she told the people at work and later on told Handsome Moshe as well that she had slipped in the street. Moshe took her to see a barber-surgeon, who cleansed her wound and bandaged her head. "You see, Binele," Moshe pressed her to his chest firmly, "whether you like it or not, you live in the spirit of the revolution." He spoke elatedly of the upheaval about to spread all over Europe, whispering enthusiastically in her ear, "And Germany, too, will soon be swept off its feet by the storm. The tides are rising. The seas from the East and West will meet and together make the entire world explode in the deluge. Poland will get back its freedom, and we Jews will finally have a Jewish homeland."

In fact, soon after that day Moshe came running to her with the news. "Binele!" He was beside himself with excitement. "They've signed the Balfour Declaration! We're going to have a Jewish homeland!" He pressed her forcefully to his chest, his face nuzzled the blue beret on her head.

Peace came to Europe. Like a white seagull it rose from the seas of destruction and soared victoriously toward the calm blue of the sky.

Handsome Moshe, rejuvenated and overjoyed, dragged Binele through the streets and whispered feverishly in her ear. "Binele, do you realize what's going on? A new world is about to hatch, to peel itself out of its shell right before our eyes. This has been the war to end all wars. Now mankind will take its fate into its own hands and lead the world back to the Garden of Eden." Moshe was inspired. He kissed Binele. "Our children will live in a happier world."

And so it happened that Poland, doomed by its geography to be constantly torn into pieces, cut up by the knives of oppression into halves and quarters, woke up one day born anew and liberated. At The Harp, during a mass meeting, Binele heard a speaker expound with great enthusiasm, "What had been sighed for and dreamed of by Poland's devoted sons, by her poets, by her workers, by her peasants and Jews has come to pass. Yes, by the Jews too!" the speaker called out and raised his fist in the air. "Throughout generations we, the Jews of Poland, have also earned the right to call this soil our homeland. We earned it by the sweat of our brow, by our participation in the struggle for Poland's freedom, and we earned it through our blood, blood that this earth has absorbed during pogroms."

On one of the mornings that Binele went out into the street to meet Moshe, she saw a million white spread-winged eagles decorating a million red and white flags hung from windowsills, walls, and gates, and pinned onto people's hats and lapels. Moshe took her to watch the first parade of free Poland's army. Moshe was as devout a Zionist as he was an ardent Polish patriot. In addition to that, he loved parades. He hated the army, and as a socialist hated any expression of militarism. Yet the heart of the actor in him swelled with jubilation at the sight of the street becoming transformed into a stage. He just could not miss out on the historic occasion.

As he and Binele stood on the curb, waiting for the parade to approach, he whispered in Binele's ear, "A state is being born, Binele, and we witness it with our own eyes. We will have something to tell our children." He explained to her how the Polish army had come into existence. He told her about Josef Pilsudski, its founder, the leader of the struggle for freedom. "As soon as he was released from the Magdeburg Fortress," Moshe said, "he gathered around him the Polish battalions of the disbanded Russian Army and of the army of General Haller that had marched in from France, and so he created this army of a free Poland."

The first columns of the parade were approaching. Fanfares were sounded. The street responded with a roar of jubilation and applause. Moshe glanced at Binele as she indifferently pushed strands of wayward hair out of her eyes. "You haven't got the slightest sense of history, Binele," he reproached her cheerfully.

"I've no sense for nonsense," she countered, smiling. "If you want to know, all this hoo-ha scares me stiff. You should have known by now that I hate spectacles of this sort. As I stand here with you on this street curb, I cannot help remembering when I was small, and how the people of Bociany were frightened of Christian processions and of men in uniforms. And, as a matter of fact, just look about you and tell me whether you can see even one Jew in traditional dress in this crowd."

But after a while Binele's spirits rebounded. Gradually the street crowd infected her with its fever and, in spite of herself, drew her into its mood of jubilation. She abandoned herself to it, and she too broke into applause.

The columns of parading soldiers, dressed in their new Polish uniforms, wearing four-cornered caps embroidered with white and decorated with the Polish eagle, marched by—column after column. Orchestras played. The throngs of thousands upon thousands who filled the sidewalks waved handkerchiefs or small red and white banners, sobbing, shouting, throwing flowers at the soldiers. After the parade was over, the waves of people streamed in the direction of the churches to offer thanks for the lifting off of a yoke that had lasted for a hundred and fifty years.

The hungry, exhausted city smiled like an invalid who has just been given the promise of a cure and could already see the day when he would stand on his own two feet. Empty pockets and the specter of starvation lost their terrifying aspect. There was hope. Frozen and dulled for so long, the city's imagination came to life and started to seek the means of creating something out of nothing. Inspired by the sight of the empty factories that cut into the depths of the sky with their smokeless chimneys, people's minds began to design fantastic projects. And as time wore on, smoke did in fact begin to spew from a chimney here and there. It had a sweet smell. Little by little the city began to cover itself with a thin shawl of smoke. Again the sirens began to divide the day into hours of toil and rest. The rhythm of prewar times resumed and pulsated through the arteries of streets. With increasing haste Lodz tried to make up for time lost, and to reach out for the future.

The Russian Bear, preoccupied with itself, had fenced itself off, withdrawing into its self-made cage. The Russian markets remained closed. Lodz had to find new markets within Poland's own boundaries. The country was in dire need of all kinds of essential products. So, in the same panic in which they had once fled from the city, the rich and poor now flooded back in order not to miss out on the golden opportunities that awaited them. And along with the returning citizens of Lodz there arrived thousands upon thousands of Jews and Gentiles from the shtetlekh and villages, all set on making their fortunes, on spreading their wings, and on playing roulette with Mother Luck. The game of life was on. Already the streets were packed with the clinking of trams, droshkies, wagons, and carts, while the sidewalks overflowed with the restless masses of the unemployed. Drunk on its dreams, the city's populace was in the meantime ravished by starvation.

Binele found work in a newly opened factory. Jewish men were refused work in the factories of the newly liberated country, but the Jewish *shtoperkes* were made an exception of and they enjoyed the same privileges as before the war.

Moreover, Binele could now boast of having some family in Lodz. The wave of Jews returning to Lodz from Bociany swept along with it a number of local residents. One such Bociany resident who settled in Lodz was Raisele, Binele's eldest sister, who came with her husband and children.

Raisele had a much better head for business than her father. She was a stout woman not easily frightened by work or hardship, and she was meticulous and frugal. She relied on no one and had her eye on everything. After her marriage she had become her husband's equal partner in his wood and coal business, and she had managed her father's chalk and lime store as well. But she had been fully aware that all her labor and sacrifices would lead her nowhere as long as she went on living in Bociany. She had managed to weather her hard existence and to live a life "without a future" with fortitude, as long as she had had no other choice. Now, however, she saw a way to better her lot. She had nothing to lose, and it seemed a pity not to respond to the call of hope that had reached Bociany from distant Lodz. Informed by her knack for business matters and her practicality, Raisele sensed that it was now possible to make a modest fortune in Lodz. Raisele was no coward. She had the courage to dare, and she courageously tore herself away from her roots in her home shtetl. She took her family, came to Lodz with her meager belongings, and moved into a basement apartment at the very end of Piotrkowska Street in a district where there lived more Germans than either Poles or Jews but where the rent was cheaper than anywhere else.

Raisele had arranged her affairs so that some of the peasants whom she had known on the Potcheyov in Bociany would be supplying her in Lodz with fresh vegetables, fruits, cheese, butter, eggs, and cream. She opened a cheap food store in the front part of the basement where she lived. Her customers were the Germans of the neighborhood. They knew how to appreciate Raisele's punctiliousness and honesty and they did not react when she gradually raised the prices of her merchandise. Her tiny shop was clean and the food articles were fresh, so it was not worthwhile to make an issue of paying a groschen more for a product.

At first, the success of Raisele's enterprise was marred by her husband's attitude and demeanor. He, the son of the Bociany *melamed* Reb Shapsele, who as a young man had shown such sharpness of mind both in his studies and in his business, had become strangely confused after his arrival in the big city. The continuous rush and his having only strangers to deal with made him feel like a nonentity. So he devoted himself more to his studies than to the business. Fortunately, as time wore on, he began to feel himself more and more at home at the Hasidic *shtibl* in Lodz. He made friends with many people and he learned about his new surroundings, gradually becoming infected by the other men's daring way of thinking. He began to "send his ears into the streets," to register with great sensitivity the earthly desires and needs of the local Germans, Poles, and Jews and, more and more often, he pushed the sacred books aside in order to open Raisele's account books and study them. So, imperceptibly, the general business fever caught up with him and swept him along.

Raisele's husband displayed a great gift for knowing both what the customer wanted today and what he might want tomorrow. Through his friends at the *shtibl* he soon found a way to procure such foodstuffs as flour, sugar, beans, cereals, tea, and coffee at the lowest prices, and he also learned whose palms needed greasing, for one purpose or another. So it happened that before long he and Raisele opened another shop in the very center of town. Fate smiled on them. The hungry city threw itself on their food, and paid well. It was not long before Raisele could afford to rent a two room apartment complete with kitchen, close to their shop on the fashionable Piotrkowska Street.

Raisele wielded much power over her sisters, and she succeeded in talking two of them, Rochele and Mashele, who found themselves in great straits in Bociany, into moving to Lodz as well. She gave their husbands employment as managers of the new shops that she opened. She wanted badly to persuade her father and her younger sister Dvorele, who had married Berele the Sleepwalker, to also come to Lodz. But Yossele refused to hear of it. He and Dvorele and her husband continued to live in the family house in Bociany.

Binele had found out about her sisters' presence in Lodz accidentally. A girl from Bociany who worked with her at the factory had mentioned the

fact. That same day, after work, Binele set out for Raisele's shop on Piotrkowska Street.

She had trouble recognizing Raisele. She saw a woman before her who
only vaguely resembled the sister that Binele remembered. Raisele had
grown heavy. Her creased tired face was dour, expressing both bitterness
and stubbornness, as if her father's bitterness and stubbornness had been
kneaded into the shape of her down-turned mouth. She was wearing a
fashionable blond wig and a spotless white apron. Her gaze acknowledged
familiarity but remained ice-cold when she recognized Binele. So Binele
stood there staring at Raisele over the heads and shoulders of the customers, waiting for the ice in Raisele's eyes to melt and reveal at least a
spark of the maternal warmth of her nature. After all, had not Raisele, despite her harshness, substituted as a mother for her siblings in her role as
eldest sister? When Binele could wait no longer for Raisele's face to
brighten, she waded through the crowd of customers, made her way to
the counter, went around it, and spread her arms, ready to thrust herself
into Raisele's embrace.

Raisele pushed her away. "I have no time," she muttered hastily, not
taking her eyes off the scale on which she weighed a bag of peas. Binele
remained standing beside her until, between serving one customer and another, Raisele turned to her and added in a hiss, "Get out of my sight! Because of you, Tateshie has nearly been killed. Because of you, he's gone
completely blind." Raisele's rage and heartbreak made her eyes swell with
tears. Binele moved away from her and ran out of the shop.

But the thought that her sisters were living in Lodz without seeing her
gave Binele no peace. After a fortnight she set out again to see Raisele. It
was a Sabbath that fell on a Christian holiday, and the factories stood still.
Binele put on her Sabbath dress, braided fresh ribbons into her hair and
left for Raisele's apartment on Piotrkowska Street. Rochele and her husband and Mashele and her husband and children had come by for the
cholnt meal. The air in the room was still permeated with the aroma of the
cholnt. Binele noticed that Raisele and Mashele's children had grown beyond recognition. They approached her shyly. She hugged and kissed
them, trying to remind them of the games she had played with them. Except for Raisele's eldest boy, none of them remembered her. She could
not tear her eyes away from them and was afraid to do so. The children,
tittering, tugged at her dress, pulling her in the direction of the large table
where the adults sat. She felt two pairs of arms embracing her, Rochele's

and Mashele's. She looked at the table but her eyes saw only Raisele, who was dressed in a solemn black dress, a large brooch pinned under her chin and fancy pins in her Sabbath bonnet. Raisele was sipping loudly from a glass of strong tea. Rochele and Mashele held handkerchiefs to their eyes.

Raisele's husband, amazingly robust, looking as if he had grown in height and breadth during the time that Binele had not seen him, sat majestically at the head of the table with the two brothers-in-law on either side of him. Having watched the scene with a frown on his pouchy face, his cunning eyes shifty, he pounded on the table with his clenched fist. "Stop wailing on the Sabbath, women!"

The women pressed their handkerchiefs more closely to their eyes. Rochele pulled Binele into a chair. Mashele brought her a glass of tea, and they all moved closer to Raisele.

"Oy, Binele," Rochele sighed, dabbing her eyes. "It's no good with Tateshie. He's just as stubborn as he ever was. He refuses to join us. And he has, poor soul, gone completely blind."

"All because of her!" Raisele, on the edge of tears, cast Binele a scathing glance.

"Yes," Rochele continued softly. "He almost got himself killed when he came to Lodz to take you home. He fell under a wagon in the dark street and barely made it back to Bociany."

Choking on her tears, Rochele was unable to continue, and Mashele took over. "The Bociany girls who worked in Lodz were telling stories about you when they came home for the holidays." Mashele said. "They told us and told Tateshie everything about you. He would have come for you long before, had he known where to find you. Finally they brought him your address. But his predicament is not only your fault," Mashele added as if to ease Binele's conscience. "It happened also because of Hershele."

"Where is Hershele?" Binele stirred.

Mashele sobbed. "They say that he's in Russia, that he's gone there to make the revolution. Tateshie's only kaddish, woe is us! We're forbidden to even mention Hershele's name in Tateshie's presence." Binele riveted her attention on Raisele, who responded with a tearful stare full of reproach and resentment. Binele could not bear that stare, so she suddenly rose from her chair and went down on her knees beside Raisele. She hastily shoved away the hair on the top of her head and exposed the place on her skull where Yossele had hit her with his stick and where no hair had ever grown back.

"Good for you," Raisele barely deigned to look at the scar. "Because of you Tateshie will, heaven forbid, soon be gone from this world."

The three sisters, mincing no words, now embarked on recounting the details of the stories that they had heard about Binele. The brothers-in-law pursed their lips judiciously. Binele wilted under the onslaught of general hostility. Finally she could take it no longer. She jumped to her feet and left them all without saying good-bye.

But she could not refrain from coming back to visit Raisele. She was especially drawn there on Friday nights when her heart yearned for the Sabbath atmosphere, for the bowls of chicken broth with noodles served on a white tablecloth, all lit with candles. Raisele, perhaps moved by Binele's persistence, which she took as a sign of repentance, finally deigned to receive her and let her join the family for the meal. But along with the chicken soup Binele had to swallow such a large portion of moralizing from Raisele and the brothers-in-law, and so many tears on Rochele's and Mashele's part, that she soon lost all her enjoyment of their company and once more ran away.

Nonetheless she continued to visit her family at Raisele's home. After a while she grew used to the litanies of reproaches and minded them less. And so she confided to her sisters one Sabbath afternoon that she was engaged to be married. In order to convince them that she was not lying, she brought Handsome Moshe along to Raisele's apartment on her next visit. That day her sister's resentment of Binele, although not completely gone, was shoved under the table.

Not that Handsome Moshe pleased Binele's family all that much. After all, he was a nonbeliever and a complete ignoramus as far as the Sacred Books were concerned. But he possessed means to win their hearts in other ways. First of all, he was a genuine citizen of Lodz, having been born and raised there, and this was one of his great advantages. Moreover, he was not an actor, as they had heard, nor was he a mere weaver. He was a supervisor, a good wage earner. He had every chance of working his way up and, with a bit of financial help, might one day be able to open a workshop or even a factory of his own. In Lodz such things could happen overnight, especially if a man had the right connections, which indeed

Moshe seemed to have. And then Moshe had a polished tongue and could ingratiate himself with his amiability and his clever compliments. He was better informed than any of them on the subject of the textile industry of Lodz as well as on the subject of politics in the new Poland and in the world at large. It was pleasant and interesting to be in his company, both for Binele's sisters and her brothers-in-law, not to mention the youngsters who clung to him. He knew songs and dance steps that were the latest crazes in town.

After one such visit by Handsome Moshe, Rochele, who was still given to frequent fits of weeping on account of her barrenness, burst into tears as she was saying good-bye to Binele. "Don't worry," she exhorted her and kissed her, "even a girl who behaves like a silly goat before marriage settles down afterwards. With God's help, you'll become a *mentsh* after your wedding, you'll see."

When after such a visit Binele went with Handsome Moshe to the theater or to a lecture, or to listen to a young Yiddish writer read from his works, she was so moved that every word she heard took on a personal meaning for her. Afterwards she would sit in her loft until late at night, studiously copying the words that the teacher at The Harp had taught her to write. She hoped that by educating herself she would become wiser. She was impatient for her knowledge to help her untie all those knots that were entangling her life more and more.

She avoided meeting Yacov at The Harp. She told herself that it was better for her not to see him at all. Nonetheless she had become a member of the women's "circle" at The Harp, having been unable to refuse the woman who had come to talk her into joining. She found herself in agreement with the woman a hundred percent on all the issues she discussed. Her own plight, the plight of Ziporah and of working-class girls in general, and even the plight of the "brides" on Faiferovka—these were matters that only a woman could understand. So she spent additional evenings at The Harp and could not avoid noticing Yacov now and then at a meeting, or in the tearoom.

Once in a while she would notice Yacov in the crowd that passed her in the street as she walked arm in arm with Handsome Moshe. Every time she saw him, her heart skipped a beat. She grew agitated, she could not stop herself from blushing, but she kept repeating to herself, "I don't remember him." She forced herself to chatter with Handsome Moshe more animatedly than before, and she responded to his kisses with a particular tenderness when he pulled her into the shadow of an arched gate. Moshe would never come up to her room. "I'm afraid of myself," he had told her. He and Binele had already set the date for their wedding, and there was not much time left before they would be together "for life."

One evening, while he held Binele in his arms in the dark of a gateway, Moshe said to her solemnly, "Wish me *mazel-tov,* Binele. I've been accepted as a full member of the Drama Circle! I'm going to become a real actor!"

Moshe was after all a man of great determination, a man who doggedly pursued his goals! At this moment Binele's respect for him had jumped to an immeasurable height. "Soon you'll become an orator for the Poale-Zion, too!" she said proudly.

He pinched her nose. "No, that's out. To be a regular member of the Poale-Zion is good enough for me. An artist must devote his life to his art. Because you should know, Binele, that art is in service of muses who are awfully jealous."

⊚ *12* ⊚

THE STATE OF MIND of Yacov's friend Baruch Weiskop was in accord with the state of mind of many an enterprising citizen of Lodz. The war was over and he was ready to spread his wings. He was, however, more fortunate than the majority of the others of his kind. The seemingly groundless castles in the air that he had built during the war when he had amassed shares and bonds of practically no value, had now turned out to be the works of a genius. Overnight he became a man of fabulous wealth and his name spread through the town with the speed of lightning. Conditions were also favorable for his once-disgraced father, who quickly recovered from the wartime shocks and helped his son in his financial undertakings.

The less Baruch occupied himself with his wealth, the faster it grew. He himself had patience only for sudden ideas, for hazardous business deals, and for risky investments. He enjoyed recklessly throwing himself into one "impossible" enterprise after another. He had an excellent nose for people's weaknesses, for the psychological nature of the business world of Lodz in its relationship to the economy of Poland and Europe at large. Moreover, he had a special feeling for the ups and downs of the stock market and for the rise and fall of currencies.

Yet in his personal life he was inclined to retain his status quo, and more or less to continued to live in the same manner as he had always lived. Thus he remained a bachelor who, having freed himself from the shackles of religious restrictions, welcomed his unlimited possibilities in the sphere of amorous endeavors. A slight improvement over his former life was that he now owned a fashionable spacious apartment, richly furnished, complete with a staff of servants. He also had new friends. He felt himself drawn to the financial and intellectual elite of the town, and it was from its midst that he picked his friends to replace those whom he had used to meet at the Hasidic *shtibl*. In general he did not consider himself a man given to intimate relationships with either men or women, and he kept himself aloof from becoming deeply involved with anybody. He considered close relationships an infringement on his personal freedom. And freedom from any kind of emotional shackle was now the motto of his life. However, on a superficial level he loved companionship; he loved intellectual exchange as much as he had loved pilpulistic debate in his yeshiva years; and he loved to savor the beauty of women, both in their physical and spiritual aspects.

Baruch, the newcomer, was well liked by the Jewish elite of Lodz. True, he still lacked the polish and suavity of manners, and his education left a lot to be desired. However he was welcomed in their midst like a breath of fresh air. He was young, enthusiastic, original in thought, and eager to learn. Most of all, he was an excellent listener. This was a priceless quality in the eyes of those who had much to say but who themselves lacked the ability to listen to others. Consequently, Baruch was frequently surrounded by his new friends who enjoyed gathering in his quaint apartment, the atmosphere of which projected a mixture of respect for exquisite traditional art and a weakness for "bad" new taste. On Baruch's brocade-covered sofas and armchairs, which seemed to be transferred directly from Venetian palazzos, were thus perched the "flowers" of Lodz's high society and the "butterflies" of the city's intelligentsia. Besides Polish and Hebrew, Baruch's guests spoke the most important European languages. A large concert grand stood next to the arched Venetian window that was hung with drapes of an oriental design. Besides good music and good conversation, Baruch's salon boasted the best wines from Europe's wine cellars just as it boasted the most beautiful women of Lodz, a city famous for beautiful, well-bred women.

As a special treat to himself, there were always among Baruch's guests a sprinkling of the most eccentric "erudites" in the fields of art, science, and philosophy, those who were an elite to themselves, the elite of spiritually rich paupers. In Baruch's salon these people were not only accepted, but also respected. The times had changed. Democracy was in high fashion.

Yacov had met Baruch for the first time after the war at a hall where Bal Makhshoves, the famous literary critic, was giving a lecture. Yacov was struck by Baruch's appearance. The difference in age between Baruch and himself, hardly noticeable during the war when Baruch's figure had had a more or less clearly delineated shape, was now blatantly obvious due to Baruch's corpulence. In his flashy, elegant dress coat, he looked like someone's prosperous uncle from America. Yet he greeted Yacov with the same spontaneous friendliness as in the past. He looked closely at Yacov, who was dressed in the same clothes that he had worn during the war, and teased him warm-heartedly, "You see, if you had become my partner . . ."

Yacov smiled back at him without a hint of regret. "If I had become your partner, you might not have been so lucky. Money doesn't like my company. That's a hereditary streak that runs in my family for generations."

Baruch's protruding eyes lit up with a scornful twinkle. "Yes, I know the psychology of you paupers. Your vision is the size of a penny, and your concepts are just as small. You approach life as if it were worth a farthing. I wonder what the arrival of socialism would do for someone like you?"

As in the past, Yacov was not offended by Baruch's talk. "If socialism were to be established," he answered calmly, "and the masses became rich, I, the *schlimazl*, would have come along, don't worry. As for appraising the worth of my life, leave that to me."

They stared at each other searchingly. A moment of silence passed. Then Baruch grabbed Yacov by the lapels of his coat and shook him, "Yacov, do you hear how we talk to each other? We haven't seen each other for such a long time, and already we indulge in class struggle. Remember, if you allow my good fortune to come between us, I will never forgive you."

"I would you took care of your side of the coin!" Yacov answered dryly. Baruch's words had begun to vex him.

"I don't consider you my class enemy," Baruch shrugged. "You consider me to be yours. You're still a Bundist. I can read it in your face. And I suspect that they've already messed you up good and proper."

"Don't give yourself a headache about that."

"We are still good friends though, aren't we?"

"It depends on what you mean by being good friends. It's a fact that we lost sight of each other, for whatever reason. But the Bund certainly doesn't dictate my choice of friends." Yacov brushed Baruch's hands off his lapels. "I hate to have to say it, but it strikes me that you've acquired a trait that I don't particularly care for. You've gotten yourself into the habit of telling people who they are and what they think. I don't much enjoy being lectured by you."

Cordially, Baruch gave him his hand. "Agreed. No lectures."

Yacov smiled. "In that case, why don't you come with me to a celebration in honor of a group of young Yiddish writers, the heirs of Peretz?"

"Are you still the same great admirer of Peretz?"

"Very much so. Now we can easily evaluate Peretz's achievement. He has laid the foundations of modern Yiddish literature. He has helped shape the new face of our people by making us conscious both of the treasures of our past and of our present. I am no supporter of breaking with the past as you know. No one can build a new life without holding on to the thread of the old."

"For Heaven's sake!" Baruch cried out. "You talk like a newspaper column! And why are you making such a big *shpil* about Peretz? And what is there in your hollow chant about the people here and the people there? Did Peretz manage to lead our people out of the ghetto—I mean their spiritual ghetto—with his starry-eyed adoration of the Hasidic way of life? There is a wide open world out there, brother, a world filled with art and beauty. There is a world literature and a world culture to be savored and contributed to."

More and more Yacov sensed the change in Baruch and felt himself hurt by it. "You're wrong," he shook his head vigorously, "in saying that Peretz has not opened a gate to the wide world. Isn't he the one who has helped to modernize our way of thinking by modernizing our own literature, by propagating the founding of the new Yiddish schools? Don't you think that it suffices to open our doors and windows to let the fresh air in and to breathe it? Do we have to abandon our own home for that purpose? Why shouldn't we allow our own voice to reach the outside world?" He exclaimed heatedly, "Let me tell you this, Baruch. Beware of jumping out of your own skin, because you may lose both worlds." He checked himself and asked in a calmer tone of voice, "I sound like a newspaper column again, don't I?"

"Yes, I can see that you've learned the art of bombastic speech making." Baruch grimaced. "Let's not kid ourselves. How can you compare Peretz to Tolstoy, or to Dostoyevsky, or to Nietzsche and Schopenhauer, or to Maeterlinck and Verhaeren?"

"Who says I want to compare him to them?" Yacov answered heatedly. "Peretz is beyond comparison. He is what he is, and that is enough for me." He forced himself to calm down. He fixed his earnest, scrutinizing gaze on Baruch's face and hastened to add, "Are you pretending not to know that the Jewish masses are in the process of just awakening? That they have no worldly education and must be taught? That we have been taught the *alef-beys* at the heder for the sole purpose of studying religious literature? And how many are there who never even finished the heder or attended none at all? What do Jewish women, one half of our people, know? They live in ignorance. Have you really forgotten everything, Baruch?"

"No, I haven't forgotten," Baruch shook his head. "And I can prove it! For your information I've just founded a high school for Jewish girls that has gone into operation at the beginning of this school term, and what's more, as president of the board, I am its factual director, too. But rest assured, dear friend, that I'll never let my girls be taught Peretz or any other literary mediocrities."

"And how about the Yiddish language? Will you teach them Yiddish at all?"

Baruch guffawed. "Don't be ridiculous. I won't even teach them Hebrew. First let these girls become dignified Jewish daughters of Poland. Polish is the language of their studies, and German and French are obligatory courses." Baruch relaxed and patted Yacov's shoulder. "Believe me, Yacov, the most sublime creature in the world is a cultured, well-bred Jewish woman. Her charm, her intelligence, the titillating elegance of her spirit and her physical attractiveness render her irresistible—the embodiment of beauty. Take for instance a certain Miss Polcia, a student at my school. She is still very young, but . . . "

"And what relation do these girls have to their own people, to the Jewish masses?" Yacov interrupted him peevishly.

"I just told you how they relate!" Baruch was clearly annoyed by Yacov's indifference to what he had just started to confide to him. "And stop harping on the masses. The masses can never be elevated to appreciate finer things anyway. Give them a buttered roll, as your own Peretz says or give them *panem et circenses* as the Latins say." He leaned over to Yacov. "You'd better have a good look at your own self and see what your involvement with the masses has done to you. Ask yourself whether it has not crippled you already. We've only been talking a few minutes, and I can already smell the change in you. Forgive me for saying it, but you reek of triviality. You've stifled your sense for things lyrical, winged, and lofty. You've forgotten the mystical, the cabalistic, the exciting, and limitless delights of the spirit, and instead have dressed yourself up in a straitjacket. You've broken your wings in order to creep on the ground, and all that is left of your dreams is one great yawn. You've become the typical party man, filling your head with belly philosophies, with Karl Marx's kitchen and housekeeping business, with the petty economy of pots and pans. You've harnessed yourself to your ideological bandwagon and have become a preacher of bombastic sermons. You offer me artificial paper flowers and then resent me for not smelling their perfume!"

Yacov flung up his head and waved a finger at Baruch. "Let me tell you one thing, brother! Until these 'kitchen philosophies' bring about a solution to hunger and want, we have no right to play around with any other philosophies. I've changed you say? So I have. And I'm not afraid of where this change will lead me. It is you who are afraid of your changed self. That's why you warned me from the start that your mirror, silvered by your great fortune, might come between us. You've transferred your own fears onto me."

Baruch smiled smugly. "I can see you have already gotten a taste of Freud."

Yacov shrugged, "No, I haven't, not yet."

Baruch's face grew somber. They were silent for a while. Then, in a renewed effort to recapture the warmth that had once vibrated between them, Baruch livened up and embarked on describing his new apartment to Yacov. "You must come to see it," he said. "There's no particular style prevailing in its arrangement. It's a hodgepodge of everything. Because, you see, there is no particular style in my love life." He gazed meaningfully at Yacov. "Every woman, every girl who passes through my rooms leaves her imprint not only on the style of my cuisine, but also on the arrangement of my home in general. One style, you understand, follows the other. I like the mixture. The chaos reflects the state of my mind. There is, however, one girl, a young student at my school, Miss Polcia . . . " He was about to say more, but checked himself yet again, since Yacov's face still expressed neither understanding nor curiosity. It rather expressed a kind of dismay, as if Baruch's talk about women had annoyed him.

In fact, Yacov preferred not to broach the subject of women. His heart was still too sore after the loss of Binele's love. He was still completely wrapped up in her. And as he had during the time before he had met her in Lodz, he was still hounding the streets, looking for her. At times it seemed to him that his and Binele's encounter and her forthcoming marriage to Handsome Moshe were all a mere figment of his imagination— nothing but part of his former fear that he would never find her—rather than facts that signified the end of his search. He found it impossible to continue with his life lying fallow as it was; he had to keep waiting for her, looking and longing for her.

Yacov and Baruch went together to the celebration in honor of the new generation of Yiddish writers. Baruch was immediately attracted by the handsome, imposing Shalom Asch, and that same evening he presented Asch with his calling card and an invitation to visit him at his apartment.

"You will, of course, come, too?" Baruch asked Yacov in a wavering tone of voice which Yacov immediately detected. "I think of inviting the magnate Asher Kohn for the occasion. Let's see how literature gets along with really big money. But you must come to see me before the others arrive, so that we can be alone and chat like in the good old days. And this time you will have to change into one of my suits. It will make you feel better."

Yacov grinned, "Don't give yourself so much trouble. I won't come. Nor will I invite you to my place."

"You took me along to meet your friend, what's his name?"

"Vove Cederbaum is his name. At present, I doubt whether I will ever in the future take you to see him."

"Are you starting up with me again, Yacov?"

"I started up with you a long time ago." Yacov laughed harder than ever, a kind of laughter that sounded strangely unfamiliar to his own ears.

No other opportunity ever presented itself again for Baruch to take Yacov to his new home. Now and then he and Yacov ran into each other at lectures given by visiting famous personalities. When they met, there was pleasure and amiability at first, then, in the course of their conversation, they unfailingly became entangled in an argument that muddled up their true feelings for each another.

Baruch and Yacov were of the same mind in regard to one thing. Both rejoiced in the fact that Poland was free again. Whatever the revolution in Russia might bring—and Baruch was of the opinion that it would bring nothing good, while Yacov believed that it would bring a great deal of good—both agreed that in the case of Poland, justice had prevailed. These were the days when the liberated Polish people, intoxicated with their newly won freedom, abandoned themselves to jingoism; they loathed everything that was not purely Polish. The soldiers of General Haller's army, just returned from France, began to attack traditionally clad Jews in the streets, cutting off their beards as well as parts of their cheeks. Baruch and Yacov told themselves that these were times of transition. Soon the process of building a truly liberated Poland would begin—a Poland founded on the spirit of western liberalism, in Baruch's opinion, or founded on the spirit of socialism, as Yacov hoped—and an atmosphere of brotherhood and goodwill would come to reign in the land.

Baruch nudged Yacov, "You don't stop talking about renewal. Why don't you start renewing your own life a bit? What future is there in warming the bench, weaving cloth all your life? You say that you are not made for business. Fine. But between being a weaver and being a businessman there are a thousand other possibilities."

"Such as?" Yacov asked.

"Find yourself a job that allows you to keep your back straight. If you don't want, heaven forbid, to become a rich man, then at least don't become your own murderer. Do it for my sake, so that I can be friends with a normal human being and not with a piece of loom. If you agree, I can look around and find you an occupation that would at least be slightly better than the one you have now."

Yacov shook his head. "There is no point. I'll be drafted into the army anyway soon."

Yacov had little time to devote to the thought of his inevitable conscription to the army. He was feverishly involved in his party work. Unions were being organized, workers' councils were being established, and cultural institutions had sprung up like mushrooms after a rain. At his workshop considerable changes had taken place. Vove Cederbaum had resigned from his job at Reb Saivel Malkes's and had started a workshop of his own in the room where he lived with his girlfriend Balcie. Laibel the Hump had left to work for him. By doing this, both men had acquired the freedom to devote themselves to party work whenever they thought it necessary, while Reb Saivel Malkes had acquired the freedom to deal with Yacov as he chose.

There was a great rush of work at Reb Saivel's plant. He had annexed a floor of the neighboring house to put in new looms. There was no shortage of weavers looking for work. Many experienced workers had arrived with the masses of people from the provinces. So, as soon as he was offered the smallest provocation, Reb Saivel threw an ultimatum at Yacov's feet: either Yacov submit to the rules of the workplace or else find himself work elsewhere. Yacov's contract with Reb Saivel had long since expired, and he finally agreed to allow Baruch to find him a job to tide him over until his conscription.

A couple of weeks later, when they next met at a lecture, Baruch, his face all smiles, shook Yacov's hand enthusiastically, and said, "I'm telling you, Yacov, life is stranger than fiction! The day after you asked me to find you a job, I visited a diamond dealer, a good friend of mine, whose daughter, Miss Polcia, has become a student at my school. It is she whom I had in mind when I mentioned the attraction of well-bred Jewish women. She is still very young, of course, but one day she will become the kind of irresistible Jewish beauty I've been dreaming of . . . dreaming of molding at my school. Anyway, as I was leaving their home, I saw Reb Itchele Hittelmakher's shoe store, which is located downstairs, beneath their apartment, and I remembered that Reb Itchele had once told me of his origins in Bociany. So I went to see him and the result of my démarche is that you can start work at his shop tomorrow."

Yacov became a salesman of ladies shoes at Reb Itchele Hittelmakher's fashionable shoe store.

Reb Itchele Hittelmakher was born in Bociany and was a brother of the Bociany wood merchant. During the great pogrom after the assassination of Tsar Alexander II, when Reb Itchele was still a young boy, his parents had managed to send him away from home. He had grown up at an uncle's house in Lodz, attended the yeshiva there, and earned for himself an ordination to become a *rov;* but instead of becoming one, he allowed himself to be drawn into the shoe business. As the years wore on and his business expanded, he rarely found the time to visit his family and his home shtetl.

Like many of the antebellum rich Jews, Reb Itchele was a Talmudic scholar who made use of his brilliant mind to secure a prominent niche for himself in the mundane world of trade and commerce. True, he had lost a large part of his investments during the war, but as soon as the hostilities were over, he moved heaven and earth to get himself back to the heights that he had reached before the war. At this time he belonged to those successful Jewish men of Lodz who, although they kept both feet firmly planted on the ground at all times, still dreamed of affording themselves the time to roam the realms of both the Torah and Hasidic lore. Diligence and imagination, intelligence and cunning, quick orientation and emotional endurance were wonderfully linked with a gift for spiritual ruminations in Reb Itchele's personality. But as soon as the war ended, he put all his talents to work on servicing his great business undertaking—to shoe the "bare" feet of the elegant ladies of Lodz and those of the entire Polish republic—while, to his regret, his spiritual needs were left unattended.

By no means did Reb Itchele Hittelmakher live only for himself. He was constantly besieged by relatives, acquaintances, and the acquaintances of acquaintances, both local and out of town. People came to him with pleas for money to help them get through the week, for money for a dowry, for money to start a business, for money to pay a doctor or for money to support a widow. Apart from that, the representatives of every possible charity came to him for contributions, which he dealt out with a generous hand.

Of late, Reb Itchele had found himself so drawn into his successful enterprises that he had less time than ever to devote to communal religious activities or even to the Creator of the Universe Himself. He was constantly busy counting promissory notes and sending his nose, eyes, and ears into the changing world. He personally traveled to every important town in liberated Poland to "smell the air" and to orient himself in the local manufacturing world. So it happened that the styles and fashions of ladies' shoes occupied his mind more than the paragraphs of Scripture or their commentaries. There was so much news concerning inventions in the fabrication and advertising of shoes! He had to catch up with the new trends as soon as they became known, lest someone else made use of them and hastened to offer the results to their customers. His shoe store on Piotrkowska Street in Lodz served Reb Itchele both as a testing ground and as a showcase.

In order to be considered a modern man, Reb Itchele dressed as fashionably as his conscience permitted. His grayish beard was trimmed by shears in the German fashion, and he wore a three-quarter length jacket and a black felt hat. However, he was not one of those who could adjust their conscience to the requirements of the moment. Despite his dress and his devotion to business, he suffered profound feelings of guilt, and deep in his heart he yearned for the past when he had lived a harmonious life as a complete Jew.

Reb Itchele took to Yacov right away. Not only did he feel as close to him as to a relative—on account of the fact that they both hailed from Bociany—but also because he saw in Yacov a kindred soul, a young man who had trespassed the religious barriers, and had gone even further than he himself had gone—perhaps because Yacov was the younger man— and who did not take these trespassings lightly. Reb Itchele could talk to Yacov not only about Bociany, but also about more profound matters. He could talk to him both in the language of the *besmedresh* and in that of modern times. Right from their very first encounter, Yacov pleased him so much that, although he barely had a moment to spare, Reb Itchele engaged him in conversation about the Wurker Rabbi and Hasidism in general. When he heard that Yacov was a chess player, he invited him for a game of chess on the next Saturday after havdalah.

Reb Itchele had the high forehead of a scholar and a pair of dark eyes whose gaze, direct and clever, made it obvious that he could be fooled by no one. His sharply defined mouth was prominently visible through the brush of his neatly trimmed mustache and beard. His intelligence seemed to radiate from his entire bearing. He had no children, yet there was obviously a well of untapped paternal feeling in his heart that was reflected in his attitude toward all those who came to him for help. And so he also took Yacov under his wing.

"There's nothing in the world that I wouldn't do for you," he told

Yacov one day when Yacov, having worked the first few months for him, had come up to his house for a game of chess. "Just tell me what you need, my boy." And being a man loath to postpone anything he undertook, Reb Itchele got up from his armchair, went into the room adjoining his *kantur,* and, as if he were mimicking Baruch Weiskop, he reappeared, holding up a fashionable suit on a hanger. "Here, try it on," he said.

Yacov blushed. "Thank you very much," he muttered. "But I don't need it."

Yacov often heard such proposals. People offered to do things for him, to fit him out, to improve his situation, to help him with whatever they thought he needed. He found this distasteful and irritating. It filled him with shame. What was there in his demeanor, he asked himself, that made people look on him as if he were a helpless creature? He could not understand what was wrong with him. At times he felt himself put in a bind. It was difficult to refuse these favors and not hurt people's feelings.

Just as in the case of Baruch Weiskop, his acquaintance with Reb Itchele muddled Yacov's concept of class differences, blurring the distinction between "we" and "they." He was supposed to hate Reb Itchele, the class enemy who treated the workers at his shoe factory so ruthlessly that every so often they found themselves forced to resort to strikes. But when he visited Reb Itchele's home, Yacov found people constantly milling around. There was always a great deal of coming and going by temporary free boarders, all of whom were made welcome at Reb Itchele's table, which was always laden with food. He watched Reb Itchele engage in charitable deeds and heard him listen attentively to everyone's problems. So the theory of class struggle remained in Reb Itchele's case only a theory. Yacov liked the man. He liked to visit him in his house for a game of chess, he liked to sit in Reb Itchele's room in a comfortable leather armchair, while a servant brought in two glasses of strong red tea with slices of lemon as well as a sugar dish and a dish of preserves. After the game, Reb Itchele and Yacov would chat leisurely and affectionately about anything of interest to the two of them, about anything—except politics.

Politics was anathema to Reb Itchele. He detested it with all his heart. To him politics was the game par excellence of the Evil One, a game of bluffs, a breeding ground for petty ambitions liable to lead to the downfall of the world. Yacov, for his part, was not particularly anxious to enlighten Reb Itchele about his own views on politics. He had come to believe that each man looked on life according to what he had in his pocket, that is, according to which side of the barricade he found himself on. For that reason any effort to proselytize a person who found himself in a life situation different from one's own was a ludicrous proposition. No one wanted to have his worldview at variance with his private interests. And then, chatting with Reb Itchele about anything in the world but politics gave Yacov the opportunity to relax and refresh his mind; it procured him a respite from the tensions of his party life.

Yacov's deplorable command of the Polish language, which he spoke with a Bociany peasant accent, had not made the best impression on Reb Itchele, who himself spoke a not much better Polish, but who appreciated people who spoke the language well. So Reb Itchele had insisted, right on the first day he hired Yacov as a salesman, that Yacov put his head to learning the Polish language properly and that, in order to hasten the process, he should pay attention to the polished manners and Polish pronunciation of the chief salesman, Mr. Morris.

"Mr. Morris speaks a classical Polish," Reb Itchele informed Yacov with a tinge of irony in his tone of voice. "That is, in his youth he prepared himself to attend classes at a gymnasium. Of course, being a Jew in tsarist times stood in the way of a brilliant worldly career. Yet Mr. Morris is so well-bred that he refuses to speak a word of Yiddish, and seems, in general, to have forgotten that he has been circumcised. My problem with him is that he is a second cousin of mine and that he has a wife who is just as well-bred as he, with two daughters, may they be well and healthy, who attend a gymnasium. And on top of it all, he's a man, alas, who knows no other trade but selling shoes. So, since he's useful to me and since our town swarms with individuals of his kind who haven't got the means of earning a living, I haven't got the heart to let him go, understand?" Reb Itchele's eyes lit up warmly. "Perhaps, who knows, Mr. Morris may become a bit more of a *mentsh* by working next to you. You're probably not aware of it, my boy, but I have the feeling that if the greatest scoundrel spent some time with you, he would become a bit more of a *mentsh*."

Yacov felt embarrassed. "Don't say that, Reb Itchele," he pleaded.

"Why shouldn't I say it, if that's how I feel?"

Yacov took leave of Reb Itchele before he gave in to the impulse to inform him of his affiliation with the Bundist movement. Reb Itchele's exaggerated expressions of affection left him with a bad taste in his mouth and an uneasiness in his heart.

Yacov's earnings at Reb Itchele's shoe store were not much higher than what he had earned as a weaver, but the work itself was child's play in comparison. It gave him the feeling of being paid for doing nothing. The work was pleasant and the work day much shorter than at the workshop. He wore a fancy suit at work, white cuffs, a stiff collar, and a necktie. The fancy suit was actually a brown uniform that all the salesmen wore, and because Yacov had inherited his uniform from the previous salesman, the pants were a little too short on him.

Mr. Morris was a serious, prim-looking man who exuded an air of dignity and self-importance. There was an aura of aristocratic refinement about him. He wore frameless glasses and sported a small dribble of yellow mustache on an otherwise neatly shaven face. Instead of being grateful to Reb Itchele for his position at the shop, he nourished envy and resentment against him in his heart. Mr. Morris betrayed his negative feelings for his boss by periodically mentioning the name of the salesman whom Reb Itchele had fired in order to hire Yacov. The fired salesman, Mr. Morris would inform Yacov sullenly, was a wizard of salesmanship and a first class *Polonist*. Apart from that, he was a man with a family to support. Reb Itchele had discarded him only because he had taken a fancy to Yacov, who was a greenhorn and an ignoramus. Mr. Morris did not explicitly state the words "greenhorn" and "ignoramus," in relating the story to Yacov, but he implied them so clearly that Yacov could, without the slightest difficulty, guess whom Mr. Morris had in mind.

So Yacov was not surprised that polite Mr. Morris bore him no great affection and that the other salesmen also viewed him with distrust. It was strange. Here at the shoe store, Yacov realized that he had become the boss's man and he found himself on the other side of the barricade. As a result, he began to suffer from remorse and from a loss of self-respect. The thought of the fired salesman whose bread he was eating constantly preyed on his mind, especially when Mr. Morris informed the other salesmen that the fired man had still not found a job, and with unemployment being as high as it was, there was nothing left for the poor soul to do but to go abegging along with his entire well-bred family.

Whenever Yacov caught a glimpse of himself in the mirror that the lady customers used for inspecting the shoes they tried on, it seemed to him that he beheld not himself reflected in it, but Reb Itchele. He could clearly hear the words that Reb Itchele had said to him one day in his warm, fatherly voice, "Remember, Yacov," he had said, "if you ever step into the swamp called politics, I am finished with you. I will be ruthless with you, because I am still a Jew, body and soul. These slogan-yelping hordes might, heaven forbid, bring about our people's destruction, even though we live in a free Poland."

"What are you talking about, Reb Itchele?" Yacov answered his boss in his mind, frowning at the mirror with self-disgust. "Here I belong only to your party."

Yacov kept his political activities a secret and tried not to betray himself, so that his co-workers would not tell on him. He was attached to Reb Itchele and was reluctant to lose him. The fact that his dead older brother's name had also been Itchele only strengthened his sentiments for the man. But these very same feelings filled him daily with shame. It was a kind of love of which he was not overly proud.

In spite of the fact that the pants were too short on him, Yacov looked impressive at work. He was slim and supple. The skin of his oval, fine-featured face was of a smooth chestnut hue. Thickly waving brown hair framed his high forehead, and his mother's faint winning smile hid in the corners of his mouth, the mouth of a dreamer. He attracted people's eyes. Noticing him once, they would usually turn their heads for a second look. A warmth radiated from his youthful, masculine figure and there was a pleasant refinement in his bearing. The air of sadness and bewilderment about him awoke in others the impulse to take hold of his strong, work-tested hand, as if it were the hand of a child, and console him, assuring him that life was much simpler than it seemed to him. But there were others, as for instance Mr. Morris and his colleagues, in whom Yacov's qualities evoked strong feelings of revulsion, or even hatred. Even among Yacov's comrades, who generally liked and appreciated him, there were some who considered him stupid, and there were others who considered him phony or a hypocrite.

The aristocratic lady customers who came into the store to shop for shoes were clad in expensive fur coats, or in silver foxes, and were wrapped in clouds of perfume. Depending on their age, they showed Yacov a great deal of either maternal or sisterly attention whenever they offered him their foot to fit on a shoe. As he bent over their legs, they peered deeply into his eyes. Despite his limping Polish, there were some ladies who would by no means allow any other salesman to attend them. The other salesmen would smirk, both with envy and satisfaction.

"Mr. Polin!" they called, snickering, addressing him by his family name, "You're wanted!" and ever so lightly, they pushed Yacov in the direction of the customer who had asked for his assistance.

The women's caressing gazes exacerbated his sense of humiliation. "They're taking me for a puppet," he raged inwardly. But occasionally a young woman, as she entrusted him with her shoeless foot encased in a silk stocking, glanced at him in such a way that it made his bitterness mix with drops of sweetness. He was confused and enchanted. The contact of his hand with the young woman's delicate sole and ankle was electrifying, although there was nothing as mundane as fitting on a pair of shoes. Yet such tactile contact had an air of closeness about it that a mere handshake rarely produced. A woman kept her foot hidden from people's eyes, whereas a hand, even when gloved, was free to be looked at. Taking hold of a shoeless foot, to be clad in a shoe that would protect and shield it against the cold and mud, created a bond of momentary intimacy.

He considered older feet to be easier to handle. To the older women he responded without any particular tension. Nonchalantly, he bestowed on them a warm gaze and a friendly, filial smile. However, with the older women there were greater problems concerning the feet themselves. More then once was he overcome by compassion at the sight of a shapeless foot. And so, by observing their feet, he began to learn about the women themselves. He would form an idea about a woman's life, gleaned from the sight of her twisted, bumpy toes, of her protruding gouty sidebones, her fallen arches, her corns, her ingrown toenails, and her calluses. All these were the milestones on a woman's road through life, indicating how far she had gone, how much youth there was still left around her ankles, how much joy she could still absorb with her toes, how much restlessness was left in the balls of her feet, and how far she was from eternal rest.

He was often amazed by the fact that he never viewed these female clients, the wealthiest women in town, as belonging to the enemy camp. The fact that he despised himself on account of his work had to do more with the role that he himself played at the shop, than with the functions he performed. He knew the names of many of these ladies. It was against their husbands and fathers that he marched at the mass demonstrations. But toward the women themselves he felt a tenderness of the kind reserved for caged birds. They belonged to a different class from that of their men, to a different class even from that of the women who were his comrades.

Dark-haired Miss Polcia had a pair of very large, very black eyes whose gaze was tinged by a glint of sadness mixed with arrogance. She stopped by at the shoe store even when she had no need for a pair of new shoes. She was the only daughter of Baruch Weiskop's acquaintance, an assimilated, Polish-speaking jeweler who lived on the first floor in the flat directly above the store. On quiet afternoons Miss Polcia's light footsteps could be heard through the ceiling along with the muffled sounds of the Polish ballads that she sang, accompanying herself on the piano. Every so often the ringing echo of her laughter reached the ears of the salesmen downstairs at the shop.

There were hours at the store during the afternoon when no customers showed up. Then Yacov ran out for half an hour or so to attend to his party duties, or he sat in the storage room and read. He never brought any socialist literature along to the store. The better he got to know his co-workers, the more careful he became. They considered him their enemy, Reb Itchele Hittelmakher's spy. But at the same time they looked down with disgust on the Jewish mob that brought shame upon the entire community with its demonstrations and strikes. They despised the Yiddish language that the Jewish "riffraff" spoke; they hated the sound of it more violently than did the fiercest anti-Semites. Whenever a lady customer who belonged to an orthodox family and wore a wig came into the shop and began to speak in such broken Polish that it was impossible to understand her, these courteous salesmen would just stand there and listen amusedly, refraining from helping her out with even a word. If she tried to explain her problem in Yiddish, they shrugged, pretending total ignorance of the "jargon." Smirking politely, they entertained themselves by allowing her to struggle with her tortured Polish, until at last they deigned to repeat to her in elegant phrasing what she had just said, making it clear that they had known all along what she had wanted. The salesmen firmly believed that if a person lived in the Polish Republic, it was that person's patriotic duty to speak the Polish language decently.

Miss Polcia was a student of the graduating class at the gymnasium that Baruch Weiskop had founded, to which her parents had transferred her from a Catholic school. On her way home from the gymnasium, if Miss Polcia was in the mood, she would drop by the shoe store for a flirtatious chat with the intelligent and cultured young salesmen. The first time Miss Polcia noticed Yacov, she saw him sitting in the side room with a book on his lap. She came over to him, bent down over his shoulder, and exclaimed, "What on earth is that?" She bent down so low that Yacov could smell the fragrance of the soap that she used. She asked in a playful, sarcastic tone of voice, "You read books in exotic languages, Mister, what's your name?"

Yacov immediately knew who she was. "My name is Polin, and it's not an exotic language. It's Yiddish," he answered her calmly. Since he did not dare push her away, he closed the book and stood up. He waited for her to leave him alone. She did not interest him. He wondered how Baruch Weiskop could have talked so flatteringly about this girl who behaved herself as if she were everyone's spoiled only daughter. Her mannerisms and her lack of manners irritated him. He did not consider it his duty to entertain her.

"And what is it that you are reading in Yiddish, Mister Polin?" she asked in the same tone of voice, exchanging meaningful glances with the other salesmen.

"*Jean Christophe,*" he said curtly. He put the book away and, turning his back to her, busied himself arranging the shoe boxes on the shelves.

A few days later when she came into the store again and saw Yacov reading in his corner, she again approached him, "You are still reading *Jean Christophe,* Mister Polin?"

"I am," he snapped back.

"Then read to me a sentence or two. I want to hear how it sounds in Yiddish. I will understand it. I study German."

He wanted to tell her outright to leave him alone. Then for a long while he hesitated. Finally he flipped through the pages, combing them intently for a passage that had particularly moved him. Slowly he began to read to her: "The Bible that his mother had given him to take along as a companion in his exile became a source of dreams to him. Although he did not read it with religious feeling, the vital energy of that Hebrew *Iliad* became the spring in which he bathed his naked soul in the evenings from the grime and mud, and from his suffering."

Yacov raised his head slowly and saw before him a transformed Miss Polcia. Her huge black eyes were full of astonishment, an astonishment that children display when confronted by the mysterious aspects of a story. "How strange," she whispered. "I've copied that same excerpt into my notebook." Coming back to reality, she added, "In Polish of course. I don't read French fluently yet."

Yacov's curiosity was sparked. The girl had two faces—one, for every day, and the other, the face she showed him now. And he had passed judgment on her so quickly, had taken her at face value, so to speak, without having suspected the duality of her nature. He nodded. "It *is* preferable to read in the original. But a work like *Jean Christophe* sheds language like a shell, because what really matters is its content."

"That's true," she agreed. She was serious. As she stood there before him with the delicate oval of her olive face, with her refined Semitic features, her long black hair glistening over her shoulders, she looked Like a Jewish princess, like a young bewildered Queen Esther. "But what surprises me," she went on, "is that these things can be expressed in Yiddish, which is not a language at all." She shook her head lightly at him, waved her hand at the other salesmen, and, swinging back and forth the heavy schoolbag that she was carrying, she left the store with an uncertain step.

Miss Polcia visited the store with increasing frequency, each time coming over to Yacov to check what he was reading. She would lean over his shoulder and frown. "Again Yiddish!" and the mischievous, mocking little flame would light up her eyes.

Yacov was more patient with her. One day he replied calmly to her expressions of ridicule, "Yiddish is my mother tongue. There is so much to read. In Yiddish I find the going faster. And Yiddish literature must certainly be read in Yiddish, don't you think?"

"Yiddish literature!" she cried out, the fire that kindled in her eyes pierced him with needle-sharp sparks. Yacov had often noticed similar sparks ignite in the eyes of other Jewish people who disliked the Yiddish language. It was not just that the language was not pleasing to their ears, it was that they hated Yiddish with a fierce personal hatred. "Aren't you ashamed of using the sacred word 'literature,'" Polcia raged, "in reference to a jargon of the lowest kind? Are you out to make of fool of me!"

"It is you who are making a fool of yourself," he answered composedly.

"Pray tell me why I'm making a fool of myself, if you don't mind?" She swung her hip forward and planted her fist on it.

"Because you are ignorant," he answered. He wanted to add, "and arrogant as well," but he restrained himself. He felt like grabbing this monster of a girl by her shoulders and shaking the sick, self-righteous chutzpah out of her. At the same time he felt a compulsion to stroke the lustrous hair that cascaded down her shoulders. He wanted to ask this angry girl-child why she was hiding her true face, to ask her what worm was eating her and making her spit out the venom of despair through her hatred for her people's language.

Miss Polcia tittered bitterly, "I am ignorant! I am ignorant, while Mister Polin, who doesn't know when to say *dwie* and when to say *dwa* is not ignorant! Perhaps you can tell me, dear Mister Polin," she mockingly curtsied before him, "what language should citizens of the Polish Republic speak? Should they be blabbering away in Yiddish and hiccuping in Polish?" She noticed the delight written on the faces of Mr. Morris and his helpers and, as if she were an actress playing for the gallery, her voice rose to an even higher pitch, sounding shriller and more aggressive. She drew herself up indignantly. "Is this how we respect ourselves and our newborn father-land?" she declaimed. "Is there any wonder that the Polish people detest you and spit on you?"

Yacov smiled sadly. "And you they don't detest?"

"Of course they don't!" she flung her head up high and shrieked, beside herself with rage. "I speak a better Polish than many a yokel of theirs. And I know Mickiewicz and Sowacki and all of Polish literature better than many thousands of them do! And I am a better patriot and a better citizen than many of them, too!"

Yacov cast another glance at Miss Polcia's flowing black hair and at her eyes that were still ablaze with frenzied despair. He thought that Queen Esther, when she had felt herself helpless, had probably looked like Polcia did now. "You're screaming so loud, Miss Polcia," he said, "but the color of your hair and the blackness of your eyes scream even louder. They contradict every word you yell out."

"Not true!" she rejoined with vehemence. "The color of my hair has nothing to do with it. I can bleach my hair blond if I like."

"And your eyes? Can you color them blue? And what will you do with that quaint tormented gaze of a Jewess that betrays you?"

"Don't you dare make idiotic wisecracks about me, Mister Polin!" She laughed bitterly. "You groaning and moaning good-for-nothings see only gloom and doom wherever you look. Always coming out with that funereal tone! My eyes aren't tormented. They're screaming with rage at the likes of you, that's what they're doing! You want to drag me back into your stinking swamp. But bear this in mind once and for all, Mister. I'm not Jewish, and I refuse to be Jewish, and no one can force me to be Jewish, understand? I am a Pole and a proud one at that!" She grabbed her schoolbag and dashed over to the other salesmen who had delightedly been watching the scene. "Did you hear that, Mister Morris?" she raved. "Did you hear that treacherous, scandalous, and archaic piece of verbal garbage?"

Mr. Morris and the other salesmen shook their heads mournfully. Mr. Morris said, "That, unfortunately, is the situation."

"But it cannot go on like that!" Miss Polcia pounded her small fist against the counter top, unable to calm herself. "We must fight against those who abuse our dignity. We must root them out, destroy them to the last, until there is not a trace of them left!"

When she had gone, Yacov remained sitting—thunderstruck. Never had he heard anyone express so venomously the hatred of one's own people. He mourned his friendship with Baruch Weiskop. If this was how Baruch was educating his female students, then he was destroying everything that he, Yacov, stood for and believed in. If this was true, his and Baruch's antagonisms had grown to formidable proportions; they had become irreconcilable. Not only was Baruch no longer his friend. He was his enemy. Yacov felt a lump in his throat. The truth was hard to swallow. He decided never to speak to Baruch again, although in his heart of hearts he could not help but admit that he still harbored tender feelings for the man. There was also great uneasiness in his heart. He was holding a job that Baruch had provided for him. He stared at the shoes that he was wearing, the shoes that Baruch had given him. Fortunately they were disintegrating.

The next time Miss Polcia visited the store, she made a point of not looking in Yacov's direction. If their eyes met, she frowned and quickly turned her head. She chatted loudly with the other salesmen, broaching her favourite topic, books and literature. She was a great expert on Polish writers and felt euqally at home in European literature and in the Greek and Roman classics. After all she was about to take the *matura* examinations. Miss Polcia, her classmates, and her teachers, not to mention the director himself, had been working very hard to establish the renown of the newly founded gymnasium as a first-rate institution of learning.

As for the polite salesmen, they actually had no idea what Miss Polcia was expounding so fervently. In order to cover their ignorance, they responded to her deliberations with an affectionate pat on her arm, with a deep meaningful gaze into her eyes, or with a fine-sounding, elaborate compliment. Miss Polcia, well aware that she was wasting her time on them, began with increasing frequency to shoot arrows of angry glances in Yacov's direction. He suspected her of being a very lonely girl.

One day, when she had grown badly annoyed with her listeners' left-handed response to her lecture and could bear it no longer, she approached Yacov. As was her habit, she bent over his shoulder and called out, "Naturally! Yiddish again!"

It made him laugh. He raised his head and said, "Look what I am reading. *Quo Vadis?* by Sienkiewicz."

She wrinkled her nose and grimaced. "I knew that *Quo Vadis?* was translated into all the languages in the world, but . . . "

Her eyes met his. He asked amusedly, "*Quo Vadis?* Miss Polcia?"

As if a veil had been peeled from her face, its expression changed. Embarrassment mellowed her black eyes, giving them a warm velvety luster. Her lips drew together in a red knot as if she were forcing them to keep back a secret. She did not answer his question, but remarked in a changed tone of voice, "It seems to me that you and I both suffer from the same madness, books." She leaned against the shelves laden with shoe boxes and scrutinized him. After a long moment of silence, she embarked on telling him about what she was reading and what she intended to read. She could not overcome her amazement at the fact that, of the many books she mentioned to Yacov, he had read most of them and had heard about the others.

Little by little Miss Polcia's loyalties to the store's employees began to shift. She stormed in during the quiet afternoon hours, greeted the salesmen with a nod of her head, and made her way straight to Yacov's corner. The salesmen cast sharp glances in their direction. When Miss Polcia passed them on her way out and refrained from stopping at the counter, they called after her, "Watch out, Miss Polcia, we'll tell your mama that you're flirting with young men!" Smiling sweetly, they tried to hide how badly hurt they were by her neglect of them.

After a while, Miss Polcia came in to invite Yacov to her home in order to show him her library. To her dismay, he did not respond to her invitation at once, and when he did, it was with an impolite shrug of the shoulders, "As you know, Miss Polcia, I don't read Polish," he said.

His behavior was outrageous. She found him badly wanting both in tact and manners. Yet she kept her hurt in check and insisted, "I will read to you. Polish poetry compares well to Russian," she assured him.

He shook his head and quipped, "I don't read poetry in the middle of the day, not even in Yiddish. During the day I must be sober and poetry is liable to intoxicate me."

Although the quip amused her, she frowned. "Yiddish poetry! I'm sure it's nothing but vaporous babblings produced by senile brains!"

"The Jewish poets are handsome *young* men." Yacov's smile broadened. "What's old about them is the tradition that they have inherited." He waited for her anger to ignite, which would save him from seeking excuses for refusing to go upstairs with her. He was not in the least inclined to make the effort to persuade her to an affection and respect for the Yiddish language. She knew nothing about the people who spoke it. Moreover, he considered himself unsuited for the role of a knight; he was not ready to undertake the valiant task of freeing the sleeping princess from her glass tower.

But he misjudged the strength of Miss Polcia's determination. The following day as he was leaving the store after work, he found her standing outside, waiting for him. He was about to cross the street when she grabbed him by the arm and the next moment she was dragging him into the stairwell that led up to her home.

They entered a spacious dwelling the windows of which were hung with tulle curtains. Massive pieces of furniture, sparkling mirrors, crystal chandeliers and candelabras, gilt-framed paintings, sculptures, porcelains, Gobelins and tapestries filled the rooms that Yacov peered into as Miss Polcia led him through a long corridor with doors opening off on both sides. He wondered how a family of three could manage to live in such an enormous flat and feel cozy.

"Mama and Papa are in Italy," Miss Polcia informed him. "We are alone, thank heaven. There is only my nanny in the kitchen." She led Yacov into her room, half of which was taken up by a piano. "You're looking at the piano?" she asked and shrugged off her coat, leaving it along with her heavy school bag on the piano stool. "Its usual place is in the salon, of course, but when they are gone . . . How can I tell you? Sometimes I need its company, not in order to play, but just to be in its presence, like wanting to be with a friend yet not having the need for conversation." She was wearing her navy-blue school uniform: a pleated skirt and a blouse with a wide, white, sailor's collar which contrasted vividly with her black hair. She looked even more girlish and more vulnerable than when he had seen her in her coat. "So why are we standing around like this?" she cried out and threw off her shoes. She wore thick brown school-girl stockings. She jumped onto the sofa and drew up her legs so that only her feet stuck out from under the umbrella of her pleated skirt. Automatically, Yacov noticed the soles of her feet. They were small and of a fine, delicate shape. He could discern the outline of each of her tiny toes through her stockings.

Haltingly, as if in fear that he might crush the sofa with his weight, he sat down on its opposite end, and utterly embarrassed, stared at the piano in front of him. Polcia observed him shamelessly for a long while. Then she embarked on a monologue, talking about her school, her girlfriends, her studies, and her teachers. She immersed herself in a hodgepodge of details, sprinkled with clever remarks and peals of laughter, whose purpose, Yacov guessed, was to make him feel at ease. When she mentioned the founder and chief authority of her school, Mister Weiskop, Yacov did in fact forget his discomfiture for a while. He was on the verge of blurting out to her, and betraying himself by telling her, that this great man, this idol of Polcia's gymnasium, this most noble human being in the entire world was no stranger to him. It was not something that he wanted her to know.

The fascination with which he listened to her as she talked about Mr. Weiskop did not, however, escape Miss Polcia's notice. So she continued with increased enthusiasm to chatter away about the great man and the particular relationship she herself enjoyed with him by virtue of his being a friend of the family.

"All the girls are jealous of me," she giggled, "because all of them are head over heels in love with him." She waited for a moment, beaming at Yacov with laughing eyes. "Aren't you going to ask me whether I'm in love with him, too?"

"Are you?" he asked, flushing.

"He's in love with *me!*"

"You were supposed to read to me," Yacov reminded her.

"Of course. But why are you in such a hurry, Mister Polin?" She curled her underlip, pretending to be offended.

He was not only embarrassed, but also irritable and hungry, yet he did not want her to offer him any food. He felt himself stifled. He wondered what argument to use in order to get away from her quickly and smoothly.

He saw Miss Polcia raise her small hand and pull at a bell that was suspended from the wall by a heavy silk cord. An old woman dressed in black, wearing a white apron and a white bonnet on her head, entered the room. "Bring us tea, Nianiu, and some chocolate cookies!" Miss Polcia commanded. The nanny's watery eyes stared at Yacov questioningly. He saw her shake her head distressfully before she left the room. Miss Polcia jumped down from the sofa. Her mane of black hair cascading down her back, she dashed toward the mahogany bookcase and drew out a thin volume from amidst the books on one of the shelves. When she returned to the sofa and sat down, the expression on her face was extremely serious. "We will start with Kochanowski, of course," she announced to Yacov. "Have you ever heard of Jan Kochanowski, Mister Polin?"

"I've heard something," he muttered.

"You can tell me the truth, have you or haven't you really? And why are you staring at me as if you were afraid of me? I don't bite. Look, I have weak teeth." She snarled, showing him the two rows of her tiny teeth.

"All right," he grinned. "I know nothing about Kochanowski."

Polcia became even more serious. She wrinkled her forehead. "We should have started with a much earlier period. Kochanowski is already part of the Polish Renaissance." She held up the booklet and showed it to him. "These elegies . . . lamentations on the death of his little daughter Ursula . . . these are his swan song."

The nanny came back carrying a tray. She put down a silver jug, two glasses, and a plate of chocolate cookies on a small table. Casting horrified glances at Yacov and scrutinizing his threadbare clothes, which were suited for a bagel vendor rather than for a friend of Miss Polcia's, she poured the tea with a trembling hand. She offered Yacov one glass and Polcia the other. Yacov responded to the old woman's frantic gaze with a comradely look, as if to let her know that he himself did not know what he was doing there. But the moment the nanny left the room, he fixed his attention on the plate of cookies. As he sipped the hot tea, he thought of Queen Marie Antoinette's dictum, "Let them eat cake." He waited for Miss Polcia to offer him a cookie. As soon as she did, he gave himself entirely to the delight of the chocolate cookie's taste. To his chagrin, the cookie melted in his mouth much too rapidly.

Meanwhile Miss Polcia continued with her lecture on the subject of Jan Kochanowski. At length she pushed a long strand of wayward hair out of her eyes and began to recite *The Elegies on the Death of Ursula*. Yacov shoved himself closer to the plate of cookies, becoming engrossed in their various shapes and forms. One after the other, he stuffed them into his mouth. Consumed by his desire for the cookies, he stopped worrying about whether or not he was behaving properly. The white empty spaces that soon began to appear on the bottom of the plate filled his heart with indescribable regret.

Miss Polcia looked up from the book. Yacov turned his head away. To his surprise he heard her say, "Do you see how much alike our tastes are, Mister Polin? I, too, am mad about chocolate cookies."

It was at this moment that Yacov grew fond of Miss Polcia. "They have a heavenly taste!" he exclaimed with genuine sincerity.

"Then we shall have some more!" Polcia pronounced triumphantly. She picked up the empty plate and in her stocking feet, glided out of the room. Soon she was back, and with her came the plate filled with double the amount of chocolate cookies. "Eat!" she commanded, and picked up a cookie herself, biting into it with her small sharp teeth. Yacov listened to the crunching munching sounds coming from her mouth and watched the brown chocolate crumbs appear on her thin lips. She licked them off with the tip of her tongue. Her lips shone with a crimson shine. The next moment, these lips were moving, carving out musical words. She was back at reciting the *Elegies*.

Yacov threw himself at the cookies without great ceremony. Finally, his stomach bearably satisfied, he interrupted her and said, "You must read the whole thing all over again. My understanding of poetical Polish is worse than I thought."

She agreed readily and began to read from the beginning, explaining the poetry, talking about the tragic yet purifying love of a father for his deceased little daughter. The *Elegies* were an outcry of grief at the loss of a child, grief so powerfully expressed in poetic stanzas that it transcended the centuries. At another time Yacov might perhaps have been deeply moved by such a lyrical outpouring of a man's sorrow, but now he listened more to the sound of Miss Polcia's lilting voice than to the words of the verses themselves. Somehow the flow of her voice harmonized with the flow of her brilliant black hair. The dark yet glittering cascades of sound overshadowed the meaning of the cascading mournful words.

There was something that disturbed him greatly and kept him from concentrating. It was obvious that Miss Polcia had undertaken the task of educating him by starting with the Polish literature of the Renaissance.

Not that he minded her efforts. On the contrary. It fascinated him to inhale the air of these unfamiliar surroundings, to be sitting in this room that was permeated with a kind of spiritual perfume, and to look at this creature. In looking at her and listening to her voice, he could forget his political duties for a while; he could forget about the Polish-Bolshevik conflict that had disturbed him so of late. What bothered him at this moment was the question of where Miss Polcia's lessons might lead him.

He no longer felt uncomfortable in Miss Polcia's presence. She was spontaneous and direct, not the way he himself was, but as he liked people to be. She was almost too direct, too aggressive for his taste. But this emboldened him. The same evening he told Polcia a story by Panait Istrati that he had just finished reading.

Miss Polcia waited for Yacov in front of the shoe store more and more frequently. If he was not too hungry and had no particular party duties to attend to, he went up with her to her room. Her parents were not yet back from their extended vacation. Polcia seemed to be used to their absence. Nor did Yacov have anything against being alone with the girl. He minded not in the least that his friendship with her was nothing but one of her pastimes, the pastime of a spoiled, lonely girl.

One day Miss Polcia discovered that the bar in the salon was not locked, and ever since that day she and Yacov shared a glass or two of liqueur when he visited. As the alcohol spread pleasantly through his limbs, Yacov would tell Polcia stories that he made up on the spur of the moment, much as he used to do on his walks with Abrashka, when, inspired by the beauty of Bociany's landscape and by Abrashka's curiosity, he had given free reign to his imagination. While telling Polcia his stories, he would occasionally look at her, absorbing the luster of her dark devouring eyes and the partly dreamy, partly playful expression of her face. He had the feeling that a little girl was sitting at his side and that he himself was a child, and he would abandon himself to the enchantment of the moment.

Once, when the raveled threads of the tale that he was spinning had dissolved into an undefined and vague ending, Polcia remained sitting transfixed as if she were still listening. Then she said in a whisper, "You must write this down, Mister Polin. Such beauty must be captured."

"The beauty of my Polish?" Yacov asked in jest.

"Oh, your Polish. I didn't even notice it."

"That's quite a compliment, coming from you."

"Stop jesting. You must write down the story. I will help you."

"That would make me into a writer, Miss Polcia, and becoming a writer is not one of my ambitions."

Her dark eyes pierced him through. After a moment of silence she asked, "What are your ambitions, Mister Polin?"

He shrugged, "I haven't formulated them clearly yet."

"But you must have formulated your personal ambitions, at least the main ones."

He stared at her as if he sought the answer to her question in her face. What indeed were his personal ambitions? Miss Polcia's face faded from his sight. He peered into the vague distance within himself and saw himself walking down the Wide Poplar Road with Binele at his side.

"I do have one perhaps," he conceded. "I don't know whether you can call it an ambition, though. I would like to be able to love well. I find this very difficult to do."

"Difficult? To love?" She knotted her thin black eyebrows. "But loving is easy. It comes by itself, doesn't it?"

"I said to love well."

"It is well . . . to love." She looked him straight in the eye.

He fidgeted uneasily on the sofa. He was getting himself involved in a conversation that he should have avoided. He knew he ought to explain to her what he had meant by his words. But he was loathe to get deeply into the subject. Some profound-sounding platitudes would suffice, he decided.

"Love can be good," he ventured smugly, "but very often it is selfish, even destructive both for the person who loves and for the one who is loved. A great many contrasting feelings collide in love, some are the opposite of love itself, and they all hide under the cloak of that magic word."

Miss Polcia was all afire. She too shifted uncomfortably in her seat and moved her arms restlessly, intrigued by the topic that had so unexpectedly sprung up in their conversation. Yacov smiled to himself. This schoolgirl had probably been spending much of her time with her girlfriends, philosophizing about the nature of love. She had probably underlined all the passages dealing with the topic in her books. She no doubt discussed "love" with the male students with whom she flirted. But why then did she look at him so avidly—as if he were the first man with whom she had ever had a chance to tackle this delicate subject? Why then did she become so agitated and so gravely serious? She looked decidedly as if her life depended on the outcome of their conversation.

He felt her heart tremble in the tremor of her voice as she asked, "What then does it mean to you, to love?"

Her nervousness was contagious, yet he managed to answer her more or less calmly. "To me it simply means to help another person to live. My mother, for instance, helps me to live."

Miss Polcia stood up, looked about the room, let her eyes rest on Yacov, then, in her stockinged feet, with soft, cat-like steps, she glided over to the piano. She stroked the keys with caressing hands. Over the musical sounds that she produced, her voice reached Yacov in a hoarse whisper, "I want to help you to live, Yacov."

Startled and frightened, he jumped to his feet. "Thank you. Thank you very much. I must go now," he muttered, staring at her blouse in order to avoid her open devouring gaze. He did not want to ever see her again. He had no business here. He stretched his hand out to her. She offered him hers, curled into a small fist, like the hand of a child in pain.

"Already?" Slowly she uncurled her fingers and responded with a limp handshake.

The following day Yacov found Miss Polcia waiting for him in front the shoe store. She took his arm as if nothing had happened between them the day before. He noticed that the skin under her eyes was puffy and he realized that she had been crying. He firmly refused to go up to her room. He had no time, nor was he in the mood to exchange more than a few words with her in the street. The Polish-Bolshevik war had broken out and a storm was raging in his heart.

Polcia would not let go of his arm. She chaffed him. "I am no longer bothered by your obsession with Yiddish. I swear it. I don't mind any of your obsessions. You may go on having your lofty opinions about the riffraff of Baluty. So please come!" She tugged at his arm frenziedly. Her voice changed. It became tremulous and pleading. "I don't understand," she finally said, turning up her face to him, her features twisted into an expression of anguish. "Is it because I told you . . . because I let you know that I'm in love with you, that you are punishing me?" He bit his lips. She grew more aggressive. "Had I kept quiet about it, we would have still been friends, wouldn't we? Why shouldn't people express their good feelings? I want nothing from you."

"Forgive me," he rejoined. He was sore inside himself and there was an edge of harshness in his tone of voice. "I'm sorry, but I can't." That was all that he could say. He tried to free himself of her hand around his arm, and added, "You must not fail your *matura* exams."

She would not let go. "I will not forgive you, ever, if you don't come upstairs, so that I can prove to you that I will never again make a fool of myself. We can read together, just read. And don't worry about my exams."

He gave in to her. Once in her room, they drank tea as usual, munched chocolate cookies, and sipped some liqueur later on. Polcia read Polish poems to him. They discussed books. Miss Polcia was intelligent and truly well read. It was instructive and delightful to talk to her. She even made him forget about the war with the Bolsheviks and his impending conscription, as well as all his other worries and obligations. But her black hair was too slippery and her eyes were too deep, too dark, and too devouring. She had a graceful figure, thin beautiful legs, delicate small feet, and her tread was like that of a cat. Her every gesture, every flight of her small pale hands through the air when she talked, called him to her with the allure of a flame teasing a moth. Whether she was aware of it or not, there was a heat concealed in her cool sensuous body, a demon lying in wait for him, in order to claim his unconditional surrender.

In order to keep his mind clear, he, for the first time, directed their conversation onto the paths of hard, cold reality. Sacrificing these moments of temporary oblivion, he concentrated his thoughts on the outside world and spoke to her of the Russian Revolution and discussed the war with the Bolsheviks which had broken out because of squabbles over the common Russian-Polish border. Up to now he had never broached such subjects with her. Nor did it make much sense to do so now, unless he could make her see what he called the real world around her. Yet he could not stop talking. The more her body appealed to him, the more animated he became, lecturing her about the hopes of millions of people, telling her about the times of tremendous social change that were fast approaching, times of true brotherly love, times of friendship among the nations, and times filled with the joy of children who would never go hungry. He even told her how upset he was about this war between the Soviets and Poland.

"I am just as passionate a Polish patriot as you, Miss Polcia," he said, "although I consider myself a Jew and want to live as a Jew according to my beliefs. That's why my feelings are split, I mean, as far as Poland and the Soviets are concerned. Because in the Soviet Union a new way of life has come into being, the first great social experiment. And, you understand, it will not be easy for me to join the Polish Army and fight against an army of peasants and workers who are out to protect their renewed hopes, hopes we all have nourished for so long in our dreams."

Miss Polcia seemed not to be listening any longer. She fixed her eyes on him. "You, to fight? In the war?"

He grinned. "Why are you so surprised? I don't look much like a fighter or a soldier, I know. I don't feel much like one. Never mind. Greater schlemiels than I have mastered that art quickly enough. Killing is one of the easiest skills to learn. You need no brains for it. So I am waiting for my conscription call."

The color ebbed away from her cheeks. "How strange . . . " she whispered. "I am in fact a great patriot, yet I loathe the idea of you leaving for the front." Before Yacov could manage to respond, she had thrown herself into his arms, her body tightly glued to his, her eyes open and burning. She wrapped her arms firmly around his neck. "I can't help it," she burst into sobs. "I love you. I want nothing bad to happen to you!" She pressed her head against his chest.

He felt a weakness in his limbs as if he had lost the strength to stand and were about to fall to his knees. He put his hands on her hair and then took her face between them. "Thank you," he whispered.

She raised her wet, tear-stained lips to his mouth. "I would do anything for you, Yacov." She sealed her words with a salty kiss.

"I don't want you to . . . I don't need you to do anything for me." He returned her kisses, his fingers buried deep in the black cloud of her hair.

"I want you . . . I want you to be my first and my last . . . " Her words sank heavily into him.

He did not want to be either her first or her last. He did not want to be her lover at all. But it was so easy to let himself be swept away, to cease being "captain of his own ship." Fragile and thin though Polcia was, it was she who was carrying him to the sofa, while he saw himself running away, pounding down flights and flights of stairs. But it was only his heart that raced away. He lay on the sofa, covering her with his body, she so fragile, so light, he so heavy, about to crush her. Looking at her, seeing and not seeing her, he saw Comrade Bronia, the seamstress whom he had met at the library and with whom he had been spending most of his nights. He recalled when he had first tried to kiss Bronia. "Shame on you, Comrade Polin," she had pushed him away. "The hydra of capitalism is involved in its desperate struggle for power. A war will soon be raging. In Baluty tiny babies are daily dying of starvation. And you have such things on your mind." But later on she also wanted to do "everything" for him. And through these two, Bronia and Polcia, he expressed his yearning for the girl with the golden hair who had escaped from him forever. "My goal has been never to hurt anybody," a voice sounded mockingly in his head.

෬ *13* ෬

FOR THE PASSOVER HOLIDAY Yacov left for Bociany. This time he took along gifts of shoes for all the members of his family. This had been a project of his ever since he had begun working at the shoe shop. He had sent a letter home to that effect, asking his youngest sister, Shaindele, to cut out paper sole-forms for all of them, his brother Shalom and his wife and children included. As long as Yacov could remember, shoes had been a most serious problem in his family. His mother had always tried to save up some money in order to fix the holes in the shoes of one child or another. Yacov himself had never had a new pair of shoes, but had always worn Shalom's, who first inherited his deceased brother Itchele's shoes, and then those of his deceased father.

The shoes at the elegant shop where Yacov worked were not at all suitable for the female members of his family, and they were too expensive. But thanks to his friendship with Reb Itchele Hittelmakher, who had contacts with many shoemakers in town, Yacov was able to purchase the right kind of shoes at a bargain price. He made sure that they fitted the forms that he had been sent. The colossal sum of money that such a purchase, even at a bargain price, required, was far above Yacov's means. He himself was still wearing the disintegrating shoes that he had received from Baruch Weiskop a long time ago. Food and the rent that he paid for his lodgings in the room of an old couple in Baluty left him with hardly any money to save of his earnings. In fact, the undertaking had been sheer madness. But ever since he had begun to make himself inwardly ready to be conscripted and sent to the front, the extraordinary idea of leaving such a gift behind for his family had taken on a particular meaning, and he had only reinforced his determination to go through with this project which had begun to obsess him. In this venture Reb Itchele (to whom Yacov, after a game of chess, mentioned his money problem) had again come to his rescue. Moreover, Reb Itchele had encouraged Yacov to acquire all the gifts at once. "First of all," Reb Itchele had said to him, "the more pairs of shoes you buy, the less they'll cost you. Second, your people need the shoes now. So why wait until you save up the money, which may take who knows how long, especially with the war at hand and the times being uncertain? I'll lend you the money. We'll take it off bit by bit from your weekly salary, and you won't have to worry about paying me back."

"And what if I'm sent to the front, Reb Itchele?" Yacov asked.

"So you'll repay me when you're back."

"And what if I don't come back?"

"A Jew must not live with such thoughts in mind. Our trust in the Almighty's providence must never falter."

Bociany was not in a particular holiday mood that year. Many young men had been sent to the front. Nonetheless people made the effort to celebrate Passover in a positive frame of mind. So Yacov's gift of new shoes for every single member of his family did not go unnoticed in the shtetl. It even created a kind of sensation. On the first Passover day, as the family promenaded about the Potcheyov and the Garden, people came over with congratulations to Hindele and her children and to admire their shoes. Shalom's daughter boasted to her little friends that her Uncle Yacov had brought shoes for everybody in her family from his shoe store. And so the rumor spread that, just like it often happened in America, Yacov had overnight become a prosperous shoe merchant and was the owner of a fashionable shoe store on the elegant Piotrkowska Street in Lodz.

Yacov's extraordinary presents had, of course, created a tremendous sensation in his own family. Although they all remembered Yacov having asked to be sent forms of their soles, they never expected such results. They thought that, in the best case, Yacov would bring along a pair of secondhand shoes, first for Hindele, and then, at another visit, for someone else in the family. But such a feat—new shoes for each one of them—

bordered on the miraculous. Thus the merriment at the family reunion around the seder table was doubled. Although all their hearts fluttered with worry for Yacov's safety, not a word was mentioned on the subject of the war. Yacov felt the grateful loving glances from around the table. They warmed his heart and made him feel good, while at the same time they filled his heart with sadness and compassion. So little was needed to make his family happy.

This time during his visit, Yacov spent little time at home with his mother, as he had on his previous visits. Nor did he go to visit Reb Faivele the Miller and inquire about Abrashka. He was busy conferring with his friend Ariele, who was the leader of the Bund in Bociany. Ariele too expected to be drafted into the army any day.

The Bund in Bociany had its own clubhouse now, just like the other parties had theirs. The clubhouse consisted of a large room in one of the peasant huts on the fringe of the shtetl. During one of the intermediary weekdays of the holiday, Yacov and Ariele headed in the club's direction. There was a crowd waiting for them. Yacov, as the guest from Lodz, was due to deliver "greetings" from the organization in Lodz and to make a speech. Such was the rule, regardless of whether or not he, the guest, had the qualities of a public speaker. Yacov's heart pounded. He loathed speech making. He had no gift for it. What he normally enjoyed was serious conversation with another person, eye to eye.

There was however no escape from this function, which was generally considered a great honor. In a jocular manner Ariele introduced Yacov to the crowd who remembered him well. And so it came to pass that Yacov stood all alone at the head table, facing a roomful of people. Friendly, attentive faces were turned toward him, curious eyes looked at him. He focused his gaze on a young man who wore a traditional gabardine and who, for some reason, reminded him of Yoel the Blacksmith. Yacov spoke to this face.

He launched into his speech and expounded on the theme closest to his heart. He talked about the Jewish religion, explaining how it had led up directly to Bundism, and how Bundism gave a new meaning to the moral teachings of the Scriptures as well as a new meaning to Jewish life in exile. He said that the prophet Isaiah's dream of forging weapons into plowshares and the dream of the lion lying down with the lamb were Bundist dreams. He said that Rabbi Yochanan Ben Zakai, who had received permission from the Roman Commander Titus Vespasian to found the

Yeshiva in Yavne, had been the first Bundist because Rabbi Yochanan Ben Zakai had believed in the moral and spiritual power of the people whose main weapon was the word of the prophets. He reminded his listeners of Rabbi Isaac Luria, the great cabalist and great human being.

"The Almighty has done a righteous thing to disperse the Jewish people among the peoples of the world, Rabbi Luria said, because in this manner we can assist the Almighty in bringing salvation to the world. Rabbi Luria asked his students to 'love thy brother as thyself' by praying not only for the Jews but also for the Gentiles. We Bundists reject the concept of the chosen people, we reject the idea of one people being singled out among the nations, but we do *not* reject the obligation of every individual to contribute to the redemption of man!"

Yacov spoke about how intertwined Jewish fate was with the fate of non-Jews, how the struggle against evil in the world had to be accomplished by the joined forces of those who sought justice, and how, in a world of evil, there was no hope of redemption for the Jewish people alone. He spoke about the Bund being the heir of Hasidism. He said that attachment to one's language—and to all forms of creativity in that language—was an expression of a Jew's completeness as a human being. It led to respect for other people's individuality. Yacov recounted the achievements of the party in the city of Lodz and then opened the general discussion on the subject of the Soviet-Polish war.

After the meeting, the crowd poured out of the clubhouse and strolled through the shtetl, following the Narrow Poplar Road up to the manor court. There were many young men in the crowd who, like Yacov and Ariele, expected to be drafted any day. But for the time being there was festivity in the air. Yacov taught his companions the new songs that were sung at party functions in Lodz, trying as best he could to conceal his thorough dissatisfaction with himself. He had not spoken well at the meeting. His arguments had been too entangled and chaotic, his manner of delivery too old-fashioned. What he so strongly believed in had sounded, when pronounced aloud, like hollow phraseology. It was not the first time that this had happened to him. Whenever he had to address a crowd of people, whenever he discussed politics in general, something inside him locked itself up and only the upper layers of his thoughts surfaced in his words, sounding simplified and smug. He was not like Laibel the Hump who could transform the simple and superficial into near poetry. Yet Yacov knew well that he would not give up speaking in public whenever this was required of him. He had to serve his new faith as best he could. So he linked arms more tightly with the other strollers and elatedly, continued singing.

He could not believe his eyes and marveled at how much Bociany had changed since the end of the Great War. It seemed to have suddenly woken up after a sleep of hundreds of years. During the holiday the shtetl gave the impression of belonging entirely to the young, who in noisy clusters streamed back and forth through the streets and alleys. Small as Bociany was, all the existing shades of Jewish political life, all the movements and trends that had sprouted during the last few years in Poland, were represented in its narrow confines.

All these various groups and organizations did not live in peace with each other. But as a rule everyone honored the gray-haired leader of the town's Zionist movement, Shmulikl, the barber-surgeon, who still had his barber shop on the market place and still practiced his profession, although a real doctor now resided in the shtetl. Shmulikl and his wife, the latter having been miraculously cured of her migraines, had more time now to devote to their work for Zion. Ariele, who had taken his first ideological steps in Shmulikl's dining room, accompanied Yacov on a visit to Bociany's venerated veteran of modern Judaism. And old Shmulikl, who had lost little of the passion and fervor of his youth, immediately involved his two young visitors in a heated discussion.

However, side by side with the new, the old Bociany was still alive. The beautiful "new" synagogue had sunk considerably to one side. It was stooped and cracked, and as worn as an old man. But it was still the center of Bociany's life and it still harbored its soul—a split soul, a tormented soul. For just as the new Bociany flourished and thrived, the old kept doggedly to its ways, but with grief and pain. The new were the children, the old—the parents. Between both yawned the chasm that the young tried to camouflage by continuing to wear traditional clothing, by going to the synagogue, and by going through the motions of piety. Outwardly they still respected the Sabbath, but secretly they smoked cigarettes on that sacred day. They pretended to fast on Yom Kippur, but actually stole away to remote villages to buy peasant bread and, even, ham. There was no bridge on which the two generations could meet in reciprocal understanding.

Yacov experienced a similar split at his home. He felt himself both familiar and alien. His older sister, Gitele, had grown up to become a vivacious temperamental young woman. She was tall, slim, and agile, with a head full of thick brown curls, a fine milk-white skin, pink cheeks, and a small, thin nose. Her charming little mouth was full of talk and laughter. She had not the least interest in social problems. She was cheerful and light-hearted and only went where she could enjoy herself. However, his younger sister, Shaindele, who with her dainty figure and dreamy disposition resembled Hindele, had become a member of the Zionist Shomer Hazair. Almost every evening she and Yacov immersed themselves in long, serious discussions, while their mother often stood at the window and listened to their arguments with a mixture of pride and regret. As he talked to Shaindele, Yacov felt his mother's presence acutely.

On the surface the air was still clear and bright between Hindele and Yacov. Yet they both knew that she could mentally accompany him only to a certain point, that beyond that point she remained behind with a trembling heart. "I am beginning to see you through a haze, my son," Hindele would say to him in her mind.

"Perhaps this is because we have been separated for so long, because we don't take part in each other's day-to-day life," Yacov told himself. Still he refused to acknowledge the parting of their souls. "Such things may happen nowadays, but they must not happen between Mameshie and me. We are bound together in an indivisible union."

Hindele and Yacov never talked about it, but never again did Yacov sit down with her and talk until some late hour of the night. Even if an opportunity presented itself, they pretended not to notice, as if they feared that in spite of their love for each other, their words might cast a still darker shadow between them.

During these days, it frequently happened that as they sat around the table, chatting, Hindele would stand up, put a pot of hot food under the folds of her plaid, and leave the room. On one such occasion, when Shalom had joined the rest of the family for a visit, and her children were engaged in a conversation about Bociany, their childhood, and their shared memories, Hindele again left the room. After she was gone, Gitele looked meaningfully at Shalom and Shaindele, then she leaned over to Yacov and said, "She's going to see Yossele Abedale. You know Mameshie, don't you? She must have someone to nurse and care for."

Shaindele explained, "Reb Yossele is not a man who would allow himself to be nursed and cared for so easily. But what can he do? His daughter Dvorele, with whom he was living, ran away from her husband, Berele the

Moonwalker. She left for Argentina with Henechl the Broom-maker's son, so Yossele has been left all alone. His rich daughters want him to come to Lodz, but he won't hear of it. And he's gone blind. So Mameshie pities him. He chases her away, but she too is stubborn. She feeds him and takes him home from the shop. She helps him out at the shop, too. I wouldn't mind it, but more often than not she comes home all in tears."

Shalom, who as a rule had remained a man of few words, commented dryly, "Mameshie likes to overdo things. So her devotion to him is also overdone."

Yacov saw his mother's behavior in an entirely different light than his siblings did. To him it seemed that in a mysterious way Hindele had sensed his own relation to Yossele. It was as if with some inner ear she had heard the tune of his yearnings and was humming it along with him. "Perhaps we should invite him for the seder," he proposed.

Gitele waved a dismissive hand. "Don't be silly. The man's like a rock. No one except Mameshie can even pity him. Who wants to have a stranger like him at the table? Such a sulking bore would spoil the whole pleasure of having the family together for once."

The seders were conducted by Shalom. Yacov could not take his eyes off his elder brother, who was still devoutly traditional and had changed little; he behaved as if nothing had happened in Bociany. "Between him and me," Yacov thought, "the wall of silence has gone up long ago. Who knows, perhaps this has something to do with the different ways in which Mameshie has loved him and me." He fixed his gaze on the face of Shalom's wife, who was a modest, quiet woman. She and Shalom were so similar in character and they harmonized so well with each other that they seemed like twins. Shalom still worked as a porter on the Potcheyov, yet his wife, so noble in her bearing, looked like a young Mother Rachel. She seemed to radiate the love that she and Shalom bore for each other. The sight of her awakened Yacov's former jealousy of his brother.

At the table general attention was focused on the Passover Haggadah and the conversation dealt mainly with Shalom's children and with the delicious seder meal. Everyone's tongues were loosened, all were united in song. Three generations. A family. Elijah the Prophet drank from the goblet of wine that stood waiting for him on the table, and all their hearts were like "the hearts of dreamers."

It was unusually painful for Yacov to take leave of them all. Hindele, her face bathed in tears, could not tear herself away from him. Gitele and

Shaindele also wept shamelessly. Even Shalom's eyes were misty. During all the past days when they had been together they had not once mentioned the possibility that nagged at their minds, that they might be seeing each other for the last time, that any day Yacov might be leaving for the front. This thought made of every word uttered, every tear shed, every gesture shown—a memory to be cherished, a recollection to be sealed in the mind forever.

In order to demonstrate their freedom of spirit, the Jewish bohemians and artists liked to parade through the streets of Lodz, wearing the strangest outfits. Some dressed like hunters in high boots, riding pants, and German-style hunting jackets. Others walked around in broad daylight, wearing shabby dress coats, tuxedoes, or evening clothes. Still others wore loose capes and hats with broad rims and wide cockades, as if they had just stepped out of one of Rembrandt's paintings. The more modest amongst them satisfied their whims by wearing Pushkinesque clothes or the garb of Russian revolutionaries.

On May Day Yacov decided not to go to work but to participate in the May Day parade and then claim illness at the shop. In order to disguise himself he had chosen a Rembrandtian outfit that he borrowed from a painter, a Bundist sympathizer who, along with the poet Moshe Socrates, was a steady visitor at Vove Cederbaum's. To complete the costume Yacov put on a pair of dark glasses and carried a walking stick.

The May Day demonstration marched past Reb Itchele Hittelmakher's shoe store on Piotrkowska Street. Hidden deep in the cortege Yacov cast stealthy glances at the store. Its door was bolted but, in the window above the shoe display, he could see the faces of the salesmen, including Mr. Morris, peering out at the spectacle. Yacov had the feeling that he was a buffon, a clown dressed in a skin not his own. He felt ashamed, not so much before his friends or even before Mr. Morris and his assistants, as before himself. He felt not a fraction of the zest and the élan that normally carried him through a demonstration. Rather than keeping his head high and marching with his chest expanded, singing the marching songs loudly and with passion, he tried to shrink, to vanish into the mass of people. Not only did he not sing aloud, he barely moved his lips, as if in fear that Mr. Morris might hear him.

When he arrived at work the next day, Mr. Morris asked him in an overly friendly tone of voice, "So you were ill yesterday. Do you feel any better today, Mr. Polin?"

Yacov flushed. "Much better, thank you."

"What exactly was wrong with you?" Mr. Morris moved his head closer to Yacov. "Was it the red fever by any chance? I presume you know as well as I do that Mr. Hittelmakher loathes his employees becoming ill on the first of May."

Yacov turned away from him. He felt relieved that Mr. Morris and the other salesmen had recognized him and would probably tell on him to Reb Itchele Hittelmakher. That would teach him once and for all that he was a bad actor, a clumsy liar, and that dressing up in other people's clothes made him look ridiculous, especially in his own eyes. Wasn't he living in a new liberated Poland? If he could not show the world his true face now, what sense was there in all his actions?

But the incident was quickly forgotten. The truth was that neither Mr. Morris nor the other salesmen were a hundred percent certain that they had in fact seen Yacov in the May Day demonstration. Not that they found it difficult to connect this supposedly dreamy former Hasid, Mr. Hittelmakher's pet, the favourite of the shop's lady customers, and Miss Polcia's "weakness," with the vulgar, arrogant slogans screaming down from the placards and red banners. But they considered him too much of a schlemiel and coward to ever have the guts to participate in even such a legal adventure.

Yacov continued with his work at the store. Miss Polcia never entered the store again, but at the end of his work day she often waited for him outside. He adamantly refused to go up to her room despite her tears and pleading. She insisted that she had something very important to tell him. His heart sore with shame, he told her flatly that he would not have her failed exams on his conscience, since the date of her *matura* exams was at hand—or he used other such excuses. He also let her know that he was an active member of the Bund Organization and that he was busy with party work. He was not afraid that she would betray him. Recently he seemed, almost on purpose, to be leaving clues behind at work. Once he had left behind a book with compromising contents at the shop, another time he had thrown a party publication into the wastebasket by mistake.

He was not lying to Miss Polcia when he said that he was immersed, almost drowning, in party work. Despite the war, the party was expanding. A network of children's nurseries had been founded. Yiddish folk schools were growing in number, new institutions were being created, and new unions were being organized. And then there were the endless meetings with their long, heated discussions about the party's stand with regard to the Soviet Union and Poland. Yacov quarreled with Laibel the Hump and Vove Cederbaum. He agreed to a dot over the "i" here, disagreed with a dot over the "i" there. His head boiled over with all things that he was doing or had to do; he felt that he was defending his point of view even in his sleep.

Yet his conscience bothered him about Miss Polcia. He owed the girl the truth. So when she stepped up to him in the street one day, pleading with him, and telling him how urgent it was that they meet, he forced himself to say to her bluntly, "Polcia, let me tell you this one thing. There is no future for us together. So let's part ways and please, leave me be for once and for all."

He said good-bye, made a gesture to shake her hand, then gave it up, and turned away from her. A few times during the following days he left the store, expecting her to be waiting for him outside, but she was not there.

Despite his active life, scenes from the Passover holiday spent in Bociany lingered in Yacov's memory not only at night but even during his busiest days. He walked around with the fragrance of Bociany's air in his nostrils. His longing for home, for everything he loved, was so powerful that a few times he walked to the house where Binele lived and waited for her outside, so that he might at least see her from a distance. But he had no luck.

Then, one day he saw her through the display window of the shop walking in the street arm in arm with Handsome Moshe. He caught a glimpse of her face, of the sparkle in her slanted eyes, of the light playing on her sensuous mouth. He went out and stood in front of the door, so that he might follow her with his eyes. He admired her graceful well-rounded figure and the way her braids were wound around her head like a wreath. She put the entire weight of her body on the soles of her feet as she walked, yet her steps were light and nimble. The way she walked, the way she swayed her hips, betrayed that magnetic mysterious something about her that had always held him spellbound. Her whole body seemed to know that someone was following her with his eyes. The sight of her evoked a sensation of unbearable tension within him, as if she emitted a kind of ray that electrified him from a distance. "There she walks," Yacov said to himself. "Like the light of a star she has crossed my path and vanished."

Long after he had seen her, Yacov carried this image of Binele in his mind's eye. It found its place in his memory alongside his memories of home. He recalled the first glimpses that he had had of her as she had sat near the mill on top of the Blue Mountain, a wreath of bluebells on her reddish-yellow hair. In his daydreams and ruminations all the images that he had of her mingled and became fused together to produce new ones that had no basis in reality. He saw himself sitting with her at a Sabbath table. She was wearing a white bridal gown and he was dressed in black, like a groom. Between them stood two lit Sabbath candles. Together they both raised their goblets filled with wine and saluted each other, as the Creator of the World and His bride, the *Shechina,* saluted each other on her return home from her long wanderings to celebrate the Sabbath with Him. God's breath hovered over an earthly bed, transforming it into a crucible where the divided halves merged into the infinity of one.

He had chanced to have another glimpse of Binele's face in a crowd of workers during a benefit celebration for the Yiddish Folk Schools, organized in the gardens of Helenovek on the outskirts of town. She wore a white peasant dress of a flowery pattern and on her head was perched a straw hat, its hat band a wreath of shiny artificial flowers and its wide brim becomingly shading her face. She was looking up at the outdoor stage where a drama group was performing fragments of a play by Shalom Aleykhem. Yacov followed Binele's gaze toward the stage. A tall handsome young actor stood there, reciting his lines. Yacov recognized Handsome Moshe. He slid his gaze back to her and let his eyes rest on her back and neck, which were exposed by her pinned-up hair and cut-out dress. Her neck and back were veiled in the faint shadow created by the wide brim of her straw hat. Yacov wondered whether Binele and Moshe were already married. Her face glowed with a quiet radiance, a feminine softness. There was an air of calm and contentment about her. "She is fine. She seems to be happy," Yacov told himself and wandered off.

Weeks passed. Then, on an autumn day during a strike of the textile workers, Yacov saw Binele again. The striking workers marched past Reb Itchele Hittelmakher's shoe store. Yacov dashed toward the door to have a look at the demonstration, and saw Binele marching with a firm gait, her bosom raised, her arms linked with those of the people next to her, part of a row of men and women. She sang loudly and with feeling. He reminded himself of the first political conversations he had had with her.

As he looked on, an unexpected noise and confusion suddenly disrupted the ranks of the marchers. Mr. Morris shouted at Yacov, "Mr. Polin, get inside! We are closing the shop!" Mr. Morris jingled the keys like an alarm bell. But instead of rushing back into the shop, Yacov threw caution to the winds and moved further out into the street. The disturbance in the ranks was caused by a column of workers that had marched too quickly and had bumped into the column before it. The front rows rushed ahead, followed by others, so as to make room for those coming behind. Yacov pushed himself through the rows of marchers, looking for Binele whom he could no longer see.

"Yacov!" he heard a triumphant shout. He turned his head and saw Binele separated from him by about ten rows of heads. He tried to reach her through the chains of linked arms but could not. The forward thrust of the marchers swept him along, yet he managed to get himself a little closer to her. "How are you?" he heard her call as she pushed forward with the rest of the people in her row.

"I'm working at Hittelmakher's shop!" he shouted back, his head turned in her direction, as the human mass dragged him along.

"What did you say?" The crowd had begun to sing "Red Banner," and she could not hear him.

"He's a slave of the bourgeoisie! He works for Hittelmakher, the bloodsucker, is what he said!" a cheerful youth behind Yacov loudly transmitted the information to Binele.

"Down with Hittelmakher the bloodsucker!" another worker shouted.

"Where do you live, Binele?" Yacov yelled, marching forward while his head was turned back toward her. "Did you move?"

She did not hear him. The crowd was roaring, "We demand justice! Long live the working class! Long live the working woman! Long live a socialist Poland!"

Yacov, caught in the tangle of marching feet, stumbled. A robust placard bearer prodded him in the ribs, bellowing loudly, "You, comrade, either you get out of here or you join the ranks!"

Yacov gathered all his strength and cut through the ranks, breaking up one row after another until he joined Binele. Before he even linked arms with her and the others, he burst out and asked, "Have you gotten married?"

"Not yet," she laughed and pulled her arm through his. "But you know what, Yacov? I've been elected to the board of the women's circle!" She beamed with pride. "Can you believe it? They elected me! I can't even read or write properly yet!" It was obvious that she had been saving this piece of news, which meant so much to her, to tell him. Only then did she ask, "And you? Have you gotten married?"

"No, no, we won't carry arms! No, no, we don't want a war!" someone in front of them began to sing. Then the entire crowd burst out singing the "Internationale."

Yacov and Binele, arm in arm, glued to each other, closer than they had ever been in their lives, sang along. Dazed by each other's closeness, one body with one voice, they were carried forward by the force of the crowd, swept away by its passion and enthusiasm. Binele thought that if such a feeling as bliss existed, than she was experiencing it right now, at this very moment. Yacov thought of nothing. All of him was dissolved in the sensation of having Binele beside him. His senses were tense and sharp. He had only one craving: to come still closer to her, to take her into his arms and raise her above the heads of the crowd, so that her unbraided sunny hair should flutter over the town like a banner.

In another few minutes the ranks loosened. Linked arms were disentangled. The demonstration, flowing now like a tame river between the facades of houses, poured into the Train Garden where a mass meeting was about to take place. All fired up, Yacov whispered in Binele's ear, "You see, Binele, the times of hope have finally come."

Handsome Moshe appeared beside them as if he had emerged from underground. "Good-bye!" Binele waved at Yacov, as Moshe took her arm and made his way with her through the knots of people, pulling her closer to the speakers' platform. Yacov followed them with his eyes until the last reddish shimmer of her yellow braids set behind the sea of heads.

The following day Reb Itchele Hittelmakher sent for Yacov. Reb Itchele had for a long time been hearing from Mr. Morris that something was seriously suspicious about Yacov's behavior. Now, after what had happened the day before during the demonstration, there was no need to investigate the issue any further, especially since Reb Itchele himself had begun to have suspicions of his own concerning Yacov. All the Jewish people who belonged to political parties developed a distinctive style of speech. They used a particular set of phrases and expressions and, in general, one could detect a certain pattern of behavior which differentiated them from other Jews. And Reb Itchele had a fine eye and a fine ear. He was a sensitive and clever man. During his conversations with Yacov, he had gradually come to discern these peculiarities of speech of which Yacov was obviously not aware.

But the issue of Yacov disturbed Reb Itchele much more than any other such case would have disturbed him. The more often Reb Itchele had talked with Yacov, the dearer this young man from Bociany had become to him. Usually when Reb Itchele met someone and formed an initially positive opinion of that person, it so happened that the more familiar he had become with the person, the less favorable became his opinion of him. In Yacov's case, however, the opposite was true. It was not so much a question of an opinion as of the sentiments that Yacov had aroused in him.

A man like Reb Itchele, always surrounded by family, by all kinds of acquaintances and business people, was seldom alone. Nevertheless he was haunted by a great sense of loneliness until the day when he had met Yacov, to whom, for some reason, he was able to talk with great ease and frankness. He was not even ashamed to confess the shoddy sides of his own nature to him; he was able to uncover the shady nooks and crannies of his soul and find understanding without the slightest hint of condemnation in Yacov's eyes. It had given Reb Itchele a sense of atonement to be able in Yacov's presence to set out on these painful voyages through the maze of his own inner troubles, to investigate his guilt feelings concerning his failures in relating to both God and man, and to ponder about his unquenched cravings to achieve more and more in his business undertakings. Sometimes Reb Itchele thought that even if he had had a son of his own, it was questionable whether this son could ever have understood him as well as Yacov did.

For these reasons Reb Itchele had tried to disregard Mr. Morris's innuendoes and had tried not to heed his own suspicions. When Mr. Morris suggested that, aside from everything else, Yacov might also be responsible for the tragic situation concerning Miss Polcia, the jeweler's daughter, Reb Itchele flew into such a rage that he showed his own relative, Mr. Morris, the door. That far Reb Itchele would never have gone in his suspicions of Yacov. He knew him too well. However, this time he could not avoid summoning him to his *kantur*. All the salesmen had seen Yacov leave the store to join the demonstration. Reb Itchele had to face the truth and take action against Yacov, which, to his profound regret, meant in a way taking action against himself.

When Yacov appeared before Reb Itchele in his *kantur*, Reb Itchele did not ask him to sit down. Nor did he immediately come to the point, at least he did not do so directly. "I would have invited Baruch Weiskop to our meeting as well," Reb Itchele began slowly. "After all, it was Baruch who recommended you for the job. I would have asked him to judge between you and me. But as you probably know, Baruch left Lodz in a great hurry."

"Baruch?" Yacov was startled.

"Didn't you know? I thought that you two still kept in touch with each other."

"What happened to him?" Yacov took a step closer to Reb Itchele's desk.

"I'm surprised that you didn't hear about it. All of Lodz is talking. You know how people love to gossip. Mr. Morris even suggested that you have been friendly with the girl."

"What girl, Reb Itchele?"

"The only daughter of the jeweler who lives above my shop."

Yacov gasped. Without being asked, he slumped down into an armchair across from Reb Itchele. An inner voice goaded him, "Force yourself to be an actor! Pretend! You must! Act indifferent!" He raised shifty eyes to Reb Itchele and said hoarsely, "Please, tell me what happened."

"Well, it's an ugly story, and I didn't call you here to indulge in gossip. To make it short," Reb Itchele looked Yacov straight in the face, "The girl was very spoiled. She had some doings with a young man from Baluty, and he fixed her up good and proper. The parents left with her in great secrecy for Vienna, probably to rid her of the 'thing'—you understand? Then came the news that the girl was gravely ill. Obviously, she had turned Baruch's head, too. People say that he was head over heels in love with her, may God have pity on him. So he followed her to Vienna, and that's that. Now let's get back to the problem I'm having with you, my friend, that is, at least up to now I've thought you to be my friend. I thought that there was not the slightest shadow of dishonesty between the two of us. I know now for certain that you've concealed from me the fact of your active involvement in politics. So first answer me straight to my face, to what party do you belong?"

Yacov had lost all sense of reality. He found himself diving into a deep dark pit. Yet he managed to answer Reb Itchele's question.

Reb Itchele rejoined, "You do remember my conditions, don't you? So I must now face you with an ultimatum. Either you stay on the job, or you stay with your party."

Yacov tried to recall the details of his last meeting with Polcia but could not. He only remembered the moments on the sofa in her room. Had she offered him any liquor on that day? Most probably she had taken up with God knows whom after he had refused to see her. Yet all his limbs, all his being cried out, "It's me! Me! My fault!" Then he suddenly remembered the money that he still owed Reb Itchele for the shoes he had bought for his family and he wondered why Reb Itchele had not mentioned it.

Reb Itchele had to remind him that he was waiting for an answer. So, in his rage against himself, Yacov jumped to his feet and lashed out vehemently, "You know very well that your ultimatum is ridiculous. To hell with the job!"

Reb Itchele's face twisted into a grimace of pain. "You needn't be so arrogant," he remarked falteringly. "I wish you would think over your decision properly. In the present situation . . . how will you earn a living? And I hope you remember how much money you still owe me." He swallowed and said with a groan, "I was like a father to you."

Yacov's mind was working feverishly. "I must forget about Polcia now," he said to himself. "I have a lifetime left to carry the burden." He shook his head at Reb Itchele and asked, "Do you remember the story of the idol worshiper, Reb Itchele, whom Abraham our Father threw out of his tent? The Almighty said to Abraham, 'I have tolerated that heretic for seventy years, and you cannot tolerate him even for one night?'" Was this example to the point? Never mind. It had happened to pop into Yacov's head, so he had used it. He would keep on talking. Or better still, perhaps he should run out, slamming the door behind him? What did he care about anything any longer? What mattered was to find the money for Reb Itchele and pay him back as soon as possible. But he also wanted to come out now and tell Reb Itchele the truth to his face. He straightened himself and moved his chair closer to Reb Itchele's desk.

"If you consider yourself to have been like a father to me, then please, also consider that I was devoted to you like a son. Yes, you were kind to me, but I saw your other deeds. You treat your workers at the factory like vermin. And in spite of it, I continued to bear good feelings for you in my heart. Not because you were my boss, but as one person to another. I remembered your generosity toward all those who depend on you. Granted, I didn't tell you the truth about my being a Bundist, but neither am I free of weaknesses or faults. I was afraid to tell you. I did not want to lose my job. And I felt good in your company. I didn't want to lose you. I lost my own father so early in life. Oh yes, you were kind to me. But perhaps my comrades are right. There is no common language between the two sides of the barricade. All I can do now is give you my word of honor that what I owe you I'll pay back. Do you trust me with that at least?"

"Of course I do," Reb Itchele muttered. "But it is not money that is the issue here."

"Then why did you mention it? Didn't you trust that I would pay it back no matter what?"

"I thought that the debt might help you make up your mind to stay on the job."

"Did you think me capable of giving up my beliefs for the sake of money? Good-bye, Reb Itchele." Yacov turned toward the door.

"Yacov!" Reb Itchele called after him. Yacov stopped and turned his head. What was he seeing? Were his eyes playing tricks on him? He took a step back into the room and looked at the patriarchal man on the other side of the desk. Reb Itchele's eyes were misty. "I don't want you to leave, my boy," Reb Itchele said softly.

Yacov's eyes opened wide. Humble, downtrodden, at the bottom of a pit of darkness, and filled with blinding shame, he stared at the man. His heart pounded. For a long while he did not know what was happening to him, his heart was full to overflowing with tenderness. Then he heard a voice within him, his own innermost voice. It dictated the words to him. "Thank you, Reb Itchele," he said. "But anyway I decided a long time ago that I cannot stay on the job. I cannot look at myself in the mirror anymore."

"But . . . " Reb Itchele stretched both hands out across the desk. "I can find you another place."

"Thank you, Reb Itchele, but it's not necessary."

"Well, but you can come by once in a while for a game of chess, can't you?"

"Many thanks. I'll have no time for it. I'll come to pay you back my debt." Yacov quickly left Reb Itchele's *kantur*.

☺☺ 14 ☺☺

YACOV JOINED THE RANKS of the unemployed. He moved in with Comrade Bronia, who was ready to share with him whatever she had. She greeted this opportunity for self-sacrifice with great enthusiasm and made him feel even more disgusted with himself. Finally he could bear it no longer, and a few days after he had moved in with her, he moved out. He did not love her. The fact that each was the answer to the other's loneliness was not good enough. Moreover, he was afraid of hurting her, too—although he did hurt her by moving out of her room. Obviously the guiding principle that he had chosen for his life—to hurt other people as little as possible—was a convenient one. What did "As little as possible" mean? It was a door left ajar.

He went to live with Vove and Balcie Cederbaum, who occupied a large room in a house in Baluty near that smelly canal, the Lodka River, from which Lodz derived its name.

In the ensuing weeks, Yacov was like someone frantically trying to save himself from drowning. He allowed his love for Binele to entirely repossess his consciousness. He no longer tried to cover up his feelings for her with denials nor to dismiss them with a shrug of his shoulders. His former boyish yearning for her had grown into a man's love. And for him as a man, even though an imperfect one, these were no times for self-delusion. The truth about himself and his life situation confronted him even when he sought to shut his eyes to their reality.

Among all the questions that he asked himself each morning, the most overwhelming one was whether the day would still belong to him or whether fate would knock on the door and bring him his recruitment slip, demanding that he enlist in the army. The thought of joining the army filled him with a twofold dread. Besides putting his life in jeopardy, this war he was about to fight in was not his war. It no longer presented him with the dilemma of having to fight for "half" of his ideal, for Poland, while lending a hand to the destruction of the other "half," the new society growing in Soviet Russia. He had had the time to ask himself about this new society in Bolshevik Russia, a society built on the corpses of millions of people, and also to ask himself about this new "free" Poland in which so little had changed since Poland's leader, Josef Pilsudski, the dreamer of a just republic, the member of the Polish Socialist Party, had declared to his comrades, "I am getting off at the station called Independence." So was this disappointing reality the ideal that Yacov should be ready to die for, to kill for? It seemed like a mockery. He felt fate was sticking its big tongue out at him. This war about the border of two countries—two countries that had just won their freedom—was an indication of something unclean and offensive permeating the air of the "new" world. And this truth was what doubled his dread of it.

In order to cleanse himself of his bitterness, Yacov deliberately gave himself over to thoughts of Binele. He also thought about Handsome Moshe, with a mixture of envy, curiosity, and a certain amount of admiration. He had not the slightest inclination to compete with Moshe. They could not be rivals, not now when Yacov was shattered by remorse and ugly feelings about himself. And then each man's love for a woman had its own coloration, its own intensity, and thus could not be subject to comparison. Yacov thought of himself as belonging to Binele's past, a past that no longer existed except, perhaps, in her memory. But Moshe, noble Moshe, was a part of her present. And just as nobility was superior to baseness, so the present was superior to the past. Thus, Moshe had the upper hand in his love for Binele. Yacov saw himself as a loser on all fronts.

But Yacov had reached all these conclusions concerning Binele exclusively by way of his reason. In his heart of hearts he could not free himself of the certainty that what bound him to her had nothing to do with any qualities of character, or with the past or the present, but had to do with the uniqueness and timelessness of two souls speaking the same language. Of course, Moshe had the right to have exactly the same convictions with regard to his own feelings, but an inner voice told

Yacov that even if Binele were not fully conscious of her unique bond with him, she somehow was aware of it. She did not have to spell it out. Her face, her body, the air about her made him sense it whenever the two of them met.

"So what?" he asked himself. The fact was that Moshe was about to take her away from him forever. The fact was that the cobweb-thin threads of communication that were still binding him to her were almost completely torn. That was the truth. He was perfectly clear about that. And yet he felt he had to do something to bring this truth into a sharper focus, if, in spite of everything, he wanted to go on with his life. For even if he were destined to die tomorrow, he had to think of his life as an entity with a future. His problem was that he did not know what to do. Should he stand up and challenge Moshe to a fight—as if they were two male animals competing for the favors of the same female? That seemed ludicrous, and such behavior would have been an offense against Binele. Moreover, he had not the slightest desire to fight Moshe. He had nothing against him. If Moshe had any rights to Binele, it was because she herself had given him those rights.

Gradually, it began to dawn upon Yacov that Binele must at least once hear from his mouth, clearly and explicitly, what he felt for her. And she must, at least once, answer him clearly and explicitly about her choice and thus determine her fate as well as his and Moshe's. It seemed odd to be a free individual, and yet allow someone else, a woman, to decide one's fate. But that was the way it was. Binele held him and Moshe in her power. The freedom of the bird in the cage was limited by the other birds inside it.

But first he had to see Baruch Weiskop. He had to clarify an important issue that concerned the two of them, and he had to find out what had happened to Polcia. As far as his conscience was concerned, he had killed her, destroyed her, whether or not she was still alive. He was obsessed by thoughts of what could have happened to her and he had to know the truth. He was superstitious. Without that knowledge he had no chance, no hope, no courage.

He had never visited Baruch in his new home before. Now he climbed the stairs to Baruch's apartment every day, entered the corridor hung with mirrors, asked the handsomely dressed male servant whether Mr. Weiskop had already returned from abroad, or when he was expected. One day the servant told him that a letter had arrived from Vienna with a forwarding address. Yacov took it down. He wrote Baruch a letter and waited for an answer. So he was now waiting for two letters, one from Baruch and the other from the recruiting office of the army.

Finally he could wait no longer for news from Baruch. He began to look for Binele.

His long waits for her at The Harp availed him nothing. The outbreak of war with the Bolsheviks had interrupted the reading and writing courses as well as the meetings of the women's circle. He was convinced that Binele no longer lived at the address where he used to wait for her. If she had ever told him her new address on the rare occasions when they had run into each other, it failed to register in his mind; perhaps he had feared to let it register. He began to look for her all over town, walking the streets. But the town hid her from him. It teased him with apparitions, with women of a similar gait and a similar hair color. Binele was a speck of dust in the sea of humanity, he another speck of dust. Specks of dust never meet at will but are brought together by sheer coincidence.

Finally, it occurred to him to look up Handsome Moshe first. Handsome Moshe enjoyed some popularity as a young actor with a "great future." He was known for his successful appearances at the review theater and the Poale-Zion functions. Yacov also knew that Moshe was presently employed as a functionary of a branch of the textile union.

In fact, Yacov found Moshe easily on the first late afternoon that he waited for him in the street in front of the union house. Moshe was leaving the building. His hair was fashionably long and he was dressed in a fancy manner, with a cape thrown over his shoulders. He held a walking cane in his hand and gave the overall impression of having just stepped off the stage. Yacov followed him from a distance, and so Moshe helped him find Binele.

She came out of a factory gate and linked arms with Moshe. The two of them walked down the street at a leisurely pace. Yacov was not overly proud of himself for following them. A few times he thought about turning back. What a crazy idea this was! He, the defeated moralist, the refuted preacher of noble socialist ideals, was trying to disrupt the harmonious relationship of two people! But his heart and his entire being carried him forward. He refused to be noble today; he did not want to be a *tsadik*. He wanted Binele. In order to talk with her, he had to follow her and let her decide his fate. He had no patience for waiting. He could not bear to wait and see whether Binele would take leave of Moshe, or whether they would both vanish inside the same house. Still he forced himself to wait until they both stopped in front of a gate. It was the same gate in front of which Yacov had so often waited for her and had never chanced to see her. He summoned up his courage, crossed the street, and rushed toward the pair. He stopped them with an arrogant grotesque gesture, unwittingly jabbing Moshe with his elbow. He noticed the color fade from Binele's face.

"I'm sorry." He grinned apologetically at Moshe. "I didn't mean to hit you." He turned quickly to Binele and said, "I must speak to you in private."

Silence reigned. The ground swayed beneath Yacov's feet. The faces of Binele and Moshe swam before his eyes. Finally he heard Binele say, "I will meet you at The Harp."

Yacov shook his head stiffly at Moshe and crossed the street. Only then did he realize that Binele had not told him when she would meet him at The Harp. It did not matter. He would wait for her today, tomorrow, the day after tomorrow. A question cut through his tangled thoughts. And when she came, what would he tell her? That he wanted to marry her? That he had destroyed another girl's life? That he was a pauper without work and a large debt on his head, who lived at his comrade Vove Cederbaum's place like a parasite because he was waiting to be conscripted into the army? Did he not deserve to be spat at, he, the bombastic preacher, the hollow dreamer who was nothing but a selfish imbecile?

A few hours later that same evening he and Binele met in front of The Harp. He felt his heart hammer away in his mouth. His limbs trembled with weakness. His skin burned and prickled as he shuddered with tension. He had not the strength to prolong the scene. She too seemed stunned and adrift, her mouth open but soundless, as if she had lost the power of speech.

"I just wanted to tell you," he said in a dry, grating voice, "that I love you." It was difficult to look at her pale face, yet he held his gaze fixed on the open sensuous mouth that expressed her helplessness, as she made herself ready to pronounce the verdict. He looked at her so intently that her face seemed to have become distorted.

Suddenly Binele burst out, "Is that what you asked me to come here for?" Her eyes were ablaze with fierce, maddening desperation. Before he could manage to catch his breath, she had turned around and walked off.

He ran after her and grabbed her by an arm. "I had to tell you this," he panted. "It's important to me."

"To you!" she exclaimed. "But not to me. Let go of me!"

"No! I won't! This is the second time you've run away from discussing important matters."

"What important matters?" She wrested her arm free. "Moshe has already rented a room."

"So what?" Saliva appeared in the corners of Yacov's mouth. "You must answer me straight to my face. What are your feelings for me?" Passersby who heard his question turned their heads and smiled, amused. "Do you love me?" he repeated in a calmer tone, again taking hold of her arm.

"No! No! I feel nothing for you!" She tore herself out of his grip but remained standing, as though nailed to her place, looking at him through slitted eyes, her lower lip moist, pouting like a child about to cry. "Let me be, Yacov." She struggled to control her voice. "Leave me alone," she pleaded, although he was no longer holding her. Her eyes filled with tears. Slowly she turned away from him again and walked off with unsteady steps.

Yacov heard the voice of Yoel the Blacksmith echo in his mind, saying to him, "Let her be. Don't cling. Don't violate . . . ever again . . . not even in your thoughts. Don't do harm to her—or to yourself."

Hazy days followed. Yacov's heart turned into a battlefield where self-respect wrangled with despair and hopelessness. The war with the Bolsheviks seemed to be lasting an eternity. Out of work, Yacov dragged himself through the streets, a member of the army of unemployed. The factories stood still. Those who could afford to had again left for the villages and shtetlekh.

Then came the day when the words of Lev Trotsky's slogan came forth, thundering threateningly through the land: "*Dayosh Warshavu!* Give me Warsaw!" General Tuchatchevski's red battalions were approaching the Vistula. In Lodz, bands of Polish patriots opened a local front to do battle with the Bolsheviks—that is, the unprotected Jewish population. They attacked Jews in the streets, in their homes, and in their shops. The houses of the leaders of various Jewish political parties were searched and the leaders themselves were sent to the prison camp in Dombia. Yacov and Vove joined the Bundist self-defense unit.

Yacov had avoided conscription during the tsar's reign as well as during the German occupation. Aside from hunger and cold, he had not really experienced the vicissitudes of war. Now, in liberated Poland, war had finally caught up with him, dragging him out of his abyss of personal defeat as well as away from the haven of his political dreams. One fine day he found himself with a conscription slip in his hand. He was assigned to the second division under the command of General Rydz-Smigly.

He had been expecting this for a long time. Yet the actual order requiring him to sign up immediately, to fit himself out in a soldier's uniform and a four-cornered hat with the Polish eagle, and after two weeks of training, to go to the front, hit him like a bolt from the blue. He was crushed, devastated, yet in a strange way he also felt relieved, as if all his problems had been solved. Still his sense of devastation was much stronger, much more overwhelming than any other feeling. He ascribed his sense of shock to the fact that he had never really faced up to the reality of conscription. All his efforts had been geared to losing himself in ways and means of escaping that reality, even when he was preoccupied with day-to-day battles. He had tried to escape the fateful threat through immersing himself in his party activities, in a sea of books, of new ideas, of discussions. He had succeeded in blotting it out of his awareness by engaging in reckless sexual activities. It had all been to no avail anyway.

Recently, only one good thing had happened to him. He was living with Vove Cederbaum and his girlfriend, Balcie, and could, at least physically, escape his loneliness. Vove's room was more like a club than a private dwelling. It was easy, superficially at least, to lose oneself in the noisy companionship of constant visitors.

The last evening before signing up, Yacov spent with his comrades at Vove's home. He wrote a letter to his mother atop the edge of the cluttered table. Then, when everyone had left, he and Vove, who also expected to be drafted shortly, became engaged in conversation.

It was a night for intimate, meaningful talk, but Vove had no idea of what had been going on in Yacov's heart, so their conversation was rather one-sided. Vove talked with ease about himself and his life. His personal affairs were an open book. He had no secrets and seemed not to know what privacy meant.

"Do you know what I have to tell you?" he said to Yacov, as he sat close to him at the corner of the table, his eyes and forehead veiled in a cloud of cigarette smoke. "A man's home is like a living thing. I mean a *real* home. My home. You'd say it looks rather like a streetcar, with all the comings and goings. Of course, that's because others feel at home here, too. And that's how I like it to be." He motioned to the bed where Balcie lay covered with a shoddy down quilt, fast asleep. "It's all thanks to her, to Balcie. She's breathed her soul into it. So if I am drafted, it will be both harder and easier for me to leave. It will be harder to tear myself away and easier because I know that she will keep the place going." Vove was anything but a sentimental man. Never before had Yacov seen him display any softness of heart. So Vove's words moved Yacov deeply, so deeply in fact, that he stood up from the table and threw his coat over his shoulders. He told Vove not to wait up for him and left the room.

Without engaging in any inner debate, with not a conscious thought in his head, he walked briskly through the dark night in the direction of the building where Binele lived. It was after eleven o'clock and the gate was locked. He rang the bell. The sleepy janitor appeared before him. Yacov pushed a coin into the man's hand and asked for Binele's room number. Slowly he climbed the four flights of stairs to her loft and rapped on the door. It was quiet on the other side. He understood that she was already asleep. He bent down and whispered through the keyhole over and over again, "Open up, Binele, I came to say good-bye."

Finally he heard her busying herself on the other side of the door. She opened it on a tiny room steeped in shadows. It took some time and Yacov's help before she managed to light the naphtha lamp. She stood before him disheveled, her hair, like long glowing candlewicks, spread in chaotic strings over her white fustian nightgown. The light of the moon pouring in through the roof window and the light of the naphtha lamp combined to illuminate her face.

Before she could manage to make a move or utter a word, he told her, "I've been drafted. If you happen to leave for Bociany, go and see my mother. Give her my regards." He grinned. "I went to see your father when you left for Lodz, remember?"

Binele tried to meet Yacov's eyes through the blinking light of the naphtha lamp. He stepped back toward the door, mumbled good-bye, and waved his hand as if she were miles away. He heard her answer him "Good-bye" through a muffled sob. She stood in front of him. As if with a will of their own, her arms encircled his neck and her face and body fell against his. So they stood, glued to one another, unable to move or to open their mouths.

Later that night they were lying on Binele's bed, still clutched in each other's tight embrace. Only now did Yacov clearly understand what it meant to desire someone so much that one ceased to feel any desire. Glued to one another with their mouths, with every cell of their bodies, they lay awake. Neither spoke. Binele did not tell Yacov about Yone Svolotch or about Geiger or about Moshe. He did not tell her about Wanda or about Miss Polcia or about his lonely nights at the side of Comrade Bronia or about the prostitutes of Faiferovka. There was an air of eternity permeating this single night which erased everything, cleansed everything; there were neither tears nor smiles, neither light nor darkness.

The dawning day shone in graying softness through the window. Binele and Yacov got dressed and left the room. Binele accompanied Yacov to Vove's home. Vove, Balcie, and a few unemployed comrades who had come to join them in their regular breakfast of coffee and black bread, sat around the cluttered table. There were no questions asked. Balcie, who had known Binele from the women's circle at The Harp, insisted that they stay and eat something. When they refused, she broke off two chunks of bread and handed them to the pair. Yacov embraced them all.

Vove made an attempt at a joke, "I give you my proletarian word of honor that I will replace you as best I can, until I come to join you," he said to Yacov and winked at Binele.

Yacov and Binele left for the caserns. They were exhausted after that night of wakefulness, exhausted by their fear of death and by their hope for life. Now as they walked and nibbled on the chunks of dry bread, they talked a great deal. But in their confusion they did not hear each other's words, or even their own. Only the language of their interlaced fingers was clear. Everything around them seemed distant, unreal, as if they were walking through the streets of a looming city lost in the depths of a nightmare.

The streets were full of feverish activity. Bearded Jews scurried quickly by, hugging the walls, vanishing first into one gate, then into another, as if they were being chased. "Watch out, children!" a frightened man accosted Binele and Yacov. "The goyim are splitting heads! There is a massacre going on at Freedom Place!" He ran off in a hurry.

Yacov and Binele stopped in front of the caserns and joined the crowd of recruited men and their families who were clustered at the entrance. Here pandemonium reigned. Noises and weeping were all around. People embraced, women hugged their sons, brothers, husbands, friends; Jewish women in wigs, Polish working-class women with plaid shawls over their heads—all with faces filled with total bewilderment.

Binele and Yacov stared at each other. Nothing more was given them than the past night of peace and this morning of violence and parting. That was all. Suddenly Binele's face lit up. She opened her purse, drew out a knotted rag, and undid it. She took the two kopecks out of the rag and handed them to Yacov. "Take them," she said, "wear them as an amulet. Parting money. They are the same ones that you gave me when I left for Lodz. I've warmed them on my heart all this time." Tears ran down her face.

"An amulet?" He smiled, took the coins, and tightly curled his fingers over them. Then he remembered something, put his hand into his pocket, and drew out a piece of copper covered unevenly with carved letters. "You must take this. An amulet. Reb Senderl the Cabalist gave it to me."

A kiss on numb lips, a handshake, a last look, a wave of the hand.

For a long time Binele stood all alone in the noisy crowd. Then she left, heading for the building where Moshe worked. She climbed up the stairs to his small office. She found Moshe sitting bent over a pile of papers, calculating something. He raised his head and his face lit up. Before he could say anything, she pulled the fake platinum ring from her finger and placed it on the pile of papers in front of him. "I'm going back to Bociany," she said to him. "I can't marry you." Before she left, she added, "Be careful, they're beating up Jews in the streets."

Within an hour she was passing the Train Garden where she used to meet Moshe. On her way to the train station she sensed the anxiety and confusion lurking in every corner. Violence was chasing fear through the streets. Shouts of "Death to the Jews and the Bolsheviks!" could be heard coming from all sides. Like escapees from a madhouse, Jews, their faces white, their eyes wild with terror, were running back and forth, stopping each other, warning each other where it was dangerous to pass, and then rushing on.

At the train station a woman in tears, holding two children by the hand, came up to Binele. She asked her for the time, although there was a large clock right above her head. She took note of Binele's accent and her face relaxed. "Do me a favor, my dear," she pleaded with Binele. "You look like a Pole. Please stay with us until the train pulls in."

As soon as she arrived at the newly built train station in Bociany, which faced the plush factory, Binele, bundle in hand, set off down the Narrow Poplar Road. She passed the fence of the manor where she and her friend Yadwiga used to wait for the landlord's son to pass them in his carriage or on his white horse. She remembered how at later times she had walked home in melancholy sadness from the plush factory by way of this road. How sweet that bygone sadness had been, in comparison to what she now felt. It was with the eyes of a stranger that she stared at Bociany's new school building. The school bell chimed. She saw bands of barefoot children racing from the yard and the surrounding fields toward the school house. Then she saw the new city hall on the edge of the marketplace, by the church. Across from the marketplace was the Potcheyov. There her father would most likely be sitting in his shop. She did not want to see him and walked around the marketplace on the side where the church stood. People in the streets and alleys stared at her. Some recognized her. Others did not.

She climbed the broken stairs to Hindele's loft. The door was unlocked. No one was inside. She went in. Soon Gitele staggered in with a pail of water. "I am Binele, Yossele Abedale's daughter," Binele approached her. "I'm Yacov's bride-to-be. He was taken into the army this morning."

Gitele let out a muffled squeal and covered her mouth with her hand. She put down the pail and calling out, "Wait here!" she ran from the room.

Binele went over to the window and looked out on the shtetl. Across the yard she could see two storks standing on the roof next to the wheel which housed their nest. They looked like her storks, Mendl and Gnendl, unchanged since her childhood. She peered down into the nuns' garden. She had seen it before, she could not remember when. As she was looking at this green flowering island of peace, she saw approaching from the other side of the fence an old woman and her two daughters. They started climbing up and the stairway began to groan, as if it were cracking under the weight of their anguish.

As on many sad occasions in the past, that day in the fragrant loft became reminiscent of the day of mourning over the destruction of the Temple. Hindele was overcome by a trembling that she could not control. In utter confusion, she stared at this girl, Binele, who was to become Yacov's wife, and thus become related to herself. Fate was playing an awesome game, teasing an old woman's heart with both fear and hope. And it was in fact Binele's presence that finally helped to calm Hindele's nerves. She had to make the girl feel welcome. So she first filled a basin with water for her so that she could wash up. Then she busied herself, preparing something for her to eat. There were many questions that she wanted to ask the girl, but she finally relinquished asking them as she had not yet mustered up the courage to listen to the answers. Only one question did she manage to ask Binele after a while, "Have you seen your father yet?"

Binele shook her head. "I don't want to see him." She looked questioningly at Hindele and her daughters. "Will you let me stay with you for a while?"

"Yacov's bride," Gitele answered with feigned cheerfulness, "must not ask such questions."

Hindele nodded. "You can sleep on Yacov's pallet tonight. But don't forget that you have a father in Bociany, may he live and be healthy." She wrapped herself in her plaid. "Don't come running after me," she said firmly to her daughters. "Put the coffee on." And she left the room.

She hurried in the direction of Yossele Abedale's hut at the other end of the shtetl. Yossele was sitting inside the room by the open door. His neighbor, Peshele the Slob, a tiny, stooped old woman, was puttering around by the stove. Hindele sat down on the threshold beside Yossele and burst into tears, trying to smother the sounds of her sobs by pressing the edge of her plaid shawl against her mouth. "Yossele," she said haltingly. "Your Binele is at my place. And . . . and they have taken my Yacov into the army."

Yossele barely stirred. He sat on his chair, dressed in his chalk-smeared gabardine over which his white beard was spread out in all directions, and stared in front of him with open blind eyes. "Hindele," he tried in his awkward manner to console her. "And if you tear your heart apart with grief, would it help you? There is no way of fighting destiny. And as for her, tell her—"

Hindele interrupted him. "She's Yacov's bride-to-be. She told me. That's what she said."

Yossele bit his underlip. He stroked his beard with his hand for a while and then took one of its tips into his mouth and chewed on it. Finally, he removed the beard from his mouth, and slowly his full, sharply defined lips took on a form that they had never before managed to bring into shape—the form of a smile.

"How dare you, Yossele?" Hindele was beside herself. "My heart is breaking into pieces, and you sit here, smiling!"

"Heaven forbid, Hindele. My heart is also not of one piece. And go and tell Peshele the Slob that she ought not to mix into people's affairs, when not asked to."

Peshele was just then approaching them with a steaming bowl of potato soup in her hands, a spoon inside it. "Careful, it's boiling hot," she warned Hindele as she handed her the bowl. "What a man this Yossele is!" She shook her head. "Won't let a soul do the slightest thing for him."

"God bless you," Hindele mumbled, turning her head away, so that Peshele would not see her tears. "Go in good health, Peshele. I will stay with him for a while." Peshele went back for a slice of bread and pushed it into Yossele's hand. After Peshele had left, Hindele fed Yossele the potato soup and poured her heart out to him.

Hindele and Yossele had been sharing a secret for quite a while now. Before the Polish-Bolshevik war had broken out, Hindele had had a complicated conversation with Reb Menashele the Matchmaker. She had begun the conversation with a long preamble, the purpose of which was to remind Reb Menashele of their long and lasting friendship. She punctuated her talk with many reminiscences of the past, in order to further soften his heart toward her. She continued talking on and on, using tangled phrases. She seemed unwilling to come to the point, which was not normally her nature.

At length her chatter, along with the strange expression of her face, made old Reb Menashele, who had cut his teeth on pairing Bociany's youth, divine the purpose of her visit. The matchmaking profession had undergone a serious crisis of late. It had virtually become useless in Bociany. The shtetl's youth had taken to guessing the Almighty's intentions by making matches of their own and had renounced Reb Menashele's help. So Reb Menashele presently inferred that his old friend Hindele was intent on helping him preserve his self-respect and had come to ask him to find suitable bridegrooms for her daughters, who were about to reach their twenties and would in former times have been mothers of children by now.

Before Hindele had managed to finish with the introduction to her request, Reb Menashele had drawn out the fat black notebook from his breast pocket. Although he lately transacted few important matrimonial businesses, he still conducted himself as before. He inscribed all the names of the newly available candidates for marriage in alphabetical order, black on white, in his black book. There he also listed all the good qualities of the candidates, omitting the bad, because, according to him, bad qualities were not important as long as crooked parents could produce straight offspring. In his black notebook he quickly found the names of two young men who were exactly right for Hindele's fine daughters, even though the girls had not a groschen to their dowries and were already old maids. These however were modern times and a modern matchmaker, such as Reb Menashele had always been, knew that such bridal qualities as beauty and intelligence had recently grown in value and could, with luck, substitute for a dowry.

"Here I have a match for your Gitele. Perfect!" Reb Menashele kissed the tips of his fingers as he interrupted Hindele. "And here I have a young man who is just made for Shaindele."

Hindele, oblivious to his words, continued talking as if she had swallowed a glass of windbag water. He let her talk on, while he put his hand into his other breast pocket and first drew out an envelope swollen with photographs of bride and groom candidates from Chwosty and other shtetlekh, and then pulled out another envelope, fatter still, with photographs of the young men and women of Bociany provided him, in secret, by their parents.

"The times are such these days," he again broke into Hindele's speech and sighed, "That the young people refuse to rely on the matchmaker's taste or even on the taste of their own parents. They want to see a face."

Hindele interrupted Reb Menashele by pushing away his hand filled with the notebook and envelopes for her to look at. "I have someone in mind for myself," she finally declared, calm and composed.

Reb Menashele leaned away from the table as if he wanted to have a better look at this old woman of whom "nothing was left," as if he wanted to decide whether she had not by any chance lost her mind. "What do you mean for yourself?" he asked.

"I mean," Hindele answered without blinking, "that I would like to marry Reb Yossele Abedale."

"What!" Reb Menashele jumped to his feet.

She pulled at his sleeve to make him sit down. "Relax, Reb Menashele. The skies have not fallen in, heaven forbid. All I want of you is that you should, with God's help, go to see Reb Yossele Abedale tomorrow morning and propose the match to him."

"You must be out of your mind!" Reb Menashele gasped.

"Big deal to be out of one's mind these days," she answered with, as it seemed to Reb Menashele, a coquettish smile on her wrinkled lips. "If, as you claim, you are really my good friend, Reb Menashele, then be so nice and do as I ask."

"Never! You can be as crazy as you like, but I am not! I won't move a finger to bring this calamity about!"

"For me, for Hindele, your devoted friend, you won't do this, Reb Menashele?" she asked, looking at him wistfully with her large dark eyes that had changed little through the years, except that they had become fringed with red rings from frequent crying.

"I refuse to do you a disservice, and I will not do a disservice to myself either by disgracing my honor and my profession." He fidgeted in his seat. "I'm glad I've finished with Yossele for once and for all."

The times that Reb Menashele had had to deal with Yossele had obviously remained indelibly printed in his memory. Ever since the unfortunate marriage of Yossele's daughter Dvorele, who had left her husband for another man and had fled to Argentina with him, Reb Menashele had rarely exchanged a word with Yossele, except during the High Holidays when they shook hands and wished each other all the best. Otherwise, he avoided him like the plague. Even after he had gone blind, Yossele had changed so little in demeanor that people often forgot that he *was* blind. And now Reb Menashele was confronted by Hindele, who had come to him with a proposition devoid of even a speck of reason, with an idea that was so out of place that it was not even ridiculous. Granted, his own wife had proven to Reb Menashele that the most inconceivable thoughts could suddenly pop up in a woman's head, even if she were the most decent and reasonable member of her sex. But an idea like Hindele's was truly uncanny. As Hindele's good friend, Reb Menashele considered it his sacred duty to do something that was in direct opposition to his role as matchmaker, namely, he had to talk her out of her crazy intention and not allow such a match ever to take place.

But here she was, sitting beside him, demanding that he do his job and intercede on her behalf. Of course, a sane man would never have obeyed a good friend who had come to ask him for help in hanging herself. Yet it did not look like Hindele would ever give up and leave him alone. Also, despite her being a woman, he considered her to be one of the most valuable and impressive people he had ever come in contact with. So who knew? Perhaps she could succeed in having a beneficial effect even on as unmanageable a man as Yossele and bring about an improvement in his character. Had she not in the past often talked him, Reb Menashele, out of his own hostile feelings toward one neighbor or another and calmed his anger with her wise words, like a dedicated friend should? After all, her life was her own business.

At length, having washed his hands of any responsibility and leaving the burden of Hindele's decision on the shoulders of the Almighty and Hindele herself, Reb Menashele promised to repay her for her kindness in the odd manner that she wished. Fully aware of what he was about to expose himself to, Reb Menashele summoned up his courage, took his umbrella, and the next morning went to pay blind Yossele a visit.

It all happened just as Reb Menashele had expected. As soon as Yossele had understood the proposition with which Reb Menashele had dared to come to see him, he flung his arm, stick in hand, into the air and called out, "Off you go, or else!" Thanks to Yossele's blindness and his own umbrella, with which he warded off the blows, Reb Menashele was able to escape into the street with all his bones intact.

That afternoon when Hindele came over to Yossele's shop to help him attend to a customer, Yossele spoke not a single word to her. Later, when she brought him food, he refused to touch it. Feigning innocence, Hindele asked, "Is something the matter, Reb Yossele?"

"Yes! Something is the matter—with you, woman! You're out of your mind!" he burst out.

"I know," Hindele answered calmly. "Reb Menashele told me the same thing."

Yossele pounded his stick against the ground. "Oh, no! I'll let no one make a fool of me, not on your life!" She left the shop without answering him. When she returned at dusk to help him lock up, he said in a somewhat calmer tone of voice, "And I thought that you were a woman with a kosher Jewish heart."

"As far as my heart is concerned, I am myself not sure that it is so kosher, Reb Yossele," she said as she helped him cross the gutter. "Because . . . for instance, the day after Fire Chief Vaslav Spokojny hung himself, I was overjoyed. Yes, despite the tragedy of the pogrom, I came back to my house a new person, as if the Almighty had supplied me with a brand new character and a brand new zest for life. And that does not seem so kosher to me. But as God is my witness, Reb Yossele, my intentions with regard to you personally are quite kosher. And if you don't want to marry me, we can still remain good friends, and that's that."

"I have no friends!" Yossele shook and for a moment removed his hand from Hindele's shoulder. "Pity has nothing to do with friendship." Hindele walked Yossele home every day, and they were now heading toward Yossele's street. One of his hands rested on her thin shoulder, a hard, heavy hand, but he kept the rest of his body at arm's length from her. In his other hand he held his walking stick. He never allowed anyone else to see him home, and Bociany had gotten used to the sight of these two old people walking home after the shops closed. No one paid them any attention. "Had you, heaven forbid, been stricken by blindness, neighbor, I would have taken you home, too," Yossele added.

"I *am* blind," she whispered back. "Who knows who's leading whom, Reb Yossele? More than once you've said something to me, and it has opened my eyes. You have often given me things to think about for days. Every time we are dealt a blow we are blinded. We become confused, because we don't understand what . . . or why. We don't see others or ourselves properly. Yes, take Vaslav Spokojny, for instance. When he saved our lives during the pogrom and I thanked him and kissed his hand, he said to me, 'Remember, Hindele, there is only a small step between being the Angel of Mercy and the Angel of Death.' Oh, I cannot tell you, Reb Yossele, how mad I went with joy when, after my ordeal with him, I understood that he had hung himself. I was grateful to him. I clapped my hands like a little girl. Oh yes, it was as if I had been reborn. That's how blind I was. And that's what it is, Reb Yossele. You and I, we are both two badly burned survivors, saved from a ship that is continually sinking, a ship that the Almighty nonetheless keeps forever afloat. Our children are far ahead for better or worse, and we can never change that. What we had to give them to take along, we have given them already. So . . . " She shamelessly turned her head and stared at him as if he could see her. "In my opinion, Reb Yossele," she pursued, "this bit of time left to us . . . it's practically a sin not to use it properly. Tell me, for example, what the Almighty could have had against the two of us holding on to one another in the dark? We would have done harm to no one, would we? And I wouldn't have to run to you on winter evenings to ease my heart. And you wouldn't have to wait for my coming, in case you needed something, because if I ask a neighbor of yours to cook some food for you when I can't make it on time, it's common knowledge how you receive them."

"Because they lack the talent to do a favor properly," Yossele murmured. "Right away they start to boss me around and mix into my business, supposedly for my own good."

For a long time Hindele thus tried to talk Yossele into marrying her, with no result. Finally she gave it up and the two of them carried on as usual. Hindele thought that Yossele had forgotten the whole idea.

Owing to his blindness Yossele was no longer able to move around much physically. He spent entire days sitting on a chair in his shop or at home. But a man has to move his limbs, and if he physically cannot, then he has to move them in his mind. The world had vanished from before his eyes, yet it existed inside his head and there he began to travel. He transferred his energy to his mind and became a carpenter again. He constructed edifices of thought concerning the world, the Creator, and mankind and concerning his children as well as himself. He grew increasingly amazed at his own former stupidities. Things that had once seemed of major importance to him, now appeared ridiculous. Things that he had treated with extreme seriousness, now seemed laughable.

It had all started with his return from Lodz, where he had gone to bring Binele back home but had had to come back without her. He had fallen under the wheels of a wagon, when, blinded by rage, he had tried to cross the street. He had suffered wounds, but his life had been miraculously saved. At that time his eyesight had not completely failed him yet. Not long after this accident, his daughter Dvorele had run away from her husband and from him. When he had found out that she had left with the broommaker's hoodlum son and gone to Argentina, Yossele had burst out laughing, inwardly, for the first time. Life had revealed its grotesque face to him. "To hell with it!" he said to himself. "I am not like Job, the fool, who went with a list of complaints to the Almighty!" And so Yossele went completely blind without complaint.

When Hindele would come into his shop and ask him in her soft voice, "How are you today, Reb Yossele?" he, who had never before betrayed any sense of humor, would answer, "No change, neighbor. I am still best friends with the Almighty, and He is still just so-so with me."

He allowed the great darkness to embrace him like a soft featherbed. He was ready for it. Not that he had not raged at first and tried to fight it. He had even gone to Shmulikl the Doctor for advice. Shmulikl had taken him to Chwosty to consult another doctor, who had stated that even an operation at a hospital in Vienna would not yield any definite results. That was the verdict. So, when the great darkness came, Yossele gradually made peace with it, until it turned into a soft black featherbed that covered his soul and smoothed out the sharp edges of his impulses, erasing them little by little. His former edginess and irritability sprang back to life only when it seemed to him that his helplessness was being mocked at by those who exaggerated their expressions of pity.

Hindele the Nag, as he called her with a certain degree of affection, seemed to have just the right measure of compassion, and she dispensed it in such a manner that it did not irritate him. He chased her away from him only when he was fed up with her nagging or when her talking to him made him feel that she could clearly see what went on in the privacy of his mind—that seemed a tactless intrusion. And then, what sense did it make to let a woman talk to you for so many hours, day after day? But if she stayed away from him for too long, he grew restless. Sometimes when she was sitting in front of her shop and he in front of his, her voice would reach him, thin and rustling, soft and balmy, and it appeared to him that he was not blind. He could see her in her voice. He could feel her touching him with it.

He never thanked her for anything. Words of thanks were too trivial and cheap. She not only took care of him, but of his shop as well. True, most of the time the customers served themselves, and he was rarely cheated. But he knew Hindele kept an eye on his customers, watching from the side, even after he had learned to attend to them himself and was able to count the money, making out its value by the size of the coins.

The matchmaker's visit had come as a shock to him. He could not for-

give Hindele for it. The woman wanted to sacrifice herself for him! So low
had he fallen even in her eyes! He could not swallow the insult and could
find no peace thinking of it. The only solution was to forget it, to delete it
from his mind. He tried to do so without success. The greater his efforts
at ridding himself of the thought, the more it boiled over within him,
until he heard the strange new self within him burst out with boisterous
liberated laughter. Suddenly he felt the featherbed of darkness grow
lighter—his mind acquired the weight of a feather! Hindele's outrageous
idea began to sit increasingly better with him and even began to please
him. To play fate such a trick suited his present-day mood perfectly. There
was a quality of spitefulness and mischief about it. He remembered how
Hindele the Nag had arrived in Bociany. As a bride, she had had a heavy
bun of brown hair on her slender neck and she had barely touched the
ground with her feet. Of course, his own Mariml had pleased him more.
But Mariml could no longer touch him, while with Hindele he had danced
that unforgettable dance in the middle of the marketplace on the night of
his daughters' wedding. Hindele touched him with her voice and with her
shoulder to which he held on as she walked him home every day.

Then it came to pass that Abele the Town Fool suddenly reappeared in
the shtetl—a much older Abele, his hair whiter than before, his body thin
as a stick, worn, and withered, but there was the same silly smile on his
face. No one could find out what had happened to him, where he had
been or how he had found his way back to Bociany. All of the shtetl ran
after him as soon as he was noticed. People pulled at him from all sides.

"Abele, where have you been?" they asked.

Just as in the olden days, he answered, "There."

"Where is there?"

"Near the cherries."

"What cherries?"

"Behind the cemeteries."

Big and small accompanied him to Yossele's shop. Abele could barely
drag himself along. He was barefoot; the soles of his feet were covered
with festering boils and wounds. As soon as he reached Yossele, he sank
down by his feet, snuggled up against Yossele's legs, and the next moment
he was snoring aloud. Yossele felt the weight of the fool's body against his
legs, felt his warm breath against his skin. He heard the people talking in
front of his shop, speculating how Abele might have come back to Bociany and concluding that an amnesty had probably liberated him from a

prison somewhere in Russia or in Poland. But no one could figure out how such a complete blockhead could, just like a dog, have sniffed his way back home. Yossele uttered not a sound. Only after the people had dispersed and he himself had gotten over the shock of surprise, did he start to titter, muttering, "Abele, with all my seven gone, I am left with you alone."

Yossele and Abele communicated with each other by some additional sense. There was an odd affinity between the two of them. It was a simple matter for Yossele to train the fool to help him with his comings and goings and turn him into a kind of seeing-eye dog, an extension of himself. Yossele tried to take Abele into his home so that the two could live together. But Abele ran away every night to sleep in his shed on the Potcheyov. In the morning he was back to take Yossele to the shop.

In his own mind Yossele explained Abele's reappearance in Bociany as a wonderful and mysterious event. It was then that true contentment and a brightness of thought began to hum within him, as if he had crossed some border and had entered an entirely new kingdom where people walked about with their souls unharnessed, their hearts bared, and their talk free and spontaneous. Thus it was with unrestrained pleasure that he now greeted Hindele whenever she dropped by his hut to sit with him. Ever since Abele's return, Yossele had been spending less time with Hindele. Even the food that she cooked every day for him was sent over with Abele and warmed up by Abele or, rarely, by a woman neighbor. That was how Yossele wanted it to be.

One particular evening, as Hindele sat next to him, Yossele all of a sudden said to her playfully, "Tell me, neighbor, what do we need Reb Menashele the Matchmaker for?"

Hindele stared at him flabbergasted. For a long while she sat there, pondering what he might have meant with his question, and she did not answer him. She wondered whether he was not making fun of her. Finally she said, "That's how Jews conduct themselves."

Yossele stroked his beard. "And did not the matchmaker tell you that I am as blind as a bat, that I'm not easy to live with either, and that I wouldn't be of much help to you in earning a living—and that all that I am capable of is to add another burden to your load of worries?"

Hindele was still not sure in what vein Yossele was talking to her. "What do you mean by that, Reb Yossele?" She stared at him.

"I mean," he answered, "That now we can set the date of our wedding, may it be in a propitious hour, and we shall keep it a secret until we no longer have any choice."

Thus, Yossele and Hindele became engaged. They set the date for their wedding, keeping the whole thing a secret, so that not a trace of suspicion entered anyone's mind. Then the war with the Bolsheviks broke out, and Hindele was so preoccupied with worrying about her sons that she barely knew what was happening to her. Consequently, they decided to postpone their wedding until after the war, with the Almighty's help.

Now that Binele had returned to Bociany with the news that Yacov had left for the battlefront and that she was Yacov's bride, Hindele could not do without Yossele. At his side she could let go of her tears and allow herself to be consoled by him. Nowhere else could she recharge her heart with hope. There was a brightness to Yossele's silence. Just sitting with him for a while made her feel better. Sometimes they would wonder together at the way fate had woven the threads of feeling between them. They mused on how fate, sometimes with strange humor and at other times with painful beauty, had twined their destinies together—like in a storybook. But since Hindele knew that life could play games with people more cruelly than any storybook could tell, she feared that it might play a horrible trick on her—and she continued to tremble for Yacov's safety.

In order to conceal this major worry, Hindele resorted to her nagging nature to the full. She constantly harped on Binele and Yossele, insisting, "It's high time that you two made peace with each other, believe me."

As usual, she read Yossele's mind. She knew that ever since the day that Binele had arrived in the shtetl, the thought of her was never very far from his mind. She knew, too, that Binele was at the core of whatever torment there was left within him. The bitterness that had accompanied his rejection of his only son, Hershele, had long since faded. He had forgiven his Kaddish as one forgives the dead. As for Dvorele, he had already been partly desensitized by the time she fled to Argentina, and he felt almost no hurt when she was gone. But Binele was still very much alive within him. It was as if the guilt feelings that he had always nourished with regard to her had kept her near to his heart. All the softness and tenderness that he harbored beneath the hard armor of his rigidity bore Binele's name. At times it seemed to him that he owed his happiness with Hindele to the sparks of love that Binele had kept alive within him. The mysteries of the human heart, the enigmatic ways it found to express itself, were extraordinary. He was not surprised that Hindele knew how frightened he was of meeting his daughter, how much he wanted it, and also how much he needed Hindele's support.

Finally he managed to bring the words to his lips. "Send her in," he told Hindele.

Day after day Binele wandered about Bociany and the countryside, thinking herself to be in a world that she remembered from a dream. Bociany was the place where she had chosen to wait for Yacov's return. He too was unreal, a stranger whom she had left in a dream to roam the twisted roads of her life and to whom she then had returned in a dream, in order only to part with him again. She was waiting for him just as she had used to wait for the arrival of the storks or the arrival of the Messiah. All that was left of her relationship with Yone Svolotch was the sheepskin coat, and all that remained of her relationship with Handsome Moshe was the silk scarf with the design of forget-me-nots. She kept the scarf at the bottom of her bundle of belongings, a souvenir of Moshe, a reminder of the harm that she had done him. She owed him a debt that she would never be able to repay. But she could not help it. She was Yacov's, and Yacov was hers. She wore the amulet that he had given her suspended from a ribbon around her neck.

Whenever she walked into the loft, she met Hindele's questioning eyes. "Have you been to see your father?" Hindele would inquire.

Binele could barely keep from telling Hindele off, asking her to mind her own business. Why should this old woman care whether or not she had been to see her father? The fact that she was Yacov's bride gave his mother no right to mix into her affairs. "I have not," she answered, "and I won't see him, ever!"

Hindele was not impressed. She saw that Binele's nerves were stretched to the breaking point, yet she kept on insisting. The gift of a caress, a kiss, a warm word, a bit of tenderness—that was what she badly wanted for Yossele. So again and again she repeated, "Go to see your father, child. Grant him a little pleasure." As Binele turned on her, ready to explode with anger, Hindele embraced her, trying with a pat or a stoke to soften the girl's stiffness, her stubbornness. "I know, my child," she muttered, "It ain't easy to break the ice."

And so, as she stood savoring the sweetness of Hindele's embrace, Binele came to realize how badly she herself wanted and needed what she so vehemently refused. She knelt and showed Hindele the spot on her head where her father had struck her with the stick and where no hair had ever grown. "I will never forgive him for that. Every morning when I comb my hair over this bald spot, I remember what he did to me," she raged, but she knew that every morning when she combed her hair, she also remembered that her father was blind.

"Remember the bareness of his life," Hindele did not give up. "If you forgive a loved one, you also forgive yourself. Believe me, he may be blind, but his heart is not."

So Binele finally went to see her blind father at the chalk-and-lime shop. They hardly said a word to each other, but the mere fact of her presence broke the dam of tensed-up hostility that they bore toward each other. Something was being finalized and discarded. Binele sat down in front of the shop, on a box next to Abele the Fool, who spent most of the day leaning against Yossele's legs, and she began to converse with Abele in "his language," as she had done in her childhood.

She stayed on, living with Hindele and her daughters, but every day she went to her father's shop and helped him attend to the customers. She took Yossele to the synagogue, to the *shtibl* and back, or wherever he wanted to go, and found herself amazed at the strength that he still commanded. He was still her powerful father. The only contact between the two of them was the touch of his hand, large, hard, and as dry as parchment, the same hand that he had used to beat her. Now he held onto her with that same hand. Sometimes he tightened the grip of his fingers around her shoulder, perhaps to support himself better, or perhaps to let her know how much he regretted . . . She was his youngest and best loved one.

However, things did not happen quite as Hindele had wished. No fount of emotion broke the ice and allowed tenderness to flow freely and spontaneously between father and daughter. Even talking did not come easily to them. Yossele refrained from questioning Binele, and she told him nothing. Only once, when she could no longer overcome her restlessness and worry about Yacov, did she ask him whether he knew that Yacov was her fiancé.

He coughed, then startled her with his hoarse giggling. In his mind Yossele was already capable of loud, clear laughs, but his voice was still learning how to bring out the sound of laughter. He squeezed her hand and asked, "Does Reb Menashele know about it, too?" She stared at him in wide-eyed amazement. Her father, Yossele Abedale, joking! Moreover, a childlike delight radiated from his creased leather face. He did not let go of her hand, but took hold of the other one, too, and gathered them both into the palm of his. With his other hand he grabbed the tip of his beard as if about to put it into his mouth, perhaps in order to prevent himself from saying more, perhaps to keep his own secret from rushing to his lips. She became totally confused, when a while later, he pulled her down beside him and said, "Nu . . . let me see how you look." He put both hands on her face and his rough fingers touched her as lightly as a fine brush. He began ever so softly to trace her forehead, eyes, nose, cheeks, ears, and chin. He had never stroked her like that when he could see her. Her father's first touch. Tears trickled out of her eyes. He felt their moisture on his fingers and quickly withdrew his hands as if they had been burned.

"A bride ready for the wedding canopy must not cry before the veiling ceremony," he said and coughed. His ashen eyes without a spark were misty.

෯ 15 ෯

THE SUMMER WAS GONE. Binele and Hindele continued to receive letters from Yacov mailed from localities like Yablonny, Hrubieshov, and Zamosc. Hindele's letters from Yacov were read aloud to the family, while Binele only reported on the contents of hers. At the entryway of her father's shop she would sit down to write an answer. When she could not remember how to spell a certain Hebrew word used in Yiddish, she asked Yossele, and he would call out each letter and draw it in the air with a motion of his hand.

For the approaching winter Binele bought her father a hand-knitted woolen vest from her childhood friend Yadwiga. Yadwiga was now the mother of four small girls. This year she was not pregnant because her husband was at the front fighting the Muscovites. Just like Yacov he belonged to the Second Division and his letters arrived from the same places as Yacov's. Yadwiga and Binele shared every bit of news they heard about the war. Yadwiga helped herself earn a living by knitting vests at night. Binele offered to sell them for her and thus earn a bit of money herself.

Once in a while Yadwiga's mother, the still agile and handsome Yankova, invited Binele to supper. Again Binele felt herself at home in Yankova's kitchen. She told the peasants, who would come in for a chat, of the wonders she had seen in the big city of Lodz. They could hardly get over their amazement that people managed to live in such a cramped, smoky beehive of a place with not a field or tree in sight. Binele was in turn puzzled by the peasant's attitude toward life. They all had sons or husbands at the front, and it amazed Binele to observe the fatalistic stoicism, the calmness of mind which with they accepted their lot, while she herself was boiling over with impatience, with anxieties, with frustration and anger. On the whole she was irritated by time moving so slowly in Bociany and by its people going about their daily affairs so complacently.

Then came a week that shook the Jewish inhabitants of Bociany out of their complacency good and proper, as Binele would say. A company of lancers arrived and was stationed in the shtetl. The lancers took to entertaining themselves by attacking the Potcheyov and the Jewish homes. The Zionist leader, Shmulikl the barber-surgeon, and old Zelig the Tailor, who acted as leader of the Bund in place of Ariele, who was at the battlefront, quickly organized groups to defend themselves and their families. But as soon as their groups appeared in the streets, they were all arrested for alleged communist sympathies and were sent to a prison camp in Dombia near Krakow. Shortly thereafter the lancers left and calm returned to the shtetl.

In order to occupy her time, Binele helped out with the housekeeping chores at Hindele's home, did the cooking and washing for her father, and walked around peddling Yadwiga's sweaters. Yet all these chores still left her with many idle hours every day. Sometimes, when she had nothing to do, she sat down at the window in Hindele's loft and peered into the nuns' garden. She observed the nuns strolling among the trees and flower beds. If everything in Bociany moved in slow motion, in the nuns' garden time seemed not to move at all. Binele, although unlike the nuns in her emotions of impatience and restlessness, still felt herself related to them. She felt herself as pure at heart, as innocent and maiden-like as they were.

She slept under the window on Yacov's straw mattress. Before they fell asleep, the four women frequently talked about Yacov. Their fears for his safety continually hovered in their minds like a black bat that flapped its wings above their heads. After they received a letter from him, their worries would subside and Hindele would tell them stories about him as a dreamy and distraught little boy. She remembered the funny questions he had asked and the games he had played with his little sisters. When the hearts of the four women were soothed by the news of the approaching end of the war, Shaindele would, from her bed where she slept with her mother and sister, embark on reciting poems by Mickiewicz or Sowacki, or the sisters would hum the song that Wanda had used to sing:

> You will go through the mountain,
> Go through the mountain,
> And I through the stormy sea.
> You will blossom like a rose,
> Blossom like a rose,
> And I like a windswept tree.

The months dragged slowly on. The rumors about the approaching end of the war had stopped. The seasons changed. Binele still busied herself selling the woolen sweaters and vests that Yadwiga and other peasant women knitted. Another winter was approaching and the knitwear sold well among the temporary residents from the big cities. Binele was glad that her work kept her from being a financial burden to anyone.

It was on a windy day in fall that she set out for the Blue Mountain with a bundle of sweaters that she intended to sell to Zirele, Reb Faivele the Miller's wife, or to their relatives, city people who had moved in with them. She entered the gate of the enclosure near the mill and was about to walk up to the white wooden house when she noticed a four-wheeler being loaded with luggage by an elderly peasant. Zirele and Reb Faivele were sitting in the back seat, their heads turned toward a young man who stood by the wagon embracing an elderly peasant woman—Fredka the housekeeper.

"Abrashka, hurry up, the train leaves in an hour!" The loud, impatient voice belonged to Reb Faivele, who, although old and gray, still looked robust. The young man turned around, and Binele saw his face, the face of Abrashka. It had changed, and yet she recognized him easily, in particular by his lively black eyes, which reminded her of the mischievous little boy with whom she used to play in front of this yard. His build resembled that of Reb Faivele, he was thickset and sturdy, but he looked taller than his father, and there was a gracefulness in his bearing that his father had never had.

Without thinking, Binele ran up to him and grabbed hold of his sleeve as he was about to climb into the four-wheeler. "Remember me?" she asked.

He leaned back and furrowed his bushy eyebrows. Running his fingers through his mop of black hair, he asked, "Aren't you the girl who used to roll down the hill with me? You always had a wreath of bluebells around your neck." He laughed, displaying two rows of sparkling white teeth; each tooth seemed to produce a smile of its own.

"Abrashka, for heaven's sake!" Reb Faivele bellowed as the elderly peasant, Fredka's husband, climbed up to the front seat and took the reins in his hand.

"I must go." Abrashka made a motion to raise his foot and climb up, but he seemed reluctant to part with Binele. "I am going to Paris, to study," he informed her.

"To study . . ." she repeated, not knowing what she was saying, so overwhelmed was she by the sight of him.

"Yes, I am a sculptor," he said boastfully and climbed into the front seat beside the elderly peasant.

She dashed toward him. "Yacov is at the front!" she called out.

The peasant's whip swished through the air. The four-wheeler moved forward, but Abrashka jumped off and ran back to her. "You know Yacov? Yes, of course!" He panted, grabbing hold of her hand. "Tell him . . . tell him . . . " he choked on his words. He squeezed her hand, turned back and raced after the four-wheeler.

Binele's second long autumn in Bociany began. The storks had departed. The weeks leading up to the Days of Awe had been full of rain and fog, and this particular day was no different from the others. Hindele was at the Potcheyov. Gitele and Shaindele were in Chwosty shopping for merchandise for the pre-holiday rush. Binele cleaned the loft and scrubbed the cracked, uneven floor. She hummed a song by I. L. Peretz, "The Eyes Red, the Lips Blue," which had been one of the favorite songs of her comrades at the women's circle of The Harp. The haunting melody and the story the song told of three seamstresses worn out by life had always moved her deeply. She hummed the song as she looked out the window at a gray sky with not a ray of brightness. True, a new year was coming, but she felt no speck of promise or hope. Her eyes began to burn. Tears trickled down the tip of her nose and fell onto the soapy floor.

And so, in the midst of her melancholic humming and weeping, Binele heard a sound, a distant echo of a voice. The sound seemed to be reaching her from outside, as if it were coming through her limbs and skin rather than through her ears. The sound of her name, mingled with the soft rustle of the leaves in the nuns' garden, reverberated in the room.

"Binele . . . "

Only one pair of lips could utter her name in such a tone of voice. Nearly turning over the basin of water, Binele jumped to her feet, and thrust herself toward the window. At first she could see nothing. Her nervousness and the fog outside blurred her vision. And then: She saw him!

In the yard beneath the window stood Yacov, in the flesh, dressed in his soldier's khaki uniform, the collar unbuttoned. His uncovered head, its short brown curls trembling lightly in the breeze, was raised to her. In one hand he held his four-cornered cap with the small white eagle, in the other he held some papers, and both arms were stretched out as if he were waiting for Binele to fly down from the window and land in them. The call of his eyes was so powerful that she almost did so—so dizzy had she become with the fragrances that reached her from the nuns' garden.

It was a moment of total bliss. An explosion of boundless joy. A moment impossible to measure with the usual measurements of time. A moment that seemed to rise above the boundaries of both life and death. It took place in the stairwell, on the crooked stairs leading to Hindele's loft. Clumsily Binele and Yacov fell into each other's arms, clumsily they held on to each other, and together they stumbled and rolled down the stairs. Together they tried to stand up on their entangled legs and then sat down on the first stair, arms linked in embrace, face against face, mouth against mouth. There was magic in each other's touch, the realization of long-endured yearnings. But the tension between Binele and Yacov was so great that it dulled their senses, deprived them of the faculty of speech, and came so close to pain that it was impossible to bear it for long. There was no breath left in their lungs to breathe. They withdrew slightly from one another and, in the half-darkness, relied on their eyes to bind them to each other.

Binele took hold of Yacov's arms, made him stand up, and pulled him upstairs into the loft. The grayness inside was now as dazzling as the strongest light. But the air inside was sticky, the walls were too narrow, and again Yacov and Binele fell into each others arms. Again they moved away from each other to allow the tension to subside.

Binele's heart hammered. Before her stood a flesh and blood Yacov, her Yacov, the nearest to her heart. And yet he was different, not quite the one for whom she had been waiting as she had wandered through the streets of Bociany, as she had wandered through all the paths of her life. It was he whom she had hoped to see, and yet not exactly he. For some reason he aroused a fear in her heart. Was it the fear of facing a love that was now no longer a dream, a dream that with Yacov's presence had become reality? Or perhaps it was the fear of what she was reading in his eyes, eyes which no longer resembled two bowls of honey. His eyes flickered between light and shadow, his gaze was both tender and hard. Nonetheless she was ready to serve him with all the impassioned devotion that she was capable of. Perhaps it was this readiness to serve him that so frightened her.

Yacov's heart hammered. Before him stood his Binele, the wandering, escaping bright comet that he had followed for so long and that he had now conquered but would never truly possess. She remained free, frightfully free. In fact, she was not exactly the woman to whose image his memory had clung as he had lain in the trenches. She seemed more powerful than ever in her submissiveness, as she looked at him now, her eyes full of tenderness and pain. She was more mysterious, more alluring than ever. It was she who had conquered him and forced him to surrender. As they stood there facing each other, he was overcome by a desire to kneel down at her feet, to bury his face in her dress, and to sob out all his sins.

Gradually they became aware of their surroundings. Yacov looked about the room. It had changed little, yet everything in it was different, smaller, more decrepit than ever—yet precious. For some reason the sight of the room brought back his remembrance of the repository of the sacred scrolls in the village synagogue where the tired Jewish soldiers of his battalion had found shelter after a long march during the night. In the autumn grayness, the fragrance of lilac, acacia, and jasmine seemed to be issuing from the straw mattress on the floor under the window, where he used to sleep as a child.

Binele noticed the basin of water on the floor and the puddle that she had made when she had knocked it over in her excitement at hearing Yacov's voice. In the puddle swayed the reflection of the white curtain, newly washed in honor of the New Year. Yacov, his eyes on Binele, came closer to the puddle. She giggled hoarsely, "Watch out, you'll drown in the water!" She picked up the basin and poured the water out the window. She stepped on the rag that lay on the floor and rubbed her foot back and forth on the boards to dry them. Finally, she took hold of Yacov's hand and pulled him toward the door. "Let's go!" she called. They ran to see Hindele on the Potcheyov.

From the distance, Hindele saw them arriving. For a moment she stood thunderstruck. Then she heard voices calling to her from all sides, "Hindele! Hindele, look who's coming!" People called loudly, as if to revive her, pointing their fingers in the direction of the approaching pair. She roused herself and ran forward. The plaid shawl on her shoulders, spread like a pair of wings, seemed to be lifting her up. "My son!" she shrieked in a voice not her own. A moment later her tiny figure was wrapped in Yacov's arms.

"Send someone for Shalom!" Binele ordered the people who had gathered around them. She dashed into the chalk-and-lime shop where Yossele sat on a chair, staring into the distance. "Tateshie, he's here!" she cried and sank to the ground at his feet.

"I know, I know," Yossele patted her on the back. "Blessed be His Holy Name."

"I know, I know," echoed Abele the Fool, who sat on the other side of Yossele's legs, his smiling mouth drooling.

Binele and Yacov made certain that they would not be alone with each other for the rest of the day. Together they loitered on the Potcheyov, letting people stop them and ply Yacov with questions. Parents queried him about their sons, whether he had seen them or heard about them. Peasants too came over to question him about their sons, sons-in-law and neighbors. Bands of boys, gentile and Jewish, caroused excitedly around him. Geese and ducks quacked, dogs barked, a couple of storks flew overhead as they readied themselves to leave and catch up with their kin that had already left the shtetl for the winter. There was a deafening clamor all around. Yacov and Binele allowed it to engulf them. Kindness and patience filled their hearts. They could permit themselves the luxury of being taken hostage by this festive world buzzing all around them. There was so much time ahead of them, so much time to be alone with each other.

Toybe-Kraindele, the women's ritual bath attendant, a shrunken little woman wearing a pot of "bobe" beans suspended on a cord from her neck, pushed her way through to Binele and prodded her with an elbow, "I hope you at least appreciate your bridegroom, Marzepa dear. I heard he'll get a medal for bravery, sure enough. That's why they let him come home for New Year in the first place, isn't it? The whole town is talking. The burgomaster himself is said to have said so."

"If the whole town is talking, then it must be true!" Binele exclaimed. Pride swelled in her bosom. But then she felt a tug at her heart. A medal for bravery? But medals were awarded only for putting one's life at risk. Then hadn't Yacov risked not only his own life but hers as well, risked their love that had been so tenuous for so long that they had barely managed to save it? Her face began to flush. She was beside herself with anger. "He's the same silly head that he has always been!" She fumed inwardly. "The same smart aleck when it comes to book knowledge, and the same ignoramus when it comes to life. How could he dare to do such a thing? He's an idiot, not a hero! And I'll not marry him, because it is clear as day that all those things that are sacred to me, mean nothing to him!" But then she grew thoughtful and finally smiled to herself. "I am a greater idiot than he is. I'm just fooling myself. Of what worth would my life be, if I didn't marry him? And had he been a brute, a thief, or a swindler, wouldn't I still follow him even through the gates of hell?"

A young woman plowed her way forward through the crowd that encircled the pair. Yacov recognized her immediately. She was Rivkele, Ariele's wife. She looked aged, haggard. Her eyes were misty as she shook his hand. "Welcome, Yacov," she muttered. Yacov embraced her, and then she burst out sobbing on his shoulder, "Ariele is no more . . . no more. Felled . . . in the battle for the Vistula . . . "

Binele left Yacov his straw mattress under the window in the loft and went to spend the night in her father's hut. All night she lay awake on the

narrow, shaky, and creaking cot, her mind going over the past day, the
most important of all the days of her life. At dawn she got up, left the hut,
and set out through the awakening shtetl in the direction of Hindele's
house. The sun was about to rise and the sky was full of small scattered
clouds; there was not a trace of yesterday's fog in the air. Sleepy shepherd
boys herded cattle through the streets and alleys toward the fields. Jews
with prayer shawls under their arms hurried in the direction of the *besmedresh* or the synagogue. Hatzkele the Water-Carrier trotted past her with
two pails of water suspended from the axle that dug into his drooping
shoulders. He was now a white-haired old man. Whether or not he was
still bound by his vow of silence, he spoke to no one. At the entrance to
the synagogue stood a group of Jews immersed in heated conversation
with the *rov*, who was still a tall, handsome man although his long beard
was now streaked with strands of gray. They all looked as though they had
spent the entire night in this place.

She saw Yacov approaching her from the distance. They stopped a few
steps away from each other and smiled—ill at ease like two shy children
who hardly dared to look at each other. They stretched out their arms as if
about to embrace, but they only linked hands and began to walk at a distance from one another in the direction of the Wide Poplar Road.

Yacov had slept badly. He was mourning Ariele and could not get him
out of his mind. He went through all the memorable moments he had
spent with his childhood friend. But now as he walked beside Binele,
keeping his distance from her, he badly wanted a moment's respite from
his mourning, and he said to her with a smile, "Do you want to bet that I'll
reach the birch wood before you do?"

Instead of answering him, she roused herself and began to run. It felt
good to free the body from all restraint and let it be carried forward on
speeding feet. It seemed as if she were catching up with her childhood,
with the awakening of her passions, as if she were leaping over all the
heavy and confusing things that had crossed the straight path of her life.
Now she knew clearly where she was racing to. However, her heart raced
faster than her feet. She had grown unused to racing. The weeks and
months of waiting for Yacov, of trembling over his safety, and that past
day and the wakeful night that had followed were difficult to shake off.
Soon it all began to weigh down her limbs. Yacov was far ahead of her.
She lagged behind, her gaze clinging to his figure in the distance.

He stopped, looked around and ran back toward her. Panting, he took her hand and pulled her along.

The birch wood was alive with twitters and rustles. Its foliage was a sea of colors—bright gold, reddish brown, and rich dark green. The nearby lake shimmered between the white tree trunks, the pale autumn sun swept the tiny waves on its surface with a long broom of rays. At the lake shore, not far from where Kailele the Bride had drowned herself, stood the oaks as if steeped in prayer to the accompaniment of the singing birds. There was not a trace anywhere to show that it had been here that Yacov and Hindele had experienced the most agonizing moments of their lives, when Fire Chief Vaslav Spokojny had hung himself on one of the oaks. Not far from the oaks lay the trunk of a birch that had been struck by lightning many years before. The birch showed not a trace of the beautiful moments that Yacov had spent here with Yoel the Blacksmith, who had seated him and Abrashka on the birch's trunk, which lay horizontally raised above the ground. Stretched precariously upward, two of its branches were still alive and were covered with healthy golden leaves.

"Yoel the Blacksmith called this broken birch his friend," Yacov said to Binele as they approached the tree. He and Binele sat down on its trunk.

They kissed. The touch of their lips awoke their dormant passion for each other and liberated their arms from restraint. Their joined lips barred the confessions that struggled to escape from their mouths. Yacov felt himself dissolved in the softness of Binele's mouth. How many times in the trenches had he seen before him these sensuous protruding lips and dreamed of being absorbed into them. Now he felt the taste of the entire world awakening to a new day in the taste of her lips.

However, as he removed his mouth from hers for a moment, to breathe in more air, he grew acutely aware of another reality, of a night on the battlefield under fire. Again the specter of Ariele appeared before his mind's eye, and a feeling of shame and guilt engulfed him. He caught a passing glimpse of the lake, which glittered through the birch trunks, and in his mind he saw the fork of a river that flowed through pitch-black darkness, branching out in two directions, its lazily moving waters black with blood. Between the arms of the river lay the desecrated earth with its bowels cut open. Uprooted trees stretched toward the sky like hands with gnarled spread-out fingers. In a trampled field of ripe rye that a peasant had not managed to harvest, nestled the carcasses of horses; cows with open intestines lay between the stalks of grain. The air was permeated with the stench of human corpses, with the smell of roasting human flesh.

Here in the birch wood, as his heart exploded with salvos of joy, it also exploded, in that other reality, with the salvos of the rifle that he had learned to hold in his hands. The rifle had become an extension of his body, its rhythm as regular as his breath, the pull of the trigger as simple and easy as the blink of an eye. The more passionately he caressed Binele, the more stubbornly his memory led him back to that other reality, to the hour of his victory that had also been the hour of his defeat, when his training in sin had been completed and he had stared at his "trophy," stared at a corpse with a red-starred cap sitting crookedly on its head, stared at a pair of open eyes, at a pair of bare feet. Now, in his mind, the remembered face of the Red Army man had taken on the likeness of Ariele.

He seized Binele by the hand and pulled her away from the broken tree, leading her through the wood and the neighboring field to the ruin that had once been Yoel the Blacksmith's hut. There was not a trace left of Yoel's smithy or the shed where Yoel had kept his cow. The entire place was covered with wilting yellow grass. Wilted buttercups and bluebells on broken stems winked sadly from the faded greenery washed by sunlight. The peasants had obviously removed everything after Yoel's death and had left only the ruin of his hut as a memorial. All that remained of the hut was a rectangle of corroded broken boards, sticking out like broken teeth from the ground. The new smith, a Gentile, had built his smithy nearer to the shtetl, in front of the wood merchant's fields.

Tall yellow grass covered the ground at the spot where Yoel's cot had stood. Nearby, a pile of rubble consisting of clay, rock, and scraps of metal leaned against the skeleton of Yoel's black stove.

The bed of tall grass behind the screen of corroded boards was moist with dew. Binele spread her shawl over the grass, and she and Yacov sank down on it. Their hands clasped and their fingers intertwined as they searched for each other. He tried to remove her dress but his trembling fingers were caught in its folds and buttons. Her laughter rang out. With one movement of her arms she freed herself of the dress and of all that she wore and helped him, too, to undress. She groaned and sighed with delight at the touch of his skin. Every cell of her body responded to his, and she stopped feeling the stings of the grass and the humidity of the earth through the shawl.

Avidly, she offered him her mouth, offered him her arms to support his head, offered him her legs so that he might keep his between them, offered him all of herself, with abandon, victoriously, jubilantly, hardly knowing which limb was his and which hers. At the same time she was full of amazement and wonder at how freely she was offering herself, surrendering to him; she was surprised at how much all this resembled her encounters with Yone Svolotch and with the brute Gaiger, and yet how new, how different, how unique and how sacred this present giving of herself was.

Yacov barely knew whether he was himself or he was Binele, so completely did she absorb him into her joyful eagerness, so total was his conquest of her. At the same time the remembrance of that other night of victory and defeat continued to prey on his mind. He saw himself after the great victory, dead drunk, reveling with a crowd of drunken soldiers in a room full of naked women. Their hard breasts, their round white buttocks danced in front of his eyes like balls in the hands of a juggler. He saw the white belly of a woman with the navel in its center like a hole in a leaking basin, into which he had vomited all that he had eaten and drunk during the previous few hours. And here was Binele's belly with the navel in its center—a sacred vessel.

For hours they lay fully dressed, side by side, in silent absorption of each other, and of what went on stirring within themselves. They hardly noticed that only a few words had passed between them. When the sound of the church bell tolling the noon Angelus jerked her out of her reverie, Binele raised herself on an elbow and leaned her head against her palm.

"Aren't you going to tell me why they've given you a medal?" she asked.

His hand, which had been slowly caressing her hip, stopped moving, and he looked her straight in the eye. "It's a medal for cowardice."

She burst into laughter and began to smother him with a torrent of kisses. "That I can understand! That's smart! Medals should be given for cowardice instead of heroism! A man who goes looking for heroic deeds during a war must be a complete idiot. If he can't run away, he must at least try to protect his bag of bones, unless he wants to get rid of them altogether."

He nodded. "Life has never been as dear to me as there, on the front, knowing that I had you. Besides, I had no reason to sacrifice myself. This is not my war." He raised himself and buried his head in the softness of her belly. "Binele." His voice sounded muffled. "I killed a man. A Jew."

She did not understand. "Only one?"

"I don't know. There might have been more. But this man I saw, face to face. I can't stop seeing him, barefoot, in his Red Army cap. A short fellow, older than I. He had a thick black beard, black eyes—he was terribly frightened."

"And that's what they give medals for?" she grimaced.

"That's what they call a miracle. The Miracle at the Vistula is what they call that battle." He raised his head. "I shouldn't be talking about these things now."

"Why not? You must tell me everything right away. Husband and wife share the same life," she quoted the saying that she had so often heard from Moshe.

"There is not much to tell, really. He was on a reconnaissance mission, as I was. There was a guy with me, a Communist. It was after midnight, a few hours before the attack was to have started. We knew that a hellish time was in store for us, so I was awfully frightened. I wanted to run away, to desert, while the guy who was with me wanted to get himself through to the Reds. We quarreled, then we lost our way. He vanished from my sight. It was pitch-dark all around. Suddenly I looked up and there was this red star on a visored cap. I saw a face, a pair of eyes piercing me with such . . . such horror. He called out, '*Stoj!* Stop!' and I immediately pulled the trigger."

"How do you know that he was a Jew?" Binele asked.

"I heard him scream the *Shma*. Or maybe I just thought I heard it, because at the same moment I myself called out, '*Shma-Yisroel!*' As soon as I fired and he collapsed, I started to run like mad. I have no idea how I found my way back to the camp. I reported the whole story. An hour later we ambushed and captured another few red reconnaissance units, then the attack began. That's all. But you know what, Binele? I can give you regards from your brother."

She squirmed. "From Hershele?"

"I heard about him from a Jewish war prisoner. He told me that his commander was a fellow from Poland, from Bociany. He described him to me, said he was a thickset young man more or less my age with freckles and slightly slanted eyes, that he wore glasses. Did your brother wear glasses?"

She burst into sobs. "I hope nothing happened to him."

"I don't think it has. Rarely does anything happen to commanders. We did capture a number of them though, but none of them was your brother."

The experiences of the past twenty-four hours were difficult for Binele to bear. But then she became furious with herself. How dare she cry at such moments as these? She managed to smile through her tears, "I can give you regards from someone too. From that mischief Abrashka. You should have seen him. A full-fledged adult. I saw him leave for Paris to become a sculpture."

"You mean a sculptor," he corrected her.

"Of course I mean a sculptor. What kind of crazy trade is that anyway?" she asked wiping her wet face with her palm.

The war with the Bolsheviks was over. The Polish republic acquired its firmly defined borders.

Hindele and Yossele decided to reveal their secret to their children. For this purpose Yossele allowed himself to be taken to Lodz, a trip that he had previously refused to make year after year. He was taken there by his eldest grandson, Raisele's firstborn.

The strongest impression that Yossele brought back to Bociany from that trip was that of his train ride. He had hated it. The train was going too fast, there was too little air inside, the compartment was like a cage, the passengers were like animals rushed to a fair. How could this compare to traveling by horse and buggy or on foot? Then the road imprinted itself on one's memory with every bump, every ditch, so that a man became one with it and with the distance that God had created, a distance that was not meant to be shrunk! A train ride was like slurping down hot noodles in haste, without savoring them. Nothing good could come of these adventurous inventions, Yossele was certain.

As for the purpose of his trip, his children's reaction to the news that he had brought them was, to say the least, as disappointing as the reaction of Hindele's children. It quickly became clear to both of them that neither set of children was overly excited by their idea. Not that the children laughed in their faces, heaven forbid, but it was beyond any shadow of a doubt that their children considered this marriage a madness that only the infantility of old age could have conceived of.

Yossele reported to Hindele that his daughter Raisele had said, "Do you lack anything, Tateshie? You have only to say the word and you can have whatever you want. Do you think I wouldn't hire a servant to take care of you, if you agreed to it? And better still, why don't you come to live with us in Lodz instead of bothering with a wife in your old age? An old woman has old habits. Nor are you one of the easiest passengers to have on board. You'll be marrying into a family of paupers to boot, and what kind of *tsadikim* they are you can judge for yourself. Didn't Yacov take Binele away from a decent bridegroom just a few weeks before their wedding? They even had a room rented already."

Raisele's words were in accord with her other sisters' reasoning, and the sons-in-law agreed with their wives. "You'll become the laughing stock of Bociany," they warned him respectfully.

Hindele gave Yossele her report. Her children were also of the opinion that Yossele and Hindele would be making fools of themselves by going through the rigmarole of getting married. The daughters said that Yossele should simply move into their house and occupy the downstairs room, where Manka the Washerwoman had used to keep her cow. True, the room was so ruined that it was uninhabitable; but still, it could be fixed up as a living place for Yossele, so that Hindele could take better care of him, if she absolutely insisted on taking the burden upon herself. Then she would not have to run across town on winter evenings to spend time with him. To spare Yossele's feelings, Hindele refrained from telling Yossele the other things her children had said, namely, that she was putting a "healthy head into a sickbed"; that, apart from the fact that Yossele needed to be cared for like a child, he was not the easiest person to live with; that he was a sulking stubborn bull, stingy with words and as devoid of feelings as a rock.

Yossele and Hindele were sitting in his hut near the open door. When they had finished exchanging information on what their children advised them to do, or not to do, Yossele concluded cheerfully, "Never mind, let's set the date for the wedding." Then, as they sat there, talking about a suitable date, Yossele and Hindele were inspired by such a wonderful idea that it made them both laugh. It occurred to them to hoist two wedding canopies simultaneously, and at the same celebration marry off Yacov and Binele as well. Hindele immediately jumped to her feet, and, as if she had regained the energy of a young girl, she rushed out of the hut to find the young pair. She looked for them all over the shtetl and was finally directed to Rivkele, Ariele's wife's dwelling. Without giving Yacov and Binele any explanation, she ordered them gaily to come with her. She brought them to Yossele's hut, so that he could present the proposition to the two of them.

For a long while the young pair stood open-mouthed in front the two old people. Then they grinned and burst into artificial laughter, pretending not to be able to control it. Finally, both of them together and each of them separately, began, much embarrassed, to explain their case to Hindele and Yossele, using long involved arguments, the main sense of which was that they were not overly excited about the idea and that they wanted to make their own plans at their own pace in their own time. Their refusal gave Hindele and Yossele just the right amount of disappointment and regret that they needed to help them enjoy their celebration properly. Nothing stood in their way now, and with an air of spitefulness, they fixed their marriage date for a much earlier time than they had originally intended, that is, for one of the first days in spring, right after the storks had returned to the shtetl.

The wedding had been meant to be a modest and quiet affair. But first, Bociany of the heavens decided to mix into the event. On precisely that day the storks celebrated a wedding of their own. They fluttered and flapped their wings, raising a Hasidic storkish noise above Hindele's backyard, where the celebration was taking place. Second, Bociany on earth did not lag far behind and also managed to interfere. The entire shtetl came running to participate in the wedding.

Nechele the Pockmarked, the widow of the heroic sexton Reb Laibele, busied herself like a mother-in-law on the bride's side, while the *rov*, no longer young, but more majestic than ever, busied himself like a father-in-law on the groom's side.

Reb Faivele the Miller and his wife, Long Zirele, arrived with a wagonload of drinks and gifts. Shmulikl the Doctor, recently released from the prison camp in Dombia, arrived with his wife, the former midwife; they were followed by a crowd of cripples and beggars from the poorhouse. Fishele the Butcher came with his wife and his bands of butcher boys, wagon drivers, and firemen, but without the apple of his eye—his son Ariele—who had been killed in the Polish-Bolshevik War. The old ritual slaughterer, the late storyteller Sore-Leyele's widower, came with his two daughters and sons-in-law, surrounded by men of the clergy. The old *dian* was no longer alive, but the rest of his family came, as did Reb Shapsele, the Gemara *melamed.* After all, these two families were closely related to Yossele's. Also the neighbors from Yossele's street were there, among them Peshele the Slob and Toybe Kraindele the Women's Bathhouse Attendant, along with all their familiars. The only ones missing were the members of the late Brontchele the Mourner's family. Ever since Yossele's daughter Dvorele had run away from her husband Berele the Moonwalker, they were not on speaking terms with Yossele. But the matchmaker Reb Menashele was there, in spite of his reservations concerning the success of the new couple's union, as was of course the merrymaker at wedding celebrations, Reb Dovtchele, not to mention the Hasidim of all the *shtiblekh,* as well as the Hasidic band.

Apart from all these guests, there was no lack of representatives from young Bociany whom Yacov and Binele, Gitele and Shaindele had unofficially invited. And of course there were the starry-eyed children, the exuberant mischiefs, swarms of them. Laughing, yelling, beside themselves with delight, they cavorted all about, getting tangled up in people's legs.

And last but not least, Shalom was of course there with his wife and children, and Yossele's children and grandchildren had arrived from Lodz, bringing expensive gifts.

The Hasidic band played a jubilant wedding tune. The Hasidim from the various *shtiblekh* danced with one another. The Bundists danced with the Zionists, the Yiddishists danced with the Hebraists, the poor with the not so poor, the tall with the short, the thin with the fat. From the roofs, the trees, and even from the top of the fence of the nuns' garden the gentile neighbors looked on, clapping their hands. Manka the Washerwoman, who had helped Nechele the Pockmarked with the preparations for the feast, was now sitting in her doorway in her Sunday best, in the company of Wanda—who was fat, pregnant, and held a baby on her lap—and of Binele's childhood friend Yadwiga, and of Yadwiga's parents, Yankova and Yanek. Yanek rocked one of his grandchildren on his knee as he excitedly twisted the upward side of his uneven gray mustache. Reb Faivele the Miller approached them with a tray of glasses filled with *monopolka* in his hands.

Abele the Town Fool danced alone in the middle of the crowd of revelers, smiling his broad fool's smile.

⊚⊚ *Epilogue* ⊚⊚

THE BEGINNING

The locomotive clanked to a stop. The train came to a halt under the starry night sky. The Polish soil outside, wrapped in the scents of late summer, stopped escaping and came to rest at the station of a small sleeping town on the western Polish border. In the perfumed pungent-sweet silence, an officer of the Polish border police appeared in the compartment. He approached the young woman who sat near the window. Nervously, she gulped down a mouthful of balmy air and handed him her passport—valid for one crossing of the Polish border. The playful breeze blowing in through the window flipped the few pages of the booklet as if mischievously trying to prevent the man from scrutinizing it properly.

"Your name and recent address?" he asked in a dry hurried voice.

"Miriam Polin," she replied. "Lodz, Pusta Street, number 6."

He glanced at her photo in the passport, then fixed her with an investigative look. "How long have you been in the country?"

How long? It seemed to her that this last stretch of "the country" was speaking to her from outside the window, prompting her reply through the breeze's whisper. "Approximately one thousand years." But her eyes met the indifferent blue of the man's and she answered, "I was born here."

He pressed a seal onto the page of her visa. With a fountain pen he wrote in the date, "July 30, 1947." As he handed her back the thin booklet, his glance rested for a moment on her bare forearm, the Auschwitz number tattooed onto it. *"Dowidzenia,"* he saluted her matter-of-factly, raising a finger to his visor, and turned away.

"Adieu," she replied in a whisper, facing the navy blue darkness outside. The train moved on.

Backwards raced memory. Backwards unwound the chain of generations from the spool of time, until the knotted threads of heredity passed through a tunnel of darkness where all traces of continuity were blotted out. Then the light of survival appeared on the other side of despair, and recoiling on itself, the ring of generations advanced once more.

So did the memory in Miriam Polin's blood seek out the thread of eternity, that it might attach itself to that thread as to an umbilical cord, in order to be carried aloft over the abyss of question marks on which grief hung impaled as on countless sharp hooks. Backwards and forwards—over time and space, over home and exile, over rootedness and wandering, over the lights of faith and the bonfires of hatred, over Gardens of Eden and deserts, over mountains and valleys, over seas and oceans—raced memory.

Legends of her life dozing deep in the subconscious. Barely sensed perceptions about Father and Mother, about their forefathers and foremothers, way back until time immemorial, to the beginning that had no beginning.

Thus they had emerged from there—they, Miriam Polin's ancestors: from Somewhere, Sometime, and then from Ur of the Chaldeans. Through the valley of the Tigris and the Euphrates they had moved in nomadic vagabondage, driven by a restlessness owing perhaps not only to the aridness of the plains but also to the thirst of their minds, to their passion for what was beyond the tangible surface of things, passions for the song of all matter, for the spirituality and godliness that was in each form, beyond each form.

From the valley of the Tigris and Euphrates she saw them proceed to Haran, and from there into the Land of Milk and Honey. (How often had both the milk and the honey acquired the taste of poison—their sweetness remaining solely in the joy of creating soothing visions!) Thus they kept on wandering—vagabonds in the steppes of longing, driven on by their earthly needs and the inexpressible cravings of their souls.

Perhaps . . .

Perhaps one of her—of Miriam Polin's forefathers—had belonged to the retinue of shepherds accompanying biblical Abraham? Perhaps he had even been related as a distant cousin to Abraham and Sarah? Or later—perhaps one of her ancestors had grown up on biblical Isaac's homestead and heard the confessions of lovesick Jacob when he opened his heart to him on how he had coveted Rachel while making love to Leah?

Down to Egypt her forefathers had wandered. Thus it might have happened that their children had played the pebble game *strulkes* with Joseph's children and that these children's children had played hide-and-seek with Joseph's grandchildren in Pharaoh's palace. Until the Pharaoh who "knew not Joseph" moved into the royal chambers and the played-out children became slaves and built pyramids.

Perhaps an offspring of these children, a girl, Miriam Polin's ancestress, had stood hidden among the reeds of the river Nile, watching along with Moses' sister, also named Miriam, to see what would happen to the infant Moses who was carried off by the current in a braided basket? And perhaps a son of that girl had later on complained about his yoke to the restless Prince Moses?

Thus they had been slaves and then became a free people. Again they wandered through the wilderness of ignorance and cravings, subsisting on the manna of dreams. How many of them perished in order that the seed of heredity be saved? Who among them lived to stand at the foot of Mount Sinai and heard with his own ears . . . ? Had it perhaps been given to at least one of her ancestors to move in the circle of close familiarity with Moses, the unique leader of a people, the stutterer, the sinner, the rebellious, justice-demanding seeker of a World Conscience? And had he learned from Moses that The Law without love and respect is worse than lawlessness, and had he learned from him how to become a self-sacrificing servant of a God, of an ideal?

And later still, when their children had reached the longed-for land of Canaan at last—who among them had heard the trumpets of the ram's horn at the walls of Jericho? Who had seen the sun stand still upon Gibon and the moon in the Valley of Ajalon? To which tribe had they, Miriam Polin's forefathers, belonged? Where had they pitched their tents and how were they related to the first Judges? Had not Binele, Miriam Polin's own mother, possessed the heroic might of Samson when she had found herself at the precipice of Auschwitz?

And the most credible of all hereditary derivations—the Polin family's relatedness to the House of King David—how credible was it in fact? Was it true that the book with the family tree that Miriam Polin's grandmother Hindele had guarded like the apple of her eye was "in black upon white" tracing back her origin to King David's seed? Is this why Grandmother Hindele had always treated her sons as if they were princes, the sole legitimate heirs to the Jewish throne?

And King Solomon, the author of the Song of Songs, so dear and familiar in his storybook splendor, with his human frailties, his love of life, his vanity-of-vanities philosophy, his thirst for knowledge, and his hunger for beauty—how much of his essence had taken root in all the things near and dear to one's soul?

Might it have happened thus, that Yacov, Miriam Polin's father, in his ancestral incarnation had already befriended the young Abrashka, in the latter's ancestral incarnation; had met him there, in King Solomon's gardens? The same Abrashka from the shtetl of Bociany who would later sketch the landscapes of the Ghetto in Lodz, transform them into the landscape of the Song of Songs, inviting her, Miriam Polin, to dance upon these real yet imaginary meadows. Had he perhaps already invented a new name for her there, in Kings Solomon's gardens, and called her Rinah—Song? For his soul and hers had often housed together, perhaps already there . . .

And from there, from the glorious Holy Temple, from the thresholds that had begun to tremble, whereto had the dust carried off the threads of heredity: to the Kingdom of Israel? to the Kingdom of Judea? Had any of her forefathers listened with their own ears to the fiery words of the prophets? Perhaps one of her ancestors, barefoot, wrapped in sackcloth, had himself chanted his own winged prophecies, standing upon a hill of desert dust?

Who among her ancestors had been exiled to Babylon and how many had hung up their lyres on the willows' boughs? Had any of them sought solace from old Jeremiah? Had perhaps one of them copied Jeremiah's lamentations on parchment, so that generations later, when there were no more words left, the prophet's lament would pour out from mourners' lips? For had not Miriam Polin's paternal grandfather, Hamele the Scribe, spent his life, up to his very last breath, copying the Holy Scriptures with diligence and tender care, with faithful attention to the smallest dot, in reverence before each mark?

They, the paternal forefathers, had probably returned home from the

bondage in Babylon and settled in Jerusalem, the city where the air is permeated with holy song and every pebble on every hill speaks of the transformation of spirit into tangible substance. Thus there is a possibility that
in the increasingly darker yet spiritually brighter later times someone
among those ancestors had had at least a modest part in the creation of
the Babylonian or the Jerusalem Talmud. Perhaps this had been one of
the reasons why their passionate yearning for truth and justice had
reached Miriam Polin's father, Yacov, and kept alive the flame of hope in
his bosom even during his incarceration at the concentration camp
Kaufering near Dachau?

Of course the maternal forefathers might have been there as well—
there, in the Holy Land. But they were the salt of the earth—just like
Miriam Polin's grandfather Yossele Abedale—sages full of wisdom of
life, men and women awake with all their senses, earthly, stubborn. Perhaps they had belonged to those who for a long time continued to worship the idols of Baal and Astarte, tangible gods of every day needs,
whom they could touch, grasp. They, Miriam Polin's maternal ancestors,
had probably found it difficult to break any bond of devotion. But as
soon as their hearts and minds had been flooded with the New Light, and
the God of Israel had finally taken hold of their beings, they became
ready for self-sacrifice, for martyrdom, in the name of their faith. They
belonged to the breed of the hard-necked, the folk-people, the toilers.
They might have belonged to those who had left their plows or their
sheep in the pastures and joined the Hasmonaim, forging weapons for
Judah the Maccabean. Perhaps they had carried out more than one heroic
feat in their readiness for sacrifice. But they belonged to those heroes
whose names are never mentioned on tablets or scrolls of parchment.

Thus Miriam Polin's ancestral grandmother might have been one of
Jerusalem's stubborn daughters, who at a later time found herself among
those women who handed over pails of boiling pitch to the men on the
walls of the besieged Holy City. While her lover might have been one of
Miriam Polin's paternal forefathers who was helping Rabbi Yochanan Ben
Sakkai steal out of the city in a coffin, in order to found the Yeshiva at
Yavne, and thus salvage the treasures of the spirit.

And when Zion was destroyed—which of her ancestors had been
among the captives of Rome? What had happened to them? To where did
they turn from that crossroads of separation, the road of dispersion, at
the beginning of an exile that was still going on?

Probably then and there, almost nineteen and a half centuries ago, the parallel parental threads of heredity had parted for long generations. Those on her father's side had perhaps wound through Spain, France, Germany—through the Crusades, the Inquisition, through blood accusations and the Black Plague. The others, those on her mother's side, no doubt with similar luck—proceeded through Turkey, the Caucasus, and appeared in Russia.

Perhaps one of her mother's great-great grandmothers had been none other than the Jewish cook who had introduced kosher cuisine to the kitchens of Joseph, the Khazar King, a convert to Judaism, whose empire bordered on the Black and Caspian Seas? Or perhaps she had been the Khazar King's concubine, who night after night enlightened her monarch on the details of love making, according to the spirit of the Bible or the Talmud? Or had she translated into Khazaric language the letters that Hasdai Ibn Shaprut, the vizier at the court of the Caliph of Cordoba, had dispatched by a special diligence to the Khazar King? And who knows? Maybe it so happened—as a symbolic accident—that the vizier's secretary was none other than her father's ancestor who had written those letters with his own hand?

Then a slight suspicion might enter the mind that later, much later, the maternal hereditary thread had become mixed with an alien fiber. It might have happened during the times of violence and brutality, during the days of self-sacrifice and desperate efforts to salvage lives, during the days of the Cossacks and Haidamacks, when Jewish daughters paid with their bodies for the privilege of belonging to the Chosen People. This could have been the reason why Grandmother Miriam—whom Grandfather Yossele Abedale affectionately called Mariml, and whose name she, Miriam Polin, was carrying—had yellow hair with a reddish sheen, slightly slanted eyes, and the Mongolic cheekbones that her children had inherited.

Thus the threads of heredity meandered, some through the East, others through the West. They were passing through lands and languages, through oppression and persecutions, until just a thousand years ago, encouraged by the wise princes of the Land of the *Lachs,* who had wished to develop their domains, Miriam Polin's ancestors set foot in green Polania, Polska, a name that begged to be translated into the biblical language as "Po-lin", meaning: "Here (we) rest," a name that entered into the woe-and-wander language, Yiddish, as "Poyln," thus giving the origin to Miriam's family name, Polin.

Here, in Poland, the threads of heredity halted. They tied themselves into a knot near the opulent hills that embraced the valley of the upper Vistula, and settled in the very middle of a marshy ring, in a shtetl where storks built their nests on the rooftops. In Polish the word for storks is Bociany, thus the name of the shtetl was Bociany.

There, one day, at the very end of the nineteenth century, the stork on Grandmother Hindele's roof had brought down a baby boy from the heavens, with eyes the color of honey: Yacov, Miriam Polin's father. While a few years later the stork on Grandmother Miriam's roof had brought down a baby girl with a few yellow hairs on the very tip of her head: Binele, Miriam Polin's mother.

Miriam Polin glanced at the Polish passport that she would never use again. She straightened up and raised her eyes to the star-studded sky.

Glossary

Alef-beys: Alphabet.
Besmedresh: Prayer and study house.
Cholnt: A baked dish served on the Sabbath.
Deutsch: German.
Dian: Assistant to a rabbi who decides questions of ritual cleanliness.
Dowidzenia (Pol.): Good-bye.
Emes (Heb.): Truth.
Gabe: Warden of the synagogue.
Gemara (Yidd. *Gemore*): That part of the Talmud that comments on the Mishnah.
Golem: Dummy; artificial man created by a saintly rabbi.
Goy (pl. goyim): Gentile.
Havdalah: Ceremony at the close of the Sabbath.
Halutzim: Pioneer settlers.
Heder: Religious school.
Heimat (Germ.): Homestead, homeland.
Kaddish: Prayer for the dead; person who says the prayer.
Kugel: A kind of pudding.
"Lech lecho:" "Get thee out into the world."
Malkes: Lashes, whipping.
Matura: Baccalaureate diploma.
Medresh: Biblical exegesis.
Melamed: Teacher.
Mentsh: Human being; complete person.
Minkha: Afternoon prayers.
Mishnah: Part of the Talmud.
Molodiec (Russ.): Clever fellow.
Ochrana: Tsarist secret police.
Pan (voc. panie; fem. pani.) (Pol.): Form of address: Mister.

Patcher: Women's dance.

Pincettes: Tweezers.

Reb: Mister.

Rov: Rabbi.

Sefirot: Fundamental term of the cabala denoting the ten stages of emanation.

Shkhina: Divine Emanation.

Shma-Yisroel: The credo: "Hear, O Israel."

Shtibl (pl. *shtiblekh*): Hasidic prayer room.

Shtoperke: Female factory worker who mends damaged fabrics.

Strulkes: A pebble game.

Svolotch (Russ.): Scoundrel.

Torah: The Pentateuch.

Tsadik (pl. *tsadikim*): Saintly man.

Verruckt: Crazy.

Vitish (Yidd. slang): Honest person.

Yaptzok: Hash of potatoes and beans.

Yeshiva: Institution of higher Talmudic learning.

Zohar: The holiest book of the cabala.